Love's
FORTUNE

the
Ballantyne
LEGACY 3

Love's FORTUNE

A NOVEL

LAURA FRANTZ

Revell

a division of Baker Publishing Group
Grand Rapids, Michigan

Published by Revell
a division of Baker Publishing Group
P.O. Box 6287, Grand Rapids, MI 49516-6287
www.revellbooks.com

Printed in the United States of America

Library of Congress Cataloging-in-Publication Data
Frantz, Laura.
     Love's fortune : a novel / Laura Frantz.
          pages cm. — (The Ballantyne Legacy ; #3)
     ISBN 978-0-8007-2043-8 (pbk.)
     1. Families—Pennsylvania—Fiction. 2. Christian fiction. 3. Domestic fiction.
I. Title.
PS3606.R4226L66 2014
813′.6—dc23   2014015210

Unless otherwise indicated, Scripture quotations are from the King James Version of the Bible.

Scripture quotations marked NIV are from the Holy Bible, New International Version®. NIV®. Copyright © 1973, 1978, 1984, 2011 by Biblica, Inc.™ Used by permission of Zondervan. All rights reserved worldwide. www.zondervan.com

Published in association with Books & Such Literary Agency, 52 Mission Circle, Suite 122, PMB 170, Santa Rosa CA 94509-7953.

14   15   16   17   18   19   20   7   6   5   4   3   2   1

To my son, Paul,
who gives unending joy
on his fiddle

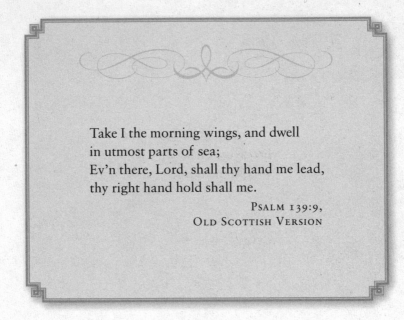

Take I the morning wings, and dwell
in utmost parts of sea;
Ev'n there, Lord, shall thy hand me lead,
thy right hand hold shall me.

PSALM 139:9,
OLD SCOTTISH VERSION

Prologue

So throw off the bowlines. Sail away from the safe harbor. Catch the trade winds in your sails. Explore. Dream. Discover.

MARK TWAIN

APRIL 1823

For the rest of his life James Sackett would remember this moment. He was just a boy, but he felt full grown. Free. Nearly winged. More master. Like the young man standing beside him.

Ansel Ballantyne placed a firm hand on his shoulder, eyes asquint in the blinding sea glare. "Ready, James? For a new adventure?"

James smiled up at him, feeling close as kin, entwined with the Ballantynes like he'd been. He didn't look back at Philadelphia's fading spires and steeples. He looked forward, beyond the ship's proud bowsprit. To England.

"You're not missing Pittsburgh, I hope."

A firm shake of James's head shot down the notion. "I want to do you proud, sir. I want Mister Silas and Mistress Eden to be glad that I'm with you."

"You're good company, James. One day I hope to have as fine a son as you." Ansel faced the wind's salty spray, the wearied lines in his face easing. "Mayhap I'll teach you to play the fiddle while we're at sea. By the time we arrive in Liverpool, you might well outshine me."

The prospect brought a keen warmth to James's chest. Together they stood, of one purpose, looking out on an ocean so wide and blue it seemed the sky turned upside down.

Oh, to be a Ballantyne.

He wasn't one, but James wanted to be.

Mayhap being a Ballantyne apprentice was a blessed second best.

1

Soon after, I returned home to my family, with a determination to bring them as soon as possible to live in Kentucky, which I esteemed a second paradise.

DANIEL BOONE

CANE RUN, KENTUCKY
AUGUST 1850

Papa had forsaken his black mourning band.

The shock of it stole through Wren like ice water. For two years her father's shirtsleeve had borne a reminder of her mother's loss, as telling as the lines of grief engraved upon his handsome face. Not once had he taken off the black silk. But all of a sudden it was missing. And Wren ached to know what stirred inside his russet head.

It had all begun with a letter from far upriver. From New Hope. She'd paid the post, wonder astir inside her as she studied the elegant writing. *Ansel Ballantyne, Cane Run,*

Kentucky. They received a great deal of mail, mostly from Europe and the violin collectors and luthiers there, or from Mama's family, the Nancarrows in England. Not Pennsylvania, with the Allegheny County watermark bleeding ink on the outer edge of the wrinkled paper.

She ran all the way home and arrived at the door of their stone house flushed and so winded she could only flutter the letter in her fingers. As it passed from her hand to Papa's, she measured his expression.

Pensive. Surprised. Reluctant.

Sensing he craved privacy, she turned on her naked feet and fled, climbing the mountain in back of their home place till her lungs cried for air. There she sank to her knees atop a flat rock and drank in the last colorful bits of day.

The river before her was no longer blue but liquid gold. Wide and unending, it cradled a lone steamboat with fancy lettering on its paddle box, a far cry from the crude canoe of her childhood. Where it was headed she didn't know and didn't want to. Her world began and ended on this familiar mountain and always had.

She didn't move till her father's husky voice cut through the sultry twilight, calling her home. The supper their housekeeper Molly made was waiting. Wren darted a glance about the too-still kitchen. No Molly. No letter in sight. Just cold cups of cider and deep bowls of hominy stew and corn bread drenched with butter.

"*A bheil an t-acras ort?*" Papa stood in the doorway to the parlor speaking the Gaelic he'd used with her since childhood, warm and familiar as one of Molly's hand-sewn quilts.

Are you hungry?

Hungry, yes. For mourning bands and Mama and explanations of strange letters from upriver. She nodded, sitting down and waiting for grace. Tears touched her eyes when he prayed. The words were Mama's own, ushering in her sweet presence again.

"Give us grateful hearts, our Father, for all Thy mercies, and make us mindful of the needs of others, through Jesus Christ our Lord. Amen."

There was a moment's hush.

"I've news from Pennsylvania." Swallowing some cider, Papa gestured to the mantel where the letter rested.

"From your Ballantyne kin?" Wren nearly choked asking it, the grit of corn bread crumbs in her throat.

"Aye. It's been a while since they've written. Longer still since I've visited. Things there are changing . . ." Misery rose up and clouded the blue of his eyes. He took another sip of cider and then pushed up from his chair, nearly sending it backward. "I fear I've been away too long."

Tossing aside his napkin, he limped out the back door, his old injury tugging at her as he disappeared among fruit-laden trees. In the heat of the kitchen, she was left alone with her clamoring questions.

All her life she'd wondered about their family in western Pennsylvania. She'd heard the romantic tale of how her Scots grandfather, Silas Ballantyne, had come over the mountains the century before and built a fancy brick house for his bride. She was sure the homespun bits of gossip whispered by Cane Run folk had been embellished over time with silken thread. Some sort of trouble had driven Papa away from there more than twenty years before. But that was a puzzle too.

She picked up his bowl of stew, set it in the hearth's embers to keep warm, and placed his plate of corn bread atop it. Though he'd gone outside, his profound disquiet lingered. She'd not seen him this *afflocht* since Mama's passing.

Darting a look at the mantel, she sighed. The letter that started all the trouble seemed to taunt her, Papa's black mourning band coiled beside it, rife with mystery.

Birdsong nudged her awake, just as it had for twenty years or better. Wren could smell coffee—and varnish. Someone was in the workshop situated across the dogtrot at the south end of the house. The instruments they crafted seemed to dry better there, soaking up the sun through the skylight in the vaulted ceiling, the room's brightness calling out the rich pine and maple grain of the finished fiddles.

She dressed hurriedly and donned an apron, then wove her hair into a careless braid, tying it off with a frayed, pumpkin-colored ribbon. It jarred sourly with her blue dress and brown shoes, giving her the look of a rag rug. She never fussed over-long about her mismatched wardrobe, not caring how she looked. A spill of varnish or a chisel gone awry had wrecked more dresses than she could count.

The workshop door was open wide, revealing a long rack stretching the length of the room, jewel-toned violins strung like beads on a necklace. The smell of varnish wafted strong but not unpleasant, competing with the tang of freshly cut wood. Lingering on the door stone, she swept the shop in a glance. Papa? No, Selkirk, Papa's apprentice. Straddling a bench, he was carving the scroll of a violin from a piece of pine, his back to her.

"Morning, Kirk."

"Morning, Wren." He didn't so much as glance up, keeping his chisel true to the wood, a dusting of sweet shavings across his breeches.

"The McCoy bow is finished," she told him. "I rubbed it

with pumice powder and oil just yesterday. But you'll need to test it first." She'd lost count of the bows that didn't pass muster. The instruments they made had to be nearly faultless. Papa's reputation as luthier depended on it.

"I won't be making any deliveries today." Selkirk's tone was low. Thoughtful. "Your father's left for Louisville. Something about booking passage upriver to Pittsburgh."

She went completely still, nearly forgetting how strange it was to be alone with Selkirk without Papa present. Just outside, Molly was stringing laundry on the line. *Mute Molly*, Cane Run folk called her. When small, she'd been choked by a slave trader and robbed of her voice.

Wren fought the catch in her own throat as she fastened her gaze on the instruments adorning the sunny room, not just fiddles but mandolins and dulcimers and psalteries, the work of their hands and hearts. "Pittsburgh sounds right far."

Kirk shrugged. "Just a few hundred miles easily managed by steamer." He looked up, his chisel aloft. "Don't you want to meet your Ballantyne kin, Wren?"

Did she? In truth she rarely thought about them aside from Christmas, when Grandmother Ballantyne sent fetching, impractical packages downriver. An enameled jewelry box. A cashmere shawl. An ivory-handled parasol. Things far above Wren's raising. "Mostly I forget all about them."

Kirk gave a chuckle. "Well, they've not forgotten you. Fact is, they've named a steamboat in your honor. She's called the *Rowena*."

Her backside connected with the nearest stool. "You don't mean it."

"Aye, I've seen her taking on cargo in Louisville. A first-rate steamer she is too, well deserving of your name."

"But . . . why?"

"Because the Ballantynes name their steamers after the petticoats—er, ladies—in the family."

"I'm hardly a lady," she replied, glancing at her varnish-stained apron and hands.

"You might be by the time you come back here."

The very thought made her smile. She reached for a finished bow and newly strung fiddle, launching into a lively jig as if it could drive the ludicrous thought from the room. But it simply ensnared Kirk, keeping him from his work.

He studied her, mouth wry. "If you tickle their ears with your fiddle, they might well forgive you for Cane Run. The truth is, Wren, you don't belong here. Not like the Clarks and Landrys and Mackens who settled this place. Your mother's people are of English stock, aye? And your father, for all his humility and homespun, is still a Ballantyne."

"I misdoubt I belong there either."

"How will you know unless you go?"

Because some things the heart just knows.

"If someone named a boat after me and begged me to come upriver, I'd be the first aboard." Kirk traded one tool for another. "It's a bit odd your father seldom speaks of his kin. Makes me wonder what drove him to Kentucky to begin with."

She rested her fiddle across her knees. "All I know is that Papa left Pennsylvania when he was young as you and sailed to England. He took up with the Nancarrows—Welsh luthiers and collectors—and wed my mother. After I was born they came to Kentucky."

"Bare facts, Wren. You'd best be finding out before you go."

She fell quiet, pondering the sudden turn of events, the steamboat *Rowena*, and Louisville, a place she'd never been. "When will Papa be back?"

"Tomorrow or thereabouts."

She was used to his absences. His violin hunting often took him away for months on end. Sometimes Mama had accompanied him, but never Wren. Since Mama's passing, Papa hadn't gone anywhere at all.

Why on earth would he now want to return to Pennsylvania?

2

Nothing is so painful to the human mind as a great and sudden change.

MARY SHELLEY

No matter where one happened to be standing on the Louisville levee, one could hardly miss the enormous steamboat with elaborate black lettering bearing her name. Heat scoured Wren's face and dampened her brow as she studied the boat's detail. There was something almost arrogant in its presentation, a garishness that made her want to slip into the muddy current and slide away.

So this was the *Rowena*.

A simple *Wren* would have sufficed.

Today, as she stood in the sweltering sun, nothing was like she thought it would be. Louisville was supposed to be smaller. Tamer. Less filthy. Words she'd never before heard bruised her ears as muscular stevedores manhandled cargo all around her, wrestling hogsheads and bales onto vessels that stretched as far as she could see. Noisy peddlers pushed their wares on every side. Roasted peanuts. Plugs of tobacco. Wilting flowers and religious tracts.

Just ahead her father moved among the crowd effortlessly, doffing his hat and speaking to crewmen. Astonishment sluiced through her. Was this truly her beloved papa? The simple luthier crafting instruments in the seclusion of their Cane Run shop? Or more Ballantyne, a man of the world, polished and pleasant?

Casting a look over her shoulder, Wren made sure Molly followed. When she turned back around she nearly stumbled over a barefoot boy, skin and eyes dark as night, small hand outstretched. He looked up at her, hunger in his gaze. Sympathy bloomed. Stooping, skirts swinging in a wide arc around her, she opened her poke and spied the two biscuits Molly had wrapped in a handkerchief alongside a few coins. "It's all I have or I'd give you more," she told him.

His eyes lit with gratitude, and he took the offerings. Smiling, Molly nodded her approval as he darted away, disappearing into the colorful crowd. In front of them on the boarding platform, Papa was greeting a man in a brass-buttoned coat and top hat, his face a sun-creased brown. The captain?

"Good to have you this trip, Ansel. I see you're traveling in company."

When Captain Dean turned her way and gave a little bow, Wren could hardly speak. The new corset she wore pressed all the breath out of her. Made her feel as flat and faded as the wildflowers she dried between the pages of her Bible.

"This is my daughter, Rowena."

Was she supposed to curtsey? Awkwardly, she extended a hand. "Pleased to meet you, Captain."

His eyes flashed something she couldn't name as he kissed her gloved fingers. "The pleasure is mine, Miss Ballantyne."

Her breathlessness heightened as they stepped aboard the boat and were taken to a grand salon, its floor-to-ceiling windows and gilt glass multiplying her reflection tenfold. They'd only had a hand mirror and small looking glass back home. She stared back at herself, stricken. Cocooned in linen and lace, she ached for her old clothes, comfortable as a second skin. She felt trussed as a game hen in her stiff damask crinoline.

The captain gave a signal to raise the stage planks from the bustling levee. "At six knots and six hundred miles, we should make landfall early tomorrow. Until then the Ballantyne line's finest New Orleans chef is on board, and you'll occupy the best staterooms." He turned in Wren's direction with a practiced smile. "Your grandmother gave special instructions as to your quarters. If you have need of anything else . . ."

"I'm sure we'll lack for nothing," Papa replied with the ease of a man who'd done this dozens of times.

Though she tried to mirror his calm, it seemed a basketful of kittens had been let loose inside her.

A steward led them up a graceful double staircase to a wide sunlit deck. Wren put a gloved hand to the painted wooden railing as the roar of machinery sent the steamer away from the dock. The paneled wall before her was lit with frosted lamps, the wainscoting elegant and polished, the carpeting beneath her feet lush as lamb's wool.

A stateroom door was thrust open on a room made rich with bird's-eye maple and gold-plated hardware. Her head swam with the scent of blooms. Sun-worn damask and wide windows awaited, a lush backdrop to a great many pink and cream roses in cut-glass vases. Mama's favorite flower. The hitch of sadness in her chest seemed sharper in so strange a place.

"Dinner is at seven," the steward said with a little bow.

By the time she'd joined her father in the dining room, Molly had doused her with attar of roses and arranged her hair, then stayed behind to manage their trunks.

A waiter seated her at a linen-clad table overlooking steep river bluffs. A dozen or so tables surrounded them, all empty.

"Papa, are we the only ones aboard?"

"Aye, just us, the crew, and a great deal of cargo from New Orleans."

Perched on the edge of her chair, she let the lonesome fact take hold, watching a spindly legged heron along the far bank.

"Blue becomes you, Wren." He was looking at her as he'd not done in days, preoccupied as he'd been. "All grown up. More like your mother when I first met her."

She glanced down at the ice-blue folds of her skirt, one of a dozen dresses hastily gotten from a Louisville seamstress the day before. "It's mostly Molly's doing. I don't know that I'd ever get in or out of this without her."

"You'll likely have a lady's maid at New Hope."

"A maid?" The prospect was as unappealing as corsets and crinolines. "But what about Molly?"

She read the answer in his eyes before it reached his lips. "Pennsylvania—Pittsburgh—isn't like Kentucky. We will do things differently there."

She fell silent as a creamy soup was served alongside bread and small molds of butter in the shape of swans. Awe faded to confusion as she counted four spoons engraved with an elaborate *B*. She copied Papa as he chose one, her other hand clutching the napkin in her lap. Serviette, the waiter had called it.

Mindful of the staff watching, Wren followed Papa's lead and bowed her head. But here, amid such stilted grandeur, his humble Gaelic prayer seemed out of place.

Papa leaned back in his chair, looking chagrined and no hungrier than she. "I ken this trip is something of a shock for you. The letter came—what, a week ago? I'm realizing you've been too sheltered. Too hemmed in. Your mother always said I should have taken you upriver years ago . . ."

She tensed, soup spoon suspended, moved by the sheen in his eyes. Any mention of Mama usually made him founder. "I'll be fine, Papa. Don't you worry about me."

"It's time you met your family . . . Past time." Taking a letter from his pocket, he pushed it toward her. "This will help explain things."

She set down her spoon and opened the letter. Grandmother Ballantyne's writing hand was lovely if fragile, a spidery weave of words that all but begged Papa to come home.

> *You're needed here, Ansel. We need to see*
> *Wren again. We are growing older and can no*
> *longer manage without you. I worry so about*
> *your father's health. He stays strong but the*
> *years have taken a toll. Please come if you can.*
> *And if you are willing, stay . . .*

Folding up the letter, she put it between them. Her eyes wandered to his sleeve and she felt a wrench. Though his mourning band was missing, he was still broken. Grieving. She needed that reminder. She needed to let go of her reluctance about this trip. She needed to help him to wholeness or forever feel like she'd helped him to an early grave.

"I remember once, when I was small, a dark-haired lady came to visit us." Groping for a dusty memory, she tried to smile. "She wore a gown the blue of a robin's egg and a string

20

of pearls. She was the most beautiful woman I'd ever laid eyes on save Mama."

He gave a nod, eyes on the roses at the table's center. "That would have been your aunt Ellie."

"Ellie?"

"My sister Elinor." He took a drink of water but made no move to eat. "She's mistress of River Hill, not far from New Hope. At last count she and Judge Jack had eleven children, most of them sons."

Her jaw went slack. Nearly a dozen to Papa's one. And a girl at that. Another course was set before them, something swimming in pastry and cream. Wren willed herself to eat. "Was it just you and Ellie growing up?"

"There's Andra and Peyton. But I was closest to Ellie."

His terse words kindled her curiosity if not her appetite. She sampled the offering, pleasantly surprised. "I'm not sure what this is, but it just might keep body and soul together."

He smiled and forked a bite. "Catfish, but not as you and Molly make it."

She nodded absently. "Tell me about Aunt Andra."

"Once, Andra was said to be the belle of Pittsburgh, but she spurned every suitor who came her way." His words lacked the warmth of when he'd talked of Ellie. "She lives at New Hope with your grandfather and grandmother."

Wren made note to be chary of her unknown aunt. "And Uncle Peyton?"

"I'll let you draw your own conclusions about my older brother and his heir."

The grim tenor of his tone couldn't be ignored. Selkirk's voice sprang to mind, challenging her ignorance.

Bare facts, Wren. You'd best be finding out.

She took a deep breath. "Papa, I'd rest easier if you told me more. Like why you left Pennsylvania in the first place."

"I owe you an answer. But where to begin . . ." His face clouded as if she'd touched a nerve. "Years ago, when I was young as you, our family sheltered runaway slaves at New Hope and helped them to freedom. After a time we were suspect, and I became the target of bounty hunters and the like. Some of the slaves we helped were caught and sent south again. Things became more and more dangerous. I decided to go to England after an attempt was made on my life."

Wren went cold, sifting through the carefully crafted words to the crux of the matter. "Someone meant you harm? Is that why you limp?" He'd always made light of such, telling her it was an accident.

He met her eyes, and she read the answer. "I thought, after being away in England, the danger had passed. But one night on a road outside Pittsburgh, shots were fired and I was injured. You and your mother were with me, and I knew beyond a shadow of a doubt that I had to move you to safety. Kentucky seemed the best refuge."

"You wanted to shelter us, protect us." That she could understand. He'd always loved his family deeply.

His gaze held hers. "I was willing to let go of anything to ensure that you'd grow up beyond any danger."

"Are you in any danger now—in Pennsylvania?" She lowered her voice, all too aware of the ship's staff hovering. "Do the Ballantynes no longer help runaways to freedom?"

"Their involvement is different now. But since it doesn't concern you and likely never will, there's really no need for you to know more. I don't want to fill your head with unnecessary fears."

She shifted uncomfortably in her chair as Captain Dean

reappeared, top hat tucked beneath one arm. "I trust supper is to your satisfaction?" At Papa's praise he smiled his practiced smile and said, "If I might be so bold, perhaps you and your daughter would care to join us later in the grand salon. Some of my officers have a particular fondness for string instruments."

"Of course," Papa replied cordially.

Wren looked at him. "But we didn't bring the Cremona violins—"

"The Cremonas are in my cabin." There was an apology in his eyes. "I intended to tell you . . ."

She set down her fork, feeling he'd pulled the finely upholstered chair out from under her.

The captain turned back to her father. "I've heard about your violin hunting in Europe. I'm particularly interested in your Amati. The Nightingale, I believe it's called."

Papa smiled, seemingly blind to her dismay. "Yes, Rowena prefers it to all others. I'll accompany her on a Bergonzi. I've brought them all."

Robbed of speech, she looked to her lap. So the Italian Cremonas were on board, the cream of their collection, the fruit of countless hours and untold wrangling to acquire them. It could only mean one thing.

Papa had left Kentucky for good.

3

*The Mississippi River will
always have its own way.*
MARK TWAIN

James Sackett stood in the wheelhouse of the *Rowena*, steering into the twilight, alert to the slightest alteration in the river's mood or appearance. The sonorous music drifting up from the grand salon below made him slightly melancholy. It was his birthday. Only he didn't know how old he was. Over thirty, he guessed. The sun lines framing his eyes bespoke a good many years but on a good day were chased away by a boyish smile. He supposed age didn't really matter if the soul was eternal, as Silas Ballantyne claimed.

"Sackett, sir?"

At the sound of his name, he glanced down. A lean shadow strode across the texas deck and began a slow climb to the pilothouse. The lead engineer appeared in the doorway, expression smug. "The *Molly Dent* is chasing us. Feel like a bit of racing?"

"Not with the cargo I'm carrying."

"The Kentucky Ballantynes, you mean? The ones making all that racket in the salon?"

James nearly smiled. "It's a wee bit sweeter than your yammering."

"Sweeter to look at, you mean." With a wink, Perry fished a flask from his pocket and took a sip. "I've never heard such violin playing."

"Nor have I."

"Miss Ballantyne is the talk of the entire ship. Did you know Ansel had a daughter?"

James fixed his eye on the flag flying from the jack staff. "No." He'd returned to Pittsburgh soon after Ansel's marriage to begin his pilot's apprenticeship and lost track of him. Ansel's subsequent homecoming was hazy—and had likely been secretive given the danger.

"Makes me wonder what else he's hiding."

"I like surprises."

Perry chuckled at the blatant falsehood. "She has the look of a wood nymph, if you ask me. All sun-browned and wild-eyed. Not like a Ballantyne."

"She takes after her mother's people—the Nancarrows in England."

"Does she now? I suppose you'd know more about that than anyone."

James gave a slight shrug, eyes on the far wooded bank. "That was a long time ago."

Taking out a handkerchief, Perry buffed a brass lever. "I wonder what she thinks of her namesake? None finer than the *Rowena* . . . though that brag boat is sure to trump her if Bennett Ballantyne has his way."

At the mention, James wanted to spit over the railing. The polished walnut wheel grew damp beneath his grip. "Brag boat?"

"Floating circus is more like it. Word along the levee is that Bennett is determined to have it—and you as pilot."

Setting his jaw, James put an end to the conversation. "I'm going to call for the lead."

At the boat's deep, throaty whistle, the violin music stilled. By the time the second engineer called "Mark four," or four fathoms, the salon had emptied and Captain Dean and guests had emerged onto the hurricane roof.

"No bottom!" came the welcome call, confirming the river beneath them was more than four and twenty feet deep. At this rate they'd see Pittsburgh by dawn.

James took his eyes off the water just as Miss Ballantyne emerged from the salon onto the polished promenade below. In the glimmer of moonrise, her blue dress was silvered. She'd removed the bonnet she'd worn when boarding, rewarding James with an unhindered look. Somehow she seemed out of place. A fragile wildflower in a stifling hothouse. The poignancy of her expression reached out to him like a woman drowning.

Home, she seemed to say. *I want to go home.*

He understood. It had been his heart's cry over the years. Pittsburgh was home . . . yet it wasn't. He knew what it was like being at sea in a situation, surrounded by strangers. He'd not forgotten. The wrench of it made him want to take her aside, into some quiet corner. Tell her who to cling to, who to avoid.

Her father might have wanted to protect her by keeping her secreted in the hills and hollows of Kentucky. But there'd be no protecting her now.

There were times Wren suspected Molly was deaf as well as mute. This was one of those times. Light from a paper lantern fell over her lithe figure like gold dust, reassuring Wren she was asleep—something of a miracle since the steamer shuddered from stem to stern in convulsive heaves. Chaos loomed beyond their cabin, but Wren didn't care. She was desperate for air and wanted to be sick over the railing in the dark, not in the stateroom's elegant marble sink.

The confections her grandmother had ordered, a great beribboned box of them, had kept her company since their concert for the officers in the ship's salon. She and Molly had sampled far more of the French bonbons and ribbon candies than good sense allowed, the cloying taste of them now lingering on Wren's tongue. If her stomach was at sea, she was more to blame than the rocking boat.

Cracking open the door, she found the grand salon empty, the entrance to the promenade deck ajar. She nearly forgot her queasiness as she stepped outside into a night so sharply beautiful the stars resembled shards of glass.

All around her, sweating deckhands who'd been busy working scattered like cat-stalked mice as the boat pulled back into the river. They'd just taken on wood again. This great beast of a steamer liked to be fed every thirty miles or so, Papa said.

She shut her eyes. Tried to savor the cool wind against her heated skin. A sudden noise made her press her back against a paneled wall. An officer took a stair to her left. The ship's clerk? She wasn't sure if he was more prince or pauper. Whoever he was, he couldn't compete with the figure crowning the *Rowena*. Her gaze swept upward and held fast. She knew nothing about steamboats except they were noisy and proud and served too much supper. But she knew somehow that the man standing at the wheel high in the pilothouse could do *something*.

Or so she hoped.

James caught the movement of a passing shadow on the bare promenade deck below. Miss Ballantyne? She stood near the churning paddle wheel, looking like she wanted to jump in the frothing water. Still clad in the lovely gown, her gloveless hands clutched the railing, the light from the firepots calling out the misery in her expression. No father. No maid. Alarm bells tripped inside him.

He tore his gaze from her, hopeful the clerk would intervene. He couldn't be distracted, especially heading upstream in the dark when vessels were at the most peril. Buchanan handled all passengers with a good deal of grace, reassuring them and returning them to their rooms. As James thought it, his practiced eye met the mast of a wrecked packet poking through the black water, starboard side. A slight adjustment of the wheel took them around it, but the sobering sight remained locked in place.

He fought the nudge to look below a second time, thinking it the end of the matter. And then with that sixth sense every good pilot had to have, he felt a presence, the hair on the back of his neck tingling.

Rowena Ballantyne stood in the pilothouse doorway. Silent. A bit white about the mouth. James went hot then cold. He tensed as she stepped inside, invading his world of glass and leather and brass. Her gaze swept the floor's oilcloth and corner stove before resting on the costly inlaid wheel he stood beside. Wonder filled him. He was having a hard time coming to grips with this young woman he never knew existed.

"I'm James Sackett, lead pilot of the Ballantyne line."

She gave a small nod. "My name's Wren."

Wren. How they'd wrested that from *Rowena* bemused

him. There was a touching simplicity to her speech, so unlike the formalities he was used to. He'd expected a proud reference to being Silas Ballantyne's granddaughter. Or even a prim *Miss Ballantyne*. "Is there anything I can do for you this evening?"

A slight pause. "I'm just feeling slightly . . ."

Homesick. Heartsick. "Seasick?" he said.

She came closer, nearly pushing him off the cliff of composure. "But how can that be? This is only a river."

"The motion is the same. And it's all water besides."

"The steward gave me peppermint drops." She looked down, eyeing a small tin in her palm. "If I was home I'd chew on gingerroot."

"I could have some ginger beer brought to your stateroom if you'd rather."

"No need." She smiled at him, clearly relieved. "Up here the boat doesn't seem to rock so."

"You get used to the motion in time. A few hours' rest should cure you." A polite curtness had crept into his tone, a subtle cue she needed to go below.

But she was clearly having none of it.

"You've been on the river a long time, Papa said." She was studying him as if he was the most interesting thing in the world, or till now her world had been very small and so everything was of interest. "You apprenticed with the Ballantynes."

"We go back a long way, your father and I . . ." He left off. Now was hardly the time to talk ancient history. Not with fog creeping in. He adjusted the wheel, making a wide arc around a white snag in the midnight waters. His pulse had hardly settled when she came to stand beside him.

This close she was even tinier than he'd thought. She barely cleared his shoulder. Keeping his eyes on the water, he guessed at all the rest of her. Though he couldn't see her eyes, he wagered they were like her mother's, the color of sea foam, that mesmerizing green on the curl of a wave. He caught a hint of peppermint on her breath and lost himself in the gentle rhythm of her Southern speech.

"Do you pilot by the stars?"

"The stars, yes—and memory. A pilot has to know every bend and shoal in the river, be it daylight or dark."

Reaching out an ungloved hand, she touched the great wheel, her soft shoulder brushing his arm. A start shot through him at her nearness—and her audacity. The wheel was almost a sacred thing, handled by a chosen few. His was likely the first in steamboat history to feel a woman's hand. Hiding a wry smile, he forced his attention back where it belonged.

"Being up so high reminds me of home." Her voice was thick with wistfulness. "There's a mountain in back of our house with a view of the river. On summer mornings the sunrise is a sight to behold."

He knew it well—the very mountain. The same winsome twist in the river. He felt a sudden urge to tell her about the privileges of the pilothouse, particularly the hallowed four o'clock watch, the most favored time of all.

Or order her to go below.

She turned to him, a beguiling light in her eyes. Sea foam, just as he'd suspected. Her ungloved hand came to rest lightly on his sleeve. "Might I stay here with you till morning?"

The gentle question rocked him much like the river current far beneath his feet. He looked at her longer than he should have. Speechless. "Miss Ballantyne, I—"

A sudden shadow snatched his words away. Captain Dean cleared his throat and filled the pilothouse doorway. For once

James hadn't observed his approach. "Sackett, a word with you, please."

His solemn tone, cordial with an undercurrent of authority, sent Rowena Ballantyne scurrying to the waiting arm of the clerk.

And then she vanished from sight like the wood nymph she was.

4

Pittsburgh entered the core of my heart when I was a boy and cannot be torn out.

ANDREW CARNEGIE

Long before the Ohio melted into the Monongahela and Allegheny Rivers and ushered them into the city, Wren took in the pall of Pittsburgh. Immense. Dark. Industrious. Enormous smokestacks belched black clouds, overshadowing the distant spire of a church steeple. Soot and grime lay over a crush of brick and timber buildings that rarely saw the sun and seemed to sag in protest. She shuddered. If this was what Papa had run from years ago, she need never wonder why again. Kentucky seemed a sort of paradise.

In the feeble morning light, the steamer was alive with activity, shattering the dawn's calm. The captain stood at the wheel, preparing to nose the *Rowena* into port. Wren heard his gruff call to open the fire doors and cool down the steam. James Sackett was nowhere in sight. Had she caused him trouble by invading his midnight watch? The mere thought flipped her still-queasy stomach, the furious churning of the paddle wheel rivaling the unrest inside her. Last night Pilot Sackett had struck her as gentlemanly if a mite high-minded. As if she was a fly that bedeviled him and wouldn't settle.

This morning Molly had made her look presentable in linen and lace, her upswept hair crowned by a matching bonnet, her hands gloved. The smudges of sleeplessness about her eyes she could do little about. In such fancy dress, she felt like an imposter, sorely missing her varnish-soiled calicoes and aprons. But she read approval in Papa's eyes when she joined him at the railing, much like at supper the night before.

High above the whistle blew, sounding like a long yawn punctuated by two gasps. Boats—packets, Papa called them—lay three and four deep along the levee. On the wide, muddy shore, cargo was stacked higher than a man's head, and a great many wagons and drays rushed about. Everything was a swirling, perspiring melee as the *Rowena* entered Pittsburgh. Wren took it all in, gaze snagging on a boardwalk closest to the water. Amid stevedores standing ready with mooring lines and stage planks stood a tall figure in a top hat.

"Papa, who is that man?"

A muscle twitched in his cheek. "My father."

Silas Ballantyne.

The rush of emotion coursing through her made no sense. Her grandfather was a stranger to her, little more, though Papa was clearly overcome by the sight of the old man waiting. Something told her he'd been waiting a very long time.

"How does he know it's us?"

"He knows the sound of each boat's whistle. They're tuned to be distinguished from each other."

She scanned the levee. "Where is Granny?"

"Your grandmother is a lady, Wren. Ladies do not appear in indelicate places like levees and other unsavory situations if they can help it."

The *Rowena* was nosing into port now, all hands on deck, James Sackett among them. By day he looked entirely different than in the moon-washed pilothouse. Sun-worn. More serious. His hair wasn't tobacco-brown as she'd first thought but black as cast iron. He was flanked by fellow officers and crew, the pecking order quickly apparent.

If he was high-minded, he'd come by it honestly.

A silver pin denoting the Ballantyne line winked at her from his lapel, a replica of the one never worn in her father's wardrobe. His shoulders were squared, his hands clasped behind his back, his coattails flapping in the morning wind. He looked straight ahead, his eyes fixed on some point she couldn't fathom. She turned back toward Pittsburgh reluctantly, wondering if she'd ever see him again.

Lifting a gloved hand that hid the calluses made in the violin shop, Wren tried to make peace with their arrival . . . and fought the dizzying sensation she was being pitchforked into a world she knew nothing about.

For several long moments Papa and Grandfather stood locked in an emotional embrace. Ignoring the catch in her throat, Wren looked away, feeling like an intruder in the midst of so poignant a scene, and then Grandfather turned to her. His arms were warm and strong and steadfast. She liked that he called her Wren. He bore the same tobacco-bergamot scent that was Papa's own. Though her father had recovered his composure and was instructing the steward about the Cremona violins laid by, emotion still choked her. Ansel Ballantyne seemed a different person here with his genteel clothes and manners, admiring the waiting vehicle along the curb. Not her beloved papa but a near stranger.

Grandfather smiled as a groom opened the lacquered door. "You're just in time to break in the new coach." Trimmed in plum velvet, the rig's leaded glass windows opened and closed via pull straps. The groom showed her how to manage them, but instead of the fresh air she craved, her senses were stormed by coal dust and the potency of the levee.

She didn't draw a decent breath till the coach had whisked them beyond Pittsburgh, past the last bastion of Fort Pitt and the once-grand King's Garden and out the Allegheny Road toward New Hope. Beside her, Molly's eyes were everywhere at once. It felt good but odd to have her riding with them as a passenger, not in the baggage wagon behind. Things were indeed different in free Pennsylvania. Kentucky was very much a slave state.

"Pittsburgh was nothing but a small fort town when I arrived in 1785." There was pride of place in Grandfather's tone, a strong sense of ownership. "Now it boasts nearly fifty thousand citizens."

Cane Run barely boasted fifty souls. Sensing Molly's skittishness, Wren took her hand and squeezed. Across from them Grandfather sat shoulder to shoulder with Papa. She measured their likeness, marveling that this timeworn stranger was her flesh and blood.

"Enough of the city," Grandfather said suddenly, his aged face creased with a hundred kindly lines. "How was your journey?"

"Blessedly uneventful," Papa replied. "No sinking, no explosion, no mutiny."

Grandfather nodded in wry satisfaction. "And you, Wren? How do you like the floating teakettle that bears your name?"

She answered in Gaelic, clinging to its sameness when the whole world seemed to be shifting around her. "I liked the *Rowena* better once I stepped off her."

He laughed, surprisingly rich and deep. "No doubt you'll like a wedding better."

Papa gave him a sideways glance. "A wedding? Mother's letter didn't mention . . ."

"She likely thought I'd already told you. Bennett is to wed a Boston lass this Saturday. The first of our grandchildren to tie the knot."

"Boston? Not a local bride?"

"Charlotte is a shipping heiress. Apparently Bennett likes boats. The Ashburtons arrived last week and are staying at New Hope and Ballantyne Hall."

"Sounds a bit crowded." Papa turned toward a window, where the sooty Pittsburgh skyline was fading from view.

"Since we've added a new wing, there's plenty of room for all." Grandfather steered the conversation in another direction. "As for floating teakettles, the honeymoon voyage will be aboard our newest steamer, the *Belle of Pittsburgh*."

Papa sat back, hat resting on his knees. "How many packets are in the Ballantyne line?"

"Twenty-four at present, though some are so old they're hardly river worthy."

"I've heard of plans to build a floating palace, a showboat. Are you moving more toward passengers than cargo?"

"Not if I can help it. Cargo is always the better choice and less risky when something goes awry."

"Mother said you've begun to invest heavily in the railroad . . ."

Wren left them to their business, the gentle swaying of the coach nearly rocking her to sleep. As she leaned into a sunbeam falling through an open window, her soul lightened. No humble cabins or split-rail fences met her eye, just river and rolling hills. Soon the horses were turning, passing through open iron gates and gliding up a gently sloping hill fronting the river.

She'd been expecting something different, something far from what she knew, yet she still felt a start of surprise at the palatial brick house straddling the river bluff like an aging king holding court. New Hope was a grand dove-gray, old but well kept, dressed with sparkling glass and sweeping porches and fluted columns. An eight-paned cupola crowned the wide gambrel roof. She caught the diamond glitter of a fountain beyond yew hedges and bricked walls. People were wandering about, some sporting top hats and parasols. The wedding party? Curiosity seeped into her, crowding out resistance.

Was Papa glad to be back? Had Mama ever longed to be here?

Amid a small storm of dust, a groom helped her alight from the coach onto a mounting block. Near at hand was an unsmiling man in fancy dress who ushered them into the mansion. Molly followed close behind, her eyes still as wide as Wren's own.

The breezy foyer held a soaring staircase, a profusion of peonies in silver bowls on an immense sideboard. Servants were lined up from front door to back, their posture soldier-stiff, eyes forward, all dressed in navy and white. Wren felt a breathless bewilderment. There were as many servants as the steamboat had deckhands.

Someone was coming down the stairs, someone who seemed a part of all the polish, her gown the deep orange of a wild lily. *Andra?* Wren couldn't recall much about her save she was Papa's older sister.

"Rowena?" Appraising jade eyes peered out of a lightly lined face. Her figure was trim as a girl's, her fair hair the exact shade of Wren's own. Pearls draped her lace bodice, countless creamy rows matching the drops at her ears. "I'm your aunt Andra."

Wren opened her arms to embrace her and met nothing but air. Her aunt had moved on to her father with a starched, "Welcome back to New Hope, Ansel."

Papa returned her tight smile. "Good to see you again, Andra."

Grandfather gestured upstairs. "Your mother is resting, though she wanted me to rouse her as soon as you arrived."

The butler—was that what Andra called him?—was introducing them to servants, who curtsied or bowed at his bidding. Papa clasped hands with a few of them he'd obviously known since boyhood, their faces creasing with fleeting smiles as he called them by name.

With a wave of her hand, Aunt Andra led her beyond the sweeping staircase toward a rear door. "If you'll come out onto the veranda for refreshments, the servants will bring your belongings to your rooms. Of course, you must meet our guests, the Ashburtons of Boston. The wedding is but a few days away."

The next hour became a blur of voices and faces and first impressions.

Uncle Peyton, Grandfather's oldest son. Clutching an eagle-headed cane.

His wife, Penelope. A pale ghost.

Their son, Bennett, the Ballantyne heir. Tall. Tanned. Firm of voice.

His fiancée, Charlotte. Pale. Slim as a willow switch. Silent.

Charlotte's parents were doing most of the talking, their northeastern nasal tones unsettling. Aunt Ellie and her brood were missing. She was nearing her confinement, someone whispered, and couldn't hazard the short distance between River Hill and New Hope.

"Mayhap we'll see them on the morrow," Papa said as if sensing Wren's disappointment. "For now, feast your eyes on those old roses climbing the garden wall. They were planted in honor of your first birthday."

Wren was overwhelmed with buttery blooms the size of teacups and endless acres of flowers beyond. When she opened her mouth to ask if she could wander, Grandmother Eden appeared on the porch, leaning heavily on Grandfather's arm. Little and bent, she reminded Wren of a dried rose, the first blush long faded. But her blue eyes were warm and lively, the clasp of her hand strong.

"Rowena," she said with a contented sigh. "Ansel's little Wren."

"Morning, Granny." Or was it afternoon? Wren's reply sounded rusty. She'd hardly spoken all day.

"We've settled you in the lavender room. 'Twas Ellie's before she wed her Jack. You have a princely view of the garden and chapel." She let go of Grandfather's arm as he helped her into a wheeled wicker chair. "Your father is across from you. His bedchamber is just as he left it."

There was a telling poignancy to the words that touched Wren. So Grandfather wasn't the only one who'd been waiting for them to come. Smiling self-consciously, Wren searched for some reply but failed to find it, her gaze trailing to a maid bringing round a tray of crystal glasses topped with sprigs of mint. Lemonade?

"You must be weary from your journey." Grandmother

leaned in with a whisper. "I'll tell you a little secret. I never got a wink of sleep on a steamboat. Sometimes it seemed I'd travel from here to New Orleans wide-eyed the whole way, my stomach at sea. Thankfully you came upriver to us with nary a mishap, in part because your grandfather arranged for James Sackett to be at the wheel."

"I met Mr. Sackett." Her tongue was finally loosed. "He's . . . right fine." Somehow *right fine* seemed too humble a phrase for a handsome pilot with a silver lapel pin.

Andra was hovering with the persistence of a hummingbird, infusing the sultry air with a noticeable chill. "You mustn't tire yourself, Mother, with too much talk."

"I mustn't tire Wren, you mean," Grandmother returned gently.

"Wren?" Her aunt's voice fell below the tenor of the men as they discussed business across the veranda. "*Wren* might be permissible in the Kentucky woods, but here in Pennsylvania, *Rowena* is best."

"I doubt I'll remember," Grandmother said with a resigned chuckle. "She's been Wren ever since her christening in the chapel—and in every letter her father wrote."

"Letters? Those were precious few."

"Perhaps. But each was special to me. I've saved them all."

Wren shrank beneath her aunt's green gaze. Pondering their exchange, she took a sip of lemonade from the heavy, sweating glass, feeling she might choke from its sourness. One swallow and the glass slipped free of her grasp, splashing her skirts and shoes and drawing every eye. With an ungracious clunk, it rolled rudely across the porch and came to rest at Bennett Ballantyne's feet. He flung her a half-amused, half-aggravated glance as a maid sprang forward to right the mess, a look of dismay on her florid face.

Grandmother leaned nearer and squeezed Wren's limp hand as the conversation swirling round them resumed. "Why don't we go upstairs and I'll show you your room?"

Mumbling an apology, Wren followed on the heels of a maid, Papa and Grandmother close behind. The feminine bower that was to be hers was little more than a blur of pale purple, window curtains cast about in a wildly unsettled breeze.

A mantel clock chimed as the door closed after them. Two in the afternoon? Wren was midnight weary. Molly was missing, unable to help her with her dress. Unmindful of her lemonade-stained skirts and the corset that pinched her with unrelenting fury, she fell facedown on the bed and went to sleep.

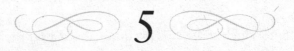

5

Never marry but for love; but see that thou lovest what is lovely.

WILLIAM PENN

Hours later, Wren awoke in a strange bed but had little memory of how she'd gotten there. Somehow, in the sleepy, humid hours following their arrival, Molly had divested Wren of her soiled dress. Now clad in a cotton nightgown, Wren roused, skin damp from the room's sultriness. The cobwebs in her head were gone, the clumsy mishap of the afternoon forgotten. An open window nearest a corner fireplace lured her with its teasing breeze. She leaned into the deep sill, ears taut. A mockingbird's song rent the air—and then a cry.

She hadn't been dreaming. Someone *was* weeping. She feared it was Molly. Molly couldn't speak but she could cry. Was she missing Kentucky too?

Slipping out the door, Wren padded down the stairs, intent on the veranda. Andra had corrected her when she'd said *porch*, as if the word was too plain. Shivers puckered her bare skin at the thought of meeting up with her very proper aunt, but not a soul was in sight. The big house was more kindly without her tonight.

Beneath her feet the floorboards were smooth, the wet mess she'd made earlier set to rights. It took a few minutes to get her bearings, but once at the edge of the garden, she felt for the latch on the ornate gate. Its answering creak set her teeth on edge.

The weeping she'd heard had given way to cricket calls and the low cooing of a dove. For several moments Wren sorted out shadows. Farther down the bricked path she spied a slim silhouette hunched over on a bench. Not Molly. Bennett's bride-to-be? Befuddled, she couldn't recall the woman's name. She'd been easily overlooked in the haze of Wren's arrival.

Should she intrude? Speak? Wren took a careful step, and the woman snapped to attention, clearly startled.

"Please—it's only me. Wren."

The full moon shone down, bright as a lantern, calling out the alarm in the woman's expression. "Bennett's cousin?" Despite the heat, the bride wore an elaborate dressing gown, slippers on her feet. "I thought you were called Rowena."

"I'm not sure what I'm to be called." Mindful of Andra's dislike of a simple *Wren*, she trod cautiously. "You're welcome to use either."

"You seem more a stranger here than a Ballantyne."

Did she? Looking down, Wren smoothed her wrinkled nightgown, almost ashamed of its plainness. "I hardly know my kin. We rarely come upriver from Kentucky. You're from Boston?" Isn't that what Grandfather had said? Something about a Boston shipping heiress? "I don't recollect your name."

"I'm Charlotte Ashburton of Boston, yes."

"You're a long ways from home, then, same as me." Feeling a twist of sympathy, Wren sought some common ground. "You must miss it."

"I do miss Boston, everything about it." The hushed words were almost swallowed by the splashing of a near fountain. "Pittsburgh is so dark. All that coal dust. The pastor who's to marry us says they'll have to wrap me in a sheet to get me to the church or my wedding gown will be blackened."

Wren drew in a sultry breath of honeysuckle as if to clear her mind of the memory. The pall of the city was all too easy to recall. "Why not marry right here in the garden?"

"I'd hoped to wed in New Hope's chapel." Charlotte gestured beyond a yew hedge to a stone wall. "But Bennett says it's too small. He wants more guests. A lavish gala."

Wren listened without comment. Kentucky customs seemed so uncomplicated. The weddings she knew were always simple, delightful, with a lively frolic of fiddling and feasting.

"The ceremony is only a few days away." Resignation weighted Charlotte's words. "Everything has been decided."

Studying her, Wren let go of her assumptions. She'd expected a happy bride, a willing bride. "You don't want to marry?"

Though respectfully spoken, it was a bold question, unfit for polite company, or so the bride's expression told her. "The match was arranged two years ago. After Bennett met my father at a business function."

"So your father is more of a mind to marry him than you are." The ticklish matter struck Wren as mildly amusing.

"My father wed my mother by arrangement, and my grandfather my grandmother. It's how my family has always done things."

"Back home I've never heard of such. People marry for

love and little else." Wren slipped onto the bench, mindful of Charlotte's lace handkerchief between them. "So if everything's been decided, and it's how your family has always done things, why are you so . . . *dowie*?"

The Scots word was not lost on Charlotte. "Sad?"

Wren fixed her gaze on the chapel wall. "It's none of my business, truly. But sometimes a body needs to unburden themselves."

A brief pause. "You'll say nothing to the Ballantynes?"

"I'm no tale-bearer, if that's what you mean."

Charlotte balled the handkerchief in a fist, her words coming slow and soft. "There's someone else . . . someone other than Bennett."

"Someone else?" Wren looked at her. "Back in Boston?"

Charlotte glanced toward the house as if fearful their voices would carry. "Christian is a clerk in my father's shipping office. We met by accident last year. He's a good man—a respectable man—though my family feels he's beneath me."

Wren hesitated. The pecking order among fancy folk was quickly coming clear. "Do you love him?" The honest question seemed the only thing that mattered.

"I do love him. And he loves me. Just yesterday a letter came. He asked me to marry him. He thinks we can make a life together. But first I must find a way home."

Wren studied her, feeling she'd stumbled into a hornet's nest. Would Bennett's bride . . . bolt? All the way to Boston?

"I'm considering asking the pilot who's to take us on our wedding journey." Charlotte's words were hurried, her tone more hopeful. "One of the maids told me he's trustworthy and might help."

James Sackett? Wren's mind raced to keep up with the details. Reaching out, she squeezed Charlotte's soft hand,

unsure what she was communicating. Sympathy, foremost—
and surprise that James Sackett and a maid were somehow
involved. "Can I help?"

"Say nothing about this—"

Charlotte's low words were severed by the creaking of the
gate. The glow of a lamp cut across the bricked path in back
of them. Andra. "What on earth are you two doing at such an
hour? And in such dishabille? What if the servants see you?"

Wren crossed her arms, hugging them to her bosom. Her
bare feet and thin shift, nearly transparent from so many
washings, seemed to draw her aunt's unwavering eye.

Charlotte stood behind her, voice shaky. "I couldn't sleep."

There was a lengthy pause. Could her aunt sense Charlotte's
misery? Had she overheard her plan to return to Boston?

"'Tis wedding jitters, little else." Andra held the lantern
higher as if calling out all their secrets. "You need your rest.
Tomorrow you'll have a final fitting for your wedding dress
and finish packing for your journey to New Orleans. As for
you, Rowena, we'll need to arrange for a dressmaker. I've
looked through your wardrobe and it's far too rustic for Pittsburgh. You're in need of a suitable gown for the wedding
especially." She paused, her tone brooking no argument. "And
you simply must have some new nightclothes."

Taking Charlotte by the arm, Andra escorted her toward
the house, which, in light of Charlotte's confession, seemed
more prison.

If not for Andra, Wren suspected she and Charlotte might
have talked till dawn. There'd been a marked urgency, a sense
of panic, about the bride that led Wren to believe she might
be missing come breakfast. The wedding was set for Saturday
morn.

Time yet to flee to Boston.

6

Things are seldom what they seem.

PROVERB

In his grip the carving knife was nearly as familiar as the pilothouse wheel with its rich inlay work, the wood smooth and warm. A mound of wood shavings lay at James's feet, and every so often a southerly breeze would stir them into a tempest, scattering their sweet fragrance.

"Morning, James." Jack Turlock lifted his hat as he passed by, intent on the house. The scent of the judge's pipe smoke was swept along on the wind. River Hill in late August always smelled of damask roses and maccaboy tobacco.

"Morning, Judge."

Usually the master of River Hill paused to talk, but this morning his long stride never lessened. James missed the judge's company. River travel required pilots to reside mostly at the Monongahela House in Pittsburgh, though it was his familiar River Hill cottage he craved. It had been his respite since he'd come of age.

James returned to his task, the tiny figure in his palm taking shape, an echo of the heron he'd seen when shearing the riverbank in shoal water. All along the porch rail were tiny animals resembling a small circus, the morning light calling out the variations in wood and design.

"If you keep carving, James Sackett, there'll soon be more animals than children in the Orphan Home."

He looked up, squinting into blinding sunlight that framed the young woman before him from head to toe.

Izannah Turlock hovered on his porch stoop, clutching a fresh copy of the *Pittsburgh Gazette*. "Now that you're on land for more than five minutes, I thought you'd like to see all the cards printed for you in the paper."

He resumed carving, intent on the tiny wing taking shape beneath his practiced hand.

Her voice dropped to a conspiratorial whisper. "Your popularity appears to be in jeopardy. Last week there were a total of ten cards for you on the society page. This week's tally is a mere six. But one of them is from my uncle Ansel, thanking you for a safe and scenic trip." She set the paper on the railing beside him, turned so he could see the printed accolades. "Why didn't you mention you were bringing my long-lost relatives upriver?"

"I didn't know I was." He recalled all too easily his keen surprise the moment they'd stepped aboard. "Not till Louisville."

She studied him, a curious light in her eyes. "I want you to tell me all about her."

"Her?"

"Cousin Rowena, of course." When he hesitated, her voice frayed with exasperation. "Come now, James. Just this once I wish you'd open up about your passengers. I don't care that you've freighted presidents and princes and Indian chiefs up and down the Mississippi. I only want to know about my Kentucky cousin. Other than Bennett, she's the only one I have."

"You'll meet her soon enough."

Taking a stool opposite, she leaned forward, her smoky eyes intent. "Will I?"

He gave a nod, thoughts still crowded from the trip and the fact he'd nearly clipped the steering oar of a trading scow en route.

"Is she . . . pretty?"

He bit the inside of his cheek. "I didn't notice."

"James Sackett!"

He stopped carving, knowing she'd not leave till she'd wrested from him what she wanted. "Her eyes are like sea foam . . . her hair is the color of hemp rope."

Izannah sighed. "Sometimes I think you're more poet than pilot, James."

He set the knife aside. "She barely comes to my shoulder."

"How would you know? Was she standing that close?"

Yes, much too close. His mind roamed backward, remembering. Trying not to. "She handles a fiddle like I pilot a boat."

"So she's musical then, like the Ballantynes—and the Nancarrows in England."

"Not unlike."

"I've heard her mother was the talk of London in her day. She's bound to be lovely if she's anything like her." A haunted look stole away her curiosity. "It must be hard losing one's mother."

He didn't remember. He couldn't recall his own. "How are things at the house?"

She looked toward the faded brick facade. "Daddy's canceled a court hearing to stay close to home. He's afraid Mama will need him as soon as he lifts his gavel, same as last time. She's threatening to ride over and see Ansel and Rowena at New Hope."

"They'll likely come here first."

"I hope so." She watched as he set the heron aside. "I'm afraid we'll not make it to the wedding with Mama like she is."

The silence stretched long, sweetened by a warbler's call.

He reached for a small, unfinished dog. "I'll be at the levee myself."

"You know you're expected to attend, James—but I doubt anyone less than Grandfather could make you appear."

Wishing an end to the conversation, he set his jaw, though his knife slipped a tad. The tiny dog lost a paw.

"Bennett's not still badgering you, is he?" she whispered.

The peaceful morning soured. "It's nothing you need worry about."

She leaned nearer. "I *am* worried. I've overheard Mama and Daddy talking about Bennett and his extravagance, his gambling in stocks and land speculation—"

"Ease off, Izannah."

"But it's true! Bennett will likely bring the Ballantynes to ruin if he keeps on—"

"Izannah."

She quieted at the soft steel of his tone. He wasn't given to such talk, even within the family. It accomplished little and set feelings on fire. Sensing someone near, he looked past the porch to neat rows of cottages identical to his own, occupied by River Hill's large staff of servants.

A boyish voice broke over them as it hailed from the front veranda. "Izzy? Mama needs you!"

Nathaniel? James squinted into blinding sunlight. He sounded just like his twin, John Henry. There were so many boys and James was gone so often he could no longer distinguish between them.

Izannah stood. "Promise you'll come for supper tonight, James. I've asked Cook to make your favorite." She moved away with a swish of her wide skirts before he gave answer. "Promise?"

"Six o'clock," he said in affirmation, wondering if he'd be the only guest.

Wren stood before a full-length mirror of cheval glass, Molly tugging at her corset strings, looks of consternation on both their faces. *The desired waist size is seventeen inches.* The Louisville dressmaker's remark now mocked her. Her waist was a generous five inches wider if cinched tightly. Too many years of eating cat's head biscuits and gravy were to blame, Molly's grim expression seemed to say.

Wren ground her teeth as the last bit of air was forced from her lungs. "Pure suffocation."

With every yank of the corset strings came fresh resolve. Soon she'd be back home in her plain dresses and aprons, far from finery and disapproving aunts, whether she had Papa's blessing or not. She'd hang her crinoline in the barn or make a cage of it for chickens. All that Pittsburgh steel and linen thread shouldn't go to waste.

Molly sighed and draped a gown over Wren's head, easing it into place and smoothing countless rows of ruffles with hurried hands. They were running late. A carriage waited outside New Hope's ornate front door, ready to whisk them to River Hill. She could hear Papa apologize for their tardiness in the foyer.

"The coachman hardly needs an apology, Ansel." Andra's voice had the unique ability to carry throughout the immense house and chill Wren to the bone. With the door slightly ajar and nearest the stair landing, she heard every word. "Are people not prompt in Kentucky?"

"Not prompt, but polite," he returned, holding on to his good humor despite Andra's needling.

51

Finished with hooking her dress, Molly gestured to Wren's hair. Tousled beyond repair, it fell in pale disarray down her back. With a quick hand, Molly twisted and turned the length of it into a bun at the nape of her neck, teasing out a few tendrils to frame her face. Gone was the plain, familiar braid that had marked her since childhood. The glass reflected a solemn, green-eyed stranger.

When at last she came down the stairs, Aunt Andra was nowhere in sight. "I'm sorry, Papa, for being tardy."

He smiled as they went out to the waiting carriage. "One can't be late when arriving unexpectedly."

She tried to smile back at him. "So we're a . . . surprise?"

"Things are less formal at River Hill than here. With ten sons running about . . ." He leaned back on the carriage seat, studying her again as if trying to reconcile the daughter she'd been with the one who sat opposite him. "Molly has done wonders with your hair and dress. I wish your mother . . ."

Wren's heart squeezed as he looked away. *I wish too, Papa.* She searched for words of comfort, but there was little to be had dwelling on the past. As the miles swept by in a green haze, she tried to focus as he pointed out a few grand houses behind forbidding gates.

"See that drive lined with trees? That's Broad Oak, the home of Wade Turlock, brother to your uncle Jack who married your aunt Ellie."

"Wade isn't wed?"

"Not to my knowledge. He's as much a bachelor as Andra is a spinster." His gaze traveled to a distant chimney puffing smoke. "Beyond that bend is Cameron Farm, where the Cameron clan lives—two of them, anyway. The heir, a young man by the name of Malachi, is often away, as he's the owner of the Pennsylvania Railroad."

She looked in the direction he pointed but couldn't see past a thick copse of trees.

"Over there we have Ballantyne Hall, where Peyton resides with his wife and son." Papa gestured across the road to yet another long lane. "You met them when we arrived at New Hope."

Imposing iron gates rose up amid the tall late summer grass. Ballantyne Hall was where Bennett lived . . . where Charlotte would live, if she lasted. Wren took a deep breath and prayed till the tightness inside her unwound. The sound of happy shouting soon chased any melancholy from her mind as the carriage rolled past half a dozen exuberant boy- ish faces. Aunt Ellie's brood?

"Do you know any of them?" she asked.

"No," he said, regret in his gaze. "I only remember Izan- nah."

They slowed to a stop before wide stone steps much like New Hope's. Behind a tangle of roses and lilacs was a grand brick house just as imposing.

A perspiring, breathless lad of about twelve flung open the coach door. "Uncle Ansel? Cousin Rowena? We thought it might be you, as you're in Grandfather's coach." He helped her down, then shook hands with Papa as the other boys looked on, shy but smiling. "You're just in time for supper."

"And you would be?" Papa queried with a smile.

"Nathaniel. My twin's John Henry." He lined up the smaller boys with the efficiency of a soldier surveying his troops. "And here you have Nicholas, Danson, Clayton, and Tremper."

The smallest Turlock—Tremper—tucked a grubby hand in Wren's. "You're pretty, like my sister." He spoke with a lisp, his gray eyes earnest. "Did you come to see the baby?"

"The baby's not been born yet," Nathaniel reminded him.

Wren smiled and squeezed Tremper's hand. "I've come to see everybody."

Nathaniel motioned them toward a brick walk as the coachman drove on toward the porte cochere. "Our older brothers are missing. Grant and Niel are away attending university in New York. Alexander and Eben are abroad hunting at Grandfather's estate in Scotland."

Grandfather's Scottish estate? Papa hadn't mentioned that. Wren fell into step beside him as he led them to the house, musing all the way.

She tried to find a place to rest her eyes as a dozen different things vied for her attention—the noisy boys, the cupola atop the gambrel roof, the string of cottages down a side lane. A profusion of roses crowding the front porch won out. Their perfume was like a presence, strong and sweet, blooming in such varied hues Wren nearly stopped on the walk, dumbstruck.

Before they'd mounted the front steps, a woman flew through the open doorway as fast as her bulk would allow. Aunt Ellie's face was joyful yet wistful, her blue eyes glistening with tears. Still remarkably pretty despite the delicate lines about her eyes and mouth, she resembled the boys in the cut of their features if not their fair hair. She nearly sent Wren's father off his feet. Next her warm arms enveloped Wren in the sincere welcome denied them by Andra at New Hope, bringing a lump to her throat. "Rowena? Little Wren?"

Wren clung to her a little too long, reminded of Mama's lavender-scented embrace. She didn't break free till a man appeared behind them, overshadowing them. There was no mistaking who'd sired ten sons. Jack Turlock's imprint was stamped on his brood as indelibly as ink. Wren found herself staring at this tanned giant, fair hair like a shock of wheat, features ruddy. He looked more gentleman farmer than judge.

"So you've come back to us." He shook Papa's hand heartily, his silvered eyes alight as he took in Wren. "I have a daughter hereabouts who'd like to meet you."

John Henry pointed off the porch. "Izzy's down at River Row."

Wren's gaze trailed west, to a leafy, oak-lined lane. A young woman walked toward them, straw hat in hand, ribbons trailing along the ground. The man beside her seemed thoughtful, his head bent as she talked, her comely profile turned toward him entreatingly.

The boys began to buzz like agitated bees, swarming to one side of the long porch. "James is coming for supper! About time too! Suppose he'll tell us another river tale?"

Wren felt a stirring of recognition as the couple came closer. Coatless, James Sackett was in shirtsleeves and waistcoat, dark trousers falling to leather boots. All bore the mark of a gentleman at leisure, not an officer of the Ballantyne line. A mere echo of the polished pilot she remembered. She'd left him behind at the levee two days past, not expecting to see him again, yet here he was, holding her surprised gaze with his own across the fragrant, crowded porch.

And next to him was . . . her cousin? Beautiful and buxom, golden-haired and silver-eyed, Izannah Turlock stood in a shaft of sunlight looking like she'd just stepped out of a fairy tale.

"Come in out of this heat," Ellie invited, threading her arms through Wren's and her father's. "There'll be plenty more talking at table." With that, she led them into the antique elegance of River Hill.

7

I met a lady in the meads,
Full beautiful, a faery's child;
Her hair was long, her foot was light,
And her eyes were wild.

JOHN KEATS

Wren swallowed down a wave of wonder. Her gaze lifted, took in lofty ceilings and crown molding nearly a hundred years old. Someone seated her at an immense table. She took care to manage her unruly crinoline, sitting down on a chair that thankfully had no arms and allowed for her skirts to settle. Wedged between Nathaniel and Izannah, she glanced about the sumptuous, lemon-hued room.

Farther down, past a runner of ivy and creamy day lilies, James Sackett and the judge sat opposite Papa and Aunt Ellie, boys sprinkled in between. So far Izannah hadn't said a word. Wren prayed their initial awkwardness would mend. She so needed a friend.

The judge cleared his throat and leveled a solemn eye at

the boys. A prayer was said. At his "Amen," the stillness gave way to chaos. Laughter and talk bubbled over as the meal commenced. Navy-clad servants darted in and out, bearing steaming silver dishes and the loveliest china Wren had ever seen. River Hill employed free blacks and whites, Papa said. They were in emancipated Pennsylvania, after all.

"I'm never quite hungry in this heat." Perspiration beaded Izannah's upper lip and left damp wisps about her oval face. Setting her fork down, she brought out a bamboo fan embellished with tiny pink and cream seashells.

"That's fetching," Wren said, thinking of her own, a humble blend of wood and paper. "I've never seen one like it."

"James brought it back to me from the West Indies."

James. There was an intimacy to the word that made Wren's flush climb higher as he looked their way. Raising her glass of lemon ice, she took a careful sip, mindful of her spill at New Hope.

Across from her, Danson was forking his chicken with gusto, murmuring to John Henry between bites. The younger boys were trading disliked items for more palatable ones, spearing deviled eggs and pickled asparagus off each other's plates when the judge wasn't watching.

"Mama, is that pretty lady coming to live with us?" At Tremper's raised voice, every eye turned toward Wren.

Aunt Ellie smiled. "Cousin Wren is always welcome here, but she's staying at New Hope for now."

"With Grandfather and Grandmother?" Comprehension dawned on his upturned, freckled face. "And sour Aunt Andra?"

A burst of laughter tore round the table. Pink-cheeked, Aunt Ellie wiped Tremper's mouth with a napkin and turned the tide of conversation. "Would you like some strawberry ice cream once you finish your supper?"

He nodded and Izannah swished her fan more vigorously. "You may be wondering why the children aren't served separately like in most large houses. Daddy won't allow it, though there are times I wish he would."

Wren set her own fork aside. Hunger still gnawed at her, but her corset wouldn't allow for another bite. "How is it having so many brothers?"

Izannah sighed. "Downright dangerous."

Wren nearly laughed. "You have in mind a baby sister?"

"Daddy believes it will be another boy. He's been right ten times out of eleven, though Mama and I still have hopes for a girl." Izannah looked at her, a curious light in her eyes. "So tell me, cousin, what do you think of Pennsylvania? Is it very different from Kentucky?"

"Different? Like silk and homespun." Wren spoke the first thing that came to mind. "You've never been?"

"Papa won't allow me to travel. He says ladies should stay near to home. And Mama needs me here given all the children underfoot."

"One day maybe you'll wander."

"Wander?" Izannah's lovely face lit up. "I should hope so. I have in mind New Orleans and Europe. I'd especially like to see Edinburgh and London."

"You should talk to Papa, then. He's been nearly everywhere hunting violins, though he's yet to find the one he's looking for."

"The Italian Guarneri, you mean. The one Grandfather sold long ago?" At Wren's nod, her expression turned more earnest. "You've never accompanied him on his travels?"

"Hearing about them is enough," Wren replied with a smile. "Staying home suits me."

They slipped into a comfortable silence, in pointed contrast to the lively conversation at table's end. Wren let her gaze wander, alighting on the pilot again. Candlelight called out the sun lines about his eyes, his stoic profile and squared jaw. She liked how his dark hair waved and fell to his collar, like a brush of ink on stark white paper. In the heat it curled on the ends, in outright defiance of a comb. In mockery of his fierce reserve. Did he never smile . . . never laugh?

Across from him, Papa had come to life. He was talking and gesturing in a way that made Wren's jaw sag. Like he was at home here, had ever been. All his melancholy had flown.

Izannah stopped her fanning. "Would you like to walk in the garden? There's usually a blessed breeze off the river." With a last look at James, she smiled. "Mama won't mind."

Wren hated to leave her rich meal unfinished and cast her aunt Ellie an apologetic glance as she followed Izannah's graceful exit from the table.

Izannah's voice dropped to a conspiratorial whisper. "Mama usually spends summer evenings in the garden but tires easily of late. My father and yours will likely shut themselves in the study and talk business, corralling James if they can, unless my brothers get to him first." She expelled a little breath. "I believe you've met everyone at River Hill except Great-Aunt Elspeth."

"Elspeth?"

"She's Grandmother's half sister." Izannah's brow knotted and she paused, as if unsure how much to share. "Daddy sort of inherited her when he married Mama. But Elspeth is now so old she doesn't make as much trouble as she used to. She lives in a stone cottage at the east end of the garden with her maid and nurse. See that far chimney?"

They stepped onto a side porch that overlooked acres of

flowers, a large fountain at its heart. Far beyond was Elspeth's domain, a safe distance from the main house.

"I've never seen such a garden," Wren said.

"It was naught but weeds when my parents wed." Izannah plucked a cluster of wisteria climbing a near column. "Daddy employs three gardeners to tend it for Mama."

"We have a small patch," Wren said. The confession seemed a shameful thing, almost laughable. Theirs was no bigger than a wagon wheel, hardly worth mentioning, though Molly tended it like a baby. "Herbs and vegetables mostly. A kitchen garden."

"We have a physic garden too, between the house and summer kitchen, but it's so full of bees and snakes I stay away. Poor Cook is forever chasing the boys out of it."

They started down stone steps into fading sunlight and cooler air when a maid appeared behind them, apology in her tone. "Your mother needs you upstairs, Miss Izannah."

"Coming," she answered, sudden alarm in her eyes. "Feel free to wander about, cousin. If you go far enough, there's a yew maze with a pond at the center . . . swans."

Swans? Wren took the remaining steps by twos, bypassing a bubbling fountain. Its music fed her unsettled spirit, its windborne spray a welcome mist on her flushed face. She'd always felt nearer to God in a garden than any place on earth. If not for the pinch of her crinoline and slippers, she'd be nearly free.

Glory, but it was a wonder to be alone.

All day long Aunt Andra had kept her busy at New Hope, cataloguing wedding gifts and arranging them just so in the twin parlors in case callers happened by, while Charlotte sat and penned copious thank-you notes. They'd had tea with Grandmother at three o'clock before resuming their unwrapping and admiring and writing. As the day wore on, Charlotte seemed more unsettled and near tears—but what was Wren to do?

She quickened her step as if to outdistance the thought, passing flowers she had no name for. Recognizing a climbing rose, she tucked one into her upswept hair. Just ahead was the promised yew hedge. She disappeared into its green folds, befuddled. Several wrong turns and dead ends later, she stumbled into the maze's middle. Twin swans glided over the pond's shimmery surface in the hush of twilight. Never in her life had she seen swans. They seemed the stuff of fairy tales. Like Izannah.

Bending down as easily as the detested corset and crinoline would allow, she shed her stockings, garters, and shoes. The sides of her taffeta bodice were soaked through, more from nerves than the heat. Oh, to shed her dress! If she was home she would.

Fists full of fabric, she waded into the water, a shiver of delight dancing down her spine. The swans drew nearer, undisturbed by her presence. She longed to be like them, to glide through her present predicament composed and queen-like. Leaning over, she studied her flushed reflection in the still water, the blossom in her hair a ghostly white.

She could hear boyish shouts and laughter back at the house as she felt her way over the pond's pebbly bottom. The urge to shuck off all her clothes and swim was strong. The sun sank lower, but she was hardly conscious of the time, unmindful of anything but the delicious coolness of the water.

When she looked up again, the yew hedge seemed to melt away.

In the shadows stood James Sackett. He looked down at the ground as she let go of her skirts. The fabric ballooned around her, riding the surface of the water like a lily pad. Without a word he turned his back on her.

Heat prickled her skin at the sight of her discarded clothes. The high-minded pilot of the Ballantynes' . . . here? There was little to be done but hurry out of the water and wring out her skirts. "I'm sorry, Mr. Sackett. Seems like the heat went to my head."

"Your father asked me to find you." He spoke over his shoulder. "Izannah would have come in my stead, but she's with her mother."

So Aunt Ellie's baby was about to be born. What else could it be? She swallowed down a sigh. She'd rather Izannah had come. It was plain James Sackett didn't relish the task. "You needn't trouble yourself on my account."

"It's no trouble, Miss Ballantyne," he said smoothly. "I just didn't expect to find you . . ."

"Wading?" She half smiled at his careful phrasing. "I suppose barefoot Ballantynes are rare as hen's teeth."

He glanced at her and she caught a flash of green. The sun lines about his eyes were chiseled deep, reminding her of mossy rocks in a millstream. Her insides gave a little lurch. His handsomeness was a heart-catching thing. Despite his wall of reserve and too-fine manners, she could see why Izannah was smitten.

"Have you never been wading, Mr. Sackett?" She drew abreast of him, missing Selkirk and their easy banter.

"Every day I'm on the river I'm in danger of wading, Miss Ballantyne. It's not a favorite pastime."

"Yet you fancy being a pilot."

"It's all I've ever known."

She bent to gather up her discarded underthings, her hair coming free of Molly's hastily placed pins. It spilled round her shoulders, the ends brushing the cool grass. What a sight she must look! Izannah flashed to mind, nary a hair out of place . . .

She fumbled with her flimsy slippers, trying to stuff her damp feet into them while he averted his eyes again. Giving up, she decided to go barefoot.

"I'd suggest you keep your shoes on while in Pittsburgh, Miss Ballantyne."

She straightened, searching for the slightest sign of teasing in his face. "I've been barefoot all my life, Mr. Sackett."

"I don't doubt it, but Pennsylvania isn't Kentucky, understand."

"I won't be staying long." She met his green gaze head-on. "Not long enough to mend my ways."

"I don't remember hearing of your return downriver."

"You will once the wedding's through." If there was a wedding . . . if Charlotte didn't run away. Unsettled, she turned and took a last look at the swans. "I plan to be back home by the first killing frost, if not before."

"The killing frost . . ." His eyes held a query.

"When the last of the tobacco is cut and the late apples get sweet." She could tell he didn't have any inkling about such things.

He gave a thoughtful nod. "Before the rivers freeze."

"Yes." She'd canoe home if she had to. Could he sense that?

He started walking and she stayed slightly in back of him, wet hem dragging. Thoughts of Charlotte crowded in, raising more questions. Had she sent the note asking for his help? If not for the curt way he clipped his words as if each one was ground out of him, she'd ask. Charlotte might have changed her mind, or—her heart stilled at the thought—James Sackett might have refused her.

They navigated the maze far more easily than when she'd entered, and it was apparent he knew it well. Once again she stumbled on her cumbersome skirts, feeling the burn of embarrassment as he reached out to right her. Warm fingers cupped her elbow, then fell away as if bitten.

"Are you all right?" His words came quiet in the stillness, surprising her, turning her a touch shy.

In answer, her hand went to the rose she'd tucked in her hair. Plucking it free, she pressed the fading bloom into his sinewy hand. He took her small token of thanks without a flicker of emotion. As if she'd done nothing at all.

Mercy, she'd never seen a man so . . . unbent. If she handed him a rattlesnake, what would his reaction be? Unlike Selkirk and the Cane Run men she knew, James Sackett seemed cast in stone.

Papa appeared in their path, smiling bemusedly when he took in her wet attire. "I knew you'd be in the garden, Wren. Our carriage is waiting." He extended a hand, which James shook firmly. "I'll see you early in the morning, at the levee."

At James's nod they parted company, though Wren gave a backward glance at the big house, thinking of Izannah.

Papa looked back too. "Pray for your aunt, Wren. Her baby is about to be born and not all is well."

The terse words erased every thought of James Sackett from her head.

"Where's Mistress McFee, the midwife?"

Izannah swung toward her father as he stood in the doorway of the dressing room, wishing she had better news. "She's been sent for but is at the Kirks'."

A flash of exasperation lit his bearded face. She knew what

he was thinking. How dare young, vivacious Kitty Kirk, who birthed babies like a cat had kittens, intrude on a Turlock at such a time? It seemed to underscore the obvious. Mama was too old. Too tired. Too besotted with a house overflowing with children. Too passionate about Daddy—and he with her—despite a union that spanned a multitude of years and should have long since cooled.

Childbirth was the only time her father showed fear. Izannah saw it now in the tight, tanned lines of his face, the grieved gray of his eyes. As a revered and respected judge, Jack Turlock was used to swaying fate with the swing of his gavel, yet here in the stifling bedchamber he appeared completely powerless. Out of place.

Lying back on a bank of feather pillows, Mama tried to smile despite the ordeal stretching before her. "Izannah, ready the cradle and make sure a warm blanket is waiting. Then we'll—" The words were snatched away by a pain so acute her face turned ashen despite the heat of the bedchamber.

Witnessing it, Papa tunneled a hand through his hair and shut the door, enclosing himself in the dressing room. Izannah turned back to the bed as Mama finished telling her what to do, her words rushed and then extinguished altogether by an anguished moan. For a moment Izannah stood stricken.

It should be me, Mama, lying in that bed, giving you a grandchild. I'd gladly withstand the pain to bear my beloved a son . . .

The thought sent her flushing and nearly stumbling as she readied the cradle. Used by countless Turlock babies, its pine edge was marred by tiny tooth marks, the interior lined with lamb's wool in winter and the softest cotton in summer.

"Open the windows wider, Izannah. And call for your father to—" Stopping again, Mama bit her lip. "To come pray with me. It shouldn't be long now. I've had pains all through supper—"

Before the last word was uttered, her father thrust open the door that separated them. Izannah fled down the hall to fetch linens, her last look capturing her strong, stalwart father on his knees at Mama's side.

In the shadows of the linen closet, she drew in a quivering breath and tried to shake the sick feeling that followed. The day had gone wrong from the start. Her brothers had been an unmanageable handful since dawn. Her maid had scorched her favorite gown. Cook had dropped the dessert she'd promised. And James had been far too preoccupied . . .

Feeling her way through the familiar closet, she latched on to what she sought, thoughts settling on Uncle Ansel. Long ago, Mama had lost her first baby from the shock of his leaving. Would she lose this babe at his reappearing? Or worse?

"Izannah!"

Her father's voice thundered through the second floor like cannon fire. Hugging the linens to her chest, she ran toward the sound, tripping in her haste.

Lord, help us, please . . .

8

Old age is not a matter for sorrow.
It is matter for thanks if we have
left our work done behind us.

THOMAS CARLYLE

James leaned back in his chair, senses filled with the newness of the latest Ballantyne enterprise. The recently finished offices along Water Street fronted the levee, the large bank of windows offering a panorama of ceaseless activity. Ballantyne steamships lay in tiers three deep as the mist rose off the river and the strengthening sun vied with black ash and coal dust in a furious play of light and shadow.

Around an immense refectory table made of oak, shareholders gathered alongside a fleet of company attorneys, head shipwrights, apprentices, and more. Silas Ballantyne didn't exclude anyone who had a hand in the business, be it the boatyard or ironworks or glassworks. Every employee owned stock and prospered—or stood to lose everything—depending on the Ballantynes' rise or fall.

To his left, the judge's place was conspicuously empty. Jack Turlock was at River Hill, about to become a father again. James had hoped Ellie's travail would be over when he awoke, but no babe's cry had rent the morning stillness when he'd left for Pittsburgh. He'd gone down the long drive, a hollow feeling in his gut, unsure of what awaited on his return.

Silas stood at the far end of the table, diverting James's thoughts. As usual, the founder of the Ballantyne fortune didn't mince words but took matters by the tail. "I've called this morning's meeting to announce two matters of importance—the return of my son Ansel to Pittsburgh and the possibility of a Ballantyne-Cameron alliance."

A murmur of approval—and surprise—rippled through the room. James fixed his eyes on Peyton, the ailing heir, and Bennett, second in line. He knew how father and son felt about both matters. They were spitting nails over Ansel's return—and could hardly contain their glee over partnering with the powerful Cameron clan.

"In the weeks to come, Ansel will assume leadership of Ballantyne Ironworks while the management of our other interests will remain unchanged." Turning toward the wall with a surety that belied his age, Silas unveiled a large map showing railroad routes crisscrossing the eastern United States in bold black lines.

"As you know, the Baltimore and Ohio is nearing completion in Wheeling, West Virginia, and will soon be a part of the Pennsylvania Railroad. The Camerons and I have nearly formalized a partnership comprised of seven Ballantyne steamers that will operate in conjunction with the line at its end point . . ."

Though his own spirits lifted at the inclusion of Ansel and

a possible Cameron tie, James couldn't keep his mind on talk of tracks and land west of the meridian and competing railroad routes. Couldn't even entertain a sliver of envy that his old friend Malachi Cameron had finally come into his own. Couldn't feel any awe as Silas spoke of the Camerons' grand plan to link the East and the West with a transcontinental railroad.

"I'm sorry, Mr. Sackett. Seems like the heat went to my head."

Raising a hand, James gave a discreet tug to his cravat. Though the room was cool, it seemed he was still standing in the heat of the garden, bewitched by what he'd never have—a Ballantyne bride—wading in the water. In his breast pocket was the rose she'd given him, dried now. Its faint fragrance reminded him of her.

As if he needed a reminder . . .

The morning inched ahead, the meeting ending on a congratulatory note as Silas turned toward Bennett. "Best wishes to my grandson and his bride-to-be, Miss Charlotte Ashburton, on the occasion of their Saturday nuptials."

Handshakes and applause returned Bennett to the center of attention. Quietly James left his seat to stand near the door, preparing to take his leave. Perhaps it no longer mattered that Bennett's longtime rival was making such strides. Malachi Cameron had yet to take a wife, and Bennett was about to marry a shipping heiress.

But for the note in James's pocket.

Though it wasn't signed, he'd been assured of its origin—Bennett's bride. One of New Hope's maids had sent it over yesterday. The help were always going between River Hill and New Hope, and he'd thought little of it till a stable hand slipped the note to him at dusk.

> *Mr. Sackett,*
>
> *Have heard you are trustworthy. Am anxious to return to Boston. Servants say you have connections. Please advise.*

Without a doubt a scandal was in the making, and he wanted no part of it. Common sense told him to pass the matter to Silas—but something stopped him.

"Ready to depart for New Orleans, James?" Silas was at his elbow, leaning on a gold-plated cane.

"A Saturday sailing, aye."

Their eyes met, communicating a great deal more than piloting and wedding journeys and the coming twelve-hundred-mile trip. Silas's keen gaze was a never-fading jade, his handshake firm. There was no sign of the man who had collapsed two weeks prior, leaving James on tenterhooks since.

"If you have need of anything . . ." Silas began.

"A prayer or two," James replied.

Silas's voice was low and measured. "Just remember to stay clear of Island 37. And take care to dock in Louisville on the midnight watch."

James gave a nod, barely registering the details, the bride's plea weighting him.

It was the perfect opportunity to show Silas the note. Excuse himself from any trouble. But he couldn't shift the burden to an ailing man. Miss Ashburton's heartfelt note was for him and no one else. Despite the scandal about to ensue, James felt an undeniable swell of sympathy for Bennett's bride. And a certainty he had to help her.

In the privacy of the dressing room, Charlotte's strained whisper turned urgent. "I must tell Bennett today."

Darting a look at the door Aunt Andra had just passed through, Wren dared a single word. "Today?"

Charlotte's eyes, a deep lavender-blue, darkened. "Another letter came from Christian yesterday. Bennett intercepted it and confronted me. He was so angry I thought he might strike me."

Wren stared at her, mind spinning. Bennett . . . angry? He looked so gentlemanly in his tailored clothes, so polite and refined, like he'd never lift a hand to anyone. Yet here Charlotte was pouring out her heart to the contrary.

"Bennett has planned an outing on the lake today at Ballantyne Hall. He says we've hardly had a moment alone together. He wants to show me his new skiff. I dread it yet feel this may be the opportunity to end things. Last night I sent a note to James Sackett through my maid—"

A stirring outside the door quashed their whispering. Aunt Andra was approaching, her brisk step unmistakable. "The bride-to-be is in here, ready for a final fitting." She showed the dressmaker in, two assistants trailing. "I trust you've also brought a suitable gown for Rowena." She glanced at Wren, her smile thin. "I took the liberty of asking Mistress Endicott to improve on your Louisville dresses and find a more fitting garment."

"And improve we did." The aging seamstress's face held satisfaction as both gowns were brought in.

The bridal ensemble was unveiled first in all its creamy splendor. Speechless, Wren pondered how Charlotte would last through the ceremony in such heavy silk when she already looked wilted in camisole and petticoats. On a near dressing table, the wedding bonnet with its mock orange flowers and matching lace veil awaited to complete her misery.

Mistress Endicott stood with hands on her ample hips. "If you'll undress to your undergarments, Rowena, we'll fit your new dress."

The rustle of tissue drew every eye. Something satiny emerged, the mint shade with its rose trim pleasing. Wren hadn't seen anything so splendid on their hurried Louisville shopping trip. Of a lighter fabric than Charlotte's silk, the dress slid over her shoulders, the frothy lace hem settling to the floor.

Wren ran a light hand over the gathered skirt. "Reminds me of spring . . . wild roses."

Andra stood back, teeth catching on her bottom lip in contemplation. "The shade seems a trifle pale. Is there nothing else?"

Mistress Endicott moved toward a muslin-wrapped bundle, clearly anxious to do Andra's bidding. "We've brought another in chrome-yellow."

The gown emerged, a glaring gold, its full skirts edged with large blue bows. *Tawdry* was the word that leapt to mind. Even Charlotte looked aghast. There was a strained pause before a knock sounded at the door, prolonging the decision.

"I've come to see Charlotte and Wren." Grandmother took a slow step into the room on the arm of her maid, smiling, ever joyful. "Ah, the final fitting. We've not had a bride at New Hope since Ellie wed her Jack."

"Yes, Mother, you were just telling Charlotte that yesterday." Andra bent and examined the garish dress closely. "This gown is far more eye-catching, don't you agree?"

Grandmother looked to Wren, hesitancy in her every feature. "I don't know that I've ever seen that shade of yellow. In my day Spitalfields silk was the height of fashion."

"Times are changing," Andra told her curtly. "Chrome-yellow it shall be."

Wren held her tongue. She didn't want to cross Andra or create a stir for her very fragile grandmother.

"How lovely you look, Charlotte." The maid at Grandmother's side helped her to a settee. "All that Honiton lace becomes you."

Did no one notice Charlotte was as pale as her dress? The alarm Wren had fought since their garden talk now filled her to the brim. Here they were discussing gowns and weddings that might never be while Charlotte looked as if she might faint at their feet.

"I've not come to discuss fashion but share some glad news." Grandmother looked triumphant. "We've just received word that Ellie has been safely delivered of a new babe, born this morning at River Hill."

Wren's spirits took wing. "Boy or girl?"

"Jack likes to tease me and never says. I was hoping you might accompany me to River Hill this afternoon. Charlotte will be at Ballantyne Hall with Bennett, so she tells me. I thought we could take her there on our way. There's room enough in the carriage for you too, Andra."

Andra ceased fussing with Charlotte's hem, brow as creased as the fabric in her hands. "Really, Mother, I can't possibly spare an afternoon, not with more gifts to catalogue and music to see about for the reception." She sighed. "Elinor's lying-in couldn't come at a worse time!"

The nettlesome remark hung in the air, causing hurt, or so Wren feared. Laying a hand on Grandmother's shoulder, she gave a gentle squeeze. "I'll gladly go. There's nothing better than a baby, surely."

Andra gave them a disparaging glance and the room stilled.

"I think a visit could wait till after the wedding. All those Turlock boys tire you so, Mother."

"Tire me?" Grandmother gave a little chuckle. "Old as I am, everything tires me. Those boys are life itself."

"You may give Elinor my best wishes if you like."

Wren studied her aunt, Tremper's words resounding. *Sour Aunt Andra.* Out of the mouths of babes . . . A chill settled over the room that not even the warmth of Grandmother's presence could thaw.

Undaunted, Grandmother smiled up at Wren. "We'll leave for River Hill after luncheon then."

Wren stole a glance at Charlotte. Still pale. Still at war within. And obviously full of dread at the coming afternoon.

Izannah stood at the window of the bedchamber, feeling like a wrung-out rag. The cloud of dust on the long drive roused her, and she pressed her forehead against the glass pane. Grandmother? A second figure sat beside her in the handsome barouche. Not Aunt Andra. Andra rarely came. Mama was always a bit sad at her absence—and Papa sullen. Yet little could dim Izannah's joy that the endless night had passed.

Across the room Mama lay sleeping, the babe bundled in her arm, the maids going about on tiptoe as they tidied the bedchamber. In the adjoining dressing room, the tardy midwife dozed in a rocking chair, snoring softly. Thankfully one of the tutors had taken the boys fishing, so everyone was spared their wild tumbling and talk.

Turning back to the window, Izannah watched Rowena step down from the carriage and pause to admire the roses. In that instance it seemed James stood near, his low voice in her ear.

Her eyes are like sea foam . . . her hair is the color of hemp rope . . . She barely comes to my shoulder . . . She handles a fiddle like I pilot a boat.

Izannah thought of all he hadn't said.

She's brown as a berry. Her hands are callused. She speaks with a backwoods drawl.

Pushing away from the pane, she smoothed her wrinkled skirts, wishing she had time to change. Mama was stirring now, and the babe gave a little cry like a kitten's mewl, bringing Daddy round. His eyes were red-rimmed from a sleepless night, his jaw unshaven, but his relief was as potent as her own, though they both knew the danger hadn't passed. Mama had a slight fever. And the babe was so large Izannah had gasped when the midwife had first placed the infant in her waiting arms.

"Her name is Chloe," Daddy had said at the sight of his second daughter.

"Chloe," Izannah echoed, moved by the sudden glimmer in his and Mama's eyes. Once Papa had had a sister named Chloe, dear to him and Mama both. Izannah struggled to hide her dismay, wishing for a less melancholy name. But Chloe it was.

Now, hours later, she supposed all that mattered was that Mama be well again. She sent up a quick prayer, preparing for a visit. "Grandmother and Rowena are here. Shall I ring for tea?"

Mama brightened. "Yes, of course. Bring the chairs nearer the bed. And the tea table, if you please." She put a hand to her plaited hair. "You've taken care of everything, Izannah, even my favorite bed jacket."

"You look beautiful, Mama."

"Yes, she does, though I can hardly believe it after she's

been up all night." Great-Aunt Elspeth stood at the doorway to the bedchamber, lips pursed as the judge went past. "Please tell me it's not another boy. A girl would be a fitting finish to all this endless procreation."

The maid leaned in and whispered something, but Elspeth simply chortled and moved into the room's center, her cane leading. "Martha reminds me I must behave or your father has threatened to send for my nurse . . . and a straitjacket."

"Would you like to hold Chloe?" Izannah gestured to a chair, knowing the answer before she asked.

"Ah, a girl! No baby holding, thank you. But I would like some tea." Despite her advanced age, Elspeth was dressed and pressed to perfection, showing little sign of the onerous malady that plagued her. One didn't discuss the French pox in polite company.

Grandmother and Rowena soon joined them, gathering round and making such a fuss over the new arrival that introductions were nearly forgotten.

Eventually Elspeth's inquisitive gaze settled on Wren in the chair opposite, her eyes alive with interest. "And who might you be?"

"I'm Wren Ballantyne, Ansel's daughter."

"Ansel's daughter?" Her eyes rounded. "So the prodigal has returned. Oh my . . ."

Izannah noted the slight lift of Wren's brows. "There are no prodigals in this family, Aunt Elspeth. Not even you." She picked up a plate of tea sandwiches and passed them round the table. "Rowena and her father have just arrived in time for the wedding."

"Ah, the wedding. I don't suppose I received an invitation." Elspeth looked to her maid, who shook her head in confirmation. "Well, I'll stay here with Ellie and the baby, then."

"You've been invited to the reception, which will be at the Monongahela House," Grandmother told her. "The bride is a beautiful girl from Boston—"

"Boston!"

"Yes, Boston. Charlotte met Bennett while he was studying at Harvard."

"But I don't believe in Pittsburghers marrying foreigners."

"Charlotte shan't be a foreigner come Saturday," Grandmother replied. "She'll be a Ballantyne."

"Sister, do you always have an answer for everything?" Elspeth returned her attention to Wren. "I suppose you'll be next—a debut ball, a groom. Izannah hasn't had much luck with either."

Izannah bit her lip, feeling a familiar bristling. *Oh, that the wedding on Saturday was my own, and a babe to follow.* Lifting Chloe out of her mother's arms, Izannah handed her to Grandmother, praying for a turn in conversation.

"She has your blue eyes, Ellie, and Jack's fair hair. And there's no mistaking the Ballantyne nose." Grandmother's pleasure knew no bounds. "Such a big baby! I do hope you'll consider a wet nurse till you regain your strength."

"The midwife said the same, but I'm not sure." Fever glazed Mama's eyes, stealing Izannah's joy.

"Why don't you let me stay here with you a few days?" Grandmother's gracious offer only fueled Izannah's worries. "I've not forgotten all the years I spent at the foundling hospital in Philadelphia. Babies have always been second nature to me."

"But what about the wedding and all those guests, Mama?"

"Andra and the staff have all in hand. Wren has been a blessing as well. I daresay I won't be missed."

With a loud harrumph, Elspeth got to her feet, cane in

hand. "All this family harmony gives me indigestion. I must go and see what might be suitable to wear to the reception, other than the straitjacket Jack keeps talking about."

Hiding her relief, Izannah bent and kissed Elspeth's wrinkled cheek, showing her out. The maid waited in the corridor, biding her time with a bit of knitting. Izannah shut the door after them and returned to Wren while Mama spoke in quiet tones with Grandmother.

"I apologize for Elspeth."

Wren simply smiled. "She's the great-aunt you told me about. The one who doesn't make as much trouble as she used to."

"Sometimes I wonder. Her tongue still seems sharp as a rapier."

"I've never met anybody like her."

"Pray you never will." Izannah reached for a tea cake, hungry again after so long a night. "How are you faring at New Hope? Isn't Mama's old room quaint?" At Wren's nod, she said quietly, "Grandmother is fond of keeping things as they used to be. Other than the new wing, the old house is quite the antique."

"Papa said it has changed little in time." Wren sat back, teacup in hand. "New Hope's beautiful, but I miss Kentucky and long to get back there."

"Oh?" Izannah masked her surprise. There'd been no talk of returning to Kentucky, not that she knew of. Uncle Ansel had even confided to Daddy his plans to build a home on acreage west of New Hope. Obviously Wren didn't know, and Izannah wasn't going to be the one to tell her.

Her comely cousin seemed to be unaware of a great many things, Izannah realized, the least of which was Wren's inexplicable hold on James Sackett's heart.

9

When sorrows come, they come not
as single spies, but in battalions!

WILLIAM SHAKESPEARE

More than seventy years of weather and the sun's glare had bleached the old building white, but James felt more at home in the place the Ballantyne legacy had begun than the ornate Water Street offices across the way. Silas had turned over his old domain to James the week before, key and all, humble as it was. Jutting out over the levee on an aged sliver of dock, the place was easily overlooked, dwarfed by piles of freight and an army of men working under the Ballantynes' renowned Irish hull builder, Anthony Dunlevy.

James couldn't help but contrast the hum of activity to the eves he sat alone with a lantern, charting the crossings and laying out the courses by compass, the levee cat winding round his boots, the night wind sighing through the drafty boards. During daylight hours, little peace was to be had at the height of the shipping season. The door's rusty hinges required constant oiling as it swung to and fro, drawing complaints, but James wouldn't replace it. He liked the look of that door. Solid. Stalwart. Steadfast. Unlike his shifting circumstances.

Leaning back in a chair in need of repair, he looked upward to a battered shelf. There Silas had driven a hand-forged nail, a reminder that the Almighty, crucified but risen, was always near at hand. It had been the guiding force of Silas's long life. Never had James needed the reminder so much as now.

Looking out the window, he took in the *Rowena* lying at landing with a score of other vessels, but it was the *Belle of Pittsburgh* being bedecked like a bride that held him. Men scoured her decks with mops and wash buckets, while inside the grand salon artists were at work painting panels of each stateroom door with scenic vistas in oils. All at Bennett's urging. As it was now Thursday, the honeymoon sailing was only two days away.

The frivolity jarred sourly with James's task and Silas's warning words to him that morning. There was much at stake. So much that James's skin grew clammy from a sudden chill, though his shirt was sweat-damp in places.

The door groaned open. James failed to hear his cub pilot's approach, though there was no ignoring the bearish shadow filling the doorway.

"S-Sackett, s-sir?" George Ealer's stutter was more pronounced in his alarm. "There's b-been a t-telegram from d-downriver." He approached the desk, looking dazed. "B-Bennett's mad as a b-bull."

Standing, James reached out a hand and clamped Ealer's slumped shoulder as if to give him anchor. "Slow down and tell it to me straight."

Ealer swallowed hard. "It happened s-six o'clock this

m-morning north of S-Ship Island, about thirty m-miles below M-Memphis—"

"The *City of Pittsburgh*?" The latest and swiftest addition to the Ballantyne line? The nod of Ealer's head was enough. James felt a sinking to his boots.

"The s-striker and s-second engineer had the watch in the engine r-room. The s-second m-mate had the watch on d-deck . . ."

All inferior crew and cargo save one. Trevor Bixby had been at the wheel. Ealer shuddered and tried to finish. James wanted to shake the labored words out of him.

"Four b-boilers exploded."

Lord, no.

"They've t-taken B-Bixby to the nearest m-maritime hospital."

James blinked back the stinging wetness clouding his vision. "Any other survivors?"

Ealer gave a shake of his shaggy head. "B-Bennett's on his way here. I w-wanted to w-warn you."

"Go to the Monongahela House and tell Captain Dean I'll meet him there for supper instead of the noon meal." James glanced out the window, feeling he'd not eat for a week, and faced another unappetizing prospect.

Bennett was crossing the street, flanked by several minions and attorneys. Leaving out the back door, Ealer made his escape.

When Bennett stepped into the old office without his entourage, the air turned oppressively still. "I suppose you've heard the news."

"Yes, just," James said.

The tick of the wall clock swelled in the silence. Bennett turned toward a shelf of ledgers, each bearing the name of every Ballantyne packet in the line. "How much was she insured for?"

How much? The words held the force of a fist. All the breath left him. A crew lay dead and a pilot lay dying. Not just any pilot but one of the best in the line—

"I said how much was the *City of Pittsburgh* insured for?"

Still, James gave no answer. His fingers clenched around an iron paperweight atop the cluttered desk. What was Bennett's creed?

Success at any cost and hang the consequences.

Bennett swung toward him, expression thick with hostility. "I want you to find out and send word to me at Ballantyne Hall. I don't have time for mundane matters." His gaze swept the room as if searching for answers before he went out, slamming the door in his wake.

Fingering the heavy paperweight, James wanted to draw back and hurl it after him, aggravated the oak door would take the blow. But it didn't dint his desire that it knock some common decency into Bennett instead.

In the flicker of gaslight, Captain Dean's face was the color of his linen napkin. "Bixby was a God-fearing man, James. Take comfort in that."

Was. Throat too tight to reply, James stared at the elaborate menu and tried to focus. But all that filled his head was the thought of his friend and fellow pilot severely scalded, his body packed in linseed oil and cotton, dying in a strange hospital far downriver.

"You know the lifespan of a steamboat is but three to five years. It's a dangerous business. That's why we're paid like kings."

"If there'd been a first-rate crew aboard, it wouldn't have happened." James kept his voice low, his eyes on the menu. "I warned Bennett more than once . . ." His voice faded. Dean didn't need the reminder of Bennett's oversight and excess. He'd witnessed it firsthand. Bennett seemed to leave a trail of it in his wake, scrimping on safety and crew while indulging in wild financial schemes, all to get ahead of the Camerons and the railroad.

"It reminds me of the time you were blown up around Madrid Bend near Memphis, right into the river from the wheel. That was no substandard crew but faulty equipment—and you came away without a scratch." Dean took a swallow of water. "Besides, none of it can be chalked up to the affairs of men. The Lord himself ordains a man's day of birth and death. Bixby said so himself."

"I was there when he said it." James found no comfort in the memory. "But I'll not dismiss the matter so easily. There's a pattern beginning of shoddy crew and careless handling, perhaps the intentional destruction of boats to collect insurance money."

"That's a heavy charge, James."

"I wouldn't voice it unless I thought it was sound."

"The Ballantyne line has the finest safety record on the river."

"Times are changing. As soon as Bennett is in charge and Silas steps down—"

"Silas has no intention of stepping down." Dean chuckled humorlessly. "Dying, perhaps, but not stepping down."

Dying, aye. James eyed Dean intently. No one else had witnessed the incident with Silas in the boatyard office that day. He'd told no one, nor had Silas. But the incident had shaken James to the core. Somehow, in years past, he'd ignored the signs of Silas's aging, dreading the day he'd no longer be with them. Pittsburgh wouldn't be the same, nor would he.

A waiter hovered, serving Turlock whiskey in crystal shot glasses. "A round of drinks for you gentlemen, compliments of the Sullivan party."

James looked across the crowded dining room and nodded to the foremost Ballantyne attorney obviously commiserating with them over the *City of Pittsburgh*'s demise. Though he rarely drank, tonight whiskey was the only thing he could stomach.

At least Bixby hadn't had a wife and children. Rivermen tended to be a lonesome breed, always on the water with no place to call home. He wasn't sure about the rest of the crew. It was no small miracle there'd been no passengers, only cargo. He'd try to take comfort from that.

"You're not considering leaving the line, I hope." Dean's hands shook slightly as he lit a cigar. "If you do you'll send a red flag from here to New Orleans that something is amiss, and our competitors will have a heyday."

This James couldn't deny. He stayed silent, gaze roaming the plush room restlessly. Tonight the heavy blue decor seemed almost funereal, the room too dark.

"Now more than ever, insurance rates on cargo are adjusted by the caliber of the boat." There was a heated warning in Dean's stern words, a reminder they were the river's elite. "Nothing is more important than the reputation of captain and pilot."

"I have too much loyalty to Silas and Eden Ballantyne to resign right now."

Dean gave a nod, his relief apparent. "There are few if any pilots who would or could transport the freight you do." He returned to the menu with renewed interest. "We sail in two days' time. Once Bennett and his bride disembark in New Orleans, we can proceed as usual."

James took a slow drink, the liquor leaving a fiery trail. "There's another matter." He reached for the note in his breast pocket, weighing the wisdom of doing so. But when he let go of the paper, it seemed a burden lifted along with it. "I received this yesterday."

"Another matter indeed." Dean was looking at the note as if it was arsenic. "I suppose this came from the bride?"

"Who seems intent on returning to Boston."

"You've not replied?"

"Not yet."

"If you do and Bennett gets wind of it . . ."

"I need to help her."

"Help her?" Dean's brows knotted like rope. "The nuptials are two days away. All the legalities have been taken care of—"

"All the legalities will be null and void if there's no ceremony," James replied.

"Let's hope it's a simple case of hysterics."

"Miss Ashburton seems entirely rational to me."

"Promise me you'll stay out of the matter." Dean's calm was eroding, his color high. Reaching for the whiskey, he nearly knocked over his glass. "James, it's a scandal in the making. There's been many a skittish bride before the ceremony. If you—"

His quiet vehemence faded as the mayor and his wife paused briefly at their table. "My condolences, gentlemen, on the loss of the *City of Pittsburgh*."

James gave a nod but said nothing. There was little to be done for Trevor Bixby and crew. But he could certainly help Charlotte Ashburton.

He rode hard toward River Hill out Braddock's Road, weighing his options with every step. The wedding was two days away. Arrangements could be made quietly for Charlotte to take a stage to Philadelphia and then a train from there to Boston. All he needed to do was send Malachi Cameron a message and the matter would be handled discreetly. Or plans could be made for travel on a packet to New Orleans and then up the coast with her lady's maid, allowing ample time for the furor to die down.

Or he could do nothing.

The latter clawed at his conscience. Charlotte Ashburton obviously didn't love Bennett Ballantyne. She was nothing but a pawn in a business deal, allowing Bennett to shore up the Ballantyne fortune and recover his losses. At Charlotte's expense.

He reined his horse toward River Hill's scrolled iron gates and slowed to a walk. The big house's facade was welcoming, but no laughter or commotion shook the stillness. Odd. By now the boys would have spied him coming along the drive, shouting and screeching a welcome. Unless . . .

Something must have happened in the hours since he'd left River Hill. Still numb from the news about the explosion, he veered toward River Row, steeling himself against the second loss of the day.

A stony-faced groom met him and he dismounted, walking the rest of the way. Before he'd passed the giant oak shading his cottage, Izannah appeared in his path. Tears wet her lashes, and he saw the echo of her mother in her. For once she was wordless, her expression telegraphing the terrible news.

Lord, no. Not Ellie too.

"James . . . this afternoon . . ." Her voice broke. He started to raise a hand to spare her the telling, but she rushed on, stunning him. "It's Charlotte—she's dead. Something terrible happened with Bennett at the lake."

His mind reeled and stumbled. Ellie . . . the baby. Safe. Sound. Charlotte . . . dead. Regret like a weeping rain washed over him. The note in his pocket suddenly carried the heft of an anchor.

"We're not sure what went wrong, but everyone at New Hope is quite shaken. I can only imagine how Charlotte's family feels." She sought her handkerchief, a sigh shuddering through her. "Daddy rode to Ballantyne Hall with Grandfather half an hour ago. Mama doesn't know yet. Daddy won't tell her as she's so weak."

His voice was wooden. "And the baby?"

A spark of relief rode her damp features. "Big as a barrel and a girl at that. Her name is Chloe."

The ordeal of a funeral—two of them—stole his joy over Ellie's safe delivery.

"I suppose you're still going to New Orleans." The lament in her tone was plain. Izannah had never liked his leaving, even when she was small and his apprenticeship required it.

"I return in two weeks." Slowly the facts took hold and rearranged his carefully made plans. The wedding journey had been an attractive cover for an increasingly dangerous cargo. If Izannah knew the particulars, she didn't let on.

"I wish . . ." She paused, eyes glittering again. "I wish you weren't leaving at such a tragic time."

He could only imagine the scene at Ballantyne Hall. His thoughts were roiling, his emotions were roiling. The boat—had it capsized? How? There'd been no wind. Bennett was an accomplished swimmer and sailor . . .

Izannah looked away from him, gaze fastening on the upper reaches of the house. "I'd best see to Mama and the baby."

He gave a nod, looking at her without focus, his mind on Bixby and Charlotte.

She turned back to him. "Don't forget to say goodbye before you go, James. Promise?"

"Yes." Yet he had forgotten—more times than he could count. One never knew when a parting would turn final.

But he was simply no good at goodbyes.

10

The very essence of romance is uncertainty.

OSCAR WILDE

"Have a seat, Wren." Papa's low voice reached out to her. The chair he offered blurred before her eyes. The news they'd just heard beat in her brain like a taunting drum.

Charlotte dead. Dead. Dead.

She did as he bade and sat, clutching the fragile arms of the upholstered chair so tightly it seemed they would snap. "It's so—hot." Her voice frayed as she picked at the high collar of her dress, loosening a button. Her too-tight corset she could do little about.

Never had she so needed her music. Slow Scottish airs and the richer, deeper laments. From the time she'd reached her father's knee, she'd had a fiddle in hand and had leaned on it in joy and in sorrow. When Mama died, she'd mourned through her music. When words, circumstances, failed her, the music never did.

"I'll fetch something to drink," he said.

Numb, she watched him go. Why hadn't he simply tugged on the bell cord and summoned a servant? Perhaps he couldn't get used to having someone do everything in his stead or rued the lack of privacy at so emotional a moment. She wanted to tell him she didn't need something to drink. She needed Charlotte. She needed to scrub the ugly news, delivered by a grim-faced servant minutes before, from her head like wash on a washboard.

I'm sorry to inform you there's been an accident at Ballantyne Hall. Miss Ashburton is dead.

Grandmother had turned ashen. Even Aunt Andra had given a startled cry. Upstairs now, they'd hidden themselves in their bedchambers, leaving her with Papa below. The house, so full of the bustle and excitement of wedding activity since their arrival earlier that week, had turned into a tomb.

Her bleary gaze traced the unfamiliar contours of the room, desperate for a distraction. Grandfather's study had the look and feel of a museum. Antiquities lined countless bookshelves, and the furnishings were from another century. Everything smelled of leather and pipe smoke and bergamot. Like the pilothouse. The reminder of James Sackett turned her stomach. Charlotte had sent him a note. A cry for help from her very soul.

And he had not heeded it.

Molly returned with a tea tray, her own dark features shuttered. Papa followed, taking a seat behind Grandfather's desk. The weary blue of his eyes tugged at her, the line of his mouth drawn taut as a bow string.

Papa, it's time to return to Kentucky.

Instead she said carefully, "Where are our violins?"

"In the music room," he replied, his gaze never leaving the window.

She passed into the foyer, sure one sip of tea would sicken her. All the rooms on the first floor were open, the twin parlors overflowing with wedding gifts. Charlotte's chair was pulled out from the desk as if awaiting her, the thank-you notes in a tidy stack.

Woodenly, Wren's steps led her to the closed door in back of the stairs. Turning the porcelain knob, she stepped into the room she'd only heard about but never seen. A rich Delft blue and cream, it exuded elegance. When Papa had left New Hope years before and Aunt Ellie had taken her harp to River Hill, this beautiful room was all but abandoned, a maid said.

In the faint light sneaking past heavy shutters, the Cremona violins lay on a long table. A harpsichord was hidden by a dustcover, mahogany music stands huddled in one corner. Here there was sanctuary. Peace.

Home, her heart said.

Early the next morning, Papa called her into the parlor and told her the news. Molly was to return to Kentucky on the very boat meant for Bennett and his bride. Charlotte's maid was to replace her. Wren read the panic in Molly's eyes, felt the grip of her bony fingers. Slightly superstitious, Molly looked like she might come apart. The *Belle of Pittsburgh* was nothing but a ghost ship.

"You'll be all right, Molly," Wren reassured her, sinking lower with every word. "The trip isn't far. You'll soon be home. Besides, Papa promised your kin he wouldn't keep you here long, and Jonas is surely missing you." At the mention of her little nephew, Molly dried her eyes but still looked mournful. Though she couldn't speak, Wren knew her heart.

I wish you could go with me.

When Molly disappeared to pack her things, Charlotte's maid began to go about the bedchamber, straightening and tidying as she went. "My name's Mariam, Miss Rowena. But you can call me Mim." Coming to the large wardrobe, she opened it wide. "Yer aunt Andra has sent your Louisville dresses to the orphanage. The wedding trousseau is to take their place."

Wren stared at the empty wardrobe, shed of all her Louisville clothes. The sight set her heart to pounding. She couldn't—wouldn't—don anything of Charlotte's. Though she wasn't superstitious, she was chary of some things, and wearing a grave-bound woman's dresses was one of them.

A look of apology engulfed Mim's face. "Miss Charlotte never wore them, if it's any comfort. 'Twould be a frightful loss if they were to go to waste. The Ashburtons dinna want them. They've just left for Boston."

Wren sat in the nearest chair, her wide skirts brushing a small table and sending a figurine to the carpeted floor. Fighting tears, she murmured a Gaelic epithet beneath her breath.

Mim spun round, astonishment on her ruddy face. "Ye have the Gaelic?"

"I do."

At that, Mim abandoned English altogether. "I'm sorry, Miss Rowena. I don't dare cross Miss Andra. She's in such a stew about what's happened."

"Please, call me Wren." Unsure of Mim or her loyalty to Andra, she felt her way cautiously. "I know you're simply doing as you're told. Trying to make the best of it."

Mim heaved a sigh. "*Och*, the best of it. It will take time, ye ken. The servants are all abuzz with the dire news. Then there are the papers, sure to announce it like a trumpet blast come morn. Mr. Bennett will be bound in black for six months or better. And the Ballantynes are such fine folk too. Yer dear granny brought me to New Hope years ago when my kin died and I came to be at the Orphan Home."

Wren stared at the glib little maid, sorting through her torrent of Gaelic. She could hardly keep up with her. "The Orphan Home?"

"It's in Pittsburgh and chock-full of bairns. Yer granny goes as often as she can. But yer Aunt Andra . . ." She screwed up her face. "Nivver!"

"But I thought you came with Char—" Wren stumbled over the name, changing course. "I thought you were from Boston."

"Nae, I've never been to Boston. Miss Andra gave me over to Miss Charlotte when she arrived. Her own maid died on the way here. From fever."

The whole affair had been ill-fated from the beginning. Saying no more, Wren excused herself and went in search of Molly, unwilling to part with her just yet.

And still smoldering over the matter of Charlotte's dresses.

"*Och!*" With one swift look, Mim took in the overstuffed valise and fiddle case Wren clutched in the heated August foyer. "Yer doing what?"

"I'm going into Pittsburgh to see Molly off." Wren's whisper fell flat as she uttered the half-truth. Could Mim see through her pretense? The maid seemed as canny as she was glib.

"Yer not thinking about running off like Miss Charlotte?" When Wren stayed silent, Mim's eyes grew wide. "*Losh!* Ye are! I ken just from the look o' ye."

Reaching into her poke, Wren pulled out a coin, enclosing

it in Mim's hand, though the money held the taint of a bribe. "To thank you."

"I'd rather have ye than a sovereign any day o' the week." Mim's eyes were glinting again. "What will yer poor da say when he finds ye gone?"

But Wren was already heading for the front door where a carriage waited to take Molly to the levee, haste in her step. If she had any qualms about leaving the lushness of rural Allegheny County, or that she'd simply left a note for her father and grandparents, all regret faded as they descended into the smoke and soot of Pittsburgh. Hot as Hades and just as crowded, the levee resembled a carnival gone wild. Looking on, Molly withered like a sun-parched leaf.

Perspiration beaded Wren's brow as the sun slanted below the brim of her straw bonnet. She wore the sole Louisville dress Andra had overlooked and Mim had rescued, a blessedly cool sprigged muslin with a background of tiny blue flowers. But its newness almost chafed her skin, and Charlotte's impractical leather slippers were a trifle tight.

"I'm coming with you, Molly, but I have to see about passage first."

Bolstered by Molly's smile, Wren crossed the expanse of mud and boardwalk, intent on any packet bound for Louisville. Freight and chalkboards were at every turn, guarded by cigar-smoking men who sang out ever-changing rates of cargo. Wren breathed in the stench of river water and livestock pens alongside more fragrant hogsheads of tobacco and molasses and coffee.

Lord, help us get home.

At the water's edge near the stage planks, a deckhand stood guard, shouting orders and epithets with practiced ease. Flanked by the imposing *Belle of Pittsburgh* and the *Aleck*

Scott, Wren's namesake appeared almost dainty despite the tonnage being loaded.

Desperate for a deckhand's attention, she realized it wasn't the notice she wanted. A gust of wind lifted her hem, and a dozen men turned her way. She struggled to keep her composure and modesty intact, her skirts down as she spoke to the nearest roustabout. "I need passage to Louisville with my maid."

He spat into the levee mud and scowled. "Do I look like a ticket taker?"

"I don't know anything about a ticket." Her shout rose above the din. "Last time I simply walked aboard. I'm Silas Ballantyne's granddaughter—"

"Well, why didn't ye say so?" He whisked a battered cap off his head and refrained from spitting again. "Ye'll have to talk to Sackett. He's in that office yonder."

Her spirits sank. Following his pointed finger, she saw a battered building fronting the levee, windows and door open wide. Taking Molly's arm, she started up the muddy incline to the office, avoiding sweating, cursing rivermen all the way. A small ramp ushered them above the melee to the entrance, where a weathered sign proclaiming Ballantyne Boatworks swung wildly in the wind.

Molly stepped beneath a shaded eave with their belongings while Wren went inside, still clutching her fiddle case. The interior was as still and silent as the levee was chaotic. James Sackett sat behind an old, scarred desk, head bent. A clock on the wall ticked a tense four times. Departure was within an hour. She felt a wide relief. Almost home.

"Mr. Sackett . . ."

He looked up and met her tentative gaze with his own, green and solid.

"I want to return to Kentucky."

Stoic, he stood and looked down at her, making her feel no bigger than the mosquito buzzing round her head. "I don't remember seeing your name on the passenger list, Miss Ballantyne."

Squaring her shoulders, she drew herself to her full height, all five feet of it. "Molly's a mite fearful. She shouldn't be traveling alone."

He looked past her as if spying Molly waiting just outside. "Your maid will be in the company of other passengers. She's been assigned a single cabin."

Had she? Such a generous arrangement was unheard of for free blacks like Molly. Most were kept to the lower decks along with the cargo. "There's bound to be room for me too."

"The *Belle of Pittsburgh* is heavily laden this trip."

Heavily laden? When the *Rowena* had been all but empty when they'd come upriver? She glanced at the wall clock again, aware time was against her.

His face held an intensity she didn't like. "Does your father know you're here?"

She stared at him. Did he think she was still a child, under Papa's thumb? "I'm a woman grown, Mr. Sackett, and hardly need my father's permission—or yours." She kept her voice calm, not wanting to rile him . . . as if she could. "As Silas Ballantyne's kin, it stands to reason I should have passage on any boat that bears his name."

"All that aside, I seem to remember you wanting off the packet more than you wanted on it, Miss Ballantyne."

"You don't understand." She swallowed, her temper rising along with his obvious reluctance. "I can't stay here any longer. Pittsburgh is so dark. It's nigh impossible to see, to get a clear breath. New Hope's little better. There are servants everywhere—watching, whispering. I can't touch things lest I break them or say a word lest I misspeak."

He studied her, his expression guaranteeing she'd get no farther than the dock, no matter what reasons she pelted him with. "I can't sanction your going downriver. But I can arrange for a rig to return you to New Hope."

"Mr. Sackett, please . . ." She raised a hand to her brow, wishing she could shed her hot bonnet. Her desperation doubled at the sound of a boat's whistle. "Would you give me no more help than you gave"—her voice cracked—"poor Charlotte?"

Something raced through his eyes, but he stayed steadfast. "We're talking about you, Miss Ballantyne. Not Miss Ashburton." Coming out from behind the desk, he shrank the distance between them, making her want to take a step back. "Say I let you aboard, and within five minutes of leaving the landing—when most accidents occur—you lose your life? That happened just yesterday to the *City of Pittsburgh*'s pilot and crew. What would your father and grandfather say to me then?"

She looked away, stung. She'd not heard of the *City of Pittsburgh*. All she could think of was Charlotte.

"I wish I had better news for you, Miss Ballantyne. I wish traveling by packet was safe. Or that you liked Pittsburgh and didn't have to come here nearly begging—"

It was the most roundabout refusal she'd ever heard. Whirling, she clutched her violin case and made for the open door, stumbling as her toe caught on the raised sill. Out she went into coal dust and foul air, only to find Molly making her way to the loading platform, escorted by a clerk. The *Belle of Pittsburgh*'s huge smokestacks were already pluming, the huge steamer shuddering along the levee, ready to embark.

Behind her James Sackett's tall shadow darkened the doorframe. "Wren . . ."

She plunged into the crowd, baggage in hand, numb and disbelieving. He hadn't called her Miss Ballantyne or Rowena. He'd called her Wren. But it in no way lessened the sting of his refusal. Or the fact she had no money and no means to return her to New Hope.

Tugging his hat lower, Malachi Cameron fixed his gaze on the winding road ahead. He'd nearly made it. Though his Edinburgh-tailored suit was wrinkled from a long railway journey piggybacked by the stage, he blinked sleep-deprived eyes and looked homeward, expectant. Cameron House was a few miles more, tucked in the bend between New Hope and Broad Oak. Impatience set in as his driver suddenly slowed his pace, the new barouche kicking up less dust as it rolled cautiously over ruts and rocks.

To the right of the road was a woman. Small of stature. Luggage in hand. Her hair was spilling down like gold ribbon beneath her straw bonnet. Clad in a summery dress dotted with blue flowers, she was all curves and bends, her full skirts swaying gently as she walked. Nearly derailing him.

This was a reminder of why he'd come back to Pittsburgh. How long had it been since he'd exchanged words with anyone but a railroad hand? He'd nearly given up on polite conversation, feminine company. Courtesy demanded he stop. Speak.

Ho there.

No, that would never do. He'd do well to remember his city manners.

She kept on just a few steps ahead of him, never looking back. Coaxing him into a game of cat and mouse. From the slump of her shoulders, she seemed as weary as he.

Pardon me, miss . . .

11

In character, in manner, in style, in all things, the supreme excellence is simplicity.

HENRY WADSWORTH LONGFELLOW

Fiddle case in one hand, valise in the other, Wren walked out the Allegheny Road toward New Hope. She heard the *Belle of Pittsburgh*'s distinct whistle at her back as it took Molly downriver, all her hopes along with it. She wouldn't turn round and watch it depart. Overcome with humiliation and homesickness, she stirred the dust with her steps, her tumbled thoughts circling round her aching head.

He'd called her Wren.

She couldn't call him James. Nor did she want to. That was Izannah's privilege.

She hadn't even had the sense to say she was sorry for the loss of the *City of Pittsburgh*, even when he was clearly reeling from it. How would it be to climb to the pilothouse knowing a fellow pilot had gone to his death doing the same? Still, it was Charlotte who stayed uppermost in her mind, her desperate predicament unheeded. She had only to think of that to dismiss James Sackett.

She walked on till her fingers ached from her stubborn hold on her baggage and her dress hem was a grungy brown. A lone wagon lumbered past but no refined rig. She gave silent thanks. If Andra or any of her Ballantyne kin were to see her, she'd be undone . . .

The sun sank beyond the treetops, throwing a golden blanket across the burnt, late-summer grass. Stopping, she knelt and drank from a trickle of creek beneath an old bridge, her parched throat aching from an emotional lump of loss and fury. She couldn't remember how far New Hope was. Couldn't think beyond the next step. Sweat trickled down her back, turning her corset itchy.

When the jingle of a harness met her ears, she stepped aside, keeping her back to the swirling dust, her eyes fixed on a far road marker.

"Pardon me, miss. You look in need of a ride."

Slowly she turned, took in a black-hatted man in a fancy carriage, and kept walking. It wasn't like her to be so standoffish, but weariness had worn a hole in what few good manners she possessed.

"At least tell me where you're headed."

The concern in his tone touched her. A bit winded from going uphill, she managed a terse, "New Hope."

"The Ballantyne estate?" He sounded slightly perplexed. "New Hope's a few miles more . . . but the gloaming will soon overtake you."

The gloaming. A Scots word. Her feet slowed. If not for the blister rubbing her heel raw, she'd have held fast to her stubbornness.

With an agile leap, he jumped down from the carriage and

swept his hat from his head. A tumble of curls gave way, as arresting as the beard that marked his jaw. The rich ginger of his hair was the exact shade of the varnish in their violin shop, as if she'd taken a camel-hair brush and applied it. But it was the kindness in his hazel eyes that struck her.

"The Ballantynes are close friends of mine. I live down the road from them." He held out a hand and, when she made no protest, relieved her of her bag, turning his broad back to her to secure it with his own luggage. "I doubt you want to part with your fiddle."

Taking her by the elbow, he helped her into the open carriage. When her backside connected with the leather seat, she nearly sighed aloud in relief, willing her wide skirts to settle. Sitting opposite, he returned his hat to his head, and the vehicle rolled forward.

She was glad he hadn't asked her name. Glad too that he knew a fiddle graced her case.

His smile was weary but warm. "I'm a patron of the arts myself and appreciate a good bow hand when time warrants."

"Do you play?"

"Nary a note." His expression was so glum she almost felt sorry for him.

"Are you of a mind to learn?"

He chuckled. "If the teacher wasn't some bewhiskered, grumpy old coot, but you, I would."

She smiled back at him.

"You're not from here. Your speech is singularly Southern."

"I'm from Kentucky."

"A good many accomplished fiddlers down there." He eyed her case. "Mind if I have a look?"

The expectant question would have cracked open the hardest heart. Setting the case in her lap, she unclasped it and took out the Nightingale. In the fading sunlight she read stark appreciation in his eyes. It warmed her like the sun itself. Papa's hard work securing it—all the years spent hunting it—seemed worth it right then.

Placing the violin on her shoulder, she shrugged aside any shyness, silently consecrating her music to her Maker as she always did. With a tap of her foot she struck the first note. Never had the Nightingale sounded so lively and high-spirited, resounding in the open air with an infectious rhythm, chasing away her homesickness and the dust of the road. She moved on to a serene piece next, partial to the haunting laments. Closing her eyes, she nearly forgot the subtle movement of the carriage and her dread at seeing Aunt Andra again.

When her bow slid off the strings, he clapped his gloved hands. "A Highland reel followed by a Lowland lament."

She nodded. So he did know something about music. Fiddle music, anyway.

"Play another," he murmured.

He was studying her with a sort of bemused confusion. Like she was no longer the disheveled young woman limping down the road but someone else entirely. For a few fleeting seconds she opened her heart to his admiration, enjoying his pleasure.

"You make me want to quit everything and pursue the violin," he said when the music ended.

A flush that had little to do with the weather snuck over her. The man before her was young, likely unmarried. No more than thirty, she guessed. Yet the faint lines about his eyes bespoke a burden or two.

"But I'm afraid the railroad takes all my time," he finished ruefully.

She eyed his suit, wondering if all railroad workers dressed so well. "I've never before seen a train. I've only just set foot on a steamboat."

"And how did you find it?"

She wrinkled her nose in answer and struck a discordant string that echoed her dislike.

He laughed, a low rumble in his chest. "Big. Smoky. Noisy. I'm afraid trains are no better."

"Is there one in Pittsburgh?" Perhaps a train could carry her home.

"One day there will be. Soon there'll be rails from coast to coast once we find a sure way to manufacture steel and span the Mississippi." He looked west as if envisioning something she couldn't see. "I've been away from Pittsburgh for a long time, studying steel mills in the East and abroad, trying to find a way to get that done."

"Did you?"

"Not yet," he replied, his mood confident, unconcerned. "But I will."

She couldn't imagine it. She wasn't even sure how far away the Mississippi was, but she was all too aware they were nearing New Hope's imposing gates. As they turned down the tree-lined drive, she felt a hitch of regret as she tucked her fiddle away. She wanted to ask him to let her walk the remainder, but the driver, obviously familiar with the Ballantynes, was lumbering down a side lane . . . to the servants' quarters.

A little well of delight bubbled up inside her. They thought she was the help. Not a Ballantyne. Not the granddaughter of one of the wealthiest men in Allegheny County, if not all Pennsylvania. The simplicity of it made her smile.

What would Aunt Andra think of that?

Mim met her near the stables, a look of astonishment on her freckled face. "*Losh*, Miss Wren! If yer aunt spies you coming down the servants' lane borne along by a gentleman and his driver, there'll be no sunrise tomorrow!"

Stepping into the shadows, Wren glanced at the big house. "I misdoubt Andra saw me, shut up in her room like she's been."

"Well, glad I am of that," Mim breathed, hurrying her in a side entrance. "D'ye have any notion who was in that *braw* coach with ye?"

"He didn't say."

"*Och*, he doesna have to say! Everybody knows who Malachi Cameron is!"

Wren rolled the unfamiliar name over in her mind, offering up the paltry tidbit she was sure of. "I believe he works for the railroad."

"*Wheest!* He *owns* the railroad—and more besides. His coming back to Pittsburgh is a bit o' a surprise. He's to be here for the social season, the servants at Cameron House say, in hopes to take a bride."

Wren's hold on her fiddle tightened. "Well, he's handsome. And kind. He likes music. It shouldn't take long."

"It shouldna, nay." Mim chuckled. "He's also rich as cream cake. And downright canny. Malachi Cameron always gets what he wants. Simply put, he's the best catch from here to Edinburgh." Looking over her shoulder, she trod down the hall, whispering all the way. "Ye put me in quite a *fangle* running to town like ye did. I went and hid all the notes ye left for yer da and grandparents. Nae need to stir the pot ahead of time. I could have told ye James Sackett wouldna let ye aboard any packet."

"I wish you would have." *And spared me the trouble.* "I thought I could sway him."

"There's few who can sway Mr. Sackett. He doesna own the line, but he owns who sails and who stays. Runs a tight ship, which is why he's the lead pilot to begin with."

"I'll have to find another way home then."

"Well, ye'd best delay. Word's come from River Hill that yer needed there to help yer aunt Ellie. A groom's readied the carriage with side lights, and I've finished packing yer bags." She sighed upon saying it, eyes wary. "I'm afraid ye'll just have to get used to wearing Charlotte's clothes for now."

The mere thought still rubbed her raw. Leaving Grandmother was another matter. Wren was nearly as fond of her as she was leery of Aunt Andra. If she had to stay on, even briefly, she wanted to be a blessing to her gracious granny. Maybe it was good Mim had hidden the notes and spared her unnecessary explanations.

With a finger to her lips, Mim motioned her up a back stair, past a quiet kitchen and butler's pantry. "Thankfully the staff's at supper below and no one is about. We'll soon whisk you away to River Hill."

"Are you coming?"

"Nae, I'll have my hands full right here with yer granny and yer aunt." Opening the bedchamber door, Mim ushered her in and began to brush the dust from her dress. "I'd make no mention of Malachi Cameron to anyone," she whispered with a sudden wink. "Not that they'd believe you if you did."

12

Delight and danger grow on one stalk.

SCOTTISH PROVERB

James turned over atop the big bed, the linens growing taut about his restless limbs. Sweat slicked his brow despite the open window as the late summer heat pressed in. At midnight the Monongahela House was quiet aside from the muffled snores of George Ealer across the hall, a habit as persistent as his stutter.

Throwing off the covers, James swung bare feet to the floor. He was often up nights, assisting fugitives in the endless labyrinth of underground tunnels that served as the hotel's escape network. Like River Hill, the staff was mostly free blacks devoted to the abolitionist cause, helping runaways off Ballantyne boats or those who'd come into the city on their own seeking refuge. Tonight there'd been little activity. All was calm but for the storm inside him.

Steeling himself, he looked beneath the bed, hooking a

leather strap with his thumb and giving a tug. The small chest scraped against the planked floor, loud as Ealer's snoring. He fumbled with the lock, a prayer rising in his heart, and raised the heavy lid. Scant light danced across old, tattered things. Remnants of another life. After all these years, Georgiana Hardesty's citrus scent still seemed to linger, as unforgiving as her memory.

At the trunk's bottom lay an embroidered scarf, tattered love letters sent downriver to New Orleans, and a silver token with their initials entwined. On the flip side were the engraved, almost mocking words . . .

When this you see remember me.

He lingered on a locket, its glass face imprisoning strands of inky hair that had once caught on his callused fingers.

Sad remnants, all. He'd kept them reluctantly, mostly as a means to guard his heart. Painful as it was, he needed the reminder to ground him anew. He needed the reminder of what Bennett had done in a fit of rage over some forgotten business matter. Riding hard on the heels of that bitter memory was Rowena Ballantyne.

On a near table was the dried rose she'd given him, alongside Charlotte Ashburton's note. It lay open, a reproach to his timing, his tendency to tread too carefully. Never would he have believed he'd have a death on his hands. Or that Wren would blame him for it.

When she'd come to the levee hours before and he'd faced her across his desk, the tug of desire he'd first felt in the pilothouse resurfaced, flowing strong and invisible as a river current beneath their heated interaction. He'd not meant to be so stubborn, but he'd wanted to cover his conflicted feelings, his outright dismay at her leaving, as best he could. It hadn't helped that her father had asked him to keep an eye on her, as if she was as willful as a spring colt and needed careful handling.

Wren was no refined Pittsburgh belle, yet she was the first woman who'd turned his head—and his heart—since Georgiana. But for all her humility and homespun charm, she was a Ballantyne. Far beyond his reach. A first cousin to Bennett and subject to his scheming.

Resurrecting Georgiana Hardesty was far more likely than a liaison with Silas's granddaughter. Remembering that was all the grounding he needed.

The inhabitants of River Hill had wasted no time in adorning the newest arrival with every feminine furbelow and gewgaw they could find. Wren felt a sudden melting as wide blue eyes looked up at her, a plump, pink hand brushing the lace of her bodice. Clad in an embroidered linen gown and cap, Chloe Rose Turlock was already a beauty, the apple of everyone's eye.

Izannah reached out and touched a flawless cheek. "I can hardly steal her away from Daddy. Even the boys think she's naught but a wee fairy."

Ellie smiled. "It was the same when you were born. No one cared a whit you weren't a boy."

"Daddy's finally had his fill of sons," Izannah said with a sigh. "Now that Wren is here, we'll both help with Chloe till you're well again."

Wren warmed at being included. Aunt Ellie did look in need of tender care, pale as she was and still abed. The fever had left her, but the birth had been a difficult one and she was confined mostly to her room.

"I'm feeling stronger by the day," she reassured them, her

smile as sunny as Grandmother's own. "Soon we'll be able to take the carriage out and have a picnic and savor an Indian summer. For now Wren will stay with us till things settle down."

Settle down? Would they ever? Charlotte's death was being investigated, the wedding gifts returned. But all that seemed distant here at River Hill. Since arriving the day before, Wren was almost able to forget James Sackett's maddening refusal and her soreness over missing Molly. Izannah did her best to amuse her, showing her about the old house and relating bits of family history.

"The boys have the run of the second floor, but up here on high it's just us two."

Wren was delighted with the privacy of Izannah's third-floor bedchamber adjoining her own, both replete with twin sleigh beds and chintz upholstery. Everything smelled of fresh flowers, with double-hung windows overlooking the gardens below.

Opening a small door, Izannah motioned Wren up steep, winding steps. "I've been wanting to show you my secret place."

The cupola? Much like at New Hope, the panorama stretched from the eastern mountains to the three rivers. All was blue and sun-drenched and calm. A stack of books lay in the window seat, a testament to Izannah's favorite pastime.

Wren leaned into the sill, savoring the view. "Reminds me of the pilothouse aboard the *Rowena*."

Izannah turned toward her, eyes wide. "James let you come up by the wheel?"

"I was feeling poorly. It was during the midnight watch—"

"The midnight watch? The most hazardous of them all?"

Her startled reply sent Wren scrambling. If she'd ever

doubted her cousin's feeling for James Sackett, she doubted no longer. "No harm was done. I wasn't there overlong. The captain came and I went back to my cabin."

"I've never been on a steamer except when a boat lays at landing." The wistfulness in Izannah's tone couldn't be ignored. "And even then I've never been invited to the pilothouse."

"Mr. Sackett was less than obliging yesterday," she confessed, putting to rest any privileges Izannah may have imagined. "He wouldn't let me see Molly home."

"Wren, you were going to leave us?" There was hurt in the words—and something akin to disbelief. "Do you dislike it here so much?"

"Well, I . . ." The thought of traipsing up the winding, leaf-littered lane toward Cane Run moved her in ways she had no words for. But it was more James Sackett calling her Wren at the last that she couldn't drive from her mind.

"James was wise to say no. Losing you after all that has happened . . ." Izannah sighed and touched her sleeve. "Let's speak of other things, like your pretty dress. Those Louisville seamstresses are as accomplished as any we have in Pittsburgh."

Wren looked down at the confection of linen and lace and smoothed a flounce, trying to master her dismay. "This is Charlotte's, not mine."

"Charlotte's? You don't mean . . ." Dismay dawned in Izannah's silvery eyes. "Is Aunt Andra insisting you wear the trousseau? Oh, Wren . . ." She turned back to the glass, the lines of worry about her eyes more telling in the light. "Whatever is she thinking?"

With a lift of her shoulders, Wren thought to dismiss the matter. "Truth be told, I can't stop thinking of Charlotte no matter if I'm clad in her dresses or not."

Izannah sighed. "I can think of little else either." She touched her forehead as if getting one of the headaches she was prone to. "The papers are already full of the news, though with Grandfather's connections, the accounts are kinder than they could be."

Wren hadn't reckoned with the scandal that was bound to ensue. Back home there'd been no paper but plenty of tittle-tattle. In Pittsburgh and Boston there would be an abundance of both, especially with two prominent families involved. She prayed the matter would be dealt with fairly, the turn of events favorable.

"We should go below," Izannah finally said, taking a last look out the glass.

The sun was setting now, the smells of supper and the clink of china carrying to the cupola's far reaches. Wren's restless gaze stretched to a sunburned pasture where Izannah's brothers rode on horseback, two sheepdogs in tow. The sight of little Tremper atop a pony eased Wren's sorrow. She longed to be out of doors with them, glorying in the start of fall like she'd done at home. Autumn had always been her favorite season.

From somewhere on the second floor, Chloe's persistent wail reminded her of why she'd come. Turning, she started down the steps, eager to be of help. "I need to earn my keep."

"I'll see to the boys, then, and get them ready for supper." Izannah tried to smile, but the worry in her eyes remained.

"You're a marked man, James."

Though he knew it was true, hearing the fact spoken aloud in confirmation raised the very hair on the back of James's neck. Just south of Memphis now, past Island 37, he and

Captain Dean stood amid the grease and sparks of the engine room. The sweltering heat of late August ratcheted up the temperature in the bowels of the *Belle of Pittsburgh* as the engines were fired with pitch.

Dean began to fill his pipe, nonchalant though his tone was taut. "My suspicion is Silas wants you off the river come October."

Off the river? Even the thought made James chafe. More of Pittsburgh meant more of Bennett and matters beyond James's control. A sort of landlocked prison sentence. The river had always been his refuge.

"Things are becoming so tense over the slavery issue, many are predicting outright war." Dean looked at him long and hard. "Silas has asked us to consider a suitable replacement for Trevor Bixby, God rest him. We need another abolitionist pilot who's not afraid to do some slave running in your stead."

"I know the man. I'll arrange for a meeting when we get to Natchez."

Dean gave a nod. "Once we're there we need to be on guard about John Madder and his cronies. They've been known to book passage on steamers heading north." Pipe smoke whitened the close space between them. "There's growing suspicion the *City of Pittsburgh* was somehow sabotaged by Madder and made to mimic a boiler explosion."

James looked at him, incredulity overriding grief. "We'll likely never know."

"Not without a confession. Word is Madder is none too happy you informed authorities of his slave-stealing ring between Natchez and New Orleans and he's vowed to make more trouble."

"So Silas wants me lying in port under wages."

"Just for the winter. The hope is one of Madder's band will betray him and he'll be charged with horse stealing and counterfeiting or some of the lesser crimes he's known for." Dean reached into his breast pocket, withdrew a paper, and passed it to James. "Matters are becoming more serious—and far more public—than you might think."

James scanned the bold newsprint, somewhat amused at the flamboyant wording. Journalists these days grasped at anything to sell a story.

The life and adventures of John Madder, the Great Western Land Pirate, and a catalogue of the names of his 455 Mystic Clan followers and their conspiracy regarding the destruction of James Sackett, the young Pennsylvania river pilot who detected him.

"Who prints this trash?"

"The yellow-jacket press," Dean replied.

Fisting it, James tossed the pamphlet into an open furnace. "I need to relieve McCormick."

"I'll retire for the night then."

James took the stairs to the hurricane deck slightly ahead of schedule. Arriving late violated pilot protocol. He'd never been tardy, though he'd seen officers refuse to speak to each other for the breach. Maritime custom was strict, and he had no intention of letting the grim news about Madder slow his steps.

A harvest moon rode the river to the south, orange as a pumpkin, the swirling water black as a cat. McCormick greeted him and stepped away from the wheel. James pulled on leather gloves while the off-watch pilot apprised him of river conditions, lighting a cigar as he did so.

Listening, James was alert to the tendrils of fog that crept in from both sides of the Mississippi and promised a tense night. Much could be gauged by the season, the mood of the river, even the temperature.

Through the mist came an occasional glimmer of light like a firefly from some dwelling near shore. Lately he'd noticed such places more than he used to, even craved the refuge they promised. His River Row cottage seemed cramped. The Monongahela House too echoing. The ornate New Orleans quarters that served the gentlemen of the navigation laughably grand.

Home. He'd never had one. Never expected to want one. Why did it hold any appeal now? Pushing aside his odd musings, he tried to drive all but the river from his mind. Yet other matters would not relent. Thoughts of Wren Ballantyne kept bobbing like corks to the surface of his conscience, outdistancing Madder and his Mystic Conspiracy by a mile.

Wren . . . Wren . . . Wren.

Somehow his infatuation with this backwoods woman had snuck up on him without his consent. And left him wishing it was anyone else instead.

Ballantyne Hall was newer and grander than either River Hill or New Hope, almost shimmery in its splendor, an orangery under construction in the extensive gardens at the rear. Wren got down from the carriage as a light rain began to fall and entered a marble foyer and ornate dining room, where Papa wrapped her in his firm, tobacco-laden embrace.

Since arriving in Pittsburgh two weeks prior, they'd hardly had a moment alone, and now they were again surrounded on all sides, a dozen eyes on them. The closeness they'd once shared as father and daughter seemed a memory. Circumstances and Ballantyne business had pushed them apart. Still, he appeared glad to see her. And once again she was thankful Mim had intercepted her note before he'd read the depths of her discontent.

Her wary gaze fixed on Bennett through the spray of roses and ivy running the length of the table as he sat opposite her. Clad in unrelieved black down to his inky cravat, he drove Charlotte's memory home. This was why they'd come. To pay their respects, so Izannah said. With her cousin on one side of her and Papa on the other, Wren was better able to navigate the maze of silverware and French dishes.

Unlike the relaxed, laughter-sated meals at River Hill, conversation here was stiffly polite, and politics and business ruled the day. Wren felt a strange tension pulse in the air. Everyone was mindful they should have been celebrating a wedding, not mourning someone's passing. Seated at one end of the table, Grandfather kept the conversation from stalling with his usual aplomb, though it was muted tonight, out of respect for Charlotte, surely.

They waded through course after course, sampling salmon en croûte and steamed vegetables and thick custard served with rich, black New Orleans coffee.

"Wren, I was thinking you and Ansel might play for us. A slow air, perhaps, or a lament." Grandmother was looking at her, hope in her faded blue eyes.

Wren met her father's gaze in question.

"I've brought two of the Cremona violins," he told her.

Had he? She hardly felt like playing. Aware of everyone's eyes on them, she simply nodded and followed him into an adjoining room, its French doors open to the garden. Soon all had assembled—the judge and Izannah, Bennett and his parents. On a near sofa sat Grandfather and Grandmother, Aunt Andra to one side.

Hands unsteady, Wren tightened her bow and applied rosin to the strings, wishing she was in New Hope's music room, where no one came to listen except Grandmother . . . or perhaps in Malachi Cameron's carriage with only him and his driver her audience.

Papa struck the opening chord. She followed his lead reluctantly. Oh, why had he picked so complicated a lament? She was all thumbs, aware of Bennett's rapt attention never leaving her for the entire excruciating piece. Hamstrung by awkwardness, her heart meting out a stilted rhythm of its own, she tried to smile at their polite applause.

"Play another," Uncle Peyton urged, turning to Papa. "It reminds me of the early days when you and Ellie used to keep us up half the night."

Wren chose a less complicated air, hoping to offset the gloom of the room. But she had little heart for playing, worn down as she was.

At last more drinks were served and they put their instruments away. Taking a glass of lemon ice, Wren was cast back to that first day when she'd had the spill on New Hope's porch and Bennett had leveled her with a look.

Now, standing with his back to them by the French doors, he was taller and broader of shoulder than she remembered, and despite the trouble that shadowed him, he exuded polish and strength and that canny quality owned by all the Ballantynes.

No match for gentle Charlotte.

Nearly wincing at the thought, she fastened her gaze on a bed of autumn asters edging the veranda, startled when he came to stand beside her. "You play very well, cousin. Better than any I've heard in Pittsburgh, perhaps anywhere."

The compliment raised her color a notch. She didn't doubt his sincerity. She just sensed he was parsimonious with his praise. "I can take little credit, being both Ballantyne and Nancarrow."

"Have you given any thought to going on stage? Performing?" His weary eyes narrowed, the sleepless lines beneath less pronounced. "A lucrative calling could be yours, especially given the Nightingale's reputation."

"Really, Bennett, don't be so gauche." Izannah passed by and whispered her rebuke before moving on to Grandmother, her fan aflutter.

Wren made no comment. Her music wasn't something that could be bought. It sprang from her very soul like the gift it was. To be given as freely as it came.

He filled the uneasy silence. "I play the cello . . . on occasion."

"Oh?" She resisted the urge to look about the music room till she spied it. Was he accomplished or simply dallying? Bennett, she sensed, didn't dally at anything.

"The violin and cello get on very well together." His voice dropped to an inviting timbre. "So might we."

She read purpose in the words. Some plan. Yet they seemed to be dancing around what mattered most of all. She took a steadying breath. "I'm sorry . . . about Charlotte."

The surprise on his tanned features was quickly reined in. "As am I." He fell silent and Wren sensed he'd say no more. But he continued on in the same low vein, surprising her. "Everything was all right . . . and then it wasn't." His jaw tensed. "She seemed strangely upset. She wasn't paying close attention to where she walked. The steps leading to the boathouse are steep . . . I tried to catch her when she slipped. But I—it was too late."

Too late. Had Charlotte told him she was leaving and some sort of struggle ensued? Had he been angry enough to harm her? Try as she might, Wren couldn't wash Charlotte's words from her mind.

He was so angry I thought he might strike me.

A gentle touch to her sleeve drew her away. "Time to go, cousin." Izannah gave her a small smile but had nary a word more, or even a glance, for Bennett. "Daddy doesn't want to be too long away from Mama, and it's growing late."

Taking a last look at the garden, Wren wrestled with a morbid desire to glimpse the lake and make peace with Charlotte's passing. But there was no peace in her heart. And the haunted look on Bennett's face assured her there'd be none.

13

Hope is grief's best music.
ANONYMOUS

In the privacy of Izannah's bedchamber, a tea table between them, Izannah pushed aside a stack of newspapers with a sigh. "A few paltry lines about James . . . and far too much about Bennett."

Wren glanced at the boldest headline, breath held.

INQUEST TO BE MADE PUBLIC IN DEATH OF SHIPPING HEIRESS.

"Why would there be news of Mr. Sackett?" Wren broached the question carefully, unsure if talk of river pilots was any safer than that of inquests. Yet Izannah always managed to turn the conversation James's way. Further proof of her affections, surely.

Izannah looked over the edge of her porcelain teacup, its delicate rim edged with roses. "There's rumor of a race between crack boats."

"Crack boats?"

"The fastest boats in the fleet and their premier pilots,

which would be the Ballantynes' *Philadelphia* and the Vanderbilts' *North Star*. James holds the record for speed on both the upper and lower Mississippi. Everyone from Pittsburgh to Louisville and beyond will be watching."

The mention of Louisville brought a tug, but more from the memory of fleeing James Sackett's office than homesickness. Wren eyed the newspapers absently, so unsettled about the coming inquest that the tea tasted bitter.

"I saw you talking with Bennett last night following supper." Izannah took a ginger biscuit but seemed no hungrier than she. "After his outlandish idea that you take the stage."

"I don't know what to make of him," Wren confessed, unable to shake free of their troubling conversation.

"Nobody knows what to make of Bennett Ballantyne." Izannah studied her teacup without focus, as if weighing how much to say. "While everything on the surface looks very civil, there are things going on you know little about. Bennett needed Charlotte's fortune and is in terrible straits."

"But he's the heir—"

"Yes, and he lives extravagantly, whittling away much of his inheritance in reckless pursuits. Grandfather maintains the bulk of control and is always diversifying, but the truth is he's very old, and though he seems almost immortal, he isn't. When he passes, his legacy will largely be Bennett's. I shudder to think what will happen then."

"Surely he'll marry in time . . . find another bride."

"Perhaps, but right now he's in mourning, firmly out of the coming social season. And after what's happened with Charlotte, I doubt any woman from Boston to New Orleans would want him."

Wren struggled to give him the benefit of the doubt. "But if it was an accident . . ."

Izannah's sharp gaze shot down the notion. "I fear it wasn't. Even the servants are talking. It seems Bennett wanted to take Charlotte out on the lake, as he has a new skiff. There's a steep set of stairs leading to the boathouse where she fell." She looked to the newspapers. "One account says a maid heard them arguing."

Wren shut her eyes. It was all too easy to ponder Charlotte pleading. Charlotte crying. Charlotte falling . . .

"Bennett's fiery temper makes him suspect. He's arrogant and argumentative to a fault." Izannah's normally pale features were pink with heat. "Don't ever cross him. And never trust him. If he has anything to do with you, it's because he wants to use you."

Heated words. Harsh words. Wren sipped her tea, trying to come to grips with all that had happened.

"I'll never forgive him for what he did to James . . ."

James again. Wren braced herself for more, but Izannah's words were snatched away by the opening of a door. Aunt Ellie came in, Chloe in arm, startling them both. With a deft move, Izannah slid the newspapers out of sight beneath the table and put on her brightest face. "Mama, you're just in time for tea."

Wren smiled and reached for Chloe, lightly clad on account of the heat. She wore a sheer muslin nightgown, her every roll and dimple on display. Smelling of talc and milk, she was a warm, weighty armful.

"I heard voices and thought I'd join you." Ellie's smile was so like Grandmother's Wren wished she could be with them. "The boys are at lessons, your father in court."

"Should you be on your feet so soon, Mama? Another few days abed is best, or so the midwife says." Pouring her a cup of tea, Izannah added sugar and a generous splash of cream. "I should have Cook make you a full breakfast."

"No need. Your father already had a tray brought up at dawn and stayed till I'd eaten every bite."

"Oh? You missed a sumptuous supper at Ballantyne Hall. Uncle Peyton is quite proud of his new French chef." Izannah's forced cheer was worse than honest melancholy. "Wren entertained us afterward. Uncle Ansel said all that was needed was your harp."

Ellie smiled. "We used to play together quite often in the old days. Before he went away to England and I married Jack."

The mention of the old days brought a rush of tender things to mind. "Some of my dearest memories are of Mama playing her psaltery and Papa and me accompanying her on the fiddle," Wren said.

Ellie's blue gaze turned wistful. "Your mother was an accomplished musician in her own right. No one was surprised when she and your father met and fell in love."

"I know so little about their courtship," Wren confessed, craving Ellie's side of the story. "Only that Papa decided to visit the Nancarrows in Cornwall because of their reputation as luthiers and collectors. Then he met Mama."

Ellie nodded. "Unbeknownst to the rest of us, the two of them had struck a correspondence. We were beginning to think he'd never marry. No Pittsburgh girl appealed to him. When he left for England, I was heartbroken. We all were. But once he returned with a bride, all was well again. After that the three of you went to Kentucky."

Wren fell silent. Till now she'd not realized the strangeness of it, how she who had been raised in quietness and simplicity had been thrust into an unfamiliar, lush world in reverse while her mother had left England to come to humble Cane Run. Mama had never complained once, not to Wren's hearing. Yet the move must have cost her something. Family. Friends.

Refinements. And Papa's limp must have always served as a reminder of the price of resuming their privileged life.

"We mustn't dwell so much on the past," Ellie's voice cut in, gently steering them in another direction. "We must look to the future."

The gentle words seemed to hold a promise—of brighter, better things to come.

If that could be had in Pennsylvania.

Wren's two-week stay at River Hill came to a sudden end, severed by a terse note.

> *Wren,*
>   *Plans have changed. Return to New Hope as soon as possible.*
>
>   *Papa*

Might Papa have decided to return home?

For just a moment she gave in to the joy of going back to the known and familiar. To the stone house and violin shop . . . her colorful garden and feather bed beneath the eave . . . Mama's gravesite atop the mountain in back of the house. Remembrances swirled through her head, potent and sweet.

The carriage that had brought her to River Hill was waiting, ready to whisk her down a rutted road that was becoming uncomfortably familiar. When New Hope's cupola came into view, she tried to prepare herself if Aunt Andra met her in the foyer, but only Mim appeared, taking her bonnet in welcome.

"Good to see you, Miss Ro—" Looking about, she finished with a whisper, "Miss *Wren*."

A quick glance into twin parlors reassured Wren the wedding gifts were gone. Where to she didn't know, nor would she ask. A bittersweet gladness filled her as Mim rambled on.

"Yer da is in the garden with a—er, guest. Yer granny is getting ready to have tea. I'm nae sure about Miss Andra."

Relieved, Wren traveled the length of the foyer, bypassing the lure of the music room to reach the back of the house.

Mim hurried close behind. "Ye'll be wanting to change first, ye ken."

"Change? Why?"

"There's a wee smudge on yer dress, and the hour calls for an afternoon gown. Even a tea gown will do. I've just the one."

Twenty chiffon flounces and a generous splash of lavender water later, Wren returned downstairs and passed onto the rear veranda. The heat of the day intensified the flowers' fragrance, filling the sultry air like potpourri. Standing beneath the shaded eave, she searched for her father amid acres of ornamental garden. It wasn't like him to leisurely stroll on a workday. Her heart tripped as she imagined the reason.

Passing a splashing fountain, she finally found him. He was walking with a woman, fringed parasol in hand, her face hidden if not her form. They were deep in conversation, her gloved hand resting on his sleeve in a way that bespoke a troubling familiarity. Had Papa known her before? Years ago? Whoever she was, she was as different from Mama as daylight and dark. Buxom. Rather tall. Lively in manner. Mama seemed no more than a ghost in that moment, as faded and forgotten as an old portrait.

"Wren, you've come at last." Papa's voice reached out in welcome. "You're just in time to meet Miss Mina Cameron."

Miss? She looked as old as Papa but was remarkably unlined. Her smile was warm, her grip on his arm never lessening. She had the same unusual eyes as the man in the carriage—Malachi Cameron. Were they kin?

"I hope you don't mind that I call you Wren. It's delightful. Memorable. And you must call me Mina."

Wren smiled and gave in to Papa's embrace. "Mina is here to have tea with your grandmother," he said. "You might want to join them, though I'd like a word with you first."

With a squeeze to his arm, Mina left them. They continued on down a gravel path to the quaint, ivy-covered chapel Charlotte had favored. Wren felt a sudden qualm. Pushing open a creaking door that looked like it had been rescued from some crumbling castle, Papa stepped inside. Reluctant, she followed after him.

Stained-glass windows shot prisms of rainbow light against walls of stone. Everything looked and felt old. Hallowed. She softened, understanding why Charlotte had wanted to wed here. It had a charm undimmed by time. A worthy place to play a violin, promising a pleasing echo.

"I've always had a fondness for this chapel." Papa shut the door behind them, hemming them in. "You were christened here, and here your aunt Ellie wed her Jack."

Wren looked to the far rafters where a dove perched. The past seemed to rise up to meet her, filling in more missing pages of her family's history. She sensed an unspoken wish in Papa's words that she take her place and continue the legacy. She was all he had, his only hope for grandchildren. Pondering it, she took a seat, the wooden bench cold beneath her outspread hands.

He sat beside her, silent for a too-long moment. "You're aware I've been working long hours at the ironworks. Business there is going to require considerable travel, more than I'd anticipated."

She tensed, unsure of what was coming.

"I'm leaving for Philadelphia tomorrow and after that will go on to New York and Boston."

"So far?" Dismay needled her anew. "I'll go with you."

"No, Wren. It's important you stay behind to manage correspondence and settle accounts from any business in Kentucky. Besides, travel is often perilous and you didn't fare well on the trip upriver. I'll be relying on the stage and train and will try to return by Christmas."

Christmas? The promise rang hollow. She'd hoped to be home by then.

"Your grandparents will be glad of your company." He continued on in that calm, quiet way that was becoming more maddening by the minute. "And Ellie and Izannah are near at hand."

Not a word about Andra. Andra who didn't want her. Who no doubt wished she'd go east too.

"I've an interested party in the Cremonas in New York."

Emotion closed her throat and nearly kept her from speaking. "Not our Amatis. Not the Nightingale."

He looked at her as if surprised she would ask. "The Nightingale belongs to you, Wren. Always. But selling the rest of our collection might be the only way to gain the Guarneri your grandfather lost long ago."

She nodded. It was her dream as much as his. Lacing her fingers together, she prayed for calm. "I thought . . . maybe . . . you'd want to return to Kentucky."

Or give me your blessing to go home without you.

"Ah yes, Kentucky. I've news on that score too." His voice held an absent note as if he'd forgotten all about it. "I've recently received a letter from Selkirk. He wants to buy our land, continue the business, as he's to wed."

"Selkirk?" She'd not known Selkirk had a sweetheart. Stunned, she stumbled for sure footing, for a grip on the past. "But Papa, that's our life. Our livelihood."

"It was, Wren. Once."

"But you're a craftsman, not a businessman." Her frantic gaze held his. "You make music and instruments, not—"

Not *iron.*

She nearly spat out the word in disgust. Yet even as she thought it, she realized how foolish it was. Papa had no need of being a luthier in the Kentucky woods. He was a Ballantyne. Heir to a fortune. Anything else was deemed second best. Yet some foolish hope, stubborn as a weed, made her cling to the way things were. "You'd turn your back on everything like that? Like it never mattered? Or never was?"

Pain clouded his eyes. "It matters to me. It always will. But it's different without your mother. Kentucky became barren, no longer home. Returning to Pennsylvania means a new life for us both, with new opportunities and choices."

She fixed her eyes on a stained-glass window depicting a shepherd and lamb. Oh, but she felt like that lamb. Small. Bewildered. Was her Shepherd still leading? Did the Lord want her in this rocky place? If so, her spirit rebelled at every step. Mama's death had brought about such change. Selkirk had moved on, as had Molly. Why couldn't she? Bending her head, she gave in to her tears, ashamed Papa could see her so undone.

"I blame myself for keeping you in Kentucky as long as I did and sheltering you from your rightful life here." His arms went around her, comforting yet comfortless. "But there's naught to be done now. We're firmly planted in Pennsylvania. There's no going back, only forward."

"But how will I manage without you, our music? I don't know how I'll fill my time—"

"It would be a great pleasure to me if you'd use every opportunity presented to you, whatever that might be. Become familiar with Pittsburgh and your family. Be of help here or at River Hill. With that in mind, I'm placing you in your aunt Andra's care, something she's fully aware of and agreeable to." At her sigh of protest he continued calmly. "I know you find her rather daunting, but you must realize she can be trusted. She'll see that no harm comes to you. Make the most of my absence and your prospects. I'll return ere long."

She stiffened, bracing herself for yet another sweeping change. Though she wanted to reassure him she would do as he wished, make him proud, pain left her with no promises.

With every heartfelt word she felt the closing of a door, as solid as the stone chapel's.

14

Sorrow is the mere rust of the soul. Activity will cleanse and brighten it.

SAMUEL JOHNSON

With her father away, Wren could count on two things. Tea with Grandmother and Mina Cameron every Tuesday, and a day spent at River Hill every Thursday. September had dawned, as crisp and colorful as an autumn leaf, ripening the apples in New Hope's orchards and frosting the fields a brittle white. Tenants and servants were predicting a harsh winter, perhaps the worst western Pennsylvania had seen in half a century.

Molly had been gone three weeks. The *Rowena* and *Belle of Pittsburgh* were again in port, their great bulk lining the Monongahela levee, their pilothouses empty. If James Sackett was back in town, Wren didn't know. The newspapers had made no mention of his return aside from a few printed cards of praise when he'd first docked, focusing instead on the belated inquest that quietly filled a small, mournful column in all the Pittsburgh papers.

> On 23 August, an inquest was held at Pittsburgh, before R Lowry, Coroner, in view of the body of Miss Charlotte Ashburton, aged 23, who on the 22nd had fallen down a flight of steps at the Allegheny County estate of Peyton Ballantyne, Esq., of which she died. Verdict—accidental death.

Wren read the ruling in the privacy of her bedchamber, her tears spattering the newsprint. Charlotte's brief life amounted to little more than a few dismissive lines while Bennett's future beckoned bright. Somehow the matter seemed unfair . . . unfinished.

Hearing a footfall in the hall, she balled up the paper and fed it to the bedchamber fire.

Mim entered through the dressing room door, eyeing the leaping flames with a knowing eye. "Ye ken the *ill-scrappit* news, looks like." Depositing an armful of clean petticoats and camisoles in the mahogany wardrobe, she clucked her tongue. "My, but yer a soft soul to be so moved."

"It's all blown over then."

"Nae. Mr. Bennett might have escaped the inquest, but he's out o' luck securing a bonny bride." Hands on hips, Mim studied her. "I hope ye dinna mind if I speak so freely. Yer more outlander than kin here, seems to me."

This Wren couldn't deny. Truth was she rather liked Mim's confidences. Armed with them she felt less vulnerable. Better prepared to face whatever was coming. Though the Ballantynes might be silent on a given matter, the large staff never ceased its tattling. Kinfolk were employed by all the big houses owned by the Ballantynes, Camerons, and Turlocks, and secrets flew between them, sometimes for coin.

"My brother's head groom at Ballantyne Hall, and I've a cousin who's in the kitchen at Cameron House. So I hear all the blether." Mim regarded Wren with a mixture of sympathy and affection. "And the blether this morn is that yer to go out with yer aunt. And ye'd best look sharp while doing it."

"Out with Andra?" The very thought turned Wren cold. "Why?"

"She never said. I have an hour to get you ready. We'll need something warm, as there's a nip in the air."

"Granny isn't coming?"

"Yer granny's at the Orphan Home. I'm afraid Miss Andra has ye all to herself." Turning her back, she began rummaging through Charlotte's dresses. "Something dark should do. But not black. We dinna want to advertise the family's misfortune."

Wren bit her tongue as Mim picked an elaborate gown with too many flounces. An appalling purple, it was made of silk brocade with garish tufts of black lace on the wide skirts. Mim shot her a dismayed glance. "I ken what yer thinking, but there's no help for it."

"At least leave my hair plain."

"A chignon will do—and a bonnet too." Uncapping a hatbox, Mim held up a straw creation with silk violets riding the brim. "Ye'll need gloves, a shawl, and parasol."

And patience.

Wren's mind traveled to her attic room, where she'd dressed without thought or a maid, even Molly. What had happened to her old work clothes? Her two Sabbath-best dresses? She'd meant to talk to Papa about a new wardrobe, but he'd left so quickly she'd left it undone.

"Dinna look so *fash*," Mim consoled her. "Yer aunt isna a bad sort. Prickly as a thistle, mayhap, but she's always had the Ballantynes' best interests at heart."

Wren sat down at the dressing table, thinking Mim wise beyond her years. The Ballantynes' best interests were just what worried her.

Steep hills rose around Pittsburgh, cradling the city and its three rivers as if fearful all that water might spill out and the stranglehold of industry would cease. Wren tried not to look long at the Monongahela levee, frantically busy at midmorning as the Ballantyne barouche cut across Water Street. Smart and efficient, their coachman soon took them beyond the crush of the waterfront and across a long, low bridge strung with wires, out of the city's haze if not above the clatter and hammer of countless mills and factories.

"The city is still recovering from the devastating fire of '45." Andra's voice rose above the din as she sat opposite Wren, dressed in deep gray. Her plumed bonnet with its veil of black lace was another reminder of Charlotte's passing. "Your grandfather donated a great deal toward the rebuilding effort, along with other industrialists. Two of our mills were lost but have been rebuilt outside the city. I thought it time to show you the full range of Ballantyne interests today. But we need to be atop Coal Hill to see them all properly."

The touch of pride in her tone couldn't be overlooked, and Wren felt a faint spark of interest. But would they ever make it up the rutted road? Their driver seemed unconcerned, hat brim pulled nearly to the end of his bulbous nose, the matching horses moving at an unbroken gait.

Wren looked beyond the wide brim of her bonnet, gladness

filling her as sunlight fell across the carriage's leather interior. "Is Grandfather partial to certain . . . business?"

Andra's mouth softened in a near smile. "He's pleased with whatever is making the most return on investment. That just happens to be the iron mills at present, though the glassworks are second to none."

They crested the steep hill, a feat that made Pittsburgh look impossibly small if just as blackened. Wren followed the line of Andra's pointed finger toward the heart of the city teeming with people and vehicles of all description. "Over there are the ironworks, the largest and most productive in Pittsburgh, with your father now firmly at the helm. Directly below, occupying the entire Monongahela waterfront, is the Ballantyne shipbuilding and packet trade."

Wren looked down at the crowded levee reluctantly, trying not to think of James Sackett. Failing.

"Just across Water Street is the glassworks and factory housing, along with the mercantile and warehouses. Father owns a great deal of other real estate in the city, of course, and is always considering other options. He's continually diversifying and is even considering extending the Ballantynes' reach to California now that it's become the thirty-first state."

Wren listened, trying to take it all in. Failing on that score too. The sweep of Andra's gloved hand never seemed to lessen.

"Lest you think it is all business for the Ballantynes, over there on Mill Street is the apprenticeship library Father had built beside the new Men's Academy. Farther up Grant's Hill is the Orphan Home."

Wren could barely make out the outline of the orphanage atop the far hill through the haze. "Granny is there today, Mim said."

"Yes, the orphanage is your grandmother's foremost

concern." Andra settled back against the seat as the driver began the descent downhill, a far easier feat than the uphill climb. "She founded it years ago when she came from Philadelphia to Pittsburgh and married your grandfather."

Within half an hour they were back inside the city, traversing a street bordered by shade trees fronting the river. But the peaceful avenue was soon forgotten as the barouche's rapid pace plunged them into a rabbit's warren of dark streets and alleys full of ragtag children and roaming animals. Here the stench rivaled the smoke and left Wren glad of the handkerchief Mim had insisted she bring. Andra looked straight ahead, her own perfumed hankie to her nose, as if the smell was a nuisance easily dealt with.

A pack of boys started after them as they drove past, palms open and begging, voices carrying on a foul wind. Andra barely gave them a glance. "They're nearly of age to be employed. Likely their families work at the mills."

"But they're so . . . small." The children of Cane Run flashed to mind, most of them barefoot and as lightly clad. But they'd had fresh air, the run of field and forest, unlike these bedraggled urchins of the streets.

"Small, yes, but employable," Andra said. "Our workers are paid a higher wage and have shorter working hours than any in the city. No labor disputes or trouble with the trade unions either. There's also a private infirmary for whatever ails them."

The particulars meant little to Wren. All she knew was that Grandfather was wildly successful, the Ballantyne name renowned. All this industry somehow mattered to Andra, who hoped it would mean something to her.

Toward noon they passed beyond high pine gates bearing bold black lettering: Ballantyne Cotton Works. A guard waved them on, tipping his hat and watching them pass. Made of brick, the immense mill hugged the north shore of the Allegheny River, acrid smoke pouring from tall smokestacks. In the shadow of the mill were blackened tenements, their starkness broken by lines of laundry strung from doors and windows and the earthy reek of cabbage.

"The unmarried factory girls live here, as it's safer and more convenient to the workplace." Andra put away her hankie as the carriage rolled to a stop. "The married folk live in row houses beyond the gates."

The mill supervisor met them, taking them into the largest building and up a flight of steps to a gallery overlooking hundreds of spindles and looms. Here the clack and rumble of machinery was deafening. Wren focused on the women and girls swarming the mill's wooden floor. Sweat beaded every face, hands never idle. A few glanced up at them, clearly curious, and Wren felt the deep chasm that separated them. But for her name, the happenstance of her birth, she might have been among them.

"Some of the girls are from the Orphan Home. When they come of age, they're given a choice of working in a factory like this one or being in service at a private residence. Everyone has a job. A purpose." Andra skimmed the mill floor with a sweeping glance before returning to her. "Even you, Rowena."

Wren tried not to frown as the steely words dissolved in the whirr of machinery, cotton fluff flying through the air like snow.

Andra's voice held steady. "You bear the Ballantyne name. You're privy to the Ballantyne fortune. With it comes privilege—and responsibility. You're in Pittsburgh now, firmly planted in our world, and must find your place."

Wren sought a proper reply, anything to ease the strain

between them, but came up short. She didn't understand why Andra had brought her here except that Andra was trying to make a point she wanted no part of.

Touching her arm, Andra gestured to a near door, her voice raised against the onslaught of machinery. "I'll take you to the Orphan Home next. If your grandmother is there, you can accompany her back to New Hope, as I've some calls to make."

Relieved, Wren followed her out, their dresses and capes dotted with flecks of cotton, Andra's words burned into her brain. Beneath a polluted autumn sky, she took a last look at the sprawling factory with its No Trespassing signs and inhospitable fences and wanted to lift a hand and block it. But it loomed too large, too proud, edging out other, kinder memories of Indian-summer days spent gathering nuts and making apple butter, tending leafy bonfires, and going barefoot a final time till spring.

These beloved things seemed to belong to someone else, to another woman in another time and place. She'd already begun to look back on Cane Run as if it was nothing more than a story in a dusty, hastily shelved book. Almost a fairy tale.

Her thoughts reeled and her heart wrenched.

Papa seemed a world away, Kentucky even farther.

The Lord more distant still.

The voices of children and the lively sight of them playing in the enclosed orphanage yard lightened Wren's spirits, as did news that Grandmother was indeed there, somewhere.

The director greeted her warmly as Andra made her exit. "Mrs. Ballantyne might be anywhere in the Orphan Home but is likely in the nursery with the infants. You may wait in the visitors' area if you like or go outside on the green till I locate her."

Craving fresh air, Wren pushed open a near door, grateful the Orphan Home had been built on a hill outside the city. A crushed stone path led to a lone oak, a wooden swing suspended from one lofty branch. Afflicted with coal dust, the tree was no longer a stalwart green but a sad gray like most of the trees within the city limits, its leaves the same stunted shade.

Mindful of her wide skirts, Wren sat down carefully in the swing and gave a small push with her foot. At the first glide came a giggle. A curly head popped out from behind the tree's withered trunk, the toothless grin wide and welcoming. "I never saw a lady swing before."

Wren smiled back at her. "I'm hardly a lady."

"You're dressed as such." The child touched her own plain frock, smoothing out a wrinkle before peering intently at Wren's bonnet. "Are those flowers real?"

Plucking a silk lilac from the brim, Wren held it out. "They're pretend."

Taking it, the girl tucked it in a buttonhole. "I like it nearly as well as what Jamie gave me." Looking down, she withdrew something from her pocket and held it aloft. Nested in her palm was a tiny carved bird. "He says it's a wren."

"Oh?" Wren touched a wooden wing, so well-crafted it returned her to Selkirk and the violin shop. "Your little bird looks so real it could sing."

"I wouldn't know about that," she replied. "There aren't many birds or trees here."

Had she never heard a bird sing? Wren nearly sighed at the thought. Pursing her lips, she let out a cheerful, trilling imitation, the song rising in pitch with a rapid cascade of notes. Making birdcalls had been as much a part of her upbringing as making fiddles, though Papa and Selkirk were far better at it than she.

The girl's eyes widened, her giggle broadening to a belly laugh.

Delighted, Wren laughed along with her. "You can tell your Jamie, whoever he is, that you've heard a wren sing."

"I will." She pushed the carving into Wren's gloved hand. "Jamie can make me another. He comes here as often as he can."

Touched, Wren thanked her, wishing she had more to give. On a whim she pulled her bonnet free, placed it atop the child's dark head, and tied the chin ribbons in place.

Small hands touched the silken strings with near reverence. "For me?"

Wren nodded. "A fair trade—your pretty bird for my pretty bonnet."

"For keeps?"

"For keeps," Wren replied. "What's your name?"

"Adelaide. I'm six years old and I've been here since I was a baby." The rushed words sounded rote as if said one too many times, or time was short. "I like it here. It's safe and warm and I'm not hungry." She took a step back at the sound of a bell. "Time for lessons."

Wren watched her go, the cotton mill fresh in her mind. She didn't like to think of Adelaide there—or at the Orphan Home. Despite the place's tidy appearance, it was no substitute for a loving family.

As the child passed through a far door, clutching her new hat, Grandmother appeared at yet another entry, a tall shadow behind her.

James Sackett?

Awkwardness choked her at the mere sight of him. Abandoning the swing, Wren smoothed her skirts, glad for Grandmother's company, at least. As they walked her way, she fought off the memory of her last meeting with James, when she'd flown out his office door, acting no older than Adelaide.

She greeted them, noticing the way Grandmother was leaning on his arm as if the day had stolen away her strength. "Afternoon, Granny . . . Mr. Sackett."

Grandmother kissed her cheek, clearly pleased to see her. "You've already met James, of course."

He removed his hat. "And I see you've met Addie."

She met his eyes reluctantly, mindful of the little wren tucked in her hand, as surprise gained a solid foothold. Was this Addie's Jamie? "I didn't expect to find you here."

He glanced toward the gray stone building. "I lived here as a boy. I'm also on the board of directors with your grandmother."

An orphan? She'd assumed he was from a prestigious Pittsburgh family, not a man without a home. She lowered her gaze, finding him less intimidating today than he had been in his office. Away from the levee he wore what she was coming to recognize as the height of men's fashion—cravat, waistcoat, frock coat, trousers, and dark leather gloves and shoes, all exceptionally tailored. Not even Bennett Ballantyne dressed so strikingly or carried himself so well.

"James has had a hand in a great many things in Pittsburgh starting when he was very young." Grandmother smiled up at him almost adoringly. "We couldn't manage without him."

"Your grandmother is a gracious woman." He spoke in that low, measured tone she was coming to know. "I'll see you to your carriage and then I'll be on my way."

He took her elbow, and heat shot through her at his touch.

Would their every encounter be one of uneasiness, at least on her part?

Once he'd settled them in the carriage, Grandmother bade him goodbye, but Wren bit her tongue. He didn't look her way again. Somehow it aggravated her that he didn't—and that she minded. He simply walked west, into a haze of soot and feeble sunlight, his silhouette tall and distinct and all too unsettling.

Tucked in the confines of her dressing room with the door closed, Wren spoke in Gaelic as offhandedly as she could. "Mim, I want you to tell me about Mr. Sackett."

"Mr. James?" Mim's needle never stilled on the hem she was mending, but Wren didn't miss the playful smile around her mouth. "Whatever for?"

"I'm just curious, is all." Wren looked down at the cotton sampler she was working, aggravated she'd missed a stitch. "I keep bumping into him in Pittsburgh. Seems like I should know more about him."

"Well . . . he's as *braw* as they come with those jade eyes and hair black as the Earl of Hell's waistcoat—"

"That's not what I meant," Wren said in a rush. "Yesterday, when we met up at the orphanage, he told me he was raised there."

"*Och*, that he was." Mim's head bobbed in confirmation. "At least in his early years. He apprenticed with the Ballantynes and was oft at River Hill after that. He's an able hand with the horses too. He and the judge have a liking for a handsome stable. But that was before the river claimed him."

Wren nodded, thinking of Izannah. That was how they'd met, she guessed. She'd often wondered . . .

"Ye hardly need reminding that James Sackett's the finest

pilot in the Ballantyne line, mayhap the finest from here to New Orleans. He's working on publishing a book charting the crossings and whatnot to help in river navigation." Mim's moody sigh gave a warning. "Of course there's nae good wi'out the bad."

Wren lifted her head.

"Years ago there was a certain lady here in Pittsburgh, of good family and reputation, who was smitten with Mr. James. He's nae one whose head is easily turned, ye ken, but ere long they were engaged to be wed."

"Mr. Sackett and this one lady?"

"Aye, her name was Miss Georgiana Hardesty. A wee bit younger than Mr. James, she was dark-headed and had the queerest eyes, a sort of violet-gray. They made a bonny pair, they did. But it was nae to be. A fortnight before the wedding, the bride was cut down with a fever. Came on her all of a sudden and then she was gone like a puff o' smoke."

"Oh, Mim . . ."

"He took it hard, he did. Never has righted himself, some say."

Wren bit her lip, mulling it over. Was Izannah smitten with James but he was still mourning Georgiana? Might that change in time? Or had he closed his heart for keeps? She felt certain she'd seen an answering spark in him when they were together, an unmistakable affection.

"Of course we dinna speak of such things much, as they're so dreary." Mim lapsed into an odd silence, as if she had far more to tell but was keeping secrets. "Best let bygones be bygones."

"I won't say a word," Wren reassured her. "I was only . . . curious."

And somewhat humbled that a man with such unsettling reserve might have come by it honestly.

15

Only solitary men know the full joys of friendship. Others have their family; but to a solitary and an exile, his friends are everything.

WILLA CATHER

The wood flat they were towing up the muddy Mississippi behind the *Rowena* looked like any other, its facade huge and hulking, full of the fuel that stoked a steamer's ravenous engines. Few knew that beneath its carefully constructed scaffolding, two dozen slaves were huddled. The *Rowena*'s crew, bound to secrecy and well rewarded for it, treated it no differently than an ordinary tow, except for the steward's strange dispensing of rations on the midnight watch.

Years before, they'd hidden fugitives in the hold amid the cargo, but lately port authorities and searches were becoming more aggressive, penalties more harsh. Death in some cases. For every abolitionist on their side, there were a dozen who were rabidly proslavery. The rivers seemed to roil from the escalating tension between the North and the South, particularly on shores of states that proclaimed slaves free.

Nearly abreast of Island 37, the nest of Madder and his Mystic Conspiracy, they sailed past precarious chutes and reefs and rock bars that challenged James's navigation skills and his temper. He'd not rest till they were in sight of Cincinnati and could offload the fugitives onto free ground. Thankfully Silas Ballantyne had forged contacts there that had stayed strong half a century. James prayed they would hold.

For now the danger was from the river itself—and the uproarious laughter from the captain's quarters on the texas deck, where an intense game of chess was in progress. Though gambling wasn't allowed in the Ballantyne line, or spirits, the officers were cutthroat competitors. Recently Silas had gifted Dean with a rosewood chess set from Scotland for his fortieth birthday.

James's melancholy wouldn't let him join them. It had taken all his nerve to maneuver past the graveyard—the site of the *City of Pittsburgh*'s explosion—half an hour before. Bits of debris still rode the water, a grim calling card in the moonlight. Trevor Bixby and crew hadn't lived long. The loss had faded to a dull, disbelieving ache.

Uttering a low prayer, he tapped the bell three times, giving the signal to land.

The *Rowena* lapsed into a lonesome silence as the engines sputtered and stilled. In breathless seconds the wood flat emptied. Fugitive slaves, some clutching small pokes, set foot on the dark Ohio shore. Freedom's shore. A few wagons awaited, their Quaker drivers committed to helping them north. No one said a word, communicating solely through hand gestures and facial expressions, ever alert to the torchlight of bounty hunters or the barking of bloodhounds. All that remained was for the wood flat to be carefully stowed in some secluded cove till needed again on a return trip.

Dean stood in back of James as he returned the steamer to the swift Ohio current. "That was a clever ruse back there in Louisville, Sackett, filling them with fear of fever. I've never seen port authorities call off an inspection so fast in all my days. They scattered like windblown leaves."

James's smile was thin, though his relief was potent. "It was more our lead engineer playing the part than anything I said or did."

Dean chuckled. "He always looks ill, poor Perry, working around the boilers as he does. Filled to the brim with typhoid, aye."

James took his gaze from the shore as the last of the wagons faded from view. "We'll have to become more quick-witted if we're to stay in the game. The stakes are getting higher."

"The latest being the Fugitive Slave Act, you mean." Dean took a seat, fishing out his pipe and striking a lucifer match on the bottom of his boot. "Now that any person can be deputized to assist in recapturing slaves, it raises the danger to a whole new level."

"Some are predicting a war between the states."

"It doesn't help that Washington is sending mixed signals, abolishing the slave trade in the capital but letting slavery continue down south." Dean grimaced and released a plume of pipe smoke. "That's bound to make for mayhem."

"Mayhem, aye." James changed course, knowing it would be a long night if he kept Dean talking politics. "I spoke with Silas before we left Pittsburgh. He wants us to join him for a few days at Lake Lanark when we return."

"His mountain retreat?" Surprise edged Dean's voice. "It's not like Silas to be away the end of the shipping season.

Though Lord knows he needs it, with the Ashburton affair and inquest."

Aye, and more besides. But James wouldn't mention the turn in Silas's health—or Dr. Hennessey's frank appraisal. As far as he knew, only he, Silas, and the doctor were privy to that. "A few days fishing and hunting should do us all good."

Dean was looking at him as if he suspected something was amiss. "Taking Bixby's death so hard you're in need of a respite yourself." His voice dropped to a low murmur. "I'm also very sorry about Bennett's fiancée, but I'm not sorry you kept your distance."

"I was going to help her." The truth of it had come to haunt him. A day's delay had cost him everything, including Wren Ballantyne's confidence. Though there could never be anything between them, her opinion somehow mattered. "I simply should have acted sooner than I did."

"Let it go, James. Think instead of what's ahead."

He gave Dean a long, questioning look. The future was hardly promising. Madder's threats . . . Bennett's extravagance . . . Silas's demise. "Lake Lanark holds little appeal as matters stand."

"Well, I'm not averse to a little fishing and hunting and dining. Who all will be joining us?"

"Silas didn't say."

Dean drew hard on his pipe. "Well, if Silas has anything to do with it, there's likely to be a few surprises. An interesting time will be had by all."

The fall season, muted in the city with its crush of buildings, was an outright explosion of color in the mountains of western Pennsylvania. Russet and crimson and gold lit the woods like fire, defying description. James was glad he'd come. Here he could see for miles and draw a clean breath, away from the hustle of the city. Even the trouble with Bennett seemed less pressing. Charlotte's passing more distant. Only Wren seemed to have followed him. Would she find the fall color here as glorious as her Kentucky hills?

"Beautiful as it is, I'd rather be in the Highlands." Dean cast his line into the lake's still waters, where a gentle mist had begun to hover. "Nothing like salmon fishing along the Tay in autumn."

James watched the lure drift lazily atop the water. "Since I've never been to Scotland, I don't know what I'm missing."

"You only need marry to go. Silas's generous offer still stands if you're willing."

"A Highland honeymoon?" James examined his line, unsnarling a kink of silk near the tip. "Doesn't that entail finding a bride?"

"Word is you have a paramour in every port, Sackett."

The timeworn rumor nearly made James roll his eyes. "If that were true, I'd likely be in Scotland now instead of listening to your lies."

Chuckling, Dean gave a shrug. "Oh, you know the papers, forever creating a story when there is none."

"Like the Madder–Mystic Conspiracy affair."

"Unfortunately, that one seems to have merit." He watched as James recast, snapping the bamboo rod back and forth in several fluid motions. Dean's amusement faded to amazement as the line tightened and jerked.

James flashed him a grin as he reeled his catch in. "If only fishing for Mrs. Sackett was as simple."

"Ah, if only . . ." Wading into the water, Dean netted the catch in one swoop and held up a sleek black bass. "By heaven,

James. We've been out less than an hour. Will you best me in the shooting match tomorrow too?"

"I seem to remember Malachi Cameron besting us both last time."

"Only you—by a hair. I didn't make it past the first heat." Bending low, he extracted the hook. "He's here, you know. I saw him arrive with his grandfather earlier. Apparently they'll be joining us for dinner."

"I haven't seen Malachi for a year or better. Not since his father died."

Dean grimaced. "Terrible calamity, that. Cut down in the prime of life, along with a good portion of Pittsburgh."

"Typhus plays no favorites," James muttered, the memory of the mass burials all too fresh. He'd stood alongside the small Cameron clan as the ornate coffin was lowered into the hard winter ground, the only sound that of the wind and Mina weeping. From the stricken look on Malachi's face, it seemed he wanted to be buried with it. He still had his grandfather, at least, though Cullen Cameron was nearly as old as Silas.

"Speaking of dinner . . ." Dean reached into his pocket and extracted a watch. "It's nearly six o'clock. If we don't start back now we'll be late, and you know how Silas likes everyone to be on time. Besides, I wouldn't want to miss whatever the evening has in store."

"My guess is there's to be some announcement. Though with Ansel, Peyton, and Bennett absent, one doubts how much business can be done."

Dean nodded and started up the leaf-strewn path to the lodge. "Shall we?"

Coming downstairs ahead of the dinner hour, James saw Silas on the lodge's front veranda. Just beyond the open front door he stood, dressed informally though finely, the walking stick he sometimes used nowhere in sight. It was unusual to find Silas alone. Usually he was surrounded by business associates, family, and friends.

The Ballantynes had purchased the surrounding six hundred acres several years prior, though the building was but three years old, its white and red exterior and polished interior a favorite retreat of Pittsburgh's elite. All who came hunted and fished and sailed, bunking in the lodge or one of the cottages along the shore, sometimes bringing their wives but most often not. James was staying upstairs in the room he usually occupied, its wide windows overlooking Lake Lanark as it spread west.

A few men were gathering, all informally dressed and talking business. The aroma of roast lamb mingled with woodsmoke, the crackling fire in the immense, ceramic-tiled fireplace the focal point of the lodge's main room.

Nodding to the attorney and chief counsel to the Ballantynes, James joined Silas on the veranda. Since his collapse, James had sensed an unspoken urgency about him, that matters be resolved and left in order, all loose ends neatly tied, whatever they might be. The growing ache in his throat . . . his heart . . . confirmed time was short.

Silas turned. "Evening, James. The Lord has given us a fine sunset, aye?"

"None finer."

"A shame Pittsburgh has become *auld reekie* like Edinburgh and deprived us of such pleasures." Not one to complain, he smiled as if to soften the words. "Everything is to your satisfaction here, I hope." At James's nod, he said easily,

"Captain Dean has been crowing about your catch earlier today. You'd think it was his instead."

"Dean has always been a good sport, on the river or otherwise."

Silas's gaze returned to the lake. "He's given his approval regarding the pilot who's to take your place this winter."

"Yes, matters are settled there."

"It's been a long time since you were last lying in port under wages. Heaven knows you've earned such." Silas looked back at him, thoughtful. "Now seems a good time to thank you for coming to my aid in my office when I fell ill recently—and for keeping the matter hushed. I've no wish to alarm anyone unduly, though the episode has made me take stock of a few matters."

"No thanks needed," James replied, suddenly troubled by the sight of Bennett walking along the shoreline of the lake. So he'd come after all. If Bennett was present, Peyton was never far.

"Simply put, I've decided to make some lasting changes." Silas spoke with deliberate care, his aged features resigned. "I'm assigning you the new Ballantyne-Cameron alliance while you're off the river, and leaving older, less significant business to Bennett and his father. Any future enterprises will be handled by Ansel and, in my absence, overseen by him completely." He hesitated as if weighing the wisdom of his next words. "I have the utmost faith in you and Ansel, James. I only wish I could say the same of everyone."

James felt nearly light-headed with relief, yet a tug of sympathy remained. Rarely did Silas speak disparagingly about family, but he had become increasingly frustrated with Bennett's disastrous business acumen and Peyton's utter lack of vision.

"I'll make the announcement tonight following supper when everyone is present."

The shrewdness of the plan was not lost on James. When it was delivered to everyone at once, Peyton and Bennett would not be able to defy Silas or circumvent the process. He breathed a silent prayer of thanks, though the unprecedented changes meant Silas was letting go.

"I hope all of this will make your respite from the river more palatable." Silas's solemnity gave way to a familiar, sharp-eyed clarity. "I'm optimistic our new agreement with the Camerons will transition into our becoming a part of the transcontinental rail system in the future and lead to further business ventures in California."

James felt a hitch of surprise. They'd talked about the gold rush in the past, of fortunes made and lost and the opportunities to be had there. "I'm on board," he said with an interest and enthusiasm he hadn't felt in months.

"Very well, then. We have much to look forward to."

Moonrise gilded the lake silver, the surrounding stillness so hushed it felt hallowed. James sat in the shadows of the veranda, thoughts racing, the cadence of his pulse as steady as the crickets' pulsating calls. Looking back on the lengthy dinner hour, he could barely recall what had been served or whom he'd sat beside. Once Silas had made his announcement, the room held a startled hush as everyone grappled with the sweeping changes, Peyton and Bennett foremost. They'd masked their discomfiture none too well, but the die had now been cast and there was no turning back.

"I'm afraid Pittsburgh is nearing the end of its heyday in the steamboat trade with the coming of the railroad," Silas had told them. Resignation tinged his tone, but it was followed by a beat of optimism. "'Tis time for a new venture. We need to be looking west. I have every confidence that these changes will solidify our standing in Pittsburgh and move us into more exciting endeavors beyond its limits."

At Silas's announcement, James's gaze had drifted five seats down to Malachi Cameron, who'd broached a different proposal a week prior. Delivered to the boatyard office, the telegram was as forthright as Malachi could make it.

> Need freight agent for the Pennsylvania Railroad. Are you the man?

Either offer was the making of a fortune. A future. Gratitude swelled inside him. How had an orphaned boy come so far? By the grace of God. And the Ballantynes.

A creak on the stair through the clubhouse's open door broke James's concentration. He went completely still. The slant of the moon told him it was half past four. Likely a servant laying the breakfast fires. Sunrise came late to the autumn woods.

A shadow darkened the moonlit veranda. Barefoot, clad in shirtsleeves and trousers, russet hair on end, Malachi Cameron looked anything but the owner of the Pennsylvania Railroad.

"Morning, Malachi."

"Morning, James. Can't you sleep?" He rubbed a hand over his eyes as if he'd been sleepwalking and was surprised to find himself out of bed. "I'm so used to working round the clock I don't know dawn from midnight."

"I can make some coffee."

"Why? So I can be up all day too?" With a lopsided grin Malachi took the nearest chair, suddenly sobering. "I'll admit it's not business that keeps me awake."

James relaxed, glad of it. He needed time to sort through all the changes. Time to prayerfully consider the future. A cold gust of wind sent a shower of dry leaves off the roof and onto the porch, leaving a scarlet trail. He crossed his arms against the chill, his own bare feet like ice.

"I thought perhaps coming here would be the respite I needed. Help me forget." Malachi steepled his fingers and looked out at the lake. The utter quiet called for confidences not to be had in a crowded dining room. "Since my father died, I can't seem to get my bearings."

"It's not been a year yet," James said, but the reassurance came too fast. Time, in this case, didn't matter. Some wounds never healed, including his own.

"Being here in autumn brings it all back." Malachi's voice was low. Oddly sentimental. "There are things I wish I'd said. Done. I don't think I told you what my father said to me at the last. That his greatest regret was to not see me married . . . know his grandchildren."

James stayed silent. There was nothing he could say to lessen what could never be.

"I'd not given it much thought till then. But lately it's all I think about."

"Marrying, you mean."

Malachi nodded. "I've even let my aunt Mina talk me into coming back for the winter social season."

"That's bound to make some Pittsburgh belles happy."

He grimaced. "The idea of an endless round of dances and dinners and making small talk leaves me cold. I want to cut to the chase. Marry and get on with it."

"What you need is a woman who makes you forget about work."

"Is there such a thing?" Frustration peppered his tone. "As

fond as I am of Mina and her meddling, it's your judgment I trust, James. You have ties to everyone in the city. You know who's worthy of courting and who's not."

"Are you asking me to turn matchmaker?"

"Just this once." Malachi was watching him, expectant, ever intense. As serious as if he was talking business. "I won't hold you responsible if the courtship is less than I'd hoped. Surely there's some woman you can recommend."

A dozen Pittsburgh belles danced in James's head at the request, most of them unsuitable. He held his tongue, willing the matter to go away.

"Name one, James."

One. James still balked. Stubborn seconds ticked by. Pushing Wren from his mind, James let go of Izannah. "You need look no further than Miss Turlock."

"Izannah?" Malachi ran a hand over his unshaven jaw. "I haven't seen Izannah in years."

"You've seen little of anyone in years, given you've been laying track."

"Last I heard she didn't finish her season."

"True enough. Someone cut her one too many times and she refused to attend another function."

"Someone?" Malachi's surprise faded to a grim smirk. "I recall hearing it involved Alice Mellon. Miss Malice, Mina calls her."

"Some of the older, moneyed families can't get past the Turlock taint." James worked to keep the bitterness from his tone. "Pittsburghers have long memories."

"I seem to remember Izannah outdistancing me in the schoolroom when we shared the same tutors in years past."

James nodded. "She's intelligent, yes. She's also beautiful, amiable, sensible."

"Her father dotes on her, so I've heard. Won't let her out of his sight." He expelled a ragged breath. "I'll admit you tempt me. If she's anything like her mother, there may be a wealth of sons in the bargain."

"Ten at last count." James took his pipe from his waistcoat pocket and felt for his tobacco pouch. "You could simply court her and circumvent the social season altogether, if she'll have you."

Malachi took out his own pipe, igniting a match. The lucifer flared, illuminating a wicked half smile. "You sound half in love with her yourself, Sackett."

With a chuckle, James played along with the jest. "I'm little more than a river pilot with few prospects, remember."

"Few prospects indeed." Malachi raised a brow. "Rumor is Silas made you an offer tonight that may well trump mine. It's also circulating that a certain river pilot bought a hundred thousand shares of stock before news of the Cameron-Ballantyne alliance was made public, and then when the news became print, the shares doubled and he sold them."

Their combined laughter was a low rumble. James shrugged. "There's no reward without risk, as Silas says."

"Well, business aside, it's time to settle down." Malachi was studying him again, all seriousness, as if they'd entered into some binding agreement. "I'm approaching thirty now and getting older by the minute."

"Then we'd best be about the business of finding you a willing bride," James replied.

16

Music is the silence between the notes.

CLAUDE DEBUSSY

In a corner of River Hill's heated kitchen, Izannah stood by the pastry table, eyeing her hard-won confection. Cook simply stared at the creation, delight creasing her plump face. Sugar crusted beneath their shoes—a slight spill upon mixing—but the finished product perched on its crystal cake stand, twelve layers high, brimming with icing and gingered apples like it had taken first place at the Allegheny County Fair.

"I've ne'er seen a stack cake." Neva's tone held wonder. "But it looks like you did the receipt proud."

"One can't go wrong with the *Accomplish'd Gentlewoman's Companion.*" Izannah blew a dusting of flour from the page and closed the recipe book, satisfaction and weariness sliding through her. Though it had taken several hours to master, and an unheard-of amount of molasses and eggs, the concoction was finally done.

"Your Kentucky cousin will be pleased, I'm thinking. Stack cakes are as coveted as corn bread to Southerners. And it's not every day a lad turns five years old—or a young miss *five and twenty*." Neva uttered the number with a sigh, as if it held the stain of spinsterhood. Her pinched expression confirmed it wasn't just Wren she was worried about either.

Undaunted, Izannah clasped her hands together. "What a happy surprise to find Tremper and Wren share a birthday. I want tonight's celebration to be memorable for Wren, especially given her father is away."

"How many are expected for supper?"

"I hope to have fifteen at table, provided Grandfather and James make it back from Lake Lanark." Izannah peered out the largest window to the weeping skyline. Grandfather and James had been expected home yesterday, but a storm had blown up in the mountains, bringing rain and high wind and delaying their return. "Of course Uncle Peyton and Aunt Penelope and Bennett won't be coming since—well, you know."

Neva's face darkened in understanding as she turned toward the hearth and gave a poke to a ham sizzling on a turnspit.

Izannah turned away as well, hoping to hide her high flush, which had little to do with the heat of the kitchen and everything to do with the state of her heart. Just that morning the *Gazette* had reported Malachi Cameron was back in Pittsburgh. Since learning it, it was all Izannah could do to keep her measuring and sifting straight. For years she'd been following him in the papers, knew every inch of track he'd laid, every business deal he'd inked, especially the much-discussed Ballantyne-Cameron alliance of late.

Untying her apron, she took a last look out the window at the late September skyline, praying James would soon come into the foyer, Grandfather safely beside him.

"Izzy!" John Henry's jarring cry brought her romantic musings to a halt.

Leaving the fragrant kitchen, she started down the hall, ears tuned to something beyond her brothers' scuffling—the barking of dogs, the crunch of coach wheels on gravel, the creaking open of the large front entry door.

But it was only Chloe's cry she heard and Mama's soft answer. For a moment she gave in to the recurring wish that Chloe was her baby and this was her house and the stack cake she'd spent the day making was for a husband instead. Foolish. Even childish, perhaps. Yet her woman's heart craved so much more.

Lord, let Malachi come home . . . to me.

At six o'clock a commotion in the foyer turned every eye. James and Grandfather appeared just as dinner was being served, bringing the storm with them. Rain slicked James from head to toe, the damp ends of his hair curling at his coat collar, Grandfather safely beside him but just as wet. The large dining room grew hushed, and all eyes turned to their entry.

Grandfather's lean figure filled the doorway, his voice racked with hoarseness as he sought out Tremper. "Happy birthday to my favorite grandson!"

Laughter erupted from all corners. This was always the greeting at every birthday, no matter which grandchild.

"Thank you, Grandfather," Tremper replied merrily, digging into his supper. "It's cousin Rowena's birthday too."

"*Och*, another favorite." Grandfather nodded to a smiling Wren as a maid whisked away his sodden coat and hat.

"My apologies for arriving late," James said quietly when

Izannah approached. "We met with some trouble along the way."

The judge was on his feet now, insisting they go upstairs to a hot bath and dry clothes.

"All in good time, Jack," Grandfather replied, eyes on the throng gathered around the candlelit table. "A meal should come first, aye? If you'll excuse my muddy boots . . ."

"No matter your boots, Da." Ellie linked arms with him, drawing him to where Grandmother and Andra waited. "You look in need of a good meal or at least some hot broth and bread. Then you'll spend the night right here at River Hill. We've readied a room and laid a warm fire."

Left alone with James in the doorway, Izannah studied him in the dim light, noting his almost roguish patch of beard, the telling shadows beneath his eyes. He looked nearly as haggard as Grandfather. "Is anything the matter?"

He glanced down at the muddy puddle in which he stood. "Better than expected, given we veered off an embankment and had to put down one of the horses."

She winced. "Then we're fortunate to have you both back in one piece. How was Lake Lanark?"

"Peaceful. Profitable." He looked down at her, a beguiling light in his eyes. "Malachi Cameron sends his regards."

Malachi . . .

The noisy party faded. Her mouth opened but no sound came. Then finally, "Oh, James, you're not . . . jesting?"

His expression softened. "Why would I make light of something so serious?"

Joy and relief sang through her. He understood. James always understood. She dared a smile. "I'd heard he'd returned to Pittsburgh, but I had no idea he'd join you in the mountains."

"He'll be here for the winter." He looked past her to the crowded dining room. "For business . . . pleasure."

Her heart caught on the last word. He meant more than Malachi's penchant for fox hunting, surely. Linking arms with him, she swallowed down her remaining questions and led him into dinner, where he took his place between her and John Henry.

Across from them sat Tremper, talking animatedly of his new pony. But Uncle Wade kept interrupting, teasing him mercilessly. "A five-year-old lad has no need of a pony. Why, you're nearly a man! What say you we make a trade? Your pretty pony, Peanut, for my thoroughbred stallion, Runs Amuck . . ."

Farther down the table, Wren was watching Wade rather wide-eyed, clearly unsure of what to make of him. To her credit, no one knew what to think of Daddy's brother. Wade Turlock was as wild as he was wealthy, full of the whiskey he distilled, saying and doing scandalous things only Aunt Elspeth would appreciate. Two birds of a feather, Mama always said.

In the background, Izannah could hear Chloe fussing upstairs, never content for long without her mother's milk. As Mama left the table, Izannah's attention kept returning to James. Would he stay on at the cottage or return to town? He seemed as in need of rest as Grandfather, yet she was anxious to know more about Malachi and Lake Lanark.

By nine o'clock they'd moved to the blue room, and Wren was asked to give an impromptu concert. Mama had returned, taking a seat at her harp, surprising them all. She'd not played during her confinement, and now the beautiful room swelled with music as they began a duet. A perfect pairing, Mama and Wren.

Izannah looked to the antique armonica in a far corner with a pang of regret. She had mastered that but little else. Reading took all her free time. She was trying hard not to think of Malachi. Folding her hands in her lap, she made eye contact with a servant to signal it was nearly time to bring in the stack cake. Around the room her gaze traveled, past all her brothers in various stages of fidgeting, to settle on Wren as she played.

Once again intuition whispered there was something between Wren and James, some fledgling attraction or denial of such. As she thought it, James's gaze cut from Wren to the floor in front of him so that it seemed he was contemplating his wet boots. He seemed to be trying not to watch Wren, just as Izannah imagined Wren was trying not to watch him.

The lovely sonata ended, and Mama did the unthinkable. "Won't you join us, James?"

He looked up from the shadows, fatigue fading to surprise. The barest hesitation—had he ever refused Mama?—and then he gave a nod and stood.

Izannah felt on tenterhooks. James hadn't played since Georgiana's passing, not to her knowledge. Was he rusty or would the music come rushing back?

Wren's open features held a question as James took a violin from a case on a near table. Was she unaware he played the violin? Testing a string, he waited to begin. With a last inquiring look at him, Wren launched into a rousing reel. Mama's hands fell from her harp strings as the violins matched each other note for note.

James was not the fiddler Wren was, but he could hold his own, his bowing bold and decisive where hers was more intricate and delicate. Not once did he stumble, ending the joyous piece with a self-effacing smile and a little trill. The room burst into applause—even the boys were clapping and hooting—as he returned the violin to its case. This time it was Wren's gaze that trailed after him, a telling delight on her flushed face.

If a heart could be won or lost in the span of seconds, it had happened right before Izannah's eyes. Her cousin may not have been taken with James before, but all that had altered. Now she could hardly look away from him. Had anyone else noticed?

The case clock struck ten, and she turned her attention to the cake as it was brought in atop a wheeled cart. As it rumbled past, Tremper swiped at the icing with a quick finger as murmurs of appreciation replaced the infectious music. Smiling, Izannah served the confection piece by piece, cutting an especially generous slice for Grandfather, who was so fond of sweets.

He stood by her, eyes alight with undimmed enjoyment of the moment. "A stack cake, you say? If so, a worthy one."

His gnarled hands reached for the offering . . . faltered. The china dish fell from his grip, shattering as it struck the hard floor, he crumpling after it.

With a cry Izannah dropped to her knees beside him, all thoughts of Malachi driven from her mind. James was there beside her, kneeling, attending to Silas, the concern in his face fanning her fears. Through it all came Mama's voice, broken yet calm, and Daddy's heated order to summon the doctor.

Four hours. Had she truly been shut away in the music room all afternoon? The place had become her refuge in the week following Grandfather's collapse, just as it had after Charlotte's passing. Fiddle in hand, Wren was almost able to forget Papa was gone and most everyone remained at River

Hill. The doctors said Grandfather could not be moved, so Grandmother stayed at his side, turning New Hope tense and empty. Just Wren and Andra and too many servants padded about the big house, awaiting word from River Hill. Every other day they visited, but it was blessedly brief as the doctors enforced quiet. The rambunctious Turlock boys and their tutors had been banished to Broad Oak, the home of Uncle Wade, who was seldom there.

As she played she kept turning the events of the birthday celebration over in her mind, sifting through them till only the barest gleanings remained. James's late arrival. Izannah's high flush. Their time together in the foyer exchanging heartfelt talk. He shed his fierce reserve with Izannah, but that was as it should be. They made a comely couple, so intent on each other. Like the turtledoves that nested beneath her Cane Run eave.

Thinking it, she felt a bit odd, even old. More at odds with everything around her. Why was it, in all her five and twenty years, that love had never worked its way into her heart? Might it be because Cane Run only boasted fifty souls? And there'd been a famine of suitors? Being unwed had never fretted her till now.

She shut her eyes, unable to dislodge the image of him as he'd faced her across the crowded parlor. How handsome he'd looked even travel worn, his hair windblown, his ruddy features stung by the cold. When he'd picked up a violin and played . . . her mind had somersaulted to keep up with him, to come to terms with his playing, to deny him entry into her heart when he didn't belong there. Charlotte sprang to mind, reinforcing the distance between them.

She was so hungry for what she'd lost, she reckoned that was the cause of his appeal. She simply missed playing with Selkirk and Papa. Missed the music they'd made in the firefly-studded darkness as night gathered in. Missed Molly's clapping and the foot-tapping of those who came by and joined in. To say nothing of missing Mama . . .

She looked down at her fingers, stiff and slightly achy from playing so long. Making music here was a lonesome thing. The thick walls of the music room cocooned her, and it seemed Andra had forgotten all about her. For that she was thankful. Mim brought a tray to her room at mealtimes, keeping her apprised of any goings-on, including her aunt's whereabouts.

Wiping the Nightingale free of rosin, she tucked it in its case before straightening the sheet music on the mahogany stand. There were other matters at hand besides her fiddling. She needed to write to Molly and congratulate Selkirk on his coming marriage. Take stock of their Kentucky accounts in Papa's absence. Pen him a letter.

3 October, 1850

Dear Papa,

You come to mind often on these glorious autumn days as I remember it is your favorite season. With the turning of the leaves I think of how time, and change, is unstoppable. I wish I could take back what I said to you at the last— my tears and too-hasty words. I want you not to worry about my being here without you. I want you to be proud of me.

I am trying to use my time wisely and well, learning to ride sidesaddle and seeing the sights of Pittsburgh with Aunt Andra. My music continues to be a great joy to me. Sadly, Grandfather is very ill at River Hill. I pray he will be himself

again by the time you return. But I am learn-
ing nothing is sure. Nothing is set in stone even
though I wish it to be . . .

She left off, fighting melancholy. She'd continue after supper and send a servant to post it on the morrow. Perhaps by
then there would be better news about Grandfather.

Leaving the music room, she found the foyer empty of
all but voices. They drifted past the parlor door, which was
slightly ajar. Andra's voice always carried, but at the moment
it was Mina Cameron Wren heard.

"She has none of the taint of the scandal. She's an outsider.
Fresh. Unsullied. Her debut will divert Pittsburgh society from
the tragedy. She'll simply arrive on the scene unexpectedly
and woo everyone with her novelty and her violin."

Andra's reply was slow in coming. "I'm unsure, Mina . . ."

"Come now, Andra, it's a splendid idea. Rowena is certainly
entitled to a debut. She won't have had such an opportunity
in Kentucky."

"But the season begins all too soon." Andra's voice held a
wary bite. "The Mellons are opening with a winter ball the
first of November."

"You have a month. That's surely adequate."

"One month? I'm afraid *six* months wouldn't be adequate.
You don't seem to understand all that is at stake. Rowena is
entirely too rough spun."

"Such things can be remedied, surely," Mina continued,
unconcerned. "Take her complexion, for instance. If she goes
about without a bonnet as you claim, she simply must learn
to cover up. And if her Kentucky accent marks her as underbred, she's entitled to elocution lessons."

"Really, Mina, those are the least of our worries. Rowena

also has the very unsavory habit of wearing every emotion on her sleeve. She even greets and converses with the servants."

Mina chortled. "My heavens, Andra, no one comes into this world with impeccable manners. All that is easily managed in light of a little training. There are a great many etiquette manuals to move her from rusticity to gentility. And my good friend Catherine Criss may well be available to help. She gives a splendid polish to all the best girls from Philadelphia to Pittsburgh. I'm sure she'd drop everything if she knew a Ballantyne debut was in the offing."

"Less than a month . . ." Andra still sounded dubious. "If Miss Criss can assist, I'd feel better about our efforts, though I'd be lying if I said I had high hopes. At five and twenty my niece may well be beyond redemption."

Wren took a step back, reeling from the distaste in Andra's tone. So she was rough spun. Underbred. Common. A rustic. In need of polish. If eavesdropping was a sin, she'd earned her punishment in spades.

"She'll need an escort, of course." Mina sounded as if they'd been weeks in the planning. "Usually the father or a brother serves, but since Ansel is away, a trusted family friend will do."

Andra's voice lightened. "That is the only bright spot, I'm afraid. There is someone who might be willing . . ."

Wren turned away, nearly tripping in her haste to escape their scheming. Up the stairs she went, feeling as ungraceful as a Kentucky colt, confirming all they'd just said. She didn't pause for breath till she'd reached the cupola and shut herself away. Today no rain splashed the pane or lightning lit the sky. The cold glass wrapped around her, sunlight gilding a spider's web above her head.

She'd never before heard of a social season, a debut. She

supposed it involved a little dancing like a frolic, just more proper. But an escort? Whoever he was, she prayed the gentleman would be wise enough to bow out of such unbridled foolishness.

She couldn't imagine who Aunt Andra would choose.

17

*There is a charm about the forbidden
that makes it unspeakably desirable.*

MARK TWAIN

The early October sun was setting, lulling the levee to sleep. Looking up from the ledgers that had held him captive all day, James noted the time before studying the numbers in a far column. His concerns about the Ballantyne line were well founded. Though they'd transported lucrative cargo like lead, Indian annuities, soldiers, and heavy industrial equipment for the bulk of the year, they'd taken quite a loss given the sinking of the *City of Pittsburgh*.

Now, with Bennett forging ahead with the building of his brag boat and importing another hull builder from Scotland, expenses were mounting. All the more with Silas lying ill at River Hill. Word was Bennett had even begun announcing that James would pilot the new packet when it was finished in spring, claiming the trek upriver could be made from New Orleans to Pittsburgh in nineteen hours, an unheard-of feat.

But perhaps it didn't matter. With Silas cutting Bennett off from any new business and predicting the demise of the steamboat trade, Bennett would likely go down with a sinking ship. And if war erupted over the slavery issue, the rivers would be closed to traffic . . .

James sat back, the creak of Silas's old chair a reminder it needed replacing. In the corner, George Ealer was examining the latest passenger lists by the fast-fading light, brow knit in concentration. He stirred and shot James a quick glance. "Are you s-staying at R-River H-Hill or the M-Monongahela House?"

"The Mon." James knew Ealer didn't care where he lodged. It was his roundabout way of asking about Silas.

"N-no change?" Ealer asked.

"Nay."

For fourteen days Silas had been bedridden, his collapse at River Hill all too public. The doctors were murmuring about his heart, but in truth he was a very old man and they couldn't be sure. James's own chest ached if he dwelled on it, so he distracted himself with year-end accounts, determined to finish tallying the season.

Setting the manifest aside, Ealer ambled to the front window, hands in his pockets. "W-what will h-happen if h-he dies?"

James hesitated. "He'll have made a will and we'll find out then."

Ealer's emotional nod was followed by a grimace. "B-blast!" He returned to his corner, burying his nose in his paperwork. "B-Bennett's on his way."

James stood, searching for calm but finding none. The only time Bennett left his ornate Water Street offices was when he wanted something. Stoic, he faced the door, preparing for another confrontation. Or word that Silas had died. He'd not thought ahead to this particular moment—who would deliver the bitter news. His spirit rebelled that it might be Bennett.

As usual, Bennett walked in without knocking, not bothering to close the door despite the chill. A log rolled forward in the corner stove, a robust thud in the too-still office.

"You're excused, Ealer." Bennett's curt tone sent the lad scurrying out the back.

James gave no greeting, gaze fixed on the line of packets lying at landing beyond the south-facing windows. If he'd ever wanted to be back on the river, it was now. Warily he looked to Bennett.

Bennett faced him across the desk, his cold features impassive, giving no hint of what was to come. He swept the small office with a dismissive glance. "This is a rather humble place for the man now in charge of the feted Ballantyne-Cameron alliance."

"So be it." The curt answer irritated Bennett, James sensed, as did the fact he had coveted the position himself.

"I'd expected you to move across the street into the unoccupied office next to Grandfather's by now."

James said nothing.

The silence turned excruciating. With Charlotte's passing and Bennett's finances draining, James detected a hint of desperation beneath his usual arrogance.

"Since you're in the Ballantynes' employ, I'm in need of your services. It's a matter of great importance to the family."

James's wariness spiked. The family was always Bennett's trump card—and James's point of weakness.

"Cousin Rowena is to have a season." He spoke slowly, enunciating each word carefully as if to make sure there'd be no misunderstanding. "Beginning with the Mellons' ball.

It's imperative that she find a suitable husband before the season ends." Bennett was unblinking in his audacity. "And by suitable I mean a Ewing or a Schoonmaker or a Cameron."

James stiffened. Other than the Ballantynes, these were the three most influential families in Pittsburgh.

"Of course, she's in need of an escort with her father away. Everyone agrees that should be you."

Everyone. James doubted that meant more than him and Andra. "What does her father have to say about the matter?"

"Very little given his absence. Arrangements are already in place. With your connections, James, your popularity and reputation, your impeccable pedigree"—the last word was laden with sarcasm—"I'm sure Rowena will meet with every success."

Marriage—or else. The stakes were high indeed. James's thoughts swung to Wren, who was no doubt unsuspecting and unwilling. And no match for what Bennett had in mind. "I'll not be privy to such a mercenary plan."

Bennett's stare was rocky. "Have you forgotten what happened with Georgiana Hardesty, James? I wonder if you'd be more agreeable to the arrangement if all Pittsburgh was to know you're nothing but the woods colt son of Wade Turlock and his doxy at Teague's Tavern."

The ground seemed to cut from under him. James leaned into the desk, palms flat against the scarred wood. "If you breathe another word of what is hearsay and not fact—"

"Hearsay is enough for people to cut you, shun you, or refuse to be ferried about by a Turlock bastard." Looking down at the desk, he picked up a Baccarat paperweight and turned it over in a gloved hand. "Once Rowena makes a suitable match, you'll be free to do as you please. I'll reward you handsomely and ask nothing more of you."

Reward him? Bribe him? The furious pounding of James's pulse seemed to rival a packet's engine. "What does Miss Ballantyne think about your arrangement?"

"It doesn't matter. She bears the family name and will do her duty." Turning his back, Bennett started to walk out, hesitating as his hand gripped the doorknob. "Your first engagement is the first of November at the Mellons' ball."

The door slammed shut. James fixed his eye on a shipping calendar pinned to a far wall. Twenty-three days.

God help him.

God help Wren.

Wren stood stone still as Catherine Criss walked round her, her expression a strange medley of disdain and admiration. Andra, Mistress Endicott, and the seamstresses looked on from a near settee.

"There are a few attributes in her favor. Given Rowena's small stature, she is a pocket Venus, quite popular in genteel circles, though she's a tad fleshy about the waist." Miss Criss's thin, elongated features and clipped British accent reminded Wren of sharpened scissors. "Lovely complexion if somewhat . . . weathered. Good posture. Her hair is a fetching shade of caramel, but her eyes are so light a green they're unremarkable."

Reaching for Wren's hands, she turned them over, palms upraised. "Absolutely atrocious! I've never seen so many calluses. Gloves are to be worn at all times during the season except when they're removed at dinner. As for her voice . . ." Miss Criss let go of her and turned back to Andra. "We don't have sufficient time to modify her speech, so I'll attempt to modulate her tone so that her dialect is less distinct. Thankfully her teeth aren't crooked but straight and white."

Wren's head spun from their blunt assessment. Was she little more than a brood mare at auction? After several more minutes she ground her teeth, torn between being obliging or mule-stubborn, and thought longingly of the music room.

Andra let out an audible breath. "The dancing master and seamstresses are expected tomorrow afternoon—the corsetiere also."

"Very well." Miss Criss was examining Wren again as if anxious to find another flaw. "Her hands are to be soaked in buttermilk nightly. And nothing sweet is to pass her lips. From this day forward she's to eat nothing but egg, broth, and bread."

So they were to starve her? If anything, Miss Criss was even more insufferable than Andra. But at least she was to have her own wardrobe. No more parading around in Charlotte's clothes, where every brush of fabric against her skin was a mournful reminder. Yet even this was fraught with peril. Not one seamstress but two—and three assistants—were on hand, for Mistress Endicott could not concoct a gown worthy of a Mellon ball, nor an entire trousseau, in so short a time without reinforcements.

"Her debut gown must be off-white—of the richest silk taffeta with a great many ruffles." Their combined voices resembled buzzing bees, discussing her as if she wasn't present. Except to prod and poke her with a measuring tape, they ignored her altogether. "And she must have a French corset, which can be tightly laced—"

"Nay!" The heated word burst out unbidden, drawing every eye. Andra looked at Wren, appalled, as Miss Criss's mouth bunched into a tight knot. Feeling outnumbered, Wren looked down at *Godey's Lady's Book*, far more interested in the printed sheet music than the hand-tinted fashion plates.

"Not long ago Grandmother showed me her old dresses in the attic. They're beautiful, all of them. She told me I could wear them, remake them. Surely that would save time and expense."

Andra bristled. "Expense is of little consequence. And now seems a good time to tell you that one must never speak of money. It's a rule of polite conversation that shan't be violated. Ever."

Wren lowered her chin. "I'll try to remember. But I'll only wear Granny's gowns. They're all beautifully crafted. Mama and I made most of our clothes at home. I can even help with the sewing."

Mistress Endicott gave a stiff smile. "While I'm not used to debutantes dictating fashion, I'm willing to take a look at these old gowns and see what can be done. I daresay you'll create a stir with eighteenth-century fashions even remade, Rowena."

Andra squirmed on the settee, looking more disgruntled than ever. "I'm tempted to end this charade here and now. It's very likely my father, ill as he is, may pass and thrust us all into mourning, and there'll be no more talk of society."

A murmur of dismay circled the room, Wren's foremost. The possibility of being clad in black and isolated at New Hope with Andra was even more frightening than the Mellons' ball.

"Well, until that happens, our plans are in place." Miss Criss stood and pulled on her gloves, preparing to go. "The gentleman we had in mind has agreed to act as escort, so we'll proceed." She smiled at Wren benignly from beneath her elaborate velvet bonnet. "I daresay Rowena will be the envy of many a Pittsburgh maiden once the season opens."

"Yes, for that we can be thankful." Andra looked visibly

relieved. "I trust Rowena won't embarrass us or cause him to rue the arrangement."

Wren looked at them in question. Who had agreed to the burdensome task? The satisfaction on their faces spelled something momentous. "Well . . . ?"

They stared back at her as if she was some mindless simpleton, incapable of the obvious. Finally Andra spoke. "It's none other than James Sackett. There's not an escort in Pittsburgh his equal."

James Sackett?

Wren stared at her as if she'd misheard. She'd expected someone else, someone older, more in keeping with her father's age. Anyone but him . . .

All around her they began talking and quitting the room, leaving her to her tumbled thoughts. What she'd begun to see as a sort of game, an introduction to Pittsburgh in hopes to gain some friends, had suddenly gone wrong in the worst possible way.

Mim remained, jarring her from her silence with a terse sentence in Gaelic. "He's nae so bad, James Sackett, though ye look like he just killed yer cat!"

Taking a seat on the nearest settee, Wren all but wrung her hands. "I don't mind Mr. Sackett. I'm just . . . skittish about what's to come."

"Well, it's nae every day a girl gets a season—or a gallant escort. Ye'll do right by Mr. James, I'll grant ye that. He never missteps, never gives rise to any gossip."

Because he's cast in stone.

Mim prattled on, though Wren was hardly listening. "Miss Criss and her lot will dance to yer tune in matters of dress, anyway. Never in a thousand years would I have expected ye

174

to take charge like ye did. If your aunt had nae pinned me with her steely gaze, I would have clapped and hooted."

"I didn't mean to make a fuss." Releasing a pent-up breath, Wren examined her calluses. "If it wasn't for the prospect of dancing, and Papa's wish to make the most of my time, I wouldn't agree to all this."

Mim chuckled. "Ye ken what may happen? Ye might find a man to yer liking. Every lass longs for love, aye?"

"Even you, Mim?"

She smiled a canny smile. "I canna marry so long as I'm in service. That's the butler's privilege."

"There's no man who suits your fancy?"

"*Och*, there's a groom at River Hill . . ." A rare flush stole over Mim's features. "I dinna see him much, but he keeps me posted on the goings-on there." Glancing at the closed door, she faded to a whisper. "And word is there may be nae more of a season for you than Mr. Bennett. Yer grandda has taken a turn. Pneumonia, the doctors say."

Wren listened as through a fog. Her circumstances were changing so rapidly she couldn't keep up, her emotions trailing. Even now she felt a latent grief. Grandfather was so ill the doctors had forbidden visitors. She'd lost touch with Izannah and everyone else at River Hill.

"A telegram's been sent to yer da in Philadelphia, but it seems he's gone off to Boston," Mim whispered.

Boston. Bereft of Charlotte. A place that had come to be clouded with loss and unhappy endings. On par with Pittsburgh.

From the cupola Wren took in every subtle shift in color as the trees slowly began shaking free of their leaves and autumn deepened. There Mim found her on what was to be one of her last mornings free of obligations and expectations.

"Since the dancing master and such won't come again till later, ye've time to sneak in a little ride like ye've been wanting. I've already sent word to the stables to saddle the mare you fancy."

Relief washed through her. "Oh, Mim, you're such a gift to me." Somehow Mim seemed to sense her every need, much like Molly used to.

"We'll have to be quick about it in case yer aunt concocts something else for you this morning. This afternoon the seamstresses and corsetiere return."

In minutes Wren was warmly clad in her riding habit against the October damp. Though it had taken time to ride sidesaddle and not astride, she felt she'd nearly mastered it. Perhaps it would be the same with the season, though such seemed a fearsome thing on James Sackett's arm. But she couldn't back down now with all the plans in place. She'd simply pray Papa home so he could take James's place, or pray he'd bring a halt to society altogether.

Riding toward River Hill, she went at a canter, wanting to get some distance from New Hope lest Andra call her back. In minutes she'd removed the veil from her hat, thinking it hardly mattered, as the lemon juice Miss Criss had recommended for her complexion didn't appear to be helping. She stopped short of shaking her hair free of its pins, pulling off her boots instead.

A weary wooziness crept over her and she gave into it, turning the mare loose to graze. In a quiet, sun-rimmed meadow she lay down atop grassy ground and dozed till the call of a warbler sang her awake. For a few disorienting moments she felt she was home. She pondered what Molly might be doing.

If Selkirk was busy with his bride. No matter. The present solitude was too pleasurable to waste on the bittersweet.

Sleepy, she sat up, spying Izannah at a distance on her roan, a white feather in her hat. Her spirits lifted. And then Izannah turned away, galloping in the direction of River Hill. Only the sight of James Sackett stayed fast . . . and he was riding hard toward her.

She began tugging on her boots and replacing her hat and veil, suddenly out of sorts. Looking for her mare, she saw it had wandered. Whistling failed to help. She could only watch, unsurprised, as the man she had no wish to see rounded up her wayward horse.

She tried not to pay him any mind—what he was wearing, the way he sat in the saddle. The tousled, windblown look of him hardly put a crimp in his self-possession as he reined in beside her. James Sackett was as unbent as ever.

"Miss Ballantyne."

"Mr. Sackett."

He looked into the distance. She stared at the ground. Their formal greeting hung icicle-stiff in the chilly air.

Finally she raised her chin, letting go of her hope that her cousin was trailing and would ride up next. "Where is Izannah?"

"Probably home by now." He ran a gloved hand along the sleek neck of his gelding, which was the color of molasses. Her little mare looked drab in comparison. His gaze found its way back to her. "You have no escort?"

She nearly squirmed. "Not till the first of November."

His eyes lit with undeniable amusement. And then he smiled—a slow, heart-catching smile, the first smile aimed at her. It reached to his remarkable eyes, creasing the corners and warming her like an Indian-summer sun. "We could ride together now . . . ease into it."

Torn, she glanced back the way she'd come, judging time and distance, certain Andra was by now missing her.

"You'd rather return to New Hope, I take it."

She looked back at him, unable to resist a final gibe. "*Rather* is a generous word, Mr. Sackett."

His smile turned wry. "No doubt you'd rather sail south but for a certain pilot who stands in your way."

She took a breath. "You were right to refuse me." The words came hard but were needed. "If I'd gone with Molly, I'd have returned to a home no longer mine. Our place has been sold, given over to someone else."

He showed no surprise. Had Papa already told him? She'd likely never know. James Sackett was a question mark of a man, revealing little. Her eyes trailed to the mourning band about his sleeve. Surely it wasn't too late to make amends for what she should have said at the levee. "You're grieving your fellow pilot and his crew . . . I'm very sorry."

"Thankfully Trevor Bixby was as fine a Christian as he was a pilot." He swung free of the saddle, landing agilely in thigh-high grass. "I'm sorry about Miss Ashburton as well."

Was he? The memory was still raw and unmended and might always be. "Charlotte sent you a note, wanting your help."

"And you think I didn't respond." He looked at her squarely as a cold wind whooshed between them. "What you don't know is that plans were in place to help her, but she went to the lake that day and it was too late."

There was a catch in his voice, a glint in his eye, that told her how sorry he was. Deeply so. She toyed with her reins, sorry she'd misjudged him, wishing time could be turned back and all made right again.

"How goes it at New Hope?"

She lifted her shoulders. "Papa is away on business till Christmas. We keep praying Grandfather recovers. I try to fill my time as best I can." She rued the prickliness in her voice, the stubborn edge that said she'd made up her mind about life in Pittsburgh and found it lacking.

"Do you ever stop to think you're here for a reason? Something beyond the aggravation of Pittsburgh, I mean?" His gaze locked with hers in question. "Perhaps your father needs to reclaim his old life. Or your grandmother a son. Or your grandfather a business ally. You have your whole future in front of you. You can leave here in time. But give it time."

Time. It hung heavy on her hands but for her music . . . and the coming season. While she pondered his words, he took the reins from her, examining her mare. "Your saddle is girthed so tightly your horse is having trouble breathing." He began adjusting the leather straps, dark brows knit together in concentration. "And your stirrup doesn't fit correctly."

She watched him work, a new awareness dawning. "I'm beginning to see why you were asked to be my escort."

He said nothing, intent on the girth, not raising his eyes to look at her. "Are you willing to make peace with that?"

Peace? She'd not felt peace since Mama's passing. She wasn't sure she ever would again. "I don't know."

It wasn't the answer he wanted. But it was honest, spelling out the turmoil inside her. He reached for her without warning, startling her much as his smile had done. His hands slid around her waist with practiced ease as he lifted her to the saddle. She found herself wishing for another of his smiles. Wondering if he set Izannah atumble the way he did her . . .

"Good day, Miss Ballantyne."

Bidding him goodbye, she bent her head, shaken by all the ways her world had been upended since Mama died. She felt torn up by the roots, transplanted from a humble place to a rigid, rule-bound world that crowded out both life and spirit.

As he rode away, fading to no more than a pinprick on the horizon, she felt a yawning, aching emptiness. Rushing in to fill that void were the words she couldn't wipe from her mind.

Perhaps your father needs to reclaim his old life. Or your grandmother a son. Or your grandfather a business ally . . .

Or Wren a new purpose. Beyond the scroll of a fiddle.

18

Love is never lost. If not reciprocated, it will flow back and soften and purify the heart.

WASHINGTON IRVING

Wren was becoming accustomed to churchgoing at First Presbyterian. Situated on Sixth Street and made of red brick, the building seemed squat and stolid as an old hen, unable to boast a towering spire like Third Presbyterian, which dominated the city skyline. But it was grand and old nonetheless, smelling of antique wood and worn velvet, the kneeling benches frayed.

At home, bereft of a church building, their Cane Run neighbors simply gathered round and had a little praise, worshiping and making music and singing at will. No numbered pews. No stained glass. No silver sacrament dishes for communion. This was another world, another way to feel at sea with her surroundings.

Behind her and Aunt Andra sat Izannah in the Turlock pew, gloved hands folded. Farther down sat Great-Aunt Elspeth, the judge just beyond, all six boys a study of stifled stillness. Only Grandmother and Grandfather were missing, and Aunt Ellie. James was never there. Why, Wren didn't know. God felt far away in such a formal place. Perhaps he felt it too.

She fought to stay awake, to feel at home in the familiar snatches of Scripture spoken by Reverend Herron in the high wooden pulpit. But she couldn't deny her gladness when Izannah took her aside at service's end.

"Daddy thinks we're in need of an outing, given matters are so serious at home," she whispered, her Sabbath demeanor switching to delight. "We're to have our luncheon at the Monongahela House today. And there's to be *no chaperone*."

They passed out of the church into a light sleet, parasols raised against the wet October weather. In minutes they'd traversed a busy thoroughfare and passed into the lush foyer of Pittsburgh's most reputable hostelry. Seated at a discreet table, Wren took in the patterned carpets and potted palms arranged for privacy around the grand room, nearly forgetting the menu in her hands. Sunday was a popular day to be out. No other seats were available, but several tables had been reserved and waitstaff filed in and out of the kitchen door in a steady stream.

James lived here somewhere, when he wasn't at River Hill. Sympathy nudged her, something that had little place in her resistant heart. Surely home wasn't to be found in a hotel, no matter how fancy. Or even a cottage at a grand country estate.

Izannah studied her over the menu. "Have you never been to a restaurant, Wren?"

"Cane Run has no restaurants, Izannah, just a simple inn."

"I recommend the chicken pie or leg of mutton, then. The pastry is good too, particularly the plum tarts and boiled custard."

Wren lingered on the fried chicken and hominy, something Molly made, then remembered Miss Criss's dictum. *She's to eat nothing but egg, broth, and bread.* Smiling up at the waiter, she said, "I'll have the fried chicken and an extra helping of hominy."

Izannah's brows peaked. "A double portion, Wren? That isn't like you."

"I'm feeling rather hungry of late." Dare she say she was nigh starved to death at New Hope? "It may be the last good meal I'll partake of till spring. You see, I'm to have a season."

"A season?" Izannah looked like she might laugh. "Says who?"

"Aunt Andra."

"Andra?" As she sat back, Izannah's somber expression resembled the judge's. "I imagine Bennett is behind this too. No doubt they're conspiring. You're a Ballantyne and must rise to the occasion and all that. You'll need an escort, of course. I'd name Bennett, but that's out of the question."

Wren's gaze shifted, disbelief taking hold as James entered the dining room. Uneasy, she reached for her glass of water, torn between telling Izannah the details or letting her cousin discover them herself.

"I'm sure the matter of an escort has been decided too," Izannah said, gaze thoughtful. "And given you keep looking across the room, I'll hazard a guess that he's here."

"It's just . . . James Sackett." *Your James.*

"Oh? He hadn't yet told me. But he's perfect for the role, I'll grant you that." She turned her head to take him in. "I daresay he'll . . ." Voice fading to a thread, she faced Wren again, looking stricken.

Wren stole another look at him. Seated at a discreet corner table across the cavernous, chandelier-lit room, he was in the company of a well-dressed man with russet hair. Recognition stirred. Could it be? The very one who'd given her a ride along the dusty road to New Hope?

Malachi Cameron.

She hadn't known the two men were friends. Malachi had come back to Pittsburgh looking for a bride, Mim had said. Somehow the prospect of meeting up with him again unsettled and excited her all at once.

A second waiter appeared with large white dinner plates bearing the Monongahela House pattern, one mounded with more hominy than Wren could manage in a week. She picked up her fork, anticipating Izannah's next query.

"When is your first function?"

"Not till the first of November." Dread nearly stole her appetite. "There's an opening dance where I'll be introduced."

Izannah nodded, placing her napkin in her lap. "The Mellons' ball, no doubt. Well, I'm sure James will serve you well, being the gentleman he is."

"Mim, my maid, will come along too." Wren's hasty words held an apology. Izannah mustn't think she was sweet on James. Mustn't think there was anything other than his acting as her escort. "Tell me about your season, Izannah, so that I can learn from it. Be better prepared."

Izannah let out a little sigh. "Be prepared not to breathe. Between fancy dress balls and masquerades, musicales and soirees, you'll be thoroughly baptized into Pittsburgh society. The newspapers are already full of what's to come." Picking up her fork, Izannah sampled her mutton. "I'm sorry your father isn't here to put a stop to such nonsense. If Grandfather weren't so ill, he'd intervene."

Wren tried to smile. "I don't see how a season could hurt. I do love to dance."

"Well, we might be worrying needlessly. This season of

yours might never come to pass. There's Grandfather's health to consider, and you'll need a suitable wardrobe. Mine was months in the making. I remember Andra complaining bitterly of your Louisville dresses."

"Some of Granny's old gowns are to be remade. They're still beautiful, hidden away in the attic like they've been. The seamstresses seemed pleased with the idea." But not Andra. No matter how hard Wren tried, Andra would always find her lacking.

Izannah lapsed into preoccupied silence while Wren pushed her food about her plate, as she'd surely do come her debut.

Nineteen more days.

Her ordeal had just begun.

Coming home from the Monongahela House, Izannah shut herself away in her chintz bedchamber. Still a bit dazed from seeing Malachi Cameron across the busy dining room, she took out a key at her writing desk and unlocked a secret drawer. Countless clippings from Pittsburgh's newspapers, some so old they were yellowed and faded, lay before her. Her prayers for a husband and family outnumbered them all yet seemed to go without answer. And then, when she'd all but given up, Malachi had returned, reviving hope.

She knew Malachi preferred to winter in Philadelphia or even his Edinburgh townhouse, not here in the semi-wilds of western Pennsylvania, grand new house or no. He was having the mansion built mainly for his aunt Mina's benefit, the servants whispered. Mina wanted him to settle down and thought such a house a fine reminder.

The memory of their last meeting clung to her, and she felt almost light-headed recalling it now. Time hadn't diminished how handsome he'd looked that day, standing on the levee in the bright spring sunlight, ready to go downriver to New Orleans. She'd happened to be in the city shopping and had picked up a little something for James in farewell. Coming by the boatyard office to give it to him, she'd run into Malachi instead.

Unused to the hustle and bustle of the waterfront, she'd nearly been upended by a dray and a heavy load of freight, the near collision sending her bumping into the man she couldn't quite shake free of. Her maid stood by, aghast, as Malachi Cameron intervened.

"Miss Turlock? Are you hurt?" Reaching out, he took her gloved hand, looking her over as if he feared she was. His touch was sure, confident, leaving a tingling trail from her head to her toes. But his studied formality hurt her somehow, as if reinforcing the years and distance that had come between them.

"I'm fine, thank you. I'd just forgotten how hazardous the levee can be." The rushed words were full of irony and angst. *Hazardous to my heart.* "Are you about to leave Pittsburgh again, Mr. . . . ?" She left off. She wouldn't call him by his surname. He was simply Malachi and always would be.

"So it seems." He broke their gaze to eye a waiting packet. "I suppose it would be too much to hope that you're leaving too?"

"I'm afraid I'm tied to home." She smiled, trying not to gaze up at him with a schoolgirl's adoration. "But I must admit, as exciting as steamboats are, I'd rather ride on your train."

He chuckled. "I'll see if I can hurry that up for you. Lay some track in Pittsburgh."

"Will you be away long?"

"Longer than I like." He studied her, hazel eyes slightly brooding beneath the brim of his top hat. "After New Orleans I return to Philadelphia and then Edinburgh."

So far. Simply hearing about such places set her soul on

fire. She was cast back to the globes and maps of their school-room and endless books filled with fascinating facts. Yet she'd never set foot beyond Philadelphia or Cincinnati. Sometimes it seemed she would burst from the desire to roam.

"You're looking at me like you want to go with me." His honest appraisal brought heat to her cheeks.

She groped for a memorable response, wanting to make the most of this very fleeting moment. His eyes held hers, as if he was wanting more too. Or had she dreamed of him so long it was clouding her usually sound judgment?

"Perhaps one day women will travel as men do," she murmured, unsure of him.

"Perhaps," he replied.

"I wish you safe travels, Malachi." On a whim she handed him what she'd bought for James. "A little something for your going away."

He'd turned swarthy as the package passed from her gloved hands to his. Only now she couldn't recall what she'd given him. Something from the tobacconist or confectioner's, perhaps. Or a book shop. She supposed it didn't matter. He probably no longer remembered it either.

Or did he?

Scarcely a ray of October light penetrated the gloom of Silas's bedchamber. Damask drapes were drawn tight, and no lamp was lit. A low fire burned in the grate, sending an occasional spark into the shadows. James sat by the bed, head sunk in his hands. The labored rasp of Silas's breathing ate away at what little composure he'd arrived with an hour earlier. For some reason the doctors had let him in, when they'd been guarded with visitors before. A bad sign. As if they'd given up hope and it no longer mattered. Aside from the occasional intrusion of a nurse or Ellie and Eden, James had been entirely alone with him.

Deep in his gut was the certainty that the time had come for Silas to leave them. Yet James stumbled on the mere thought. Silas had always been there for him. Like Pittsburgh. James didn't like to think of the course his life might have taken if there'd been no Ballantynes. No Orphan Home. No apprenticeship.

He'd always given Silas and Eden credit for what became of him. But lately, as if a light was dawning, he'd begun to think it was more God at work through the choices and actions of His people. Silas was the father he'd never had. Strong. Ever present. Silas never seemed to lose his balance, walking the tightrope of finance and industry with grace and skill, never compromising his beliefs or losing sight of a deeper purpose. James longed to be like him. But his faith was so small. His unbelief great.

A door opened softly then shut. He felt a hand on his hunched shoulder. Felt the gentle, reassuring warmth of outspread fingers through the heavy broadcloth of his coat.

Izannah? He looked up, surprise edging out grief.

Wren.

She stood just behind him, eyes on the still figure atop the bed, the faint rustle of her skirts rising above Silas's ragged breathing.

James sat back and her hand fell away. He hadn't seen her since they'd been out riding, yet they'd soon be thrust together at every turn—if Silas lived. He shut his eyes against the thought, only to open them to the sight of her on her knees.

Skirts burnished a deep plum in the firelight, she knelt by the bed, head bent, one hand outstretched to cover Silas's own as it lay limp atop the coverlet. James's throat closed and his eyes burned as she breathed a heartrending prayer into the stillness. Awe washed through him. She hardly knew this grandfather of hers while he sat close as kin, so choked by emotion he felt paralyzed. He expected her to rise, but she stayed where she was for a very long time.

Humbled, James wanted to get down beside her. Wanted to feel his knees scrape the hard floor like when he'd been a boy. Often Eden Ballantyne had come round to the orphanage back then, kneeling like Wren, taking his small hands in her own when he was sick or in low spirits. He bent his head beneath the weight of the memory as Wren's whispered prayer of moments before settled over him like a balm. He needed to get on his knees about a great many things. His grief over Bixby. Charlotte. His everlasting struggle with Bennett. The choices before him.

The figure atop the bed was all too still. Shaken, unable to keep himself in check, James went out, turning round once to linger on Silas's profile. Peaceful. No sign of struggle. Only that agonized rattling in his chest that was a punishment to witness.

He passed into the hall, taking a seat on a settee. The doctors came and Wren emerged, sitting beside him when he'd expected her to go. Still feeling choked, he endured the pained silence, the width of her skirts like a third person between them.

"Are you . . . all right?" she asked him.

He fixed his damp gaze on an oil painting across the hall. "No."

She looked to her lap, silent, and then reached for his fisted hand on the settee between them. Her touch was warm. Kind. Violating every tenet of custom and etiquette he knew. His pulse quickened. Her callused fingers were like the strike of a match, lighting a fire he feared couldn't be put out.

The familiar hum of the house went on all around them. Servants scurrying. Doors quietly closing. The ever-present kitchen smells rising to the far rafters. But all he was conscious of was the subtle pressure of her fingers against his own.

Her voice was low and melodic if grieved. "Once Grandfather passes . . . goes to glory . . . what will happen then?"

Goes to glory. The heartfelt expression tugged at him, another reminder of how differently she thought about things. Cleanly. Honestly. Almost childlike in her simplicity.

"We'll all be in full mourning for a year or better."

He could feel her taking it in, all the ramifications. He wasn't sure what mourning was like in Cane Run, but her thoughtful silence told him it was handled differently than here.

"A season seems frivolous at such a time," she said.

"It might not come to pass." Yet his own conflicted feelings left him hoping—praying—it would. He wanted the season to move forward. He wanted her to marry well. He wanted an end to the way she went to his head like wine.

"I don't want anything to happen to Grandfather, but neither do I want to meet Pittsburgh." Her voice fell to an agonized whisper. "I want you to promise me . . ." Her features turned so entreating he felt he held her future in his hands. "Promise me you'll go slowly. I've never before had a suitor. Never been alone with a man nor been kissed . . ."

He nearly winced as she laid the matter bare between them. He looked at her then, taking liberties he had no right to. He grew lost in the gentle curve of her cheek, her thick lashes, the way her hair escaped its pins, trailing like blonde lace to her bent shoulders.

His breathing was nearly nonexistent now. He cast about for the right words, trying to tread carefully. "I'm a gentleman, remember, who's been charged to introduce you to the same. Since I know so many in Pittsburgh, it stands to reason you're in good hands."

"I know all this is happening to marry me off, make a proper match. But I'm not accomplished, other than the violin. Andra says I'm rough spun, among other things."

His jaw clenched. He forced his gaze to his boots. While Andra and Bennett schemed and maneuvered about her future, did they have to drag her through the mud of their prejudices and criticisms too?

"I can't help but wonder . . ." Her voice cracked with vulnerability. "What if no man wants me or finds me pleasing?"

"Wren . . ." He swallowed past the hammering tightness in his chest, his precarious use of her given name. "Falling in love with you would be easy. You are a very beautiful woman, and a very charming one."

She sat very still, his heartfelt words falling into the stillness between them. He couldn't take them back. He didn't want to. He'd exposed his heart when he'd merely meant to bolster her confidence. But it was out there—every tender word—lingering like a vow between them.

He was on the edge of his emotions. Feeling too deeply. Revealing too much. Standing up so quickly he felt lightheaded, he excused himself, fixing his gaze on the stairwell banister down the hall just as Izannah cleared the top step.

Her surprise at finding them together was plain. She looked to him and then Wren, features pinched with worry and fatigue. He pushed past her without a word, wondering what they would say in his wake.

Wondering if Silas would make it through another night.

*Dresses for breakfast and dinners and
      balls;
Dresses to sit in, and stand in, and
      walk in;
Dresses to dance in, and flirt in, and
      talk in;
Dresses in which to do nothing at all.*
WILLIAM ALLEN BUTLER

Ordeal by fork.

There was simply no other way to describe it. But first . . . the entrance.

"You must walk in a measured gait at all times, looking neither to the right nor the left." Catherine Criss's voice filled the dining room's cold space while Andra sat in somber observation at table's end. "Remember, haste is incompatible with grace."

Wren entered New Hope's dining room, fighting the breathless feeling someone was sitting on her chest, and finally made it to the appointed chair where other perils awaited.

"Take care not to disturb the furniture when you sit down, and mind your skirts so that they fall gracefully around you." The biting censure in Miss Criss's voice was more daunting than the obstacle course before her. "Now remove your gloves and lay them atop your lap *before* unfolding your napkin."

Wren did as she bade, flushing at the next dictum. "You are to make no remark upon the food set before you, not even in praise. Nor do you acknowledge the servants with so much as a word or glance."

This was surely a pointed rebuke to her effusiveness, as her aunt called it. Making too much of every little thing. Gushing was vulgarity itself.

Andra cleared her throat. "One misstep will mark you as a social counterfeit, Rowena, a gaffe from which you will never recover."

Wren nodded, careful to keep her eyes down demurely. Eye contact, like a curtsey or a bow, was meted out carefully, the slightest glance indicating the degree or warmth of a relationship . . . and there was no kind feeling around this immense table.

"Depending on the dinner party, you may or may not peruse a handwritten menu prior to being served." Taking a seat beside her, Miss Criss turned the full force of her gaze Wren's way. "The first course usually begins with what pairing?"

"Champagne and—" Wren struggled to keep the distaste from her tone. "Raw oysters."

"Correct. After this, waiters will offer a choice of soup and sherry to be followed by fish and Chablis."

The menu would be endless and extravagant, mostly in French, comprising course after course that could feed a great many hungry souls in the dingy alleys of Pittsburgh. Try as she might, Wren couldn't help feeling a sickening sense of excess even imagining it, like eating too much icing on an empty stomach. Nor could she distinguish all the silver.

"Take up your seafood fork." The unrelenting pace of Miss Criss's lessons the last fourteen days had worn Wren to a threepenny nail.

The seafood fork? Wren extended an unsure hand, torn between two nearly identical utensils.

"Remember, the slightest hesitation will betray you."

She'd been betrayed.

"The seafood fork is the fourth fork to the right of the oval soup spoon," Miss Criss interjected firmly. *"Always."*

Wren looked at the maze of cutlery before her and wanted to raise a white flag of surrender. "There is also the dessert fork, the ice cream fork, the pastry fork, the strawberry fork, the salad fork, and the lobster fork. And I've not even begun to name all the knives and spoons—"

"Rowena!" Andra's raised voice fell harshly around them. "There's time enough to tell which is which. Eight days, to be exact. For now, Mistress Endicott is in the hall. I'm anxious to see what miracles she's worked with your dresses."

Miracles? There was thinly veiled sarcasm in Andra's tone. Before an answering dismay leapt to Wren's face, she reined herself in, remembering restraint ruled the day.

A mark of good breeding is the suppression of any undue emotion, any true feeling to the outside world.

Hadn't James Sackett taught her this? With his everlasting reserve and impeccable manners?

As soon as she thought it, she felt a check. She'd seen through his stoicism but twice, when he'd first smiled at her while out riding, and then again outside Grandfather's sickroom. In the broken, heart-shattering stillness, she'd glimpsed a part of him that stayed hidden. As her hand reached for his, his reserve had given way for a too-tender second and he'd nearly come undone.

He cared for Grandfather deeply. He'd cared for Georgiana and had lost her. She felt a catch in her throat, remembering, barely aware Andra and Miss Criss had left the room.

Sighing, she pressed clammy fingers to her temples as if to push the pain of her headache away. The added aggravation of an empty stomach made her light-headed. The egg she'd had upon rising and the broth she'd had at noon made little sense. She was expected to starve till the Mellons' ball and then stuff herself during?

Bumping the table upon rising brought a near wince. The silver seemed to chime, calling out her foible, but only Mim appeared in the doorway, worry on her ruddy face. Making a beeline toward her, Mim made quick work of a napkin, revealing a warm biscuit slathered with butter and jam.

"Yer going to faint dead away—fall right into yer soup—yer first night out. I'll nae let them starve ye to death!"

Taking the offering, Wren downed it in two bites, careful of crumbs. The scurry in the foyer was heightening as seamstresses and assistants hurried upstairs, arms full of dresses.

"As many dresses as forks," Mim whispered in sympathy.

For now only one dress mattered—the gown for the opening ball. And from the exclamations floating down from the second floor, it was creating something of a stir.

By the time Wren reached the dressing room of her bedchamber, not a sound could be heard. Cautiously she peered round the doorframe. The women were huddled round a dress form where the altered gown was on display, blocking her view.

"I believe this is the very gown my mother was wearing

when she first came to Pittsburgh and met up with my father again." Andra's voice was oddly sentimental. "The occasion was a River Hill ball over fifty years ago."

Brushing a biscuit crumb from her bodice, Wren joined them, her breath catching at the sight of so much antique silk. Every buttery line and pleat and pearl embellishment was a picture of elegance.

Mistress Endicott turned toward Wren. "I stayed true to the eighteenth-century design while embellishing with the choicest Rose Point lace from Brussels. The skirts have been cut away at the waist to retain the polonaise lines and allow for dancing. The finished alteration is far more fetching than I'd imagined. All that remains is the fitting."

Everyone seemed to hold a collective breath as the assistants divested Wren of her day dress. Her throat knotted as Grandmother's gown rustled and slipped into place, turning the moment more poignant.

Lord, let all this fuss be worthwhile.

The shining cheval glass was reassurance the remade gown was equal to any occasion. Clad so, Wren felt nearly like a bride, her skin turning pink from so many admiring glances, many of which had only been critical before. Even Mim looked a bit overcome at the transformation.

What would it be like entering a strange ballroom on James's arm? Privy to a great many appraising gazes? The prospect tore away her joy over Grandmother's generosity. She feared she'd faint just like Mim had warned. Fall face-down in her soup in a roomful of strangers.

From the doorway a maid's voice broke through the silence. "Your father has taken a turn, Miss Andra, and you're needed at River Hill."

The slightest hesitation—and then Andra left the room.

No one said a word, but it was obvious what each was think-ing. The beautiful silk gown might soon return to the trunk in the attic, exchanged for mourning instead.

Malachi eyed the stone and glass orangery situated behind the nearly finished hulk of Cameron House. The detailed plans in his hands made little sense. He was a railroad man, not an architect, and had thought building a home would be as straightforward as laying track. Apparently that was not the case. The entire operation was being held up by a ship-ment of Italian marble. Every mantel in the twenty-five-room mansion was made of a different kind—and it seemed every marble sculptor in Italy had gone on strike.

Beside him, the lead architect squinted into the gloom of midafternoon, apology in his bearded face. "Every mantel-piece is grand in scale, and each caryatid is varied. The carvers insist on selecting each Carrara block so that no unsightly veins show. Such workmanship takes time, Mr. Cameron, as befits the Italian Renaissance design."

Malachi nodded, not caring about such things, ruing he'd let the builders have so much sway. Bending his head, he scanned the plans once more as cold rain snuck past his up-turned collar and wet his neck. All his hopes for seeing the house finished, and finished in a timely fashion, fled.

"You need a wife worthy of such a house."

He turned toward his aunt's familiar voice, ire in his tone. "I need a finished house with hearths intact before winter sets in. I'll not freeze my bride to death."

Mina merely chuckled and opened her parasol against the damp. "Why not occupy the orangery? Look at all those plants!" Together they looked toward exotic lemon trees, oleanders from the Carolinas, and sago palms from the West Indies behind thick glass. "I've not seen so imposing a structure since I was last in London."

Rolling up the plans in his hands, Malachi started away from the sound of sawing and hammering. "I'm in need of a walk."

"I'll join you." Linking arms with him, she gave him her most engaging smile. "And how is my favorite nephew?"

"Your *only* nephew."

"Which is why we must get you settled soon. I need great-nephews and great-nieces. We need to fill this grand house of yours with a family. Life and laughter."

He scowled. "I'm tempted to leave for Edinburgh on the morrow. If I return in spring, maybe this monstrosity will be complete."

"Stuff and nonsense! Edinburgh is out of the question, at least without a bride in tow." She smiled again, making light of his complaint. "I've come to discuss your tailor."

He resisted the urge to roll his eyes. "My tailor?"

"I want to make sure you have the requisite number of cravats, tailcoats, and trousers needed for the season. All in the most desirable colors. The garments sent over from town this morning seem . . . lacking."

"This is Pittsburgh, remember. Not Philadelphia. Nor London."

She patted his arm. "I have such high hopes for you, Malachi. Are you sure your valet will arrive in time for the Mellons' opening ball?"

He hesitated, doubting he had the patience to make it through the first event. "As far as getting dressed, I'm nearing thirty and can manage with or without Ellis. He's mainly an assistant. A personal secretary. All that railroad correspondence gets out of hand."

They trudged up the sodden hill toward antique iron fencing, leaving deep imprints in the glistening grass. The newest gravestone drew his eye—and strengthened his resolve to see the season through. His father's name, Daniel Cameron, was chiseled in granite, 1793–1849. Beside him lay his mother, gone so long he hardly remembered her, her epitaph so weathered it wasn't visible. He made a mental note to have a new gravestone set.

His father had been right. What was life without children, some sort of lasting legacy? It was time—past time—to settle down before another inch of track splayed west.

Mina let go of his arm, perhaps to give him privacy, and he forged ahead. He hadn't been back since the burial, and his feelings were still raw. He could forgive his father for dying. What he couldn't forgive—or forget—was letting him down so grievously.

Regret wove its way across his chest, and he swung round, facing the deep valley he'd been born in. Just below on the main road lay Cameron Farm, little more than a humble heap of stone. Dwarfed by the nearly completed Cameron House on the hill, it would soon be leased to the farm manager. Mina and his grandfather would move into the new gatehouse while he and the future Mrs. Cameron would try to warm themselves by the marble fireplaces that needed finishing.

Lord, help me find a willing bride.

He felt so capable in some respects, and so hopelessly over his head in others. Railroad mergers and cutthroat competitors and the rise and fall of stocks seemed child's play in light of courtship. Marriage. The coming season.

He glanced at his aunt, thinking how shocked she'd be if she knew the dearth of his experience. Aside from an adolescent infatuation with Izannah Turlock, he'd always been obsessed with trains. Nothing so practical as matrimony. Warmth crept up his neck like a Highland scarf as he remembered a brief, awkward liaison with an Edinburgh actress.

His thoughts cut to James Sackett. Smooth, amiable, never undone. His constant milling with society as he plied the upper and lower Mississippi and his engagement years before had given him an edge. And then Miss Hardesty had up and died, shocking Pittsburgh and sending James into a well of despair. He sometimes thought his old friend hadn't recovered still.

"Everything will be sublime," Mina was saying, drawing abreast of him and twirling her dripping parasol like it was spring instead of late fall. "All that stubborn Carrara marble is easily managed, as are Ellis's eventual return and your choice of a bride." Handing him the parasol, she opened her reticule and extracted a copy of the *Gazette*, gesturing to a bevy of typeset beauties on the society page, each drawn in cameo. "This is the cream of the coming season, though there are sure to be a few surprises. Not all the debutantes have been listed. Rumor is there are nearly three dozen in the wings. Ripe. Polished. Waiting."

He nearly groaned. She spoke of them like fruit. His for the taking. Anxious to change the subject, he pulled a letter from his pocket. "This came for you earlier today . . . from someone by the name of Ballantyne."

Her eyes widened, and he caught a hint of pleasure in their depths. So she did have feelings for the man, even after all these years. Reaching out a gloved hand, she stole the post away from him. In her excitement she appeared years younger, a becoming flush invading her powdered cheeks.

"This leaves me wondering more about the state of your heart than mine," he murmured.

"Merely a letter from an old friend. 'Tis all it's ever been."

"Ansel Ballantyne strikes me as far too busy to waste pen and ink on trivial pursuits."

Her half smile faded. "Years ago he broke my heart by leaving Pittsburgh and marrying Sarah Nancarrow. I've never quite recovered."

"Perhaps this letter will do the trick."

She gave a slight shrug and drew her shawl closer against the cold. "He's a lonely man. And I'm a lonely woman. Far too old for any romantic nonsense."

Her words tugged at his heart, the wind his coattails. Unlike Mina, he was still somewhat young. Of sound mind and resources. A worthy groom. But time promised to tick on to eternity and leave him lacking if he didn't tend it well.

All around them the wind keened, shifting his thoughts to Edinburgh again. He usually wintered there, snug in his Regent Street townhouse with an old sheepdog and a faithful servant or two. He'd been content till last winter when the quiet began to eat away at him. His bed was too big. His house too echoing. He roamed about the city restlessly. In the shops they'd begun calling him the Scots-American eccentric . . .

A sudden whim assailed his conscience. Perhaps he could circumvent the social season altogether and call on Izannah like James had urged. The prospect of escaping—nay, eloping—to Scotland was so tempting he felt a rush of fresh resolve.

And stark fear.

What would her response be if he rode to River Hill out of the blue and asked to court her? What if she refused him like her mother, Ellie, had refused his father? Moreover, what would her father, the judge, make of the arrangement?

He was certain of one thing. Mina wouldn't approve.

I have such high hopes for you.

And they didn't include settling for a Turlock.

20

Izannah couldn't stop crying. Opposite her in the hall stood James, hat in hand, having just come from Pittsburgh. Chloe was clutched to her bodice, and Izannah's tears were spotting the babe's lacy cap and gown. Only a few months old, her tiny sister was too young to be much moved by the events unfolding around them. She'd never know the man who had struggled to forge a legacy and lived his life so well, never recall the warmth of his smile or the godly wisdom he'd imparted.

"Here, let me take her." Discarding his hat on a settee, James reached for Chloe.

She went willingly, her plump arms open wide. Izannah didn't miss her little sigh of pleasure or the adoring way she looked up at him. When he bent his head and brushed his shadowed cheek to Chloe's in a rare show of tenderness, Izannah shut her eyes tight.

Oh, James. You need a home. A baby to call your own.

Chloe chortled, lifting the sadness, and James almost smiled. Biting her lip, Izannah dug for her handkerchief, its lavender scent soothing. When she looked up again, her gaze filled with Uncle Wade. Dismay gained a solid foothold. Nearly as tall as Daddy but more intimidating, he walked down the gaslit hall toward them, an easy indifference in his step, Bennett just behind.

Thick as thieves, the two of them. Wade's weakness for gambling and racehorses and other nefarious pursuits had ensnared Bennett since he'd come of age. As usual, Wade's clothing was flamboyant, but Bennett had dressed the part, his deep mourning for Charlotte sufficing for Grandfather too.

No greetings were exchanged. Wade shunned James as much as he favored Bennett. Though it was no secret James and Bennett had never found common ground, Izannah wished for a few cordial words, at least, as they all stood there together and waited for the worst.

Finally James's voice cut into the silence. "The doctors are with Silas now."

Bennett slid past Wade, taking first place by the closed bedchamber door. "Father was so stricken when he heard the latest news, Mother had to summon the doctor to Ballantyne Hall to attend to him."

Izannah nearly groaned aloud. Uncle Peyton might not outlive Grandfather by much, weakened by the last typhoid epidemic as he'd been. But she was most concerned about Grandmother. So fragile. So devoted. Grandfather had been the center of her world since their humble beginnings in York County all those years before.

Chloe gave a little cry, drawing Wade's eye. He frowned and lit a cigar by the wall sconce, replacing the glass globe a bit clumsily. Smoke filled the space between them, obscuring Izannah's view as more footsteps sounded down the hall. Elspeth and her aging maid appeared on the landing, winded from the slow climb upstairs. Izannah braced herself for whatever her great-aunt had to say, the storminess of Elspeth's expression giving a warning.

"Whatever in the world is taking so long? It's like the man has nine lives." Elspeth leaned into her cane with a heavy sigh. "I've nearly worn a path to your door, I've come so many times."

Wade smirked. "If you'd had the grace to succumb first, you might have spared yourself the trouble."

"I have no intention of dying." Elspeth pursed her lips and stared at the closed door. "Not till I see Izannah and Bennett wed. And then there's Wren's debut, which might fall to pieces if Silas has his day." Her gaze narrowed and took in Wade. "What say you we go below and have a tonic?"

Blowing smoke, Wade ignored her, fixing his eye on James as if seeing him for the first time. "So, Sackett, what's keeping you from New Orleans this winter?"

"Pittsburgh business," James said, meeting Wade's rocky stare.

"Business? My guess is that Madder and his Mystic Conspiracy have you holed up in port." Wade's brash voice seemed to thunder, and Izannah detected a hint of spirits. "All that infernal slave running is finally catching up with you, so my contacts down South say."

Izannah blanched. The careless words hung between them

like soiled rags on a wash line. James stayed stoic. Silent. For once she wished he'd lash out and cuff Wade like he deserved.

"What's this about Madder?" Bennett waved away the smoke. "Madder who?"

Wade's smug expression soured. "Apparently, Sackett's stirred up some trouble downriver that may well follow him to Pittsburgh. The Southern papers are full of it—that and the news of his replacement pilot, a radical abolitionist by the name of John Gunniston."

Bennett's gaze flicked to James. "I'm not going to inherit any antislavery nonsense, is that understood? Not even a whisper of it. There's a great deal at stake here, Rowena's season foremost." He paused, jaw rigid. "Need I remind you that more than a few of Pittsburgh's leading lights oppose the abolitionist cause?"

At Chloe's sudden cry, Izannah took her from James's arms, digging for the silver rattle she'd pocketed, her heart flipping about her chest at Bennett's insolence.

Bennett continued on, unchecked. "As for Madder, shut him up by any means—"

"Enough said." James took a step back, ending the conversation.

Wade's and Bennett's stares seemed to bore a hole in his back as he withdrew.

Izannah caught the grieved green of James's eyes as he turned away, fury building in her breast. "Shame on you!" she hissed when James was out of earshot. "If you two don't behave like grown men, Daddy will horsewhip you both!"

In seconds the judge appeared, making her nearly giddy with relief. Fresh from court, Jack Turlock spoke in low tones with Andra and Wren, whom he'd escorted upstairs. Daddy was the only one who could manage Wade—and Elspeth, who was sitting on the settee, obviously having enjoyed their heated exchange as much as any tonic.

"My, my, so much drama! And we've not even been admitted to the inner sanctum yet." She aimed another pointed look at the closed bedchamber door as if waiting for the next act to unfold.

Brushing past her, Izannah moved toward Wren, losing sight of James as he gave a nod to her father and took the stairs. Wren's head turned, her attention riveted to James's exit, confirming Izannah's suspicion of some secret attraction.

Her cousin was pale. More slender than she remembered. Had it only been two Sundays ago they'd had lunch after Sabbath service?

What had Andra and Miss Criss done to her since?

"You came back." The pleasure in Addie's voice knew no bounds.

Smiling, Wren removed her hat and gloves and set them on a table at the orphanage entrance. "I hope to come every week, if I can find a few wee folk who want to play the fiddle with me." Beside her, the Nightingale rested in its case, drawing Addie's eye.

"Sometimes Jamie plays for us." Her upturned face creased in a smile. "He says he squeaks, but I tell him it's angels' music."

"Angels' music. I like that. Does he give lessons?" She had no wish to tread on his territory if he did.

"No lessons." Addie's joyful expression turned pensive. "He's away on the river too much for that."

Wren extended her hand and they started down the hall. "Care to show me to the music room?"

With a nod, Addie led the way, surprising her with a second-floor nook made bright with wide windows and pale peach walls. Mrs. Sheffield, the director, was there to greet her, warm and welcoming as always.

"Miss Ballantyne, how good of you to come on such a chilly afternoon. The other children will be along shortly. For now we have six students interested in the violin, though that may increase."

"Six sounds like a blessed start," Wren said, adjusting to the notion she was in charge. "I've been by the Sign of the Harp, the music store on Third Street. The owner says he'll deliver several quarter-sized fiddles next week, in advance of the lesson." He'd been most obliging too, heartened by what he called her patronage. Though his instruments were no match for the Cremona violins Papa owned or the Guarneri Grandfather had lost, his work was of good quality.

"Please make yourself comfortable." Mrs. Sheffield gestured to a chair surrounded by smaller stools. "Are you in need of a music stand? Anything at all?"

"I play mostly by ear, though I've brought sheet music for the children." Anxious to start, Wren unclasped her case while Addie went to fetch a stand.

"I hesitate to ask . . ." Mrs. Sheffield looked apologetic. "But I've been so concerned about your grandfather."

Straightening, Wren rested the Nightingale in her lap. "He's still very ill. We're . . . waiting."

"Of course. Our prayers are with him—all your family. I'll bring the children in so you can begin."

The afternoon flew, Wren nearly forgetting all that awaited her at New Hope. Andra had given her one afternoon not crowded with fittings and etiquette, at least. Just yesterday the dancing master had been dismissed at Miss Criss's recommendation, as there was no more need of his services. James had come instead, surprising her, leading her about New Hope's third-floor ballroom till their shared steps were nearly faultless and she had little breath left.

"I never misdoubted you could dance," she told him. "But I never thought you'd do it as well as you pilot."

"Careful with your praise, Miss Ballantyne. It might well go to my head."

They slowed to a stop, a mere handbreadth apart. Close enough for her to notice the steady rhythm of his chest as it rose and fell beneath layers of linen and silken waistcoat.

"I had some trouble with that last turn," he murmured.

Did he? He never seemed to misstep, not in word or dance or deed.

"We could try again," she ventured, aware of Miss Criss and Andra watching from a settee.

The fiddler struck a waltz and Wren gave herself up to the music, to James's clean, masculine scent and hard arms, his firm, faultless leading. Round and round they went till she grew so winded and dizzy she was little more than a puddle of pleasure.

He leaned in, his breath warm against her ear. "You remind me of your mother. She danced like she made music. You look like her too."

"You remember Mama?" Somehow the fact he did made her loss less bittersweet.

"I remember my time in England like it was yesterday. I watched your father's courtship with her play out before my eyes."

"I wondered where you learned the violin." Simply recalling their duet at River Hill turned her joyful. "Playing by ear is no small matter. You have a heart for the music. I can hear it."

"I've never given it much thought. Not till you came."

The waltz faded and he brought her to a gentle halt. The fiddler took his leave, bowing to them and going out, Miss Criss and Andra trailing after him.

Surprised, Wren looked back at James with wry amusement. "I seem to remember some rule about not being alone with a man, Mr. Sackett."

A half smile threatened his solemnity. "Your escort has liberties no other man has, Miss Ballantyne."

"Oh? You should call me Wren, then." He had, hadn't he? At last meeting?

He hesitated, his gaze holding hers for a beat too long. She half feared he would remind her of her manners. "Only if you call me Jamie."

Jamie. Not James.

Her heart gave a little leap. That she could do.

Recalling their surprising exchange now, she packed up her violin, pausing a moment to let her gaze wander the orphanage's austere walls. She still struggled with the fact he'd grown up in this very place. Did he remember his parents or even know who they were? Her heart craved answers. Happy endings. A man like James Sackett should have a home. With Izannah if need be. But that was none of her concern either. Cousin or no, she wouldn't be accused of meddling.

She left the orphanage, the success of the first lesson forgotten as thoughts of the coming season pressed in. Unwilling to return to New Hope, unable to bear the grief and tension at River Hill, she had her driver take her about the city.

Pittsburgh wasn't so strange to her now. It bore an ugly familiarity with its pall and bustle and matched her unsettled mood. Remembering it was nearing Papa's birthday, she stopped at the tobacconist and the confectioner in the market square, testing her newfound freedom. Though she carried a beaded reticule, no money changed hands. She simply told them who she was and what she wanted, and the desired item was bundled up and given over with a smile and sound thanks.

Money was never to be mentioned, Andra said. Even bankruptcy—something that happened to other people—was referred to as *embarrassment*. A Ballantyne never carried cash in town. There was simply no need when one owned the bank. Wren recalled it tongue in cheek, struck by her aunt's high-minded notions.

Where was the evidence of the Ballantynes' humble beginnings? When Grandfather had come from Scotland with scarcely twopence in his pocket? She herself was merely Wren from Cane Run and always would be. Yet she was beginning to draw notice as she went about Pittsburgh.

Perhaps it was the Ballantyne coach, as fine if not finer than any she passed on the street, or the fact she had no maid. A sudden qualm beset her. Should Mim have come? She'd only meant to go to the Orphan Home, not the market.

Clad in a ruby cape, she scurried about like a windblown leaf, her matching bonnet just as eye-catching. One man, then two, gave a slight bow as she passed. Though Andra wasn't with her, her strident voice intruded.

A lady never seeks to attract attention or form an acquaintance on the street.

Oh, why hadn't she brought Mim?

Clutching her packages, she hastened her step to the curb where the carriage waited, bringing an end to town.

If only she could do the same with the coming season.

21

*High rank and soft manners may
not always belong to a true heart.*
ANTHONY TROLLOPE

Wren entered the morning room, finding Andra stirring sugar into her tea so vigorously the china cup rattled. She looked up from the *Gazette*, expression pinched. "The weather has taken a turn and looks to be dismal the night of the Mellons' ball. We'll have to make sure you're properly cloaked and don't mar your new slippers."

Sitting opposite, Wren bit her lip before she could mumble any thanks as a lone egg was set before her. Later Mim would slip her a biscuit, but with her new French corset so tightly laced, she feared any food she swallowed would reappear.

Andra glanced at the mantel clock. "Miss Criss is expected any minute."

Oh? Hungry as Wren was, she'd had her fill of Miss Criss. The conversation she'd overheard yesterday beat in her brain relentlessly, stealing what little confidence she'd mustered.

"If we can keep Rowena dancing and playing her violin, then perhaps no one will care if she uses the wrong utensil or wears her feelings on her sleeve." Miss Criss's strident voice drifted to her from the dressing room, adding yet another layer of dread and dismay to the web of the season.

"Her dowry is sufficient enough to hush the staunchest critics." Andra's usual irritableness held a note of triumph. "There's not a debutante from here to Philadelphia who is her equal in that."

Wren pondered their words. Was Papa responsible for her dowry? Whoever it was, she was now weighted with a name and a fortune, which might somehow make up for her rusticity, her backwoods beginnings. If some man was willing.

Reaching toward a silver salver, Andra returned Wren to the present as she passed her the post. "A letter's come this morning from your father. It seems business is keeping him in Boston."

Wren broke the wax seal, ignoring the meager breakfast in front of her.

> *Dear Daughter,*
>
> *I am writing to you from Boston, which is becoming more familiar to me than I had hoped. I trust you are well and will forgive my long absence.*
>
> *Yesterday I received a letter from Mina Cameron telling me you are to have a season with James Sackett as your escort. If not for his steady presence, I would be more concerned than I am.*
>
> *Still, I question if this is wise. A debut invari-*

ably means marriage, and I must urge you to
tread cautiously in this respect. Society is not
what it seems. If you find a young man to your
liking, do nothing till I return.

It was hardly the letter she'd expected. Had Papa not received hers? She looked up at Andra. "Does Papa know Grandfather has worsened?"

Andra set her napkin aside. "We've sent another telegram but haven't received a reply."

I've been given a fair price for two of the Cre-
mona violins and have hopes this may help in
the recovery of the lost Guarneri. Meanwhile,
Ballantyne business takes most of my time.
My continued love and prayers are with you.

Papa

What, she wondered, did he write to Mina Cameron?

Setting the post aside, she bent her head and tried to summon thanks, but before she'd finished her egg, Andra started in, unveiling a stack of etiquette books on a near table. "Once Miss Criss and the seamstresses are here, we'll have the final fitting for the gown you'll be wearing to the upcoming musical soiree."

First the ball, then the soiree. Wren said nothing, mulling over Papa's letter till Mim appeared, something in hand.

Pleasure overrode Andra's moodiness of moments before. "I'd nearly forgotten your visiting cards, fresh from the printers. You're to keep them in this case."

The case was made of silver, the lid a pearly ivory depicting a turreted manor house among trees. Wren could think of half a dozen uses for the fancy case, none of which pertained to visiting. Yet visit she must.

"This is an etching of the Ballantynes' estate in Scotland," Andra told her.

Grandfather's Highland refuge? At the moment it sounded like the most pleasant place on earth.

With a flick of the lid, Andra revealed engraved cards made of choice white paper, the lettering a rich black. Removing one, she propped it against a crystal saltcellar.

Miss Rowena Ballantyne

"Once the season is under way, visiting shall begin in earnest. A tray is in the entry hall to collect cards, the most distinguished names on top. No one would ever think of seeing another person at home without leaving his or her visiting card first."

Wren passed a finger over the fancy engraving, bemused. Who invented all these rules and then cast them in iron? Pittsburgh lagged a bit behind sophisticated Philadelphia, Miss Criss said. What on earth was the season like there?

Miss Criss arrived, energized by one too many cups of tea and the lemon drops she consumed in rapid succession. As usual, she lost no time in getting to business. "Let's review what you've learned, Rowena, and make a game of round-robin out of it. Perhaps that way our lesson won't be so dull."

Wren bit her lip. Not even round-robin could enliven the humorless Miss Criss or the etiquette she dispensed. But she nodded obligingly nevertheless.

"I'll begin." Taking a seat across from her, Pittsburgh's

social maven launched into a timeworn refrain. "One must avoid extremes of shyness or boldness."

Andra set down her teacup. "Absolutely no mention of religion or politics."

Wren folded her hands in her lap, her head throbbing like the Edinburgh-made clock in the foyer. Beneath the table she plucked the little bird Addie had given her from her pocket. It was smoothed to a satiny finish by her worried fingers, and she felt like a child with a comforting toy. "Don't drum your fingers or hum a tune."

Miss Criss gave a stiff nod. "Never laugh out loud."

Be seated with ease.

Never finger your face.

Discipline your eyes.

Eat with delicacy.

Scatter no crumbs.

Weariness pressed down on her like a heavy blanket. So many rules . . . The whole lot of them were running together in her head like ants at a Sunday picnic.

For a moment all etiquette seemed to have slipped from her grasp. Next she knew she was in bed, having "cast up accounts"—thrown up all her supper—or what little there was of it.

Mim hovered over her, candelabra in hand, stark worry in her eyes. "Ye've got a fever, ye do. Plain as day! I'll go wake yer aunt—"

"No!" Mouth like cotton, Wren shook her head, wishing Papa was near. Or Molly. And Mama, always. When she was fevered, Mama would lay cold cloths upon her heated skin and sing a hymn and pray. "Not a word, Mim . . . please."

"But what if it's something dire? There's talk of typhoid

going round Pittsburgh again, and ye spent all day yesterday in town—"

"Just let me be till morning."

"Till morning? Ye might nae be here come morning." Mim's cool hand fluttered against her fiery cheek. "I'll nae let ye slip away from me like Miss Charlotte. Oh, aye, nae for a minute, if I can help it."

Alone in River Hill's breakfast room, a smaller chamber painted azure blue and dwarfed by an enormous sideboard, James pushed aside his half-eaten breakfast. A maid whisked his tray away, then opened the drapes on a wet world. He wanted to inquire about matters upstairs yet sensed nothing had changed. Silas was, no doubt, still holding on, the pneumonia in his lungs crowding out the last bit of life and air while ordinary life unfolded all around him.

Behind him the fire crackled noisily in the grate, replenished by yet another servant, the only sound in the huge house. Moments earlier the judge had left for another day in court. James missed the noise of the boys. Normalcy.

"The house is too quiet," he said more to himself than Izannah when she appeared and shut the door.

"I agree." Weariness lined her brow. He missed her winsome smile. Lately her expression stayed careworn. "With Grandfather so ill, the boys are still at Broad Oak."

The mention turned him more restless. His confrontation with Wade in the hall outside Silas's bedchamber was slow to fade. But it was Bennett's last words that bore down on him in an unwelcome rush.

I'm not going to inherit any antislavery nonsense, is that understood? Not even a whisper of it. There's a great deal at stake here, Rowena's season foremost. Need I remind you that more than a few of Pittsburgh's leading lights oppose the abolitionist cause?

Alexander Mellon, foremost.

A chill traveled down James's spine at the thought of dancing and dining beneath the Mellons' palatial roof in two days' time. But there was little he could do about it. He fought the urge to light his pipe, then gave in to it.

"Smoking after breakfast, James?" A small smile lifted Izannah's heaviness as she took the chair across from him. "That isn't like you, though I do love the scent of your tobacco. If I didn't know better, I'd think you were skittish about the coming season."

He studied her, thinking of Malachi. Wishing he'd make a move to see her. He half regretted mentioning him after Lake Lanark, realizing the false hopes he'd raised. "The season doesn't worry me. I'm thinking of your grandfather."

She nodded. "Everything hinges on him—and always has. This tragedy with Charlotte Ashburton has taken a toll. I sometimes think that alone caused his collapse. But Bennett has always been a thorn."

Their eyes met, held, as a commotion in the hall signaled someone's approach. Ellie appeared in cape, bonnet, and gloves, shutting the door behind her as a cold draft crept in.

Izannah stood. "Mama, are you going to town?"

"New Hope." Her expression, usually so genial, was fraught with alarm. "A servant has brought word that Wren is ill. I'm reluctant to leave Da, but I must. With the season starting so soon . . ." Her gaze swung to James.

"I'll go with you," he said, already on his feet at her appearing.

"No—please. I appreciate the offer, but you're both needed

here. Besides, my confrontation with Andra won't be pretty and is long overdue."

Izannah stepped toward her. "What is the matter with Wren?"

"She's come down with a fever, her maid says. I pray it's only the influenza, though that in itself is cause for worry. With her father away . . ." She kissed Izannah hurriedly and bade James farewell with a look. "I don't know when I'll return. Chloe has just been fed and is asleep."

"I'll see to Chloe," Izannah answered, following her mother out without a backward glance at him.

James moved to a window, fighting the urge to follow, as rain splashed the pane and marred his view. A sodden coach and groom were waiting by the mounting block, and soon the vehicle lumbered away, wheels splattering mud as it shrank from sight.

Setting his smoking pipe aside, he bowed his head. His pulse was racing in an odd pattern, making it hard to draw an easy breath.

Wren.

Was she overwrought about the season and had fallen ill? If so, he wasn't surprised. He was nearly sick himself anticipating what was to come. He shut his eyes, praying Ellie would summon the doctor if Andra didn't. Andra had a strange Scots stubbornness that sometimes overrode good sense. He feared it would take Ansel's return to set things right in regard to Wren.

Passing a hand over a jaw he'd not bothered shaving, he took up his pipe again but found no pleasure in it. His gaze landed on the morning's *Gazette* riddled with the usual dire news, reminding him of Madder's Mystic Conspiracy. But the predicament downriver paled next to the one he was about to begin in Pittsburgh's drawing rooms.

As long as he kept his feelings in check, acting simply as Wren's escort, the season would move forward and no one would suspect he was falling in love with her. But it would cost him dearly. And he had no idea how the season would end.

22

Someone has gone to the bright golden shore.
Ring the bell softly, there's crepe on the door.

DEXTER SMITH AND E. L. CATLIN

Wren thrust the bedcovers back with leaden arms, amazed that a fever could steal so much strength. Carriage wheels were spinning on the drive, their muffled arrival heard through the window Mim had left open for fresh air. A sick anxiety swirled through her that it might be someone with word about Grandfather. Mim had told her the servants at New Hope, River Hill, and Ballantyne Hall were readying black crepe bands and all the trappings of mourning.

Or might it be Papa? Through the hazy delirium of her fever, she'd prayed Papa would get word and come back. But there always seemed to be a delay.

She made it to her bedchamber door and then the landing on jellied legs. A feminine voice reached her first. Aunt Ellie?

Anger turned her tone almost unrecognizable. Light-headed, Wren sat down atop the highest step, gaze falling to the foyer. With the parlor door ajar she heard every heated word.

"Why all the fuss, Elinor?" Andra's placating was as jarring as Ellie's anger. "You needn't have come. Rowena simply has a slight fever—"

"A *slight fever* is not how the servants described it. Have you even summoned the doctor?"

"I'm prepared to if she worsens today. Personally I think it's a simple case of nerves over the coming ball. This morning her maid said—"

"Her maid? Have you not seen her for yourself?"

"Rowena was sleeping, and I thought it prudent not to disturb her."

The abrupt clanging of a bell brought a maid scurrying, the butler on her heels. Ellie's voice rose again. "Send for the doctor immediately." The door barely closed before the argument resumed. "The blame is yours alone for whatever is ailing her, Andra. It's no secret you've been drilling her—nearly starving and bullying her—for the season. If Miss Criss was here, I'd have her dismissed. Once Ansel gets word of what you've done—"

"What I've done?" The exasperation in Andra's tone suggested she'd thrown her hands into the air. "I've done nothing without Rowena's consent. She's not a child who needs her father. She's five and twenty—it's past time for her to secure a husband and do her part."

"Her part? Does that include rescuing Bennett from his bouts of extravagance and shoring up the Ballantyne fortune? Such conniving would certainly sicken and send me to bed."

"I know nothing of such nonsense." Andra's voice dropped nearly beyond hearing. "She's simply to have a season as befits a Ballantyne. It's as straightforward as that. We can only hope it's far more successful than Izannah's, which was and is still talked about as being a dismal failure."

Wren made it to the door, thrusting it open and bringing the heated exchange to a halt. Both aunts turned toward her in surprise. Caught in the haze of illness, she'd violated another ironclad rule. *It is exceedingly improper to enter a room without knocking.* She read the censure in Andra's eyes. The loving concern in Ellie's.

She leaned into the nearest chair, her fingers clutching the smooth rococo back. "I'm . . . all right." The lie slipped from her lips all too easily. She knew she looked anything but all right. Clad in a dressing gown carelessly tied at the waist, her uncombed hair hanging in tangles, her bare feet cold, she shouldn't have come downstairs. But she had to stop their feuding.

"Wren, we didn't mean to disturb you." Taking her elbow, Ellie guided her to a chair nearest the hearth and tugged on the bell cord. Her words were quiet but firm when a maid appeared. "Some soup and bread, and a hot toddy. I'd also like a bath drawn in Wren's bedchamber, please."

Wren looked past the andirons into the fire as Andra began a stiff withdrawal. "Well, I can see I'm hardly needed. I suppose you'll take Rowena to River Hill next. It seems you're running an infirmary there of late."

"If she'll agree to go, yes." All the ire had washed from Ellie's tone. "I'll let you know what we decide."

The porcelain tub, filled nearly to the brim with steamy water and an abundance of rose-geranium soap, seemed to open the door to recovery. Loosely clad in a camisole, Wren sat by the fire while Aunt Ellie stood behind her and combed out her tangles.

"What lush hair you have, Wren. So like your mother's from what I remember." Gently she tamed every strand, doing what Mim normally did. But Andra had Mim busy elsewhere, and Wren was glad of Ellie's company.

A tray was brought in bearing the requested soup and bread and a hot drink. Handing her the cup, Ellie smiled. "This is the judge's secret remedy for whatever ails us—honey, lemon, hot water, and a wee smirr of Turlock whiskey."

The concoction was strong but not unpleasant, and Wren sipped it slowly. "I can't thank you enough for coming."

Ellie took a seat opposite, drawing her shawl closer about her. "I'm only sorry I didn't arrive sooner."

"Is there any . . . change?"

"No." Her blue eyes glinted with emotion. "Your grandfather is very old and very tired. I think he may still be here because we don't want to let him go."

Wren understood. It had been the same with Mama at the last, holding on for Wren's sake, even Papa's, if not her own. "I don't want to keep you long from River Hill. Chloe needs you—and Granny."

"And you, Wren? I'd like to take you home with me."

The gracious offer felt like a lifeline, but one she couldn't grab hold of. "I wish I could go with you." Wren set down her empty cup, the last of the toddy stealing through her in a warm rush. "But I need to stay and see this through."

"The season, you mean."

"Yes."

"If you're sure . . ."

"Sure as I'll ever be."

Ellie nodded, her lovely face holding a dozen different

emotions. "James will be there for you—and Mim—at every turn, every function. We'll be praying for you behind the scenes. Perhaps, with the Lord's leading, you'll find someone you care for deeply."

The romantic notion seemed more fairy tale. Wren's only concern was that she push past her dread to tomorrow night.

"We'll wait for the doctor's word on whether or not you should attend the opening ball." Ellie looked toward the open dressing room door, where Grandmother's gown hung in restored splendor. "As it stands now, I'm tempted to keep you home, at least for the ball. But we'll pray about matters and see what tomorrow brings."

Home. Such an elusive word. In some respects Wren felt as much an orphan as James Sackett.

"How is she?"

The question was asked before James had put thought behind it. He'd been waiting for word of Wren all morning and had finally gone riding despite the wet weather, just returning to the stables as Ellie's coach pulled beneath the porte cochere.

As he helped her step down, her gaze held his, and for a moment it seemed she saw straight to his heart. "Come inside out of the cold, James, and we'll talk in the judge's study."

A servant took their wraps, ushering them into the empty foyer. All appeared the same as when Ellie had left three hours prior but for Chloe. She could be heard fussing from on high, no doubt waiting to be fed, but they continued on down the hall.

Ellie closed the study door and held her hands out to the leaping fire. "Wren is still ill but determined to go through with her debut."

He nearly groaned. *Determined* was not what he wished for. He'd rather she be expectant. Willing. Though he didn't blame her for balking. "It's not too late to call off the whole affair."

She looked at him again, as if sensing his reluctance. "How are you feeling about being her escort?"

"I'll do whatever I can to ensure she has a successful season." Tension wound inside him tight as a steel spring as he realized he was being less than honest about his own involvement. "If I sense she's unwell at the Mellons' ball, I'll make our regrets and return her to New Hope."

"It's not just the state of her health that concerns me," Ellie confessed. Taking a seat in the judge's chair, she spoke in that gently candid way she had. "My fear is that she's entering a world where things are not what they seem. Wren is very trusting—naïve. She may fall in love with the first man who pays her any attention, never imagining that there are those who will court her for far less noble reasons. If it weren't for you, James, I'd insist she forego the season altogether."

"There are a few good men—" he began.

"Very few, I'm afraid.'

"Not all are fortune hunters is what I'm saying."

"I want you to keep me apprised as the season progresses. We owe it to Ansel especially. If anything should go awry . . ." The anxiety in Ellie's eyes heightened his own. "If you sense she's foundering or overwhelmed, we'll put an end to this no matter what others might say."

"You have my word."

At his reassurance she brightened. "We'll pray there's someone just right for her, someone who loves her for who she is aside from the Ballantyne name and fortune." She reached for a discarded shawl on a near chair and draped it round her shoulders as Chloe's cries reached a crescendo. "Now if you'll excuse me, I'm needed upstairs."

"I'll be at the levee."

At the door she turned round, her expression soft. "I trust you implicitly, James. Our Wren is in your capable hands."

23

*It is a truth universally
acknowledged, that a single man
in possession of a good fortune, must
be in want of a wife.*

JANE AUSTEN

The bedchamber smelled of new wood and pristine paint, not the leather and Florida Water he was used to. As he stood in front of a massive looking glass, Malachi's cold fingers found the new linen of his stock soft as lamb's wool as he attempted a proper knot. Behind him the fire crackled merrily in the grate, the rain danced on the newly shingled roof above his head, and his spirits rose with every tick of the mantel clock.

Tonight I might well meet my bride.

The thought had him half smiling at his reflection as if testing his appeal, something he'd never considered seriously till now. What did women find pleasing? He was simply a railroad baron who reeked of stocks and bonds and loans. Cameron men were notoriously industrious, not charming.

He was no match for James Sackett with his gallant good looks and sophistication.

A knock at the door turned him round, and he gave a gruff greeting, sure it was Ellis. But Mina thrust open the door instead, satisfaction on her face at the sight of him in full evening dress, the gold solitaire cuff links she'd given him flashing in the firelight.

"You look surprised to see me," she said, shutting the door after her.

"It's not every day a man's aunt appears in his bedchamber."

"Where else was I to go? Yours is the only working hearth in this hulk of a house. And what a roaring fire it is!" She took a look around. "Splendid furnishings. Straight from Philadelphia, did you say? I see you're making this into your sitting room and office too."

"Just until the other fireplaces are finished."

"Where is Ellis?"

"Probably lost."

She laughed. "I nearly was. This place is echoing. You really must have a butler and a housekeeper."

"When I'm wed I will."

"Ah, welcome words." She was practically glowing. "I can hardly wait to hear how you fare tonight. The ball begins at what—eight? You mustn't be late. The Mellons like their guests to be on time. And you must make allowances for coaches getting stuck in the mud. The weather is frightful."

"That didn't stop you."

She smiled and looked down at her sodden boots. "I've finally moved into the gatehouse—a mere stone's throw away. Your grandfather wanted to come, but I insisted he stay by the fire. Having Silas Ballantyne abed is tragedy enough."

The mention dimmed Malachi's enthusiasm a notch. Some-

228

how it seemed wrong to dance and make merry when a good man lay dying. He turned back to the mirror, reminded of his father. If Mina was thinking the same, she gave no evidence of it, moving to a window as if looking for his waiting coach.

"Word is Silas wants to be buried in Scotland," she finally said.

His hands stilled on his cravat. He understood the desire. The Camerons had a long history there, as did the Ballantynes. Though Pittsburgh had many merits, Scotland had a hold like no other. "Scots roots go deep."

"I suppose . . ." She pulled away from the window long enough to circle him. "Let me have a last look at you." Snatching up a clothes brush, she smoothed away a speck of lint on his coat sleeve. "Let's not speak of morbid things on such a promising night."

"Actually, dwelling on mortality makes me even more eager to win a bride."

Her brown gaze held a warning. "Just don't let impatience deprive you of the proper wife. The proper mother of your children."

"Do you have someone in mind?"

"I'd be a fool if I said yes, Malachi. You're quite capable of choosing for yourself, provided I approve of the final selection."

He slid a hand through his freshly washed hair, setting it awry and making her grimace. "You make wife hunting sound so . . . heartless."

"It can be nothing else with so much at stake. You're not a common tradesman who can marry some local lass at will. You're choosing the future mistress of Cameron House, the wife of the owner of the Pennsylvania Railroad, not to mention that grand townhouse of yours in Edinburgh."

"Sometimes I wish I was a mere roustabout on the levee who only cared about his pay and his supper."

"Don't be ridiculous! That mere roustabout might say the same of you. The grass is always greener, remember." Reaching up, she made a quick pass over his unruly hair before he stepped away from her.

"Wish me luck." The words were more flippant than he intended. Luck had little to do with it. *Whoso findeth a wife findeth a good thing, and obtaineth favour of the* LORD . . .

He firmly believed in Providence, the God who made marriage, the originator of romance. For the first time in his life he wanted to fall headlong into it, wallow in something other than grief and regret. Since talking with James at Lake Lanark, he'd been pondering. Praying. He wanted a fuller life, a richer, shared life, with the hope of children to come.

He wouldn't settle for anything less.

"Oh, cousin . . ." In the hushed dressing room, Izannah seemed so overcome that Wren suspected something was amiss.

Looking down at the Spitalfields silk gown, Wren smoothed a pleat with gloved hands and searched for some flaw before she met Izannah's eye.

"The gown is exquisite . . . You're exquisite. Like candy in a confectionery."

Till now Mim hadn't said a word, busy as she'd been with every button and hook. She stood back, taking Wren in from the top of her head to the toes of her slippers. "Oh, aye! Yer going to set the heather on fire, ye are!"

Wren smiled, the flutter inside her never settling as the clock crept nearer eight. Raising a careful hand, she touched the curls Mim had so carefully arranged and stole a last look in the cheval glass.

Encircling her neck and wrists were Grandmother's heirloom pearls. Imbued with a honeyed hue, they complemented the silk of her gown with its overlay of tulle and lace. She looked like—what had Izannah said?—candy in a confectionery. She smelled of something called Honeysuckle Rose from Yardley of London. Even her shoes with their tiny silk rosettes seemed too lovely to touch the ground.

"Yer aunt and Miss Criss are waiting below in the parlor." Mim expelled a breath and fetched Wren's fan off the dressing table. "And the curtain coach has been brought round."

Wren looked longingly at the bed, feeling so worn out from the ordeal of dressing she didn't know how she'd make it to the hall. "Would you . . . pray with me?"

Izannah reached for her with such emotion Wren was certain she was thinking of James and wishing she could go in her place. "You're in good hands, Wren. Just rely on your able escort and Mim."

They bowed their heads, each murmuring an earnest prayer and a hurried amen before a timid knock sounded. A maid stood on the threshold, a long, slender box in her arms. "For Miss Rowena," she said.

When Wren looked at her blankly, Izannah went forward. "Is there a note?"

"Nary a one," the maid said apologetically.

Izannah passed the box to Wren. Bewildered, she opened the lid and uncovered a profusion of fresh roses. "Summer roses . . . in November?" She bent her head, breathing in their sweet fragrance. Beneath the roses rested a jeweler's case. Couched in white satin was a tiny silver vase with a mother-of-pearl handle.

"A tussie-mussie," Mim said, wonder in her tone. "And a bonny one at that."

Wren stared at the gift, unsure of what to make of it. "I've never seen the like."

"It's also called a posey holder," Izannah told her. "You can hold it in hand or wear it pinned to your bodice while dancing." With a confidence and ease denied Wren, Izannah filled the vaselike container with a few of the roses. "According to *The Language of Flowers*, pink roses symbolize passion."

"*Och*, passion! Ye've an admirer already!" Mim crowed as Izannah pressed the gift into Wren's hand. "And ye've nae yet set foot from the house!"

"A generous gift." Wren tried to smile, not wanting to spoil their excitement.

Izannah squeezed her hand. "Wren, you're not still ill, are you? Mightn't it be better if you were to send your regrets tonight?"

"And waste all my hard work?" Mim gave a mock growl. "Nae on yer life."

"I'm ready." The reassuring words rang hollow. Taking a step in her snug, never-worn slippers, Wren focused on the bedchamber door.

"I wish your father was here." Izannah spoke what was on Wren's heart. "I don't think he'd recognize you dressed as you are. A true lady."

She smiled, though the mention of Papa made her more melancholy. He'd never seemed so far away. She sensed his displeasure even at a distance, recalled every syllable of his tersely worded letter. But for the moment it was more James who filled her thoughts. She mustn't misstep, mustn't embarrass him in any way . . .

"We'd best make haste downstairs or ye'll be late," Mim reminded her.

Wren readied herself for the inspection to come, but once she was in the parlor, neither Miss Criss nor Andra could find a flaw.

"Mother should be here. A shame she's still at River Hill." Andra fingered a lace sleeve, grudging admiration in her gaze. "It remains to be seen what's to be made of your gown."

"We'll know soon enough. The details will be in every newspaper come morning." Miss Criss motioned for Wren to turn round. Slowly. Gracefully.

She did as requested, longing to sit down in the coach and collect her tattered feelings for a few quiet minutes. The fever seemed to hover, riding high on her cheekbones, or so the parlor mirror in back of Miss Criss told her.

When Wren pivoted, she saw James in the shadows. He stepped into the light, returning her light-headedness tenfold. At his slight bow she remembered to curtsey, the practiced move coming far more easily than it had at first.

"Good evening, Miss Ballantyne."

"Good evening, Mr. Sackett."

Though her gaze fastened on her posey holder and the lovely roses, the impression he'd just made remained. Black coattails. Flawless cravat. Every inch of him as polished as silver. Even the hair that loped and curled about his collar seemed tamed tonight, every strand in place.

"We should go." His voice cut through the sudden lull, reminding them it was nearing eight o'clock and they must travel to the outskirts of Pittsburgh to reach the Mellon mansion.

Wren's gaze swept to Mim, who was waiting with her cape. Oh, but she was thankful to have such a plucky maid. Being alone in the coach with James Sackett was as daunting as the coming ball. His unnerving calm was rattling, somehow reminding her of how out of step she felt with everything, nearly tripping over everyone's expectations.

Once inside the leather and velvet interior, she sat stiffly corseted, Mim and James just across, her own cologne colliding with a masculine scent she had no name for. Her full skirts, the tick of her pulse, seemed to fill the carriage like a fourth party. All was quiet. Too quiet. When the lights of Pittsburgh came into view through the cracked shutter, a cold clamminess took hold.

Lord, help me not stumble . . . please.

24

*To be fond of dancing was a certain
step towards falling in love.*

JANE AUSTEN

The stone lions at the entrance to the Mellon mansion seemed
to carry a subtle warning. Openmouthed, they looked ravenous, ready to devour those who failed the test of decorum,
the gauntlet of etiquette waiting inside. Stepping carefully
from the coach, Wren nearly slipped on the ice-slicked walk.
If not for James's steady hand, the evening might have ended
before it began. Behind her, Mim clutched the short train of
her polonaise skirts till they cleared the wide stone steps.

Inside the brilliantly lit foyer, beeswax and blossoms
stormed Wren's senses. Proud white lilies adorned countless
crystal vases, and twin chandeliers shimmered with candles in
the ballroom just beyond. Mim soon disappeared with their
wraps, and Wren felt a sudden wrench. Thankfully James
remained at her side, his extended arm the resting place for
her gloved hand.

"Just follow my lead, Wren . . . and remember to breathe."

At his use of her name, she wanted to smile up at him, thank him for taking such care of her, reassure him she was fine. Only she wasn't fine. She was trembling like the candle flames all around them, barely aware of the butler announcing them as they came to stand on the threshold of the glittering ballroom.

At the pressure of James's fingers, she gave a small curtsey, then rose to face a tall, bejeweled woman beside a florid-faced bear of a man in full evening dress. Raising a monocle, Mr. Mellon surveyed them as his wife spoke.

"Why, Mr. Sackett! You've come off the river . . . and you're escorting a lovely young woman whose name I don't know."

James smiled and turned toward Wren. "Allow me the pleasure of introducing Miss Rowena Ballantyne, Pittsburgh's best-kept secret."

"So Silas has another enchanting granddaughter? I had no idea . . ." The rest of Mrs. Mellon's reply was lost in the stiff yet effusive embrace she gave him. "You remember our daughter Alice." With a flutter of her fan, she directed their attention to a young woman to their left, her dark gaze firmly planted on Wren.

In a gesture Wren could only describe as gallant, James took Alice Mellon's hand and kissed the back of her gloved fingers. Something akin to envy slid through her at the smug pleasure in Alice's expression and her polite, "So good of you both to come."

With a nod James moved Wren farther into the ballroom. "Well done, Miss Ballantyne. We've just navigated the first set of rapids."

"Well done indeed, Mr. Sackett," she whispered when well out of earshot, "but according to the rules of polite society and genteel behavior, it is exceedingly improper to embrace anyone upon greeting, even a baby."

He sobered, his eyes never leaving the ballroom floor. "Athena Mellon is the arbiter of the rules, Wren. She doesn't abide by them. She simply exists to make sure you do."

"She seems very taken with you."

"I've shuttled her up and down the Mississippi enough times. But remember, much of what you see here is artifice—all for show."

"Then I can never let my guard down."

"Never."

The beautifully appointed room was huge, the crowd more so. Costly gowns. Ropes of pearls. Jewels of every color. Stiff white shirtfronts and snug-fitting coats. Even a tiara or two.

An embarrassment of riches.

"Can we find a quiet corner?" Her gentle question brought his green gaze back to her, still wary. Did he suspect she still had a slight fever? "Just so I can catch my breath?"

"You don't have to do this."

"Oh, but I do," she murmured, silencing the query in his eyes.

He looked away, his handsome features resuming stoic lines. With the slightest pressure of his hand on her back, he moved her into a semi-secluded alcove adjoining the ballroom. "You're not still ill, are you?"

Her heart caught at the tender question. *More heartsick,* she couldn't say. *I'm just wishing you didn't look so fine, every little detail turning my head.* "I'm feeling a bit . . . *skitterie.*"

"*Skitterie.* A Scots word." Reaching out, he buttoned the pearl clasp of her glove, the brush of his fingers causing her bare wrist to tingle. "Remember what I told you . . . at River Hill."

Remember? Trouble was she couldn't forget. It played in her head and heart like a haunting lament.

Falling in love with you would be easy. You are a very beautiful woman, and a very charming one.

Bringing the tussie-mussie closer, she breathed in the fragrance of the roses as if they could replace his virile scent. She was beginning to understand why Izannah cared for him. She knew full well why he cared for Izannah. And while she didn't covet what was between them, she dared to hope she'd find the same kind of love in time.

"The sooner we begin, the sooner it ends," he told her.

She faced the ballroom again, leaning on his extended arm. The musicians were readying their instruments, a trio of violinists among them. Beneath the tight confines of her damp bodice, the little wren was hidden but failed to bring comfort, poking her skin like a wayward corset wire.

More people flooded in, each announced by the butler, their names and faces a sorry jumble in her weary mind. They resembled little more than the wax figures Mama had told her about in a London museum. Is that how she appeared to them? Stiff? Polished perfection?

James's low voice pulled her to the present. "Do you remember what's to come?"

Did she? The opening waltz was struck, and she tried to relax in its gentle rhythm, the warm familiarity of his arms. James held her so carefully—like she was glass and might shatter—with a cool, gentlemanly ease she found all too pleasing. Young men ringed the room, poised to pencil in their initials on the empty dance card dangling from her wrist.

When the waltz's final notes faded, she found herself surrounded by a polite hustle of dance partners. Surprised, she stepped back, bumping into James as he stood slightly behind her. When she looked up again, she met eyes that were a familiar, searching brown.

The first initials on her dance card were MC.

An awkward shyness gripped her as James looked on and Malachi Cameron bent over her outstretched hand. "Miss Ballantyne."

His voice was more rumble, deeper than she remembered that day along the road. She wanted to smile, respond in kind, but the next set began, a brisk quadrille, snatching the words away as he led her out.

When they slowed to a walk, his expression turned entreating. "Before we go another step, I need to ask your forgiveness."

She looked at him in question and then they separated, the intricate turns stalling conversation. But he resumed his plea at the next joining of their gloved hands.

"I need to beg your pardon for that day you rode home in my carriage, when you were taken round to the servants' quarters." His rugged features were swarthy. "I'll lay the blame at my driver's door. I did think your dress and your fiddle too fine."

Was he embarrassed, this important railroad man? "I only remember you were kind enough to give me a ride."

"I had no idea you were a Ballantyne."

She smiled to ease him. "Sometimes I forget I am."

He led her off the parquet floor to the refreshment table, but there was barely time enough to take a sip of punch. Her gaze roamed the burgeoning room. James was lost in the crowd, though Mr. Cameron was all too close.

The orchestra struck a reel, and she glanced at her dance card, eyes widening. He'd penciled in his initials so large he'd claimed the next set. "If you lay track like you claim dances, Mr. Cameron, you'll soon cross the continent."

He chuckled, his eyes crinkling at the corners. "I plan on it, yes." His hand was warm upon her waist, his movements this time more sure, as if he was rusty and simply in need of a turn or two about the room. "Lovely flowers, by the way." He was looking at the tussie-mussie Mim had fastened to her bodice, nestled in the daring décolleté of her gown. "Do you have an admirer already, Miss Ballantyne?"

She lowered her eyes. Did she? "I don't know who sent them, truth be told."

"Nor do I . . . but I envy the man who did."

Flushing, she realized she'd just given him reason to pursue her in earnest by revealing the competition. Though Malachi Cameron was minding his manners in this heated, lavish ballroom, she sensed he had more disdain for it than admiration. His hesitancy when he returned her to James's side suggested he was none too pleased with that either.

A second partner claimed her, and she left the two men behind, anticipating the midnight hour and the ordeal to come. Winded, smile frozen in place, she had little appetite, though if James was her supper partner she might get through the elaborate meal.

If Alice Mellon would stop boring a hole in her with her black stare.

As the clock struck twelve, the butler announced supper and opened double doors onto a space nearly as large as the ballroom. Awed, Wren took in the profusion of silver and plate upon a dining table that seemed without end. Footsore from hours of dancing, she watched the assemblage file in, the Mellons foremost, biting her cheek against a sigh of relief as James led her to her place.

Four seats down sat Alice Mellon and her escort, an attorney for the Ballantynes, so James told her. Wren had lost track of Malachi Cameron. There were a number of charming young women to choose from. Just who had he partnered with for supper?

She took a discreet look about but failed to find him, gaze halting on the elaborate centerpiece instead. Six ice swans graced the length of the table, the flicker of candlelight calling out all their melting elegance. She was cast back to the twin swans gliding in River Hill's garden on a late summer's eve far removed from this one.

Gloves in her lap, she turned her attention to the small menu situated between her and James. Breast of Partridge. Fillet of Beef. Timbale of Shortbread. Fruits. Glacés. Assorted cakes.

But first the dreaded oysters.

Set before them by white-gloved waiters, the detested offering was nested in a bed of greenery on monogrammed china. Squeamish, she watched James pick up the proper utensil without a moment's hesitation. Fingering her own fork, she prayed as she took a bite, distracted by the ripple of astonishment rounding the immense table.

James leaned in, voice low. "You may well find this dish to your liking after all, Miss Ballantyne."

Befuddled, she sat back, blinking at a second detested oyster bearing a lustrous black pearl.

"Magnificent!" One guest held hers up to the light. "Our ingenious hostess is full of surprises. Mrs. Mellon has indeed outdone herself!"

Taken aback by such gushing, Wren's gaze swept round the table. Was *every* woman present the proud owner of a pearl? If so, when strung together, the gems would make a necklace of extraordinary length. Mrs. Mellon seemed not to mind all the fuss. She displayed the largest pearl of all at table's end.

As the murmuring died down, the oyster plates were whisked away. The unparalleled moment passed. A swarm of strange dishes and wines were set in front of her, and Wren willed her nerves to settle.

Another hour crept by, then two. Would the night never end? No one else appeared to make note of the time. But why bother? For now the men were being feted with cigars rolled in one-hundred-dollar bills.

In the dwindling candlelight, James held his between thumb and forefinger before putting it in his breast pocket. The grim slant of his mouth made her think he was struggling in the midst of such extravagance. Perhaps thinking of the orphans. His humble beginnings. Or hers.

Alice Mellon's eyes were on them again, lingering longest on James before moving on. As if she knew Wren was nothing more than a pretender, an imposter. Despite her Ballantyne name and her Spitalfields silk and the newly acquired black pearl.

25

Where there is great love, there are always wishes.

WILLA CATHER

Despite the late hour at the Mellons' ball, Malachi came awake just after dawn. Light caressed the Wilton carpet with pale fingers, calling out the rich dyes and intricate design. His sleepy gaze slid to the ridiculous cigar on his bedside table, and he groaned, something not allowed the night before when surrounded by a great many self-satisfied, smoking men. In the heat of the moment he'd considered riding straight to River Hill. He might yet. If Izannah Turlock would have him, he'd end the social charade.

Rolling over, his head thundering from the strange mix of spirits at the endless midnight supper, he lay on his back, scattered events cluttering his conscience.

Lilly Alexander's vexing flirtatiousness.

Judge Caldwell's tasteless jokes.

Ice swans and expensive cigars.

Rowena Ballantyne.

When the butler had announced her at the start of the ball, his high spirits had sunk to his shoes, their meeting along the road all too fresh. She'd been so gracious about his apology. No other woman in the room, mistaken for a servant, would have been half as forgiving. But she didn't seem to care. He liked that she didn't.

Within a quarter of an hour he'd dressed and was heading down the sloping drive to the newly constructed gatehouse rimmed with young oaks and elms shivering in a biting wind. A maid let him in, her cheery good morning as welcome as the tattie scones turned out by his Scots cook. The aroma of coffee filled the small foyer, luring him to the dining room. There his grandfather sat at the head of the table, Mina to his left, both their faces framed with surprise.

"What? Dancing till the wee small hours and up soon after? I didn't think we'd see you till supper!" Mina eyed him suspiciously. "You didn't leave the ball early, did you?"

"No, though I was sorely tempted." He tossed his hat onto a near chair. "I have business to take care of this morning and am expecting Ellis to come in by stage at long last. But first, why didn't you tell me about Rowena Ballantyne?"

A sly penitence stole across her pale features. Observing it, his grandfather chuckled. "Found a lady to your liking already, Malachi? And a Ballantyne at that?"

"Have some coffee," Mina interrupted, passing the sugar and cream. "I promise I won't ask you any questions about last night till you've had your breakfast."

Cullen Cameron winked, eyes shining beneath his thatch of white hair. "Don't let Mina fool you, Malachi. We're far more stuffed with news about the Mellons' ball than breakfast."

With a wave of her hand Mina motioned to the stack of

newspapers in the chair next to her. "Even you were mentioned, Malachi—and quite favorably too. You're being lauded as the catch of the season."

"My personal fortune, you mean."

Her smile remained undimmed. "No one in Pittsburgh was expecting you . . . or Wren."

"Wren?" He swallowed some coffee and glanced at the papers. "Why is she called Wren?"

"Apparently Ansel has called her that since she was small. It seems to fit well with her nature and upbringing in Kentucky."

"You talk as if you know her."

"Oh, I suppose having tea with her at New Hope on occasion counts for something."

He fixed his gaze on the far window. *Rowena . . . Wren.* What did James call her? "Rowena Cameron does have a ring to it."

Her eyes flared. "Surely you jest! You've only just met her."

"Isn't that why men and women go to these marriage markets? To meet? Marry?"

"Marriage markets indeed," Mina scoffed as he gave into temptation and reached for the *Gazette.* "Don't be crass, Malachi."

Still chuckling, Cullen pushed his chair back and rose as smoothly as his arthritic form would allow. "Let me know just who you and Mina decide on." With another wink, he reached for his cane. "I'm late for my morning walk with the dogs. I'll say a prayer for you and your intended as I go."

The door shut behind him, and Mina opened her mouth, preparing to pepper him with questions, but he silenced her with a look and returned to the paper. Splashed across the front page was a boldface headline.

SEASON OPENS WITH SURPRISES.

Aye, pearls and cigars. He read on.

Ballantyne Belle Sure to Steal Hearts.

Beneath this, the name of every debutante was listed in a long column, Rowena Ballantyne leading. He felt a swell of satisfaction that she was first. She had a lovely name. So very Scottish.

"You needn't read any further." Mina drained her cup and leaned back in her chair. "Every other word is about the mysterious Miss Ballantyne—what she wore, how she danced, who her escort was, the state of her fortune. They go on and on about James too. What a lovely pairing they made and all that. They even make mention of Silas."

"They have no shame, drawing attention to a dying man." He turned to the business section all too eagerly.

"It makes for riveting reading nonetheless," she said stubbornly.

Before he could argue, a brimming breakfast plate was set before him. He murmured his thanks, withdrawing the expensive cigar from his pocket. "Give this to Mrs. McFee and tell her I don't expect her to smoke it."

With a nod the maid disappeared, and he heard a hoot of satisfaction coming from the kitchen.

"You spoil your cook," Mina told him, setting her napkin aside.

"I'll spoil her all I like. I had a devil of a time convincing her to leave Edinburgh and come here, if only for the winter." Breakfast nearly forgotten, he turned back to the society page, focusing on one telling line.

Miss Ballantyne performed with such grace in the ballroom she drew every eye. Indeed, her dance card was insufficient to hold all the names of her admirers.

Reading it, he felt his pulse rise. Like he'd been thrust into the middle of some feverish contest, the competition fierce, the prize unattainable. He was used to winning, to getting what he wanted. Had his father felt the same challenge in his pursuit of Elinor Ballantyne, Izannah's mother? Before he'd been turned aside for a Turlock?

Gently Mina tugged the paper from his hand. "Your breakfast is getting cold. I'll be glad to tell you the highlights."

He returned to his plate, thoughts suspended between Wren and James.

"Simply put, Rowena Ballantyne is *the* debutante of the season, an honor which will no doubt continue at the musical soiree given by the Alexanders on Wednesday next."

He forked a bite of egg, counting the days. Dreading them. The Alexanders were nearly as pretentious as the Mellons.

Mina filled the silence. "She's something of a violin virtuoso."

"Yes, that she is," he replied, remembering their memorable carriage ride.

"Oh?" Mina leaned forward, curiosity catching fire. "How would you know? Is there something you're not telling me?"

He cleared his throat. "A great many things."

"Really, Malachi, I wish you'd be more forthcoming."

"No need. You said you'd tell me the highlights."

She sighed. "Rowena Ballantyne is simply a dear, bewildered young woman deprived of her mother and home, thrust into a wealthy world she cares little about."

The words softened him. Made him put down his fork. He'd sensed something sad about her along the dusty road that day, fiddle and baggage in hand. The lament she'd played in the carriage came from a place soul-deep and grieving. He knew that all too well.

"What are her father's plans?" he asked. "Is Ansel here to stay?"

"I hope so. At the moment he's away on Ballantyne business, which is why James is acting as her escort. Since assuming charge of the ironworks, Ansel hasn't much time for anything else."

The complaint buried in her words caught his notice. "Did Ansel give approval for his daughter to have a season?"

"I don't think so." She reached for the sugar as a maid refilled her teacup. "But I believe he'd be delighted by her success, the way she's charmed society."

"For one night, anyway." He fought back the sarcasm in his tone. Society was as fickle as the rise and fall of railroad stock.

"Don't be so dour, Malachi. I trust you danced with her."

"Twice," he said. "In a row."

"Back to back?" she sputtered. "But that's simply not done!"

"No one said a word."

Her smug smile returned. "Because you're a Cameron and might run them over with a train."

Grinning, relishing the thought, he returned to his breakfast. "Speaking of trains, I'm expecting word of a possible merger involving the Baltimore and Ohio. Society is the farthest thing from my mind."

Society. But not Rowena Ballantyne.

Standing by his office window, Ealer at work behind him, James scanned the packets lying in port, his unease rising like the rivers at flood stage. Only a few steamers were still plying the upper Mississippi this late in the season, the *Rowena* among them. His replacement, John Gunniston, who was committed to the lower Mississippi run with Captain Dean, wouldn't see Pittsburgh till the spring thaw.

James's focus widened and took in the pewter surface of the Monongahela. Under noon skies it shimmered like a silk skirt as it slowly turned to ice. Though his time in port had just begun, he kept thinking of his quarters in the New Orleans garden district, lush with bougainvillea and bird of paradise in late fall. Already he was chafing to return to the pilothouse, where he was isolated and in control, able to change direction at will. Not lying in port like some sort of target, unable to counter any trouble.

He hissed out a breath as the lad who'd brought him the telegram minutes before faded from sight. The message was fisted in his hand. It wasn't the easy, informative telegram Dean usually sent that shrank the miles between them, telling of river conditions and cargo and the like. This message held fear and fury and warning.

"P-pardon, sir. It's about quitting t-time and I w-wanted to ask about the M-Mellons' ball."

Turning toward him, James tried to hide his disquiet, but Ealer was looking at him—looking at the crumpled telegram—like he suspected. "The evening was uneventful." The words fell flat in the silence. "Except for expensive cigars and pearls in oysters."

"D-did you d-dance, sir?" At James's nod, he asked, "And M-Miss Ballantyne—d-did she fare well?"

"It would seem so."

Ealer returned to counting passenger receipts, leaving James to dwell on Wren. When she'd come into New Hope's parlor in her beautiful gown, so wanting to please, to do the Ballantynes proud, he'd felt wildly and unaccountably possessive of her. He was doubly undone when he realized she seemed to be seeking his approval. As if it mattered to her what he thought, hope shining in her eyes. He wanted to tell her she'd already won him over long ago, the moment she stepped into the pilothouse. He wanted to guard her tender heart and untried emotions.

He wanted to take Bennett by the throat.

Only the shock of the telegram had driven her from his mind. And now, despite Dean's dire words, she'd snuck in again, returning him to the night of the ball, where no fewer than a dozen men had vied for her attention. Even Malachi had done the unthinkable and claimed two dances. But Wren was too naïve to make much of the gaffe, and society too enamored with the Camerons to make a fuss.

Malachi . . . and Wren. He'd been willing to wager they'd meet and give each other little more than a passing glance. But somehow she and Malachi had already met. Just when that happened James didn't know, leaving him to a wilderness of wondering.

"Are you c-coming to the M-Monongahela House for s-supper?" Ealer was at the back door, ready to depart.

"No," he said, glancing again at the telegram. "I'll be at River Hill."

26

If I loved you less, I might be able to talk about it more.

JANE AUSTEN

Izannah met him at the door, joy filling her face. "Oh, James! You've come in time! It's Grandfather—he's back. Since yesterday he's been steadily improving. The doctors can scarce believe it!"

The sudden news was the last he'd expected to hear. In a heartbeat James swung like a pendulum between hope and fear. Not bothering to remove his hat or coat, he went up the stairs on Izannah's heels. The bedchamber door that had been closed, barring them entry, was open wide. Was Silas truly back? Or only rallying before death took him? Ellie's laughter and Eden's joyous voice reassured him.

In the shadowed room, the big bed was empty. Silas sat by the window in a dressing gown, looking older and thinner but upright. James half believed not even the shadow of death daunted Silas Ballantyne.

"Well, Da," Ellie exclaimed as she and Eden left the room,

"we've monopolized you long enough. James is here. Perhaps you're in need of some masculine company."

Silas turned. Smiled. "How goes it, James?" His voice was a bit hoarse, more an echo of its former strength. But the easy companionship they'd shared in years past snuck in again, banishing awkwardness. "I've been remiss, the doctors tell me, lying abed for a month."

Throat tight, James clasped Silas's outstretched hand. "I'd say you deserved the rest, busy as you've been ninety years or better."

Silas's chuckle broadened to a deep cough. Tensing, James looked toward the open door, expecting Eden or Ellie to rush back in. When they didn't, James handed him a glass of water, slightly opaque from the medicine he'd been taking.

Sinking back in his chair, Silas took a drink and drew in a shaky breath. "Time is against me, James, and I feel the need to know some things. How is being in port for the winter?"

"Well enough." The telegram in his pocket made a mockery of his calm words. "You needn't worry on that score."

"Business matters are all in hand, I suppose."

James hesitated. The new Ballantyne-Cameron alliance was the farthest thing from his mind. "Everything is proceeding smoothly, yes."

"How about matters downriver with Gunniston and Dean?"

"The same." He thought of all that Silas had missed in the month he'd lost. The news had never been so inflammatory. "The papers are full of war talk. The slavery issue must have an end."

"I won't be here to see it, but I trust you will do the right thing, the honorable thing. You always have. I have a feeling you'll enlist if it comes to that, use your piloting skills to benefit the cause." His voice faded though his gaze stayed firm. "If you'll humor an old man, I'll hazard a little meddling and ask that you give serious thought to settling down."

Blood rushed to James's face. Even at ninety, Silas was a very shrewd man. Though his body was failing, his mind remained unbroken. Did he sense the struggle buried within him? His growing feelings for Wren? His desire to see Izannah settled?

"I wish the same for all my grandchildren in time. Marriage. A godly family."

James looked down at his hat, his fingers twisting the brim in a mindless circle. "Two nights ago Wren debuted at the Mellons' ball. I was her escort. Any concerns you have about her future, a husband, are unfounded." Even saying the words tore at him, but he was in so deep he might as well confess all the rest. "I've even spoken with Malachi Cameron about Izannah. He has little time for society and is in need of a wife."

Silas smiled. "Mayhap I should lie abed more often. All seems well." The warm words came slowly, as if forced from a weary place. "And you, James? Are you content to go it alone? Is there no woman with a hold on your heart?"

The persistent question sent him scrambling for an excuse. "I've little to offer, being on the river and going to war, if it comes to that."

"You have a great deal to offer in the interim. Life cannot be lived based on what-ifs, aye?"

It was as near a rebuke as Silas had ever given him, and James felt the sting of it from five feet away. If he ever wanted to dig the telegram out of his pocket, it was now.

I'm a wanted man, he nearly said, wanting to spell out the fear and confusion at war inside him. Silas thought he was protecting James by keeping him in port, never thinking that Pittsburgh had become not a safe haven but a hunting ground. The realization brought a sort of panicked breathlessness, curbed only by bedrock truth. The Almighty was near at hand, strong of hand, well aware of the danger if Silas wasn't.

Wasn't He?

"There's another matter I need to entrust to you once Wren's season ends." Silas set the glass of water down, hand shaking slightly. "Before I took ill, I had plans in place to return to Scotland. I still hope to do so unless the Lord wills otherwise. But if I cannot . . ."

"Of course. Whatever it is, I'll see it done."

"For years I've prayed that the Guarneri violin I sold long ago would be restored to our family. Shortly before we went to Lake Lanark, I received word that a collector in Edinburgh has possession of it. It's being kept in a vault, waiting for us to retrieve it. At a price, of course."

A hefty one, James was willing to wager. Yet for the moment pointed surprise was coursing through him, and gratitude that something that meant so much to a dying man had finally found its way back again.

"I want you to go to Edinburgh and take possession of it. My nephew lives there, the son of my late sister, Naomi. He deserves most of the credit for hunting it down and will be waiting to meet you." His eyes glittered, and he looked at his hands as if recalling the hours he'd spent playing it. "The Guarneri belongs to Wren. She'll appreciate it for the treasure it is and not let it go missing again."

James gave a nod. The thought that it was meant for Wren moved him. But it was more the humble sight of Silas's branded thumbs that whittled away at his composure like a carving tool. He wished Silas had more time. Time enough to hold the Guarneri again. Time enough to give it to Wren himself.

"I've written down instructions for you to withdraw funds from the proper accounts when the time comes, authorizing you to pay the collector upon inspection of the violin." He reached into the pocket of his dressing gown and retrieved a folded paper. "Everything should be in order once you reach Edinburgh."

James glanced at Silas's heavy scrawl. The set amount was staggering. He didn't doubt the violin was worth the price, simply because it was a missing piece of the Ballantynes' past. "If Ansel returns soon, I can sail for Scotland before the season ends."

"Nay, I'll not undo whatever is in place. I have as much trust in you regarding Wren's future as I do the Guarneri's."

"I'll see both done." The only question was when. He'd not anticipated an extended trip, a long ocean voyage. Was this the Lord's provision for him, leading him away from Pittsburgh? From Wren? Scotland was indeed a safe haven, though James rebelled against the thought of going into hiding as Ansel had done.

"Grandfather, what a change!" Bennett's voice rang out, ending their lengthy discussion. For once James was glad of him as he strode into the room and took charge. With a last look at Silas, James bade him goodbye, wondering if and when he'd see him again.

Wren stood in the unfamiliar music room of the Alexanders' mansion overflowing with Pittsburgh's elite. Fans were waving languidly, and lapel pins were winking among the two hundred or so guests gathered for the musical soiree. With the Nightingale perched on her shoulder, she rested in its beloved familiarity, though her bow hand trembled slightly as the crowd swelled. She was beginning to pin a few names to myriad faces, but most stayed a confusion of Mellons and Ewings and Schoonmakers. Buttoned so high and tight, Pittsburgh's leading lights all looked the same.

When Malachi Cameron entered the room, she tried to hide her startled pleasure. He took a discreet seat in the back row beside James, hardly a prime spot for viewing, but both men were so tall it didn't matter. One quick glance and she could clearly see their bearded faces.

Try as she might, she found it hard to adjust to James's new look, though nearly every man in the room followed custom and sported a mustache or beard. She missed the open, honest angles of his features, clean-shaven till now. The beard rendered him a bit more inaccessible and harder to read, if more handsome.

A voice from behind her, clear as a bell, brought the room to attention. "Our final performance prior to intermission is by Miss Rowena Ballantyne . . ."

Ahead of her had been harps and harpsichords, pianofortes and flutes, but nary a violin. She'd caught some of the audience napping throughout the lengthy recital, though she'd been wholly entertained. She'd not let them sleep through her piece if she could help it. "Set the heather on fire," Mim always said. This she meant to do.

Striking a rousing, high E, she launched into a spritely reel full of life and spirit. Élan, Papa would say. With no music or music stand before her, she was able to look about the room, noting with satisfaction those sleepy heads had come awake and side conversations had ceased. Alice Mellon sat in the front row, her closed fan clutched in gloved hands, gaze riveted to Wren. Even the servants positioned at the doors and alcoves seemed to stand at attention.

Who could help but toe-tap to "The Reel of Tulloch" or turn teary at the heartrending "Settler's Lament"? Days—

weeks—of schooling her emotions gave way as she played. When her bow slid off the strings after a trilled finish, there was a marked, stunned silence.

Undaunted, she grabbed hold of the next melody floating through her mind. An openly passionate piece, sure to woo— or raise brows. Closing her eyes, she cradled the Nightingale like the treasure it was. Stiff formality flew.

At the last aching note, she gave a small curtsey to polite, stilted applause. Her high spirits started to ebb. This wasn't Kentucky, where music was met with appreciation heartfelt and deep. This was Pittsburgh, not Cane Run, and she supposed she was wrong to expect it to be.

Throat dry, she tucked the Nightingale away and pulled on her gloves before joining the throng moving toward a sitting room where refreshments were served. In the foyer an immense longcase clock chimed six. Would this breathless watching of the minutes never end?

A touch to her arm turned her around. Behind her was Malachi, open admiration in his bearded face. For a moment they stood like stones lodged in a brook, people eddying around them in little waves.

His eyes held hers. "I couldn't place your second piece."

"The 'Settler's Lament'?" She smiled up at him, thankful for one appreciative listener, at least. "It's an old Scots tune Papa taught me when I was knee-high."

"You play with a great deal of feeling. Much like the Highland fiddlers I've been privy to." Taking her elbow, he led her to a windowed alcove overlooking a rain-drenched garden. A cup of punch rested on the sill.

Gladness sifted through her at his thoughtfulness. "Thank you."

"Actually, it was your escort's doing. Sitting in the back of the room has its advantages, first in line at the refreshment table foremost."

She took a thirsty drink, looking away from him, unsure where James was. Rarely did he stray from her side for long. For now she felt comfortable in the company of this tall, formidable man, his friend.

He cleared his throat. "About that lament . . . It reminds me of the one played at my father's funeral."

Her gaze swiveled back to him. "Your father? I didn't realize . . ."

"I've recently come out of mourning. I'm aware you lost your mother as well."

She felt a sudden shadow. She rarely mentioned Mama.

His eyes were grave. "Does it ever get easier . . . in time?"

The open sorrow in his face touched her. She'd tried hard to forget those first dark days and weeks, when she'd groped about like a blind person in her grief. "At first it's all you think about. Nothing is like it used to be. And then slowly life rights itself, but a part of you stays missing."

"I hope one day to miss him less. Regret less."

Yes. That had been her heart's cry over time, though the soreness inside her stayed fast. She blinked, the slight movement causing a tear to fall and spot her gloved hand. She froze at the slip, feeling one too many eyes on her.

"Forgive me, Miss Ballantyne." Fumbling, he pulled a handkerchief from his waistcoat pocket. "I don't mean to make the evening a melancholy one."

She took the linen cloth, catching a bold hint of spice in its soft folds, so different from James's subtle tobacco and bergamot scent. "Think nothing of it. I like plain speaking. A sorrow shared is a sorrow halved, as they say."

He took the empty cup from her, returning it to the sill.

"I've been considering what you proposed in the carriage that day." His expression held an endearing sincerity, something she craved. "If I came to call on you at New Hope, perhaps you could teach me to play the violin. Private lessons, if you will."

She tipped her head, unsure of him. Was he willing to set aside business to embrace a little music? Swallowing, she cast about for a proper response. "Come as you wish, Mr. Cameron. I'll be waiting."

It wasn't what she'd meant to say. It was what society required of her. And the light in his eyes told her it was what he wanted to hear.

Behind them stood James, his expression inscrutable. "The Alexanders have asked that we play the finale at evening's end, Miss Ballantyne. A duet."

Oh? She'd been prepared to play a solo instead. "Just the two of us, Mr. Sackett?"

"I'm afraid so."

Malachi chuckled, the somber mood of moments before a memory. "This I have to see."

James gave a tug to his cravat as if it was too tight. "I said I would play. I never said I played well."

"I've never heard you play, period," Malachi told him.

"All the better." James looked to Wren. "The question is, what shall we play?"

"A parlor song might be best, one of Stephen Foster's, maybe the one we managed that night at River Hill." Her voice faded as the memory of Grandfather crept in. He was never far from her thoughts. "Or a love song."

Both men were regarding her, faces intent. For a few fleeting seconds it seemed they were asking her to choose, not between songs . . .

But between them.

Startled, she murmured, "I saw the sheet music for 'Sherwood Duet' near the pianoforte."

Malachi was looking past them to their host, who was signaling him from across the room. He excused himself rather reluctantly, leaving them alone.

"Wren . . ." James faced her, blocking her view of Malachi's retreating back. "Mrs. Alexander has asked that you be a little more . . . restrained."

Her eyes widened. "Less impassioned in my playing, you mean."

"In a word, yes."

"Is that why she paired us, Jamie? So you can rein me in?"

"Likely."

"Well, you don't have to look so aggravated about it." She studied him, tongue in cheek. She'd never managed to stir him yet. "I simply thought to bring a little life to a lifeless place."

His steady gaze held hers, reminding her of her manners. "Are you trying to damage your good standing, Miss Ballantyne? Because if you are, your performance here at the Alexanders' is a fine start."

"I see no need to change the way I play for Pittsburgh." Hurt crept into her voice—and a niggling defiance. "Do you?"

"I take no exception to your music or style of playing, but the Alexanders do." He smiled politely as a guest swept past them. "And as their guest you need to tread carefully. That's all I'm saying."

She looked to his shoes, shrinking from the rare rebuke in his tone, embarrassment burning her cheeks. She cared little about the Alexanders' opinion. She cared far too much about James Sackett's. "Then you'd best pick the music lest I make a mess of it."

He took a step nearer, more tender. "I promised the Ballantynes I'll do whatever I can to ensure you have a successful season, Wren. Tonight is no exception."

Unable to meet his eyes, she swallowed down the questions that threatened to swallow her up instead. Just what was his measure of success? Ensnaring a husband who thought she was someone other than she was? Losing herself in the process? Making music so watered down she no longer recognized it or herself?

He looked away from her. "'Sherwood Duet' will make a fitting finish."

She gave a stiff nod. Malachi was coming back to them, working his way across the crowded room. He hadn't upbraided her for her style of playing. On the contrary, he wanted to come for private lessons. Maybe there was more common ground between them than she'd first thought.

The next day the seamstresses convened like a covey of quail, tittering and scattering about, mouths full of pins and fingers occupied with needle and thread. It seemed every one of Grandmother's antique gowns was spread over the dressing room in various stages of reconstruction.

"There's to be a masquerade ball," Andra told her. "We need to decide on your costume. Alice Mellon is coming as Cleopatra, so we don't dare duplicate that. Perhaps you can find out what the other young ladies are wearing when you attend the Ewings' tea this week."

The tea . . . Alice. Wren withheld a sigh, then remembered a fetching dress in *Magasins de Modes*. "I'll be a shepherdess."

"A shepherdess?" Andra frowned, her gaze unblinking. "Rowena, I do not hope to ever understand you. One would think you'd ascribe to grander things, even for a masquerade."

The tea was two days away, the tea gown with its lush overlay of Brussels lace waiting in her dressing room. For now the afternoon was almost upon them when she'd go to the orphanage for lessons, then escape to River Hill. Grandfather, slowly improving, wanted to return home to New Hope. Wren prayed that would come to pass. With a small army of servants waiting on just her and Andra, the old house held an echo, despite the silver salver in the foyer laden with visiting cards. Each caller, Andra reminded her, required a return visit—or a snub.

"Oh, aye, here's another," Mim quipped that afternoon, arranging the cards from most desirable to least. "Mr. Malachi's right at the top. What think ye o' that?"

"I think," Wren said thoughtfully, "that he means to learn to fiddle."

"*Och!*" With a gleeful chuckle, Mim started down the hall. "There'll be some fiddling all right, but it willna involve the violin."

Wren sighed, her thoughts falling back to the musicale. Caught in a vulnerable moment, she and Malachi had found a sort of harmony in their grief, yet all that wove its way across her soul since then was the music she and James had made. He'd acquitted himself well, his robust playing a perfect foil to her finesse, so the papers said. Her pleasure in their pairing was short-lived when she recalled Malachi watching them from the shadows. Intently. Possessively.

Wren examined his glazed card, smaller than her own as custom required, one corner bent, meaning Malachi took the time to deliver it himself rather than sending a servant in his stead. The owner of the Pennsylvania Railroad, bending a card just to be with her.

What would her response be?

27

Do not conceive that fine clothes make fine men, any more than fine feathers make fine birds.

GEORGE WASHINGTON

"Yer missing Mr. James, I ken. 'Tis *ugsome* that gentlemen dinna take tea like ladies do." Across from Wren sat Mim, undisturbed by the coach's rocking and swaying. "Just remember I'll be a stone's throw away in the dressing room making faces at the other maids if ye need me."

Wren nearly smiled, imagining the pecking order below-stairs. She smoothed a lace sleeve as the coach gave a lurch. A basketful of nerves since rising, she tried to approach the four o'clock hour a bit hopeful. There were so many young women in society but precious little time to talk. Might some spark of friendship be found in the Ewings' tearoom?

Her hopes rose at the sight of Lucy Hurst, then fell as Alice Mellon came into view. Though no one had said an ugly word about Alice, least of all James, her sense that Alice meant trouble grew with every function.

"Good afternoon, Miss Ballantyne." Mrs. Ewing's greeting was ever formal, devoid of the warmth Wren craved. "So good of you to come on such a frightful day. I trust you're enjoying your season."

Wren smiled, saying nothing rather than lie. *I'm enjoying pondering the end of it.* What would the high-minded Mrs. Ewing say to that?

A maid came forward to usher her into the tearoom, a circular bower of blue damask lit by crystal chandeliers, drapes drawn against the chill. Lace tablecloths adorned with hothouse blooms and china held untold challenges.

"Hello, Rowena," Lucy greeted her. She was one of a dozen debutantes gathered round an ornate hearth, just far enough from the fire screen to protect their skirts from a stray spark.

"That's a fetching gown, Lucy." Wren meant it. She tried to counter the artifice around her with sincerity whenever she could.

"I daresay it doesn't hold a candle to yours, Rowena." Lucy's British accent rose above the sudden hush. "That shade of rose is quite becoming. I've not seen that sort of embroidery before."

"Miss Ballantyne is fond of wearing her grandmother's relics from the last century." Alice's voice slid into the silence, a shade too shrill. "Don't you read the papers? They're always gushing about her quaint wardrobe. There's scarcely any print left for politics or war talk and the like."

"I don't peruse the papers." Lucy's calm blunted Wren's embarrassment. "I'd rather spend my time embroidering or painting or riding."

"Speaking of riding . . ." With a wave of her fan, Jeannie

French turned the tide of conversation. "There's to be a fox hunt at Paisley Hill next weekend. We ladies are invited to attend, provided we don't prove a distraction. The master of the hunt is Henry Holdship." Her gaze swept to a blushing debutante in peach satin. "And given that fact, I know of at least one Pittsburgh belle who'll be there."

Half a dozen silken bodices shook with suppressed laughter.

Victoria Ewing moved closer, her wide skirts brushing Wren's own. "I'm surprised Preston French or Malachi Cameron aren't in the thick of things, with their English hounds and field hunters."

Wren listened, intrigued. She hadn't known Malachi was a huntsman. She doubted he hunted the sort of game she'd grown up with.

"Oh, the gentlemen you mention are far removed from such mundane matters as that." Jeannie gave a tight smile. "I believe Mr. French is spoken for—and Mr. Cameron would like to be. The coming hunt is probably the farthest thing from their minds." Her gaze touched Wren before dropping demurely. "But it's so early in the season, anything might happen."

Riddled with unease, Wren looked toward the hall as the faint squeal of wheels announced the coming of tea carts. They trundled into the room, serving maids close behind. Wren noted the small groupings of tables, the place cards inked in black. Alice was to sit opposite her, Lucy between them. Wren's stomach soured as she took a seat.

"Ah . . ." Alice eased into her chair and eyed the étagères of iced cakes and tiny sandwiches. "A sumptuous offering. And you, Rowena? Do Kentuckians take tea?" The condescension in her tone was thick as the clotted cream in its silver dish. "I've heard you Southerners are partial to frolics and square dances and such, nothing quite so refined as this."

Lucy's smile was thin. "Did you read that in the papers too, Alice?"

"Heavens no, I was told that by James Sackett himself. Plying the waters as he does aboard the Ballantyne line, he's privy to a great many things beyond Pittsburgh." Alice looked at Lucy, studiously avoiding Wren. "The Ballantynes did well persuading him to be Rowena's escort, though I feared he'd be undone by her playing at the Alexanders' Wednesday night."

Lucy removed her gloves and draped them across her lap. "Mr. Sackett isn't one to be easily undone, Alice. I remember nothing untoward at the musicale."

"Then you didn't see Miss Ballantyne perform solo, only her sedate duet with Mr. Sackett at evening's end."

"True, I arrived late, as our carriage lost a wheel." Lucy cast Wren an apologetic glance. "But neither did I hear any gossip till now."

"Not gossip . . . fact." Alice leaned in, voice low. "Our Kentucky acquaintance seemed to forget herself, playing with a sort of unbridled abandon, almost like a wild Turlock instead of a refined Ballantyne. I'm afraid Mr. Sackett had little choice but to take command of the situation lest she disgrace herself and ruin her chances in polite society—"

"Polite society?" Wren's voice lifted. "I don't know that Pittsburgh is so refined with ladies the likes of you, who make a practice of belittling others to their very faces."

The room hushed.

"I beg your pardon, Rowena Ballantyne. You're hardly one to be speaking to me of what ladies do and don't do." As she took a breath, Alice's fury surged. "One can only hope Mr. Cameron will snap to his senses before the season ends—"

"Malachi Cameron happens to appreciate my music if you do not." Though her jaw clenched, Wren failed to keep

266

her voice steady. It wavered like a loosened fiddle string and threatened to snap. "As for the rest of society, I don't give a fig what they think of me or my playing."

"Well, rest assured, they don't think much of either—"

"Alice, *please*," Lucy said, near tears.

Wren looked to her lap, thinking of James. Had he said such things? In a high-minded sort of way? Making fun of her and her beginnings like Alice implied? The imagined hurt of it sliced deep, to her very bones. Even worse was Alice's suggestion he had somehow been ensnared by Andra and Bennett to act as her escort, as if it was a punishment to do so.

Mrs. Ewing came in, seemingly unaware of the confrontation, though the chilly silence in the room couldn't be ignored. Wren was barely aware of a maid at her elbow pouring tea, likely taking in every word of the unsavory scene to share belowstairs. The tick of her pulse turned thunderous in her ears as she groped for some rule to hold on to.

Never act in anger . . . Learn to speak in a gentle tone of voice . . . Govern yourself and be patient . . . Silence is often more golden than speech.

All rang hollow.

"Would you like a tea cake, Rowena?" Not waiting for a reply, Lucy served her as if nothing had been said, no feelings ruffled, as polite talk resumed around them.

Wren kept her eyes down, a slow awareness filling her. Alice Mellon was smitten with Malachi Cameron. Or perhaps even James. That was why she struck like a rattler, poison in her bite.

Love thine enemies.

Wren nearly winced at the unbidden reminder. Alice was no friend, yet there was truth in what she'd said. Compared to these pampered belles, Wren was common. Unfit to turn a railroad man's head. An embarrassment to her genteel escort. And a hypocrite to boot, sitting at a tea table pretending politeness when she'd rather turn it on end.

A little of Alice's malice had taken root in her own heart, watered and nurtured by missing home and Mama's passing and being thrust into the thick of Pittsburgh.

Lord, forgive me.

She looked up, half hoping to make peace, but Alice was drinking her tea, triumph in her smug expression. She clearly wanted nothing from Wren, least of all an apology.

If this was society, Wren wanted nothing to do with it.

Though bitterly cold, New Hope's chapel held the privacy Wren craved, far from society's stilted drawing rooms and unfriendly teas. Here Andra would never bother her nor Mim come looking. Here she could try to regain some sense of balance.

She took a steadying breath, chest aching from the chill, her stiff fingers unfolding a letter. Papa had written again. She brought the hotel stationery with its fancy letterhead to her nose, fancying it bore his beloved scent, a trace of his presence. His writing hand had always been so elegant. An indication of the gentleman he was and had ever been. A reproach to the finesse she lacked.

Oh, Papa, I'm trying to become a lady. But I never reckoned with the time and care it would take.

Tears fell on the paper as she looked down, her warm breath pluming like a white feather and obscuring his heavy print. Biting her lip to stay her emotions, she drank in his heartfelt words like a tonic for her ongoing angst.

Dearest Wren,

*I trust this finds you well and content. I hope
you are not missing me as much as I am missing
you, hearth, and home. Recently James Sackett
sent me a letter, assuring me you are holding your
own admirably in the midst of the busy social
season. I can well imagine all that is before you
but feel reassured knowing he is by your side.*

She stopped reading, warmed by James's thoughtfulness.
He, too, was a gentleman in all the little ways that mattered.

*When I return home I'd like to spend some
time together, just you and I, away from the
rush of the city and the confines of New Hope.
There's a charming little town south of Pittsburgh where we could rest together for a few
days, you from the season and me from business.
We have much to discuss that our brief correspondence cannot convey.*

*Please write to me again when you can. I
carry your letters with me at all times, and re-
read them at every opportunity.*

Your loving papa

She bent her head and prayed. For him to come home. For
courage to take the next step.
For her uncertain future.

This time there were no blush roses from some mysterious
benefactor, their fragrance heady and sweet, but a fancy box

tied with blue ribbon, delivered by an anonymous servant slightly red-faced from the cold.

"First flowers and now this!" Mim examined the gift with a sort of bemused wonder. "Cadbury of England, makers to the Queen and Prince of Wales!"

Wren lifted the lid, exposing long fingers of chocolate in delicate ruffled papers. Immediately she held the offering out to Mim.

One bite and Mim's smile widened with delight. "*Och!* Fruit-flavored centers! I've never tasted the like. Now what are ye doing tying it back up again? Ye're nae having one? Even in secret?"

Wren looked at the box, a bit sick. "I want to share it with James."

Mim's eyes flared wider. "Mr. James? Why would ye?"

"He likes chocolates, Izannah said. And it's a small way to thank him for seeing me through the season."

Mim looked askance at her. "What if it's a Cameron who's sending ye such?"

"Mr. Cameron doesn't seem the type." Malachi, for all his merits, seemed to have a more practical than poetic bent.

"Ye canna be sure o' that." Mim looked crestfallen. "I think he'd be a wee bit *afflocht* if he were to find his candy wi' James Sackett."

Pondering this, Wren set aside the chocolates and reached for her crook. Whoever the mysterious giver was, he had a generous heart and wouldn't begrudge her being generous in return, would he?

"Ye look like ye belong in the Highlands, dressed as ye are." Mim began tying Wren's floral sash, arranging the silken bluebells and heather into place over her petticoat of lamb's wool. "A proper Scottish lass, to be sure. Except the poor shepherds would be following ye aboot and neglecting their sheep!"

Wren smiled. Scotland kept coming to mind more and more, a sort of refuge amid the storm of the season. Papa had told her it resembled Kentucky, particularly the Highlands where Grandfather had his estate.

"Well, we're off to the masquerade. Ye only lack yer mask." Handing it over, Mim led the way from dressing room to parlor, where Andra waited below.

"There's been a change in plans," Andra announced when she saw them, looking no more pleased with Wren's humble outfit than she'd been at first.

No James? One quick glance about the room confirmed he was missing. Since the Ewings' tea, the prospect of seeing him again had been Wren's one solace. Now her anticipation reared up and mocked her. Had she embarrassed him to the point he no longer wanted to be her escort? Was it just as Alice had said and—

"James is to meet you at the Bidwell mansion. I've just received word he'll be delayed, no doubt on account of the weather." Her eyes narrowed and took in the box of chocolates in Mim's embrace. "Is that part of Rowena's costume?"

"Aye, it is," Mim replied, chin tipping up. "A good night to ye, mem. I trust ye'll be abed when we return."

At Andra's curt nod, they went out into a world dusted white. Once in the coach, Wren knotted her gloved hands, misery twisting inside her. James wasn't here because he didn't want to be. He was ashamed of her, her rusticity, her music . . .

"*Och*, the snow! We'll be nigh frozen by the time we get there! 'Tis the weather that's keeping Mr. James away, to be sure." Mim's reassurances fell flat in a coach all too empty of him. "But he'll likely be there waiting for ye . . . along with Mr. Malachi."

Bending over the washbasin, James splashed cold water on his bearded face and dried off with a towel. The Monongahela House mirror reflected tense features above a flawless cravat, reminding him to hide his unease in the hours ahead. He'd sent a note to New Hope, saying he'd be arriving separately, hoping Wren would understand and Andra would attribute it to the weather. Now wary and watching his back, he could no longer accompany her in the coach. If someone meant him harm, she'd be safer riding without him.

A second telegram had come from Dean that afternoon, no less alarming than the first.

Madder's men reported to be en route to Pittsburgh before rivers freeze. Feel we're being followed in New Orleans. Trouble abounds. Watch your back.

There was no need to read it twice. Like Georgiana Hardesty's rejection, this second warning was burned into his consciousness like a brand.

He took the back alleys of Pittsburgh to the Bidwell mansion, his driver—a fellow abolitionist and free Negro—as chary as he. Lights from the east-end estate illuminated a long line of rigs on the drive. Snow was drifting down, whipped about like chaff in the wind. The biting chill snaked past his heavy cape to his leather shoes and then was forgotten when he saw Wren.

She turned his way, something indefinable filling her lovely face. It held his heart still, that look. In that instant it seemed no one else existed in the crowded, elegant entry. In her simple shepherdess costume, she looked all too vulnerable . . . all too beautiful.

Her voice reached out to him. "Jamie, are you . . . all right?"

He took a breath, the way she said his name making his heart spin like a top. "Never better," he murmured, wanting to take the worry from her eyes. He looked away from her as Mim disappeared upstairs with their wraps and a box bound with blue ribbon.

Seeing his questioning look, she gave him a pensive half smile. "I've brought you chocolates . . . to thank you for taking such care of me."

He stilled. "I need no recompense, Wren." Was that what she thought? That this was difficult for him?

Her smile faded, assuring him it was so. Taking her hand, he led her into a small, secluded alcove. "Do you honestly believe this is hard for me? To be with you?"

"I . . ." She looked up at him, her damp eyes confirming it. "Yes."

He felt his belly clamp, knowing no matter what he said to the contrary, she wouldn't believe him. He couldn't tell her that she'd laid hold of his heart the moment she'd stepped into the pilothouse months before. He couldn't prove to her how he truly felt about her by taking her in his arms. He couldn't even speak.

She reached up a small, gloved hand and touched his jaw. "You needn't say a thing, Jamie."

"Wren, I—"

She turned her back to him. "Please . . . just tie on my mask."

He did what she asked but his fingers fumbled, catching on the silk of her hair. He shut his eyes against the warmth of her, her familiar floral scent. Desire pulled at him and nearly made him groan. Still fumbling, he finally tied the mask into place.

She turned to face him. Thank him. Saying nothing, he offered her his arm, and they started for the ballroom down an unfamiliar hall. He felt like a yawl, taking the lead and hunting for the best water, testing depth and danger, having her follow in his wake. At every event she was drawing more attention, more admiring glances, and tonight was no exception.

Though the mood was one of frivolity and amiability as guests moved about in disguise, the undercurrent of showmanship and one-upmanship prevailed. Most people he easily recognized, but some were more enigmatic. Warriors. Indian chiefs. Medieval damsels. At least here in a roomful of people so familiar he knew them masked or unmasked, he felt somewhat safe. But it was a false security, ending the moment he left the Bidwells.

They stood on the cusp of the milling crowd, and he sensed Wren's continued disquiet. To their left stood Alice Mellon dressed in Egyptian costume alongside her escort, who looked to be some sort of Arctic explorer. Sir John Ross, perhaps. Or the ill-fated John Franklin.

"Mr. Sackett, not in costume tonight, I see?" Alice's voice always grated, her nearsighted eyes giving her a perpetual squint. "Not even that of famed river pilot?"

"You can't improve on a dress coat and cravat, Miss Mellon," he replied.

Wren looked to Alice. Spoke kindly. But Alice's chilly gaze traveled past her as if she wasn't present before moving on. Cut.

James felt Wren wilt. Step back. A tremor of fury shot

through him at the slight. But the act of cutting someone was within the rules of society, and there was little to be done without making more of a scene. It was left to him to redeem the situation. Though he moved Wren away from Alice's rigid back, he could do little about the onlookers or keep it from the papers come morning.

He ground his back teeth, wanting to yank the ground out from under Alice Mellon. "Pay no attention, Wren."

She simply nodded, stoic, though he sensed her battle for composure. Facing the colorful crowd, she said, "I want you to tell me who's in need of a wife."

He hesitated, wishing he'd misheard, grappling with what she asked of him.

She scanned the room, fresh resolve in her features. "Who is that portly man by the hearth? The one dressed like a bull fighter."

"Edgar Jay Allen? He's founder of the Pennsylvania Telegraph Company." Throat dry, he measured his words, the distaste of what he had to do increasingly bitter. "A graduate of Yale, he's a close friend of Bennett's. Fond of jellied eels and whist. Word is he stays up all night, then retires at breakfast and doesn't get up again till supper."

"And the tall Viking by the potted palm in the corner?"

"Americus Hutton, vice president of Peoples National Bank. Widowed with six children."

"He's more in need of a mother than a wife, then." Her expression turned more pensive. "And the fair-haired knight over there?"

"Duncan McCord, owner of the wholesale hatters McCord and Company. Friend of the Ballantynes and benefactor of the orphanage. He's suffering a broken engagement to a woman from Savannah." The mention brought Georgiana to mind. Oddly, it lacked the burn of before. "I know firsthand because I piloted him up and down the Mississippi during their courtship."

Her gaze drifted to the entrance. "And the man just coming in?"

"The Highlander in the Cameron plaid? You well know, Wren."

"In truth, I-I don't." The lament in her tone set his pulse to pounding. "We've simply danced a few times, had some small conversations. I know little about his past . . . why he's here."

He watched as Malachi's gaze swung their way. "The Camerons made their fortune in glass thirty years ago. Malachi left manufacturing to work as freight agent for a rival railroad, investing in various ventures, including iron and oil. He's now sole owner of the Pennsylvania."

"Is he in need of a wife?"

He hesitated, thinking of Izannah. The hammering tightness in his chest nearly denied him answer. "There's not another man in the room more worthy of a bride."

"High praise, Jamie."

He felt her eyes on him again, questioning, assessing. He couldn't—wouldn't—look at her. "Malachi is nearly like a brother to me. His father wanted to marry your aunt Ellie years ago, but she wed Jack Turlock instead. Daniel Cameron apprenticed with the Ballantynes and eventually took over the glassworks. But Malachi had other ideas. Like locomotives."

"Aunt Andra said he's rarely in Pittsburgh."

"He's only here for the winter. Most of his time is spent in Philadelphia or abroad."

"The papers say he's the catch of the season."

"No, Wren . . ." Dare he say it? "You are."

She sighed. "Is that why Alice Mellon just cut me?"

276

"Yes."

"Is that why Malachi Cameron is coming toward us?"

"Likely."

The dancing was about to begin. At Malachi's approach, something else wove its way through James's soul, tying a tight knot of resignation and regret. The Camerons and the railroads were encroaching on all levels, personal and private, a reminder that his days on the river were at an end. Though Wren had never been his, losing her cut deeper still. Yet he had little choice but to stay stoic and watch the drama unfold as his friend drew near.

"Miss Ballantyne."

Tonight Malachi seemed to have stepped out of the mists of Culloden. Kilted and wearing the Cameron plaid, he was drawing more than Wren's notice.

"A Scotsman, come to claim a dance?" There was a beguiling lilt in her voice, a warm light in her eyes that turned James further on end.

"If you'll dance with a Highlander, aye," Malachi said, never taking his eyes off her.

James looked away as he bowed over her hand. For all her naïveté, Wren was becoming more nimble in society and far more alluring than she knew.

"I'm afraid to refuse you," she said coyly, eyes on his scabbard.

He chuckled. "I've no quarrel with a little shepherdess. My sword is blunt, you see. Your crook is more threatening."

Reaching for her dance card, Malachi penciled in his initials as the opening waltz was struck. More men waited behind him, stealing precious seconds from their waltz. James stood by her side, contemplating what was to come.

The night would be a long one indeed.

28

The greatest happiness of life is the conviction that we are loved—loved for ourselves or rather in spite of ourselves.

VICTOR HUGO

The sun slanting off newly fallen snow gave the tearoom with its expansive windows and crystal chandelier the brilliance of a ballroom. Feeling housebound, Izannah had suggested the outing to Prim's in the heart of Pittsburgh, realizing all too late her Kentucky cousin wasn't in need of another outing. Wren sat next to her in a quiet corner, looking quite pale against the cherry-red upholstery and English floral wallpaper.

They were having a celebration of sorts, rejoicing over Grandfather's return to New Hope and Peyton's own improved health and Wren's successful debut. Thus far she was the reigning belle, the papers proclaiming her popularity day to day, though no mention had been made of her favoring any particular suitor.

"We have much to be thankful for," Mama said, Elspeth and Grandmother on either side of her. "We're only missing Andra."

Elspeth made a wry face as she unfolded her napkin. "Let Andra look after Silas for once. Though she's so vinegary it will likely send him to his sickbed again."

"Da doesn't countenance Andra's moods and never has," Mama returned quietly, too gracious to say Andra's vinegary nature was likely bestowed by none other than Elspeth herself. "He's in good hands, as is she."

"Let's talk of Christmas instead." Grandmother looked at Wren expectantly. "We've always celebrated at New Hope, and it will be a joy to have you with us—and your father if he arrives home in time."

"I pray he will," Wren said.

Izannah nodded, excitement kindling at the mere mention of Yuletide. "The better question is what does your calendar hold for December, Wren? Not too many gala affairs, I hope."

"Just a holiday tea and a ball, then the season comes to a hush till the new year."

"I'm glad of that. You're in need of a rest from all that society." Grandmother smiled and sat back as a white-aproned serving girl came round, enveloping them in the unmistakable fragrance of Grey's Tea.

"I've been remembering Christmases past when Ansel and I were at home and the Camerons would celebrate with us." Mama seemed lost in a cloud of nostalgia. "I wonder if we shouldn't revive that tradition."

Izannah felt a start of surprise. Was Mama trying to do a little matchmaking? Izannah had not spoken of Malachi or her feelings to anyone. Secrecy was always safer in a large family. If she was found out, her brothers would tease her endlessly. And then there was Great-Aunt Elspeth . . .

"We mustn't forget James," Grandmother added. "He usually winters in New Orleans and celebrates the holidays with Captain Dean and other gentlemen of the navigation."

Izannah glanced Wren's way, wishing she could read her thoughts. Perhaps she'd only imagined a spark between her and James. She'd assumed James would join them for the holidays. But Malachi? It was more than her hopeful heart could hold.

Elspeth harrumphed in protest. "I've been hoping for some announcement of an engagement by Christmas. Every morning my maid reads me the social column without fail. The papers link Rowena with a great many admirers. We're on pins and needles awaiting her choice. I don't suppose she'll end up with a Cameron. That Malachi is rich as Croesus—"

"Auntie, *please*." The steel in Mama's tone forbade further talk.

"Well, someone should snag him. Rowena doesn't want to end up like me or Izannah."

"Izannah is still hopeful of a home and family," Mama countered quietly.

"Oh my, really?" Elspeth's expression indicated doubt. "Even after a failed season?"

Izannah took a bite of pastry, swallowing down warm, hasty words. Anything she said in reply would simply dig a deeper hole. Though Mama and Grandmother always rose to defend her, the hurt of her circumstances lingered.

"Sister, after eighty-some years, one would think you'd learn to mind your tongue." Grandmother sighed with rare exasperation and gestured to the scones. "Here, have another."

"If you're trying to keep me quiet, it can't be done. Cooped up as I've been with my mousy maid and nurse, I'm starved for gossip." Elspeth's brows peaked as a bell tinkled above the tearoom's entrance. More customers entered through the front door, adding to the friendly chaos of the room, providing a blessed distraction.

Izannah cast Mama a pleading look and prayed for a turn in conversation.

"As I was saying . . ." Mama swallowed a sip of tea, heeding her look. "We've much to plan for Christmas. Everyone agrees all festivities should be at New Hope given Da's health. The doctors have given us leave to have a small celebration . . ."

Izannah tasted her scone, barely listening. Malachi trespassed into her every thought, making her feel anxious and giddy by turns. She wondered if he and James had had time to talk further or if the shallow conversation that ruled the season prevented it. She hadn't seen James to ask. He'd been lodging solely at the Monongahela House, hardly ever coming to River Hill. Lately she saw James as seldom as Wren.

"I've missed you, cousin," Izannah said, wishing it was just the two of them and they had time for girlish talk. "You look tired, and you're all too quiet."

Wren's expression was oddly blank. "The masquerade ball kept us up till the wee small hours."

"Ah, the masquerade. The midpoint of the season. Soon the social whirl will be over." Izannah's tone was consoling as she poured more tea. "It's simply a winter diversion. Pittsburgh's preoccupation with itself."

Wren looked to her lap. "I'll be glad to have it end."

There was patent resignation in her tone, something Izannah understood all too well. Expectations were high, the pressure intense. If Wren favored James, she was in a bind indeed, to say nothing of James's dilemma.

"Is there no man you fancy?" As soon as she'd mouthed the careless question, Izannah bit her tongue. "I thought perhaps . . ."

"Maybe in time," Wren replied. "I feel a bit smothered by it all."

Izannah nodded. *Smothered* was certainly how she'd felt in the thick of Pittsburgh society, the pursuit of a husband paramount. Perhaps her own season wouldn't have been so dreary if Malachi had been there . . . if she hadn't bolted in the middle of it . . . if Alice Mellon hadn't been such a thorn. Oh, to rewind time like a clock and right the mistakes she'd made. Did Malachi ever think the same? Or was he so satisfied with life he had no regrets?

Turning toward the window, she took in the falling snow dressing the sooty outlines of the nearest buildings in shining white.

Like the bride she wanted to be.

The next day the snow was still falling, filling in the carriage tracks of the doctors as they came and went attending to Grandfather, finally calling a halt to a holiday function. Andra was annoyed, but Wren felt unfettered joy. After shutting the gown she was to wear in the wardrobe, she spent the morning reading *A Christmas Carol* aloud to Grandfather before lunching with Grandmother. When the clock struck one, she hurried downstairs to the music room. *Free at last.* As her fingers closed about the porcelain doorknob, a voice from behind made her pause.

"Hello, cousin."

Dismay doused her expectation. Bennett?

"A word with you please, Rowena." The unrelieved black

of his garments lent him the severity of an undertaker. Suddenly Charlotte seemed to stand between them, a palpable, ghostly presence as they entered the music room and Bennett shut the door.

"I've been following you in the press as the season progresses." Looking askance at the violins lying on a near table, he took a chair by the glowing hearth. "There is talk about your beautiful gowns, your exquisite violin, your dancing skills and admirers, but precious little of substance."

She picked up her beloved Nightingale. "I suppose you mean a serious suitor."

"I do. The season is half finished, after all." When she said nothing, he folded his arms across his chest, his bearing nonchalant but his manner tense. "I'm beginning to fear you'll do as Izannah did and quit your season. Or follow through till the bitter end with nothing to show for it."

A tingling embarrassment stole over her at such bluntness. *Bitter end* was certainly the right wording. The thought of abandoning the season dogged her day and night. Setting down the Nightingale, she began to rosin her bow, unwilling to spar with him over something as intimate as marriage.

"You are a Ballantyne . . . and you'll do your duty."

"Duty? A sad way to speak of such things." She felt an almost perverse pleasure in crossing him. "I'm praying about matters, and I'll do nothing without Papa's blessing."

"Your father and all piety aside, there must be someone who turns your head."

"Someone? Just whom would you have me choose, Bennett?" She kept her voice low, but it in no way hid her aggravation. "The simpleton who steps on my toes repeatedly? The glutton who eats the most oysters? The scoundrel who pinches me as I pass?"

He let out a loud, ringing laugh. "Come, Rowena. It isn't *that* bad, is it?"

"*Bad* hardly begins to describe it." She tested a string, listening to the tone, fighting for calm. "Truth be told, I'm sick to death of being enslaved to fashion, hobnobbing with fancy folk so rule-bound and stiff you never get a true look at them. They peer right through me, never getting past my name, the Ballantyne fortune . . ."

His levity faded as he stood. "Then you need to find a man who cares about neither."

Wishing an end to the conversation, she struck another note. Its insolent tone clung to the air, begging for confrontation. As she turned away, Bennett's hand shot out and caught her arm. His fingers bit deep, sending her prized Tourte bow to the floor. Stunned, she looked down as he stepped on it with a booted foot, smashing the tip.

With a little cry she brought the Nightingale behind her back, out of his destructive reach. But he simply came nearer, taking her roughly by the shoulders and giving her a jarring shake. "I don't care to have this conversation again, Rowena. You're going to announce your engagement by the end of the season or there'll be a steep price to pay, understand?"

"Understand?" She looked up at him, her words coming in a frenzied rush. "I understand what Charlotte had to endure by the lake that day. I understand why she was afraid of you. Nothing that afternoon was an accident—"

"Forget about Charlotte." His fingers dug deeper. "I was cleared of all blame. The matter is closed. But your situation is still very much at play. And I want a satisfactory finish—"

A sudden knock overrode his harsh words, and he released her. At her feeble call the butler cracked open the door. "You have a visitor, Miss Ballantyne."

Shaking, she cradled the Nightingale. "I'm afraid I'm . . ." She groped for the proper word, the pain of Bennett's hands, his harshness, seared into her. "Indisposed."

Bennett locked eyes with her, daring her to defy him.

The butler cleared his throat. "I'm sorry, Miss Ballantyne, but Mr. Cameron is not a man who is turned away lightly, especially in this weather."

Malachi? She tucked her violin in its case, feeling backed into an impossible corner. "Please bring a hot toddy to the parlor, then. Mr. Cameron might be cold from his ride."

The butler nodded and Bennett turned her way. "Finish it, Rowena. And finish it well."

She hiked her chin and stepped round him like he was no more than a stick of furniture, glancing at her pale reflection in a near mirror in passing.

His cold, triumphant reflection shone back at her.

Still shaken but pinning the smile of the season in place, Wren breathed a quick prayer before she entered the parlor. Then and there, her spirit rebelling against Bennett's deceit, she purposed to be anything but a sham. If Malachi Cameron was going to woo her, he would woo her for who she really was, not who she pretended to be. Pushing aside Bennett's fury, she welcomed Malachi graciously, like she was in humble Kentucky, not pretentious Pittsburgh.

He captured her outstretched hands, his touch cold. Melting snow left his coat glistening and the strong lines of his face ruddy. "You're not the same lass out of the ballroom, Miss Ballantyne."

She looked down. He meant her dress, surely. Made of moss-colored wool, it lacked all the frills of the season. Even her hair was arranged in a humble chignon bereft of ribbon or combs. "I'm a simple woman who takes pleasure in simple things, Mr. Cameron."

She thanked the maid as the steaming toddy was set on a near table between them. Pleasure shot through his eyes as he looked about the lovely room. "I've not been to New Hope in years, but I've never felt more welcome."

"This is a gladsome house with Grandfather back."

"How is he?"

"Better every day. Still smiling."

"Silas is a remarkable man." He gestured to a rosewood chair and sat opposite her, taking the toddy from the tray. "You're looking at me rather intently, I must say."

"I was thinking of the Cameron plaid."

"My kilt? Were you expecting me to wear it again?" At her nod, he chuckled. "In Scotland, aye. Here, nay."

"Do you really have a house in Edinburgh?"

Her query reeled him in like a fish on a lure. "Yes, an old Georgian one with a half-blind sheepdog, a crusty old cook, and an overgrown garden."

"Oh?" She thought it sounded heavenly despite his woeful tone. "What more could you possibly want?"

A bride.

Their eyes met. There was no mistaking the answer. Her teeth caught on her bottom lip as his ruddy color rose. When he reached into his waistcoat pocket, her breathing stilled. Was he . . . did he mean to . . .

The flutter inside her subsided when he simply withdrew two tickets. "You've no doubt heard of the Swedish Nightingale, Jenny Lind."

"Of course," she replied, her smile resurfacing. "Papa has told me about her."

286

"She'll soon be taking the train from Philadelphia to perform here in Pittsburgh at the opera house come January. If you'll agree to go with me, I'll arrange for a private box."

"I've never been in a . . . box."

He chuckled again. His ready smile reminded her of Mina's. "It's nice as boxes go. Just you, me, your maid."

Mim. Not James. James wouldn't be needed if she took this next step. His duties were done. She hesitated, half sick as Malachi's intentions came clear. Even James's reassuring praise failed to ease her.

There's not another man in the room more worthy of a bride.

"So you'll accompany me?" he prodded, a beguiling light in his eye.

"I—well . . . yes," she answered. She darted a look at the closed parlor door. Had Bennett ridden away or was he listening in the foyer?

"I've been wondering . . ." He looked to his toddy, his voice steely yet refined and becoming all too familiar. "Is there another suitor besides myself?"

Her gaze fell to her lap. "Just you, Mr. Cameron."

Her faint reply seemed a sort of promise, bringing her one step nearer his embrace. If they'd been sitting closer, she thought he might have kissed her.

The door to her future had cracked open.

And felt so bittersweet.

29

*The heart of another is a dark
forest, always, no matter how close
it has been to one's own.*

WILLA CATHER

"What frock will ye be wearing to the opera house? Yer aunt
and Miss Criss are set on the silver brocade for the holiday
ball." Mim's hands were on her hips, her gaze ricocheting
from Wren to the immense, open wardrobe. "If ye dinna
mind my saying so, I'd pick the smoke-blue velvet trimmed in
swansdown to see Miss Lind perform. Perfect for a winter's
night. Ye have the look of an angel in it, ye do. And ye've nae
yet worn it once yet."

Wren nodded absently. Talk of clothes and outings had
become dull as old paint.

"We've a skating party to ready for come January. The
seamstresses are nearly done with yer costume for that."
Examining a pair of gloves, Mim lapsed into Gaelic as she
always did when talk took a personal turn. "Yer getting quite

288

cozy with Mr. Malachi. Is it true he's coming for Christmas dinner?"

"He and his kin," Wren said, thinking of all Grandmother had told her.

"And James?" Mim's tone was hopeful. She'd become so fond of James since the season began, Wren sometimes thought she was secretly smitten with him.

"He's sent his regrets." Even saying it came hard. Wren felt oddly hurt, if only for Izannah's sake.

"His regrets?" Mim's face darkened. "What's a man like James Sackett to do with nae kith nor kin at Christmas— and Captain Dean downriver? Hole up at the Monongahela House?"

Wren lifted her shoulders in a shrug. "Maybe he means to have a little rest all by his lonesome."

Mim shut the wardrobe doors with a sigh. "Yer in need of a rest yerself, though yer holding up well despite Miss Malice's snubs and slights. I fear there's more trouble ahead with her, to be sure. She made Miss Izannah miserable till she quit her season. I ken ye'll nae quit, but ye can always end it and wed." Mim studied her with fresh wonder. "Now wouldn't that be grand? Mr. Malachi proposing at Christmastide!"

Wren turned ice-cold at the thought.

The rolling Pennsylvania landscape, locked in winter, had a crystalline beauty as barren as Wren's heart. How could one's life be so full and yet so empty? So cluttered with things that didn't satisfy? Seated sidesaddle atop her gentle mare, she wrestled with the future. Unbidden, a simple prayer her mother had often prayed kept coming to mind, a balm for her brooding. The earnest words floated out on a cloud of frozen breath into the icy air.

"For all that Thy love has yet in store for me, O God, I give Thee gracious thanks."

Atop a gentle hill in back of New Hope's farthest boundary line, she paused. Before her lay Cameron House, its stony presence dominating the heart of the valley, so new and grand the old outbuildings around it appeared flimsy as hatboxes. The scrolled iron gates and stone gatehouse, the long snaking drive to its wide front steps, reminded her of the painting of her mother's family home in England, Nancarrow Hall.

She'd never seen so many chimneys in all her life. She lost count at twelve. Only one was puffing smoke. There was some trouble with the fireplaces, Mim said, delaying the house's completion. Though beautiful, the place looked cold. Without heart.

Nae wonder he wants a bride, knocking around in such a big house all by hisself.

Drawing the hood of her cape closer, she pondered Mim's words. Malachi needed children, a family. Hadn't that been *her* heart's cry since she was small? To have a family of her own, a quiverful like Aunt Ellie? Somehow, in the darkness since Mama's passing, that desire had gotten lost. Wren sensed Izannah hoped for the same, though she never said so. Sometimes she seemed as tightly locked as James.

Reaching into the pocket of her cape, Wren touched the little wren, Papa's letters folded beside it, now split at the seams they were so perused.

Papa had urged caution about the season. But Papa wasn't here. And in his absence, she sensed Malachi wanted to cut to the chase and settle matters between them. Christmas was coming, and with it the proposal Mim had mentioned as sure as all the gifts and wassail and mistletoe of the season.

As she pondered it, a lone figure came out of the gatehouse and looked uphill, as intent on her as she was on him. Around his legs swarmed a melee of sniffing, barking dogs. English hounds.

Malachi.

With a quick burst, she reined her horse around and disappeared over the hill. She rode hard toward New Hope, one thought trailing.

Surely there was a music room in that big house of his.

Or a promise there'd be one.

James waited in the lushly paneled foyer of the French mansion, unable to shake the feeling of being followed. The streets of Pittsburgh were mostly empty on a cold winter's eve of all but stray dogs and beggars. Usually he shared a few coins as he passed, but tonight he kept the coach windows tightly shuttered as he'd hurried down Race Street to the French residence.

At the corner of 8th and Cherry, a second rig had appeared, matching their pace and following their every turn. He'd told his driver to take a circuitous route, hoping the vehicle trailing them was pure happenstance. But when the vehicle gained on them and seemed more their shadow before fading from sight at the mansion's gates, James knew. He needed no telegram to convince him of a threat. He'd witnessed it firsthand.

Spending an evening with the Frenches was hardly reassuring. Though they assumed a polite facade, they were known to be proslavery with deep ties to anti-abolitionists in Pittsburgh and elsewhere. Word was they suspected his own leanings.

Aware of the butler watching him, he withdrew a timepiece from his pocket. At half past eight, Wren was late.

More guests trickled in. The music started. The opening waltz—their waltz—quickly passed. His pulse beat in tempo to a rousing reel. Anxiety pulled at him and took his thoughts places he didn't want to go. What if he wasn't in danger but Wren was? What if, unable to get to him, his enemies sought her out? Rigid with alarm, he waited, eyes on the ornate front doors that refused to open.

When he could stand it no longer, he went back out into the night to find the curtain coach barreling up the drive. A cold wind struck him like the lash of a whip, wreaking havoc with his coattails and cravat. Ignoring the doorman, he hurried down the steps to meet Wren.

"I'm sorry," she told him as she stepped down from the coach, as if sensing he'd been near frantic waiting. "We had some trouble along the way. Another coach nearly hit us at a crossing."

I know the very one, he nearly said. "You're not hurt? Is Mim all right?"

Her warm smile was his reassurance, as was Mim's decisive nod. As they entered the gaily decorated foyer, Christmas greenery and bright ribbons abounding, Mim began removing Wren's wraps, unveiling the most stunning gown he'd ever seen. The lush brocade with its silver embroidery caught the light of countless candles, matching the pearls with their silver clasp about her throat. He bit the inside of his cheek to keep from telling her how lovely she was, his mind still reeling from her near mishap with the coach and all its implications.

"You always look so fine, Jamie." Alone in the foyer, she reached up and smoothed his cravat, her fingers lingering as she glanced up at him. "I don't know how you manage without a valet. Seems like you need a wife."

He felt a twinge. A sudden melting. In small unguarded moments like these, he had a taste of the intimacy between a man and a woman. Of joys to be had—or forsaken. Though she wasn't looking at him as she smoothed his collar, he couldn't stop looking at her. Her face was so enticingly close, so inviting, he merely had to lean down and—

Her fingers fell away. "I can hardly believe this is the last ball till the New Year. I'd like to see you at Christmas if you would come."

Her voice was so wistful it almost made him reconsider. The butler turned their way, waiting to announce them. The foyer clock chimed endlessly. They were now very late.

He looked down at her bare wrist. "Where is your dance card?"

"I—forgot."

Reaching into his waistcoat, he produced another.

She gave him a small smile, something sad in it. "Do you always think of everything?"

"It pays to be prepared. We'll have an end to this ere long."

Her smile faded. "I know you don't want to be here, same as me." Her face held a hundred queries. "I've often wondered why you are."

"A family favor, if you will." He frowned, trying not to be irritated with her, but everything was pressing in with such ferocity he was on edge. His fingers shook as he tied the card in place. "I want you to finish well, Wren." He offered her his arm. "To wed the man of your choosing. To not be like Izannah."

"Izannah?" She fastened entreating eyes on him. "Izannah loves you, Jamie."

293

He stared at her as the conversation took a wrong turn. "We're talking about you, Wren, not Izannah."

"We're talking about love—recognizing it, returning it—"

The music began, muffling her heartfelt words, delaying his response. Flummoxed, he felt his usual calm fade as surprise colored his face. When had she gotten it in her head that Izannah cared for him that way? Or he her? He started to correct her, then steeled himself. What if Wren knew it was only she herself he couldn't pry from his mind?

He faced the ballroom again, unsurprised to find a line of suitors waiting to fill her dance card.

She gave him a last searching look. Avoiding her gaze, he scanned the room for Malachi as another man led Wren out for a quadrille, her last words lingering.

We're talking about love—recognizing it, returning it.

Vulnerability flooded his heart as the cold truth rained down on him. He could recognize love for what it was, but he couldn't return it. His hands were tied. By his own risky circumstances. Georgiana. The Ballantynes. Malachi himself. He couldn't forget he'd agreed to help his grieving friend find a bride. He'd just never imagined that it would be Wren.

Malachi had come in late as well, exchanging a few words with their hosts. Even as they spoke, he was intent on the ballroom floor. On Wren. With her card so full, he'd be hard-pressed to gain a dance.

But knowing Malachi, he'd find a way.

30

They truly love who show their love.

WILLIAM SHAKESPEARE

Addie took the little maple carving from James's outstretched hand, delight filling her upturned face. "A cat? Just like the one I've been wishing for?" Pets weren't allowed at the orphanage, but that didn't stop the children from wanting them.

"Wait, there's more," he said, reaching in his waistcoat pocket again.

"Two kittens?" Her mouth formed an O of astonishment before she flung her arms around him. "Oh, if I were all grown up I'd marry you!"

Looking on, the orphanage director smiled. "You've a devotee for life, Mr. Sackett. Now come along, Adelaide. Time for afternoon lessons."

"May I play a tune first?" Returning the wooden figurines to James's hand for safekeeping, she reached for a small violin on a near table. "Mozart's 'Little Star.'"

A few screeches and discordant notes later, she gave him

a curtsey and he applauded. "Miss Ballantyne's doing, no doubt."

"I had another lesson yesterday," she said, taking the cat and kittens back again and hugging the violin to her chest.

Mrs. Sheffield glanced at the open door. "Ah, Mr. Cameron. Adelaide's violin playing is quite a draw. Won't you come in?"

Malachi entered, looking like a bear in his heavy greatcoat, hat in hand. "I was hoping to have a word with Mr. Sackett now that the board meeting is over."

"Of course. If you'll excuse us, we'll leave you gentlemen alone." With a smile, she went out, Addie in her wake.

For the first time he could ever recall, James was sorry his old friend had caught up with him.

"You're a hard man to pin down, James."

"The board meeting was a good place to start, Malachi." He forced a smile, his affability wearing thin. "Now seems a good time to thank you for your endowment."

"You can thank Rowena Ballantyne. She's the one who made me aware of the need for a new dining room and dormitory. I'll be glad to do whatever I can."

So this had to do with Wren, then. "Thanks to her prompting and your generosity, we'll be able to build beyond that." The understatement nicked him. He was still dazed by the donated amount, the largest in the orphanage's history.

Malachi gestured to some chairs nearest the hearth. "Have a few minutes?"

With a reluctant nod, James took a seat. Malachi's extraordinary generosity hinged on something, he felt certain. Some new commitment to Wren and the cause she cherished.

Malachi sat down opposite, his gaze roaming the plain paneled walls. "Although the matter of a bride is nearly settled, I'm still in need of a freight agent."

James shot him an apologetic look, the word *bride* tearing at his forced calm. "I owe you an answer." He'd delayed long enough, wanting to gauge where Malachi's ambitions would take him. Since there was little doubt Wren was a part of that picture, James had no recourse but to bow out. "I'm afraid I'm in no position to accept, given the situation I'm in."

Malachi's eyes clouded. "The trouble downriver, I take it."

More Wren, James couldn't say, surprised Malachi knew of Madder. Leaning forward, he added a scoop of coal to the waning fire and made no reply.

"You need to leave Pittsburgh, James. Staying on, taking part in the season like you've been, makes you too easy a target. When I stopped at the boatyard yesterday, Ealer told me you aren't in the same place more than five minutes, as you feel you're being followed."

"Ealer exaggerates."

"He's concerned for you, as I am. I could put you on the next train to Philadelphia once you reach Lancaster. My town-house is at your disposal in the city. You could lay low for a time and then assume your duties there as freight agent."

"It's tempting, I'll grant you that."

Malachi rubbed his brow, jaw firming, as if prepared to make some concession. "I'm aware Silas has you busy with Ballantyne interests and has even talked to you of California. It's a long way around Cape Horn to the West, to safety, but it's a good offer as it stands."

"That door is closed."

"Closed? Why?"

"I believe there's going to be a fight and I need to stay and enlist."

Surprise creased his friend's bearded face. "Would you really go to war?"

"We're already at war, Malachi."

"You'd not pay the commutation fee and have someone serve in your stead?"

"And give in to Madder and those like him? Never." He wouldn't say he'd already been approached by government officials anticipating the need for pilots of gunboat fleets on the Mississippi. He'd devoted a decade to helping fugitives find freedom. Would he relent in the most important battle of them all? "My responsibilities lie here in Pittsburgh with the Ballantynes and the line."

Malachi stared at him. "Don't delude yourself, James."

"I wouldn't call loyalty delusional."

"You well know what I mean. As far as the Ballantyne line goes, even Silas is diversifying. He's well aware of how matters stand in business, industry. The railroads will soon be the death of the river, as sure as there is a God in Israel. We're simply too fast, too efficient—"

"Don't." The low utterance severed Malachi's words mid-sentence. Something inside James broke, went still. "I know what's coming. And I know what's to be lost."

Wren, foremost.

Pulling himself to his feet, he went out.

Christmas was bearing down on them, and Wren's thoughts and prayers centered on one thing. Her father. All she wanted was for him to come home. Despite the heavy snows and impassable roads farther north, she refused to give up hope, even when Andra scoffed at her.

"I'm afraid the Pennsylvania Railroad is at a standstill, so Mina tells me. No one will be coming or going this Christmas in such weather."

A foot of fresh snow had fallen since the night of the ball, and Wren resisted the urge to pull on her mittens and go outside. With Andra fussing she would catch cold, Wren, sheepskin around her shoulders, contented herself with the view from the cupola. Unbidden, the winter landscape brought to mind a dozen cherished things. The humble tang of woodsmoke. Roiling kettles of hot cider. The brittle snap of branches on long walks through the woods.

Her heart squeezed tight. She had lost her beloved home, but she still had her memories. They couldn't be bought or sold or bartered. They stayed locked inside her, as warm and enduring as the winter was fleeting and chill.

Her gaze glanced off the distant rooftops of Cameron House and River Hill. But it was the Monongahela House to the west she sought, the skyline smudged with soot and smoke.

Her heated words with James the night of the ball spun round her head in an unforgiving circle. She'd only meant to speak on Izannah's behalf, wake him up to her cousin's feelings for him. But she'd gone too far and come upon a wall. James's attentions had shrunk to a word or two the rest of the evening, and once again he'd taken his own coach at evening's end, securing an outrider to see them home in his stead.

"Mr. James is in a high temper," Mim had murmured at his departure. Her questioning eyes sought Wren's as if seeking explanation, but Wren was too miserable to reply.

In the hours since, she'd considered penning him a note, holding on to half a hope he would come by and she could mend that too-honest moment. Perhaps he was still mourning Georgiana. Perhaps he didn't care for Izannah as she cared for him. Lately Wren had sensed an unusual restlessness in

Izannah, a preoccupation that left Wren wondering. Might she be growing weary of waiting for James? Wanting an engagement or some sign of his affection? Perhaps they'd had a lovers' quarrel. Wren didn't dare ask. Love was a chancy endeavor, best left to two hearts and the Lord.

She leaned forward, her warm breath misting the icy glass. A lone rider cut a dark streak across the snow to the west of New Hope. Who would be out on such a *rumballiach* day, as Papa liked to say? Standing, she bumped her head against the cupola's hanging lantern, setting it swinging in her haste.

Dusk was closing in, making it difficult to determine just who raced up the drive, slinging snow beneath the horse's hooves. When recognition finally stirred, Wren's pulse picked up in rhythm.

George Ealer, come to tell of James.

Between the thickness of the study door and George Ealer's emotional stuttering, Wren could only grasp the barest details. *Accident. Mercy Hospital. Yesterday.* Listening, she pushed past all protocol and entered the study without knocking. Ealer's slim, boyish back was to her as he stood before Grandfather, hat twisted in his hands. Grandmother sat by the fire, a tangle of knitting in her lap. Wren went to her, upended by the alarm on her face.

"Once James is stable, he needs to come here. Till then a guard needs to be posted outside his hospital room." Grandfather leaned forward, his leather chair creaking as he took up a pen. "I'll send word to Dr. Moss that James is to be moved as soon as possible, no matter what the patient says."

Ealer nodded, relief easing his stutter. "Thank you, s-sir. I'll be by his s-side till then."

Grandmother gripped Wren's hand. Squeezed tight. But the gentle gesture was lost as Wren caught sight of Grandfather's unsteady hands uncapping a bottle of ink. Obviously shaken by the news, he was unmistakably ashen. Still far from well, he pushed himself despite the doctors' cautions and had been working at his desk since dawn.

"There's been an accident along the levee," Grandmother told her in a low tone. "James was crossing Water Street yesterday at dusk when he fell on the ice into a coach's path."

"Is he badly hurt?" Her quiet query turned Ealer round.

"Some ribs are broken, perhaps a bone or two." Grandmother sighed, resuming her knitting with gnarled hands. "The hospital's sure to be overrun with visitors once the news spreads. Since James knows so many in Pittsburgh, he won't get a moment's rest lest he comes here."

The pat answer failed to satisfy. Wren sank down on the sofa beside her. "But River Hill is closer—"

"I'm afraid River Hill won't do, dear. Not with all those boys trying to wrestle with James in the condition he's in. Besides, Ellie's household needs to return to normal after serving as a hospital to us of late."

This Wren couldn't deny. New Hope was quiet as a graveyard in comparison. But what would Izannah say to find James beneath their roof? An opportunity for love to bloom had been lost, though Izannah was coming for Christmas, at least. And James, despite sending his regrets, would now be here too. As would Malachi.

"We'll try to return him to being fit as a fiddle while he's with us. The staff adores James and will see to his every comfort. Your grandfather can play chess with him. You can read to him and pass the time with your violin. And I'll keep unnecessary visitors at bay."

301

Grandmother hadn't mentioned Andra. No telling what her aunt would make of the arrangement.

Or James himself.

The next day the curtain coach moved through the snow at an excruciatingly slow pace, as if it was a hearse. From the cupola Wren watched them come, another prayer rising in her heart. Mim had followed her upstairs, looking in on the maids who were preparing the third-floor bedchamber for James's arrival. A robust fire gleamed behind the copper fireback, and the bedcovers were already turned down atop the immense four-poster. Imagining James as an invalid was hard to do.

"He's worse than they're saying." In the quiet, Mim's whisper sent a cold finger of alarm down Wren's spine. "There's far more than broken ribs to fret about. The doctors make mention of a gash in his leg and blood poisoning setting in."

Wren took her eyes off the driveway. "Blood poisoning?"

"Hospital staff didn't want him to leave, but Mr. Silas insisted. He'll get better care here, he will, and needs every bit o' it from the sound o' things."

Every detail brought new worries. Blood poisoning was as fearful as typhoid or cholera. In Kentucky Wren had known several who'd lost a limb or their very lives to such. The prospect turned her to ice.

"Ye'll have to do your part to keep him here and amuse him some," Mim said, echoing Grandmother's wishes. "Play yer fiddle. Read to him like ye did when yer grandfather was abed. Learn to play chess."

"I'll leave the chess playing to Grandfather."

"Maybe ye can get Mr. James to shave his beard."

"I like his beard," Wren blurted, surprising herself. His new look had grown on her over time.

"Ye might change yer tune if he was to kiss ye." An impish smile stole across Mim's face. "My Malcolm nearly rubs my skin raw betimes."

"*Och!*" Wren mimicked, hiding her embarrassment by turning back to the cupola glass. "Surely there's some pleasure in it."

"Some, aye." With a chuckle, Mim hurried down the steps, taking all forced merriment with her.

The coach was nearly to the front steps now. Wren put a hand to her tight throat, her hopeful spirits tumbling to her feet. Try as she might, she couldn't shake free of her confrontation with Andra at breakfast.

"If he's badly injured, James won't be able to finish the season. But that's of little concern in the long run," Andra had announced matter-of-factly. "We'll simply arrange for another escort. Your father may even return in time to take James's place."

"I can't imagine stepping out with anyone but James," Wren countered. As much as she loved her father, it was James's presence she craved. Somehow he'd worked himself into her heart, her every thought, both in society and out of it. He was her constant friend. "Seems like we should wait till he's well again."

"Don't be ridiculous, Rowena. James himself will tell you that the only acceptable way out of your debut is illness, mourning, or the announcement of your engagement."

Feeling stubborn, she said, "Izannah stopped outright."

Andra all but rolled her eyes. "Quitting the season like Izannah did exacts a high price. She's now considered tainted, something of a social outcast. The Turlocks, being rogues to begin with, only add to that impression, Judge Jack's reputation aside."

"There's nothing the matter with Izannah." Tears smeared Wren's vision at the slight. "She'll make some man a blessed wife—"

Andra banished the hope with a dismissive hand. "I doubt that will ever happen. Izannah is past the first flush of youth, as are you. And given the dreadful situation over the Ashburton affair, you simply must finish well and avoid all scandal."

Wren lowered her head. She felt she was face-to-face with Bennett again, full of ire and ambition. "If finishing well means marrying a man I don't want to, while the one I care about is lying abed injured—"

"Rowena!" Andra stood so abruptly she set the china rattling atop the table. "You will do what is expected of you as a Ballantyne and as befits your family, however unpalatable it seems. You're in our world now, and there's a great deal more at stake than your petty preferences and feelings. The sooner you realize that fact, the better off you'll be."

With that she left the room, moving at a girl's pace in her fury, the fragrance of her heavy cologne lingering.

Now, hours later, the heat of their exchange was almost forgotten by the sight of James emerging from the coach. Beneath his stark white shirt bloomed a crimson stain that seemed to spread before her eyes. One arm was splinted, his right leg encased in bandages. Each agonized step had to be managed by the waiting servants. A doctor and nurse followed close behind, assisting with a waiting stretcher.

When they entered the house and faded from view, Wren measured their progress by sound. She heard the servants struggling a bit with the stretcher on the stairs, pausing on the landing to ask James how he was faring, then proceeding onward to the next floor. Why they'd placed him so high when he was in such sad shape was a riddle. Surely a downstairs room would be better. Long minutes of commotion followed as he was settled and the servants dispersed.

Mim returned to the chilly cupola, face dark as a thundercloud. "He's to have his own nurse, doctors' orders. But he's got some right terrible wounds that need more tending than any nurse can manage, even a bonny one."

Having immersed herself belowstairs baking gingerbread, cutting snowflakes from tissue paper, and arranging fresh cedar boughs and holly brought in by sleigh, Wren hadn't seen James since his arrival three days prior. As the doctors came and went, Grandmother and Grandfather visited him at intervals, but not Andra or Wren.

"It's highly improper for a woman to enter a man's bedchamber unless it's that of her husband," Andra had told her when she'd passed Wren on the stairs.

"I'm merely going to the cupola," Wren replied. She often went there to pray and ponder, leaving the door open so the warm air from the house would fill the cold space.

She wouldn't admit it afforded her more than just a view of the snowy landscape but also a tiny glimpse of their patient's progress. A door would open or close. James's voice would creep out. Sometimes the nurse's muted tones would intertwine with the doctor's deep baritone. Often there was a worrying silence.

By the fifth day Wren could stand it no longer. As dusk drew a curtain over the land, she waited till the nurse went below to have her supper and the doctor had come and gone.

Andra, thankfully, was calling at Ballantyne Hall in the sleigh despite the snow.

On tiptoe, alert to every creak in the planked floor, Wren went toward the closed door like a moth to candle flame. No knock. No announcement. Just a brazen turn of the handle. Woodsmoke and medicine stormed her senses.

And then a gruff, "Who's there?"

She felt a qualm. Had James been sleeping? Or was he drugged? She shut the door, then wished she'd left it open, if only to offset the gloom of the room. Hurrying to a window, she pushed aside a heavy drape. "The snow is falling again. It's so beautiful I wanted to share it with you."

"Wren?"

She turned, leaving the drapes open to better see his face, hoping he couldn't read the dismay in hers. He was so bruised and battered it was pure punishment to look at him. Her hand shot out, covering his outstretched fingers atop the coverlet. He felt warm to the touch—too warm—like Grandfather had been too cold. It seemed right to hold on to him, to hands that had brought her upriver and helped her navigate the perilous social season and would have seen her finished, but for this.

"Jamie." Her voice held so much. Hurt at seeing his hurt. Hope he'd soon heal. The warm, inexplicable joy she felt in his presence.

He looked up at her, pain glazing his eyes. "It hurts . . . to breathe. Otherwise . . . I'd talk."

She nodded in understanding, remembering his broken ribs, and gave him a small smile. "You know I talk enough for the both of us."

"I like the sound of your voice . . . always have."

Her gaze wandered to the bottle of laudanum on the near table. A dreaded thing, it reminded her of Mama's loss. The strong scent was uncomfortably familiar, the effects frightening. It seemed to have loosened his tongue and lent a directness to his gaze that had been missing before. Beneath his intensity, she felt feverish herself.

Spying a basin of water, she bent and wrung out a cloth, then settled carefully on the edge of the bed. His eyes closed as she smoothed his brow and the high lines of his cheekbones. She was nearer to touching his dark hair than she'd ever been. It feathered back on the pillow in wild disarray, begging for a brush . . . her hungry touch.

His eyes flicked open, catching her long, unguarded look. Startled, she ran the cloth over his bristled jaw, wondering if the nurse was tending to his beard.

Just how bad could a bewhiskered kiss be?

Face hot, she shut the stray thought away, blaming Mim.

"What . . . day . . . is . . . it?" The words unwound slowly, punctuated with pain.

Her heart fisted. "December twentieth."

"I don't . . . remember much."

"About the accident, you mean?"

"I only recall . . . leaving the boatyard . . ."

"Your mind will likely clear in time," she said softly. "All that matters is you're here now, safe and sound."

"I'm neither safe . . . nor sound." He managed a lopsided smile. "But I am . . . content."

His words were mumbled, so unlike the articulate James she knew. The laudanum, likely. She let herself look at him, filling every crevice of her needy heart and head with him, seeking some reassurance he'd soon be well. She leaned nearer, unable to keep her distance. She felt herself slipping . . . falling. Wanting to lean in and brush her lips to his.

Oh, Jamie.

His eyes were on her, lingering, searching. Her heart seemed to stop when he took her hand. At the brush of his lips to her fingers, her stomach gave way. Shaken, she shut her eyes lest he see the longing buried deep. Could he sense she wanted to lie down beside him, never to leave him? Body to body, heart to heart, soul to soul?

The click of a door brought the tender moment to an end. At the foot of the bed stood the nurse, full of surprise and caution. "You mustn't tire our patient, Miss Ballantyne."

Face hot, Wren rose from the bed, but James kept hold of her hand.

"There's nothing tiring . . . about Miss Ballantyne."

The utterance exacted a high price. Wren detected a wince with every word.

"I'll go now," she said softly, with a last look at him as he released her. "I merely wanted to see how Mr. Sackett is faring."

The door shut firmly behind her, barring her return. But the memory they'd just made was locked in place.

31

*It does not matter much whom
we live with in this world, but
it matters a great deal whom we
dream of.*

WILLA CATHER

Malachi entered New Hope's parlor, unsure whether to be amazed or amused. In a far corner stood an evergreen, its fragrant tip spiraling to the ceiling, myriad branches adorned with strings of beads and candles. Tissue snowflakes hung here and there, and a wax angel with spun-glass wings crowned the top. He'd seen cut trees for sale in the city square but had given them little thought.

Rowena appeared just ahead of the sated revelers in the dining room, surprising him. Delighting him. He gestured to the tree. "Is this a Kentucky custom?"

She smiled. "A German one, so Granny says. Queen Victoria and Prince Albert have brought it into fashion."

"I'm only familiar with mistletoe . . . and you're standing right under it."

She looked up, pink touching her cheeks. He took a step nearer, thinking it still not close enough. Although she'd sat beside him at supper, he'd been distracted by the large gathering, wishing for more privacy. At last he'd gotten his wish. For the moment they were alone. Rowena was standing in an almost providential position. The heirloom ring hidden in his breast pocket prompted him to make a bold move. He'd thought of little else through course after course of Christmas dinner, the certainty that John King Ewing and Aaron French were equally enamored of her spurring him on.

And then there was Silas, God rest him. He'd appeared at Christmas dinner and half the man he'd been, leaving little doubt the ailing patriarch was on borrowed time. When he died, Rowena would move beyond his reach for a year or better . . .

He took her hand, so small it was nearly lost in his. She looked down, seeming a bit startled, and then Mina's voice sounded in the foyer, stealing the moment. On her heels were the Turlock brothers, all ten of them, followed by Izannah, her baby sister in arm.

Rowena welcomed them in while he stood silently by, more out of sorts by the minute. If Ansel was here, he'd ask him for her hand. Putting the question to Silas had crossed his mind, but he and Silas usually only talked business, nothing as personal as matrimony.

"So, Malachi, what's this I'm hearing about the takeover of the Central in the East?" Bennett sidled up to him, offering a cigar.

He declined with a wave of his hand, preferring his pipe.

"It's hardly worth mentioning. I simply needed to merge two subsidiary lines."

"Word is you're ready to break ground for a railroad station within Pittsburgh's city limits. A bit ambitious, wouldn't you say, given there's no track laid past Lancaster Turnpike?"

"There will be by next year, terminating on the north side of the Allegheny River," he replied easily. "We'll have shortened the trip between Pittsburgh and Philadelphia to a mere fifteen hours as well."

"Fifteen? An admirable feat . . ."

Malachi watched Rowena discreetly as Bennett rambled on, intent on business when it was, for once, the farthest thing from Malachi's mind.

James had been right. He needed a woman who made him forget about work. He'd finally found her. The next merger he wanted to make was a matrimonial one, and as quickly as possible, or the Pennsylvania might suffer from his preoccupation. A shipboard honeymoon while en route to Scotland was what he had in mind. He couldn't be away from European interests and investors any longer.

Rowena was talking with Izannah now, and he couldn't help but notice their differences. While Rowena barely reached his shoulder, Izannah was nearly his equal in height, as willowy and curvaceous as a marble sculpture he'd once seen in Italy. Since the schoolroom her hair had always reminded him of butterscotch, only darkening slightly over time. He couldn't recall the color of her eyes. She smiled and spoke in that poised, charming way she had as she passed Rowena the baby.

Though he had little experience with children, he could see Rowena would make a good mother. Being so natural and unaffected herself, she was kissing the babe and making over her as if the child were her own. As he looked on, the cavern that grief had carved deep inside him began to fill. A wife would love him to wholeness again, he was certain, chase every dark shadow of sorrow and regret away.

In a few moments Rowena left the room, no doubt looking for Ellie, as the baby was starting to fuss. Izannah stood alone by the Christmas tree, fingering a glass ornament. The gifts at her feet, wrapped with colorful paper and string, reminded him of the little package she'd given him long ago at their chance meeting on the levee. He still had the finely made Taber pipe and pipe case, though the costly maccaboy tobacco was long gone.

Did she even remember?

Curious, he started across the parlor, intent on finding out.

Izannah had dreamed of this moment for years. Somehow meeting up with Malachi at Christmas made it all the more magical. At his approach she felt a bit light-headed, breathing in the bracing scent of pine and bayberry candle wax as if it could steady her. A jumble of their childhood encounters came rushing back, causing her to wonder what he remembered and what he didn't. He'd always been larger than life to her back then. Even now he was taller than she recalled and fuller in the face and chest, hardly the lanky boy of old.

Bennett had monopolized him most of the evening, but now, with a noisy game going on in the adjoining parlor, they found themselves alone. Suddenly bereft of words, she was glad when he spoke first.

"Did you get everything you hoped for this Christmas, Miss Turlock?"

She turned from the sparkling tree and met his steady gaze. "Come, Malachi, you're not in Mrs. Mellon's ballroom," she chided gently. "I'm merely Izannah of old. And no, I didn't get everything I wanted."

"A pity." He eyed her pensively and reached out to finger a fragrant branch. "I didn't either."

"There's always next year, I suppose."

"Next year I'll likely be in Edinburgh."

"Oh?" she replied, unsurprised. "Do the Scots celebrate Christmas better than we Americans, then?"

"Not necessarily." With a wink, he bent and picked up an ornament that had fallen to the carpet. "They've simply been doing it longer." Handing it to her, he watched as she returned it to a near branch. "Though they do have some charming customs."

"Let me guess . . ." She kept her voice light, belying the jitters inside her. "Yule logs, tartans, bagpipes, and the like."

"Don't forget the black bun and haggis."

She smiled. "The Turlocks, being Irish, prefer holly wreaths, candles in every window, and plum pudding with brandy butter. Nothing quite as frightening as your haggis."

He chuckled. "I must confess to liking haggis. That's reason enough to return to Edinburgh. You have plans of your own after the holidays, I suppose."

"Nothing so grand as Scotland, truly." She tried to push the wistfulness from her tone. "I have my hands full at home with my brothers and baby sister."

"A lively, happy household from what I'm told."

Her eyes rose from the sprig of holly pinned to his coat to his thoughtful gaze. Now *he* was the one sounding wistful. "It is, and I'm thankful for it."

He hesitated. "Do you ever want to . . . venture beyond Pittsburgh?"

"Yes." She felt a tad breathless saying it. Could he read her discontent, her dreams for something more? "Till then I read voraciously, live vicariously."

"A poor substitute for personal experience, Izannah."

"Perhaps," she countered, unsure of where the conversation was leading. "But women haven't the freedom you men do. Unmarried women, anyway."

"You said something similar when we met up at the levee long ago. Do you remember?"

She heated, glad he didn't know just how close she'd kept the memory. "I do remember. But I cannot recall the little package I gave you."

With a smile he reached into his waistcoat pocket and withdrew a pipe. Surprising her. Making her melt.

Her lips parted. "You . . . kept it. All these years?"

"Finest pipe I've ever had. Though I think that has more to do with the giver than the gift." He looked down to the patterned carpet at their feet. "To be honest, I came back here expecting you to be wed. Are you being courted? Is your heart not engaged?"

She gave a shake of her head, caught between embarrassment and excuses. "I have no suitor . . . none at all."

There was a clumsy pause. He swallowed and looked like he'd stepped far beyond his ken. "I ask because . . . there was a time when I—we—"

At his odd stammering, she felt a desperate need to say something, soothe the sudden awkwardness, when a voice broke over them.

"Come along, you two. We're in need of another pair for charades." Mina stood in the doorway, luring them to follow with a wave of her fan. "Izannah's brothers are stealing the show with their antics and simply must have some competition."

"Very well." Malachi took Izannah by the elbow in a manner that seemed all too reluctant and ushered her into the parlor.

At nearly midnight, Mim helped Wren undress in the shadows of the candlelit bedroom, always an onerous task so late. Her heavy velvet gown was finally shed and brushed and returned to the wardrobe, a great many pins pulled from her hair. Once the French corset was dealt with, the rest of her underpinnings were more easily managed and she could breathe again.

"I'll finish up," Wren said, sitting down at the dressing table in her chemise. "You look in need of bed."

Mim stifled a yawn. "Dinna be fooled. With Boxing Day tomorrow and the servants' ball at River Hill, I'm in fine fettle." She unclasped the pearls about Wren's neck and placed them in their silken case. "Yer looking a bit weary yerself."

"I'm just sorry James is by his lonesome tonight."

Their eyes met in the glass. "Keeping upstairs the whole time while everyone made merry below?" Mim grimaced as she removed Wren's pearl earrings. "Dr. Moss forbade him any festivities or any company save his nurse."

"I was hoping Izannah would be let upstairs."

Mim's hands stilled. "Why would ye be worrying about Miss Izannah?"

"Well, seems like James could have a caller, some cheer from those who mean the most."

"Miss Izannah . . . and Mr. James?" Mim let out a throaty chuckle. "Ye ken the two of them are more than kin?"

Wren stared back at her in the mirror's reflection. "Kin?"

"Aye, cousins. They're close as two shoes, having grown

315

up together, but they're nae more than that, truly." She gave a backward glance at the closed door, her Gaelic falling to a whisper. "Wade Turlock is said to be James's father just as the judge is Izannah's. But ye didna hear that from me. The family likes their secrets, all told."

Secrets. Wren went numb.

"Word is Miss Izannah has her heart set on someone else. Just who, I dinna ken. She isna one to wear her feelings on her sleeve like some."

The gentle rebuke was not lost on Wren. Did Mim suspect her heart? The feelings she'd tried so hard to hide? Unable to meet her eyes, Wren focused on a spent, smoking candle. Her mind began whirling, scrambling for similarities between Wade Turlock and James, some likeness in looks or nature. But all this paled next to Mim's other revelation. Izannah and James were naught but first cousins? She'd never suspected. Not once.

She barely heard Mim's quiet good night or the gentle closing of the door. She raised cold hands to her flushed face, her gaze traveling to the basket she'd prepared for James. Just a few humble gifts meant to wish him a merry Christmas, which Mim had promised to leave at his door before she went to bed. But Mim had forgotten. The lapse was odd. Mim, bless her, never forgot anything . . .

She sat for a long time, trying to settle herself, to come to terms with the truth. Izannah didn't love James. She loved someone else. And James? He belonged to no one. He was unfettered. Free. Free to love. Be loved.

If he was willing.

Facing the hearth, James stared at the glowing remains of the charred logs, the chill of his bedchamber biting his bare flesh. Bored and bedsore, he gritted his teeth against an avalanche of pain and pulled himself to his feet. The few steps to the adjoining sitting room seemed like a mile, but he made it, the last of the laudanum leaving his head.

Did he have the grit to go farther?

Emboldened, he progressed at a snail's pace to the landing, then the second floor and foyer. Finally reaching the parlor where a Christmas tree held court, he resigned himself to spending the night in a chair, doubting he could make it back to his bedchamber.

At nearly midnight, the old house had finally settled. He'd heard the merriment for hours on end, smelled roast goose and plum pudding as the scent wafted to the rafters, savored the joy of Wren's fiddle, realized Malachi and Bennett were below by the steady cadence of their voices. Now all was empty of even the servants, though the spicy smell of wassail lingered to the far corners, as did Silas's pipe smoke, rich and thick. A scrap of ribbon from an opened package lay curled on the rug, a reminder of all he'd missed.

Pondering it, he gave in to the uncertainty of what might have happened while he lay upstairs. Deep in his being he felt Malachi might have proposed to Wren. The enchantment of Christmas seemed to call for it. As the hours unwound and all the possibilities played out before him, he'd been unable to do anything but pray.

A Christmas proposal was something he'd dreamed of, if he and Wren had been in a different time and place. But she had never been his, would never be. When she'd first come to him in the privacy of his rooms and he'd nearly been out of his head with fever, he'd almost forgotten that. The feel of her fingers on his face, the way she'd sat by his side like she never wanted to leave, would never leave him.

Exhausted from the effort of navigating three floors, he settled back in a wing chair, unaware he'd nodded off till he jerked awake at the creaking of a door. It swung wide, ushering in a burst of icy air. Wren stood on the threshold, the candle she held casting her in a halo of light. She clutched a basket, and her gaze swept from him to the dark hearth. He read her thoughts as plain as if she'd spoken them.

You made it downstairs with your injuries only to freeze to death?

Setting aside both candle and basket, she knelt by the grate and fed the cherry-red embers several chunks of oak. The dry wood caught and sparked as she coaxed the flames to life, the smell of woodsmoke mingling with her familiar cologne. He nearly chided her, certain she'd soil her dress, but the heat was so welcome he held his tongue.

"I went upstairs to leave the basket by your door." Her voice was soft as she took the stool at his feet. "But it was open and you were gone."

He came fully awake, taken with her enlivened manner, so at odds with the late hour. Clad in an unadorned blue dress, she wore no crinoline, and her braided hair was ensnared with a crimson ribbon. It wended over her shoulder to her uncorseted waist, drawing his eye and his admiration. She had on no jewelry, not even a single strand of pearls.

And she wore no Cameron ring on her finger.

Looking to the basket, she took out a linen napkin, uncovering a generous portion of fruitcake, some nuts, and an orange. "Merry Christmas, Jamie."

Ignoring the sudden dampness in his eyes, he took the humble offering from her open hands, thinking it the best present he'd ever been given. "Merry Christmas, Wren."

Next she eased something onto his lap wrapped in plain

paper and tied with string. Her voice was low, but he didn't miss the emotion beneath. "These were Papa's, but he doesn't have need of them now."

He opened the gift slowly with his good hand, a sudden tightness scoring his chest and ribs. Firelight danced across half a dozen small carving tools. From their Cane Run workshop?

"I thought maybe you could use them instead." She took the little wren he'd carved from her pocket and set it on the arm of his chair. "You bring the children so much pleasure . . . same as me."

He nodded past the catch in his throat. It touched him that she'd kept the little bird close. He hadn't been able to go to the orphanage of late due to his injuries, and a small circus of half-carved animals needed finishing. Thinking it, he examined a chisel, the wood handle slightly worn, the blade sharp.

His voice held regret. "I have nothing for you." He wanted to tell her he'd sent her the roses, the chocolates, but felt a smothering awkwardness.

She looked up at him, wrapping her arms about her knees. "I have your company."

Their eyes met—held. Would she always pull so hard at his heartstrings? He looked away from her, in need of a distraction, longing for his pipe. But it was high on the third-floor mantel, well beyond his painful reach.

Unable to erect so much as a wall of smoke between them, he said a bit brusquely, "Shouldn't you be upstairs?"

"There are no shoulds and should nots at Christmastime, Jamie."

Torn, he gathered up the tools with his good hand and set them aside. She'd turn the house upside down if found alone with him. But she didn't seem to care, and what was worse, he didn't either. Having her near, away from the hustle and fuss of society, seemed a strange sort of recompense for every injury he'd received.

"I thought I might read to you like Papa always did for me at Christmas."

She was missing her father. How could he refuse her? His gaze returned to the basket. Two leather-bound books lay within, both well-worn, sparking a dozen memories. "Your grandmother used to come to the orphanage Christmas Eve and read to us. Your grandfather accompanied her. They always brought gifts, sweets."

"Were you lonesome there?"

He hesitated, a bit wistful. "Not at Christmas."

Moving the candle nearer, she ran a finger down the spine of a book. "I've been reading Grandfather *A Christmas Carol*. Or I can tell you the gospel story of Christ's birth by heart."

By heart. Everything she did was by heart. He glanced at the clock and willed its ceaseless ticking to still. He didn't want to move beyond this pleasant moment, the gift of her presence. But Christmas Day was slipping away, just as she would.

"Your choice, Wren, though personally I'm more in need of Scripture than Dickens."

The query in her eyes left him somewhat chagrined. "Yet you don't go to church."

"I stopped going years ago." Being on the river, he'd had a handy excuse. Though the Ballantyne line didn't operate on Sundays, he always found himself in a different port. "You probably expected to see me at First Presbyterian."

She nodded. "In Kentucky we had no church building. We always kept church here." She touched her heart. "It was in our music, the instruments we made, our everyday life."

"Is it still?"

Her eyes clouded and she didn't answer, making his own heart hitch. "Tell me the Christmas story, Wren. It's been a long time since I listened." The confession grieved him. That was the crux of the matter, surely. Somehow amid the pressures and protocol of business and society, he'd stopped listening, stopped responding, stopped taking the gospel to heart.

"Are you sleepy, Jamie?"

He smiled to ease her. "All I do is sleep. Some insomnia would be welcome."

"What would the doctors say?"

He gave a slight shrug and almost flinched from the effort. "There are no shoulds or should nots at Christmas, remember. Besides, I doubt you'll be the death of me when the coach wasn't." He settled back, feet to the fire, mangled arm caught in a sling across his battered chest, feeling strangely content and at peace.

Almost able to forget the danger beyond New Hope's doors.

"'In half a minute Mrs. Cratchit entered—flushed, but smiling proudly—with the pudding, like a speckled cannon-ball.'" Wren stopped reading, stifled a yawn, and stole a look at him.

Though the large Edinburgh clock in the foyer chimed three, James Sackett's eyes were bright as daylight. She'd shared the Christmas story from the book of Luke before beginning *A Christmas Carol* at his request. Now she was the one who was fading, the warmth of the hearth as lulling as laudanum. The candle at her side was in need of replacing, sputtering and smoking as it waned. Stiff from sitting, she eyed him sleepily. It was now Boxing Day.

Soon the household would wake and the morning fires would be lit. The nurse would return, and routine with her. But tonight, for a little while, she'd been able to forget expectations and obligations and fears, overcome with the truth that Izannah Turlock was not in love with James Sackett. Wren Ballantyne was.

Alone with him, beyond society's reach, it was all too easy to wish her world began and ended in this very parlor. She simply wanted to curl up on the lush sheepskin rug before the fire and go to sleep in his arms, awakened solely by his touch. Woozy, she returned the book to the basket, thinking she only imagined the flicker of dismay that crossed his face as she did so.

He pushed up from his chair as if he'd forgotten his injuries, and she saw him flinch. But he stood tall nevertheless, reaching out his good arm and helping her to her feet. Always gentlemanly, always gallant, her Jamie.

"I'll help you upstairs," she said, knowing how even a little laudanum could make a man weave like a loom.

He moved slowly, leaving her to worry he'd never be as agile as before. When he listed slightly to the left, she slipped an arm about his waist. The heft of him made her a bit unsteady, even breathless. They proceeded slowly up the staircase as if mired in molasses. When he clipped the leg of a chair in passing and nearly came off balance, she gave a startled cry. His near fall landed them both in the doorframe of his bedchamber, on their feet but in each other's arms.

Leaning back, he looked down at her, his breathing ragged. "Are you all right, Wren?"

"No, Jamie . . ."

There was no mistaking her meaning. Overcome, she rested her cheek against his chest, the linen of his shirt soft against her heated skin. The tempo of his heart beat strong and spirited, like a complicated musical piece. Mindful of his injuries yet craving his nearness, she hovered between distance and desire. Raising her head, she touched his bearded jaw, savoring the rasp of it against her still-callused palm.

He made a sound, not of protest but of pleasure, and the tautness in his body gave way. At his touch to the small of her back, she was undone. Senses spinning, she wove her eager fingers through the wave and curl of his hair as she felt her way along his broad shoulders to the knot of his sling.

He leaned in, the touch of his mouth to hers silk-soft. She gave a little sigh of surrender as he buried his hands in her loose braid, dislodging the ribbon and sending it to the floor. More kisses followed, their warm breath mingling, till they drew apart in a sort of stunned agony.

In the semidarkness Wren read yearning and regret, confusion and tenderness in his gaze. Not once had she thought of Malachi. But the look on James's face assured her he was thinking of little else.

James stayed motionless for long minutes, the taste and scent and feel of her lingering. He could hear her light tread on the stairs, the careful closing of a door. He thought he heard a sharp sob—and then silence. If he could go to her, he would. Beg her to forgive him. But the joy he'd just felt made any apology a lie. Faced with her a second time, he'd simply gather her in his arms again. Kiss her till he had no strength left or she begged him to stop.

He sagged against the doorframe and shut his eyes, trying

to recall the moment it went wrong. There was no denying the pull between them, at first a simple spark upon meeting in the pilothouse, then flaring into something warm and enduring over time before blazing irreparably tonight.

Tunneling a hand through his hair in agitation only reminded him of the gentle whisper of her touch, and he nearly groaned. He'd broken faith with the Ballantynes. He'd broken faith with Malachi, knowing how he felt about her. He'd broken faith with Wren herself. Though she'd come to him willingly, he'd been wrong to act upon it and let his heart rule.

How to undo the deep water they'd waded into was beyond him.

32

I may have lost my heart, but not my self-control.

JANE AUSTEN

Tucked in River Hill's chintz sitting room two days after Christmas, Izannah sat and stitched a particularly challenging piece of English eyelet embroidery, in no mood for its intricate design. Beside her, Mama had abandoned her own sewing to bounce Chloe on her knee. At four months of age, dimpled chin shiny with drool, Chloe chewed vigorously on a teething ring, smiling and howling by turns.

"I don't blame her for being so fractious," Izannah admitted. "I feel somewhat out of sorts myself."

Mama gave her a knowing glance and pulled on the bell cord for tea. "You've been quieter since Christmas. I feared you were getting the grippe like your brothers."

"Not the grippe, though my head is still spinning over James's injuries and the Camerons coming to New Hope for the holidays." Bending her head, Izannah examined her handiwork with a sigh. "And I've yet to recover from Uncle

325

Wade, uninvited and intoxicated, waltzing right in during Christmas dinner!"

"He wasn't uninvited, just intoxicated, and he didn't stay long." Mama swiped at Chloe's damp chin with a handkerchief. "I'm glad the Camerons were there. I saw you speaking with Malachi."

Izannah nodded, schooling her expression. "I hardly recognized him, it's been so long."

"He's quite handsome with that full beard. Looks more like his father every day."

"Daniel Cameron," Izannah mused. "The man you nearly married."

"Very nearly, yes. But the truth was I never cared for Daniel the way he deserved," Mama murmured, offering a rare glimpse into the past. "I couldn't be betrothed to him and feel the way I did about your father."

"I know you cared for Mina like a sister."

This time Mama sighed, a rare tension touching her features. "We were very close back then, until I wed. Mina never quite forgave me for what she perceived as an unforgivable slight to her brother. And then, to add insult to injury, Ansel left for England without a word. She'd hoped to marry him, you see. Sometimes I think she's renewed her hopes since he's come back."

Izannah set aside her botched embroidery, ruing the work it would take to make it right. "It would be good to have a Ballantyne-Cameron alliance. Something beyond that of business."

"Are you thinking merely of Mina and your uncle Ansel . . . or another pairing?"

Izannah nearly squirmed at the query, unsure of whether to spill her secret or keep it close. But Mama had a curious way of uncovering matters, no matter how much or how little was said. "I don't dare turn facts into fancy, but I can't quite dismiss my conversation with Malachi."

"Oh?" Chloe's teething ring fell into the folds of Mama's skirts, and she bent to retrieve it, sparing Izannah her searching gaze. "At Christmas?"

"Yes. He asked, after the usual pleasantries, if I was being courted . . . if my heart was engaged."

Mama's brows peaked. "Then he's as candid as his father was."

"He's always said what he thinks, sometimes to a fault," Izannah confessed, the delight of the moment lingering. "But I-I don't want to get my hopes up. He's immersed in the season, likely to find a bride among all those willing debutantes."

"I used to think there might be something between you before the railroad took him away."

Something. She'd felt it too, elusive as it was. Or was she woolgathering?

They lapsed into momentary silence as the tea service was brought in. Spying a plate of ginger biscuits, Chloe gave a happy shout and tossed the teething ring away. Their shared laughter banished all awkwardness, but as soon as the door was closed, Mama resumed the conversation. "What did you say when Malachi asked you what he did?"

"About my being courted?" The directness of his gaze when he'd spoken still unnerved her. He was all business, Malachi, and little sentiment. "I said there was no one else." The confession had cost her dearly. She—daughter of a highly respected judge in Allegheny County and a former belle of Pittsburgh—a spinster. "No one at all."

"Oh, Izannah." The sorrow in Mama's tone bruised her as sure as Alice Mellon's snubs. Mama had high hopes for her, wanted more for her. "You're every bit as forthright as your father."

Reaching for the sugar bowl, Izannah wondered if Malachi took his tea sweet or plain, and felt her face flame. "Would you have me be untruthful?"

"Never. I simply meant that there are ways of saying things, softening things, to cast them in a gentler light. You might have said, 'No one at present' or 'No one has yet spoken for me.'"

"I lack your tact, Mama."

"You lack nothing, my dear. My guess is Malachi appreciates such plain speaking. Admires it even."

"Perhaps." She passed Chloe a crumb of a ginger biscuit and was rewarded with a toothy smile. "I dared to hope, when he came back this winter, that we might meet up again and further our friendship. But he's entirely too busy with the season."

"Do you love Malachi, Izannah?"

The gentle question stopped her cold. "I . . ." She broke Mama's gaze, tempted to dismiss her feelings as girlish infatuation. But the truth was she'd never stopped holding him close in her head and heart and wishing he'd return to Pittsburgh. Nor had she ever stopped praying, nearly wearing a hole in heaven with her petitions. "I do care for him. I have for a very long time. But I don't want to make too much of it."

"Perhaps he cares for you too, and only needs a little encouragement."

Izannah fell silent, beset by another worry. She couldn't confess her certainty that Wren was in love with James and somehow Malachi was mixed up in that. Mama would be beside herself if she knew James's painful quandary. Though he'd said nothing to Izannah about his feelings for Wren, she sensed his ferocious struggle as the season progressed.

"I've been praying ever since you were small that the Lord

would bless you with a husband and home of your own. We'll keep praying, trusting in His faultless timing if that is His best for you. The Lord is never too early—or too late."

Izannah brushed the moisture from her eyes with a quick hand. Her mother's faith that all would turn out for the best touched her but left her ruminating.

Would her heart be broken in the process?

Wren had grown fond of New Hope's breakfast room with its butter-yellow walls and rich aromas. The promise of coffee always met her when she set foot in the foyer, the temptation of ham and biscuits a reminder of home.

"Good morning, Wren." As usual, Grandmother greeted her, beckoning her into the bright room with a wave of her hand.

"Morning," she echoed as every eye turned toward her.

Everyone sat in their usual places—Grandmother and Grandfather at one end of the table, she and Andra in the middle, Papa's place yawning empty. Until today. For the moment James occupied Papa's empty chair, his eyes on her as she entered.

James downstairs? Why?

His fever had returned the day after Christmas, giving rise to fresh fears and half-frantic prayers. With the doctors and nurse hovering again, she'd not had opportunity to go to him, though she kept vigil in the cupola when she could.

Five days had passed since their heated embrace Christmas night, and not once had they crossed paths. But it hardly mattered. He was the first man to ever hold her. Kiss her. He'd left his mark on her as plain as if he'd made her his by any other means, even marriage. Could he sense he consumed her

329

every waking thought? She could hardly breathe for thinking of him. She couldn't even sleep.

This morning he was every inch the old James in black superfine cloth and snowy cravat, the Ballantyne lapel pin winking at her. The unruly hair she'd raked her fingers through was sleek and combed, not wildly unkempt. He was on the mend. At their very table. And hiding his discomfiture far better than she.

She choked down a bite of biscuit, thankful the men were talking business, their resonant voices strong and decisive as black coffee. A far cry from the throaty timbre whispered in her ear. Thinking it, she nearly shut her eyes. The storm of longing inside her was swirling again, stirred into a tempest by the mere memory of his touch.

"Rowena, you're to continue the season with James after all." Andra's clipped announcement slipped in beneath the tenor of the men's voices. "He's much improved and wants to finish as your escort."

Wren felt a qualm. "But the doctors . . . his fever . . ."

"The doctors have given him leave to resume his duties, barring a final examination. Even his nurse has returned to the hospital as of this morning. We're very thankful James was able to join us for breakfast." Andra consulted the watch pinned to her bodice. "This afternoon we have a final fitting for your ball gown. Saturday will be here all too soon."

Across from them Grandmother was listening and nodding. "When Malachi was here at Christmas, he mentioned the Jenny Lind concert. Pittsburgh is readying for her arrival this Wednesday, and she'll be staying at the Monongahela House, the papers say."

In the tumult of the last few days, the event had slipped Wren's mind. Now it brought fresh dread.

"James is relieved of escorting you that night, though Mim will attend you." Clearly, every detail had been taken care of. Andra looked more satisfied than Wren had ever seen her. "Mistress Endicott has almost finished your fur cape. The opera house can be quite chill, though you'll be ensconced in a private box."

The masculine voices had hushed. The coffee Wren swallowed too hastily burned her tongue.

"We're so proud of you, my dear." Grandmother's tone was as warm and enveloping as an embrace. "If only your father was here to share in your happiness."

Happiness? Since she'd come to Pennsylvania, her days and nights had held challenges and miseries she'd never known. Till James had taken her in his arms, she wasn't sure she could go another step. Yet here they sat beaming at her as if she'd won some sort of prize.

"Your father should return soon." Grandfather stood, hesitating a moment as he always did, as if unsure of his bearings. "He sent a telegram yesterday to say he'd left Philadelphia. Apparently he's recovering from the influenza there and spent the holidays alone. Thankfully he's much improved and able to travel."

Wren's heart barely lifted at the news. So much was happening. One never knew what life would lay hold of next. She stared at her plate, all too conscious of James at table's end.

Passing behind her, Grandfather placed a hand on her shoulder, giving it a reassuring squeeze. "Ansel will return in the Camerons' private car to the end of the line in Lancaster, thanks to Malachi's generosity. But after that he must take the stage. I'll be glad of the day the Pennsylvania runs into Pittsburgh."

"I agree." Andra frowned and motioned the maid for

more tea. "The stage is becoming so antiquated. Much like packets."

There was a stilted pause. Wren raised her eyes to Andra, weary of her perpetual sourness. She felt a sudden burning to reprimand her aunt, but Grandfather spoke, resignation in his tone. "One day we'll say the same of the railroad, hard as it is to envision. Time has a way of pressing on and keeping us all humble."

James stayed silent, and Wren ached to look at him. His way of life hung in the balance, yet here they were talking concerts and fur capes and private railcars as if it didn't matter.

Reaching for his walking stick, Grandfather started for the door, Grandmother at his side. "I'll be in my study."

Quietly James excused himself, leaving her alone with Andra.

"Aren't you hungry this morning, Rowena?"

Wren looked at her mostly untouched breakfast, her cold egg and forbidden biscuit, feeling she'd never be hungry again. "I believe I'll go to my room till the fitting."

"Don't be late." With that, Andra left out a side door without another word.

Gathering courage, Wren quit the breakfast room and crossed the foyer, her gaze on the wide stairs soaring upward. Though his progress was slow, James had made it to the landing. Unsure of what she'd say, she gripped the banister as she followed after him, waiting till he'd reached the third floor and they had some measure of privacy.

"Jamie."

He stopped, back to her. Would he not turn round? The stubborn set of his shoulders gave a warning. At last he faced her.

"You're still not well. I know you're not." She held out a

hand to him, and it seemed she was holding out her heart. "You don't have to escort me any longer. We can be free of all that. I never wanted a season. I just want to be yours—"

A door shut below. Andra? Wren tore her gaze from his to look down, but it was merely a maid crossing from parlor to dining room. When she looked back at him again, the softness in his face had vanished. He didn't move. Didn't take her outstretched hand. It fell limply to her side like a broken bridge he wouldn't cross.

"You need to forget about us, Wren." His voice was low but stiff with resolve. "We need to have this finished—your season, this business with Malachi."

"I plan to tell Malachi—"

"There's no future to be had with me. You need to let go of anything that happened between us that night." His eyes held hers, driving his harsh words home. "The hour was late. The doctor had given me laudanum."

"Laudanum?" Stunned, she took a step back. Did Christmas night mean nothing to him, then? She wouldn't believe it, wouldn't take his cold words to heart. Tears strained her voice, but she pressed on. "It wasn't laudanum that held me close or whispered tender things or kissed me till I couldn't breathe. It was you, James Sackett."

Another door closed. Andra started up the stairs.

"Remember your place, Miss Ballantyne." Turning away, he cast the rebuke over his shoulder like a scattering of crumbs and shut his door.

Wren's ball gown took up half the curtain coach, leaving Mim to sit with James on the opposite seat. Countless yards of watered silk separated them, but it was the moody silence lurking like an unwelcome guest that was most apparent. Their stairwell confrontation of five days past was all too fresh, all too sore.

Since then James took meals in his room or worked on Ballantyne business behind closed doors, occasionally playing a round of chess with Grandfather. Wren kept mostly to the music room or made calls with Andra, sometimes entertaining visitors at New Hope. But tonight there was no avoiding the ball that thrust them together again, James's stony presence reminding her of his bitter rejection.

A sudden bump thrust her forward, causing her to nearly knock knees with him. He looked at her as if to ascertain she was all right before lifting the shutter a crack. As if her presence was a detested thing, her honeysuckle-rose scent too cloying.

Mim said not a word, sharp eyes shining in the darkness.

Another grand foyer. Hundreds of melting candles. The same stiff faces. James wondered if Wren's distaste for society was rubbing off on him. As the season wore on, the arrogance and excess seemed to escalate, each event trumping the last in terms of ostentation and display. Everything rang hollow. Futile. Empty.

When Mim retreated upstairs with their wraps, Wren looked after her as if she'd lost her last friend. Left alone with her, he took care to fix his attention elsewhere. She appeared equally determined to do the same, studying the parquet floor or incoming guests, anything but him.

He fisted his hands behind his back, fighting an overwhelming weariness. Wren was right. He still wasn't well. Beneath his pristine clothes, his injuries were concealed but still ached with his every move, requiring his utmost concentration to stay stoic. The fever had never left him, turning his color ruddy and making him feel oddly disembodied, a flimsy shadow of himself. But he was more worried about Wren. With every step toward the teeming ballroom, her pace seemed to slow. Next he knew she'd come to a stop. He tensed in anticipation as her gloved fingers fell from his arm.

"I . . ." she began slowly.

He studied her and felt a wrench that he'd not noticed how pale she was. "You need to sit down."

Taking her by the elbow, he led her to a small chamber in full view of the ballroom as the butler's announcement of Malachi Cameron intruded. Resignation lined her features—and mild panic. He sensed Malachi's attentions were both flattering and unnerving, that she was torn between affection and fear, smothered by the admiration of too many men and sinking under the weight of her family's wishes.

Or trying to recover from his heartless words to her on the landing.

"You're not yourself," he said. "I'll call for the coach."

"No . . . I'll see this through."

Their hostess appeared, inquiring if all was well. With a polite nod, he made excuses. Wren took out her fan, waving it with such vigor he felt its cooling draft from three feet away. But she still looked so fragile he tried to gauge what might follow. Fainting. A quick exit.

Malachi was across the way, eyes on the anteroom despite his talking with some business associates, obviously having scanned the crowd for Wren. Resistance rose inside James like a wall. Though Malachi was the best choice, the Ballantynes' choice, James was a long way from making peace with it.

Once again his thoughts cut to Izannah. Had Malachi

not given her a second thought, even after James's urging at Lake Lanark? They were a near-perfect pairing. Izannah could easily handle the demands of his very public life. And she was woman enough to make him forget those demands out of the public eye. But he was closing in on Wren instead.

Wren moved past him with a brush of her wide skirts to stand on the cusp of the ballroom.

He came alongside her, looking out at the swelling crowd, wondering how they'd make it through the night. "Remember, Miss Ballantyne, you can have any eligible man in the room."

"Any man?" She swished her fan, her voice thin and tired when it had been so full of life before. "Even you, Mr. Sackett?"

Dull anguish ground inside him. He wanted to reason with her. Tell her what her aunt Ellie had said. *Wren is very trusting—naïve. She may fall in love with the first man who pays her any attention.* Unwittingly, that man had been him. Wren was simply infatuated and that would fade in time. He prayed his own feelings would fall in line as well.

Half a dozen eager men encircled her, intent on her dance card, Malachi among them.

When the time came for their opening waltz, James felt like a puppet on a string, wanting to tear himself free. But a hundred eyes were on them as the first notes were struck. Embracing her, one hand resting at her waist and the other clasping her gloved fingers, he tried to ignore the intimate feel and scent of her, but it was a bitter fight and he was fast losing ground.

If Malachi—or society—suspected anything between them, Wren's future would be ruined and James would make an enemy.

He didn't need another.

33

Riches should be admitted into our houses, but not into our hearts; we may take them into our possession, but not into our affections.

PIERRE CHARRON

Wren stepped down from the mounting block as a groom gathered the reins and led her mare away. Restless, she'd been out on another ride, the frigid night giving way to a rosy sunrise, the peaceful sight easing the raw places inside her. Papa would be home soon, or so she hoped. Spring would come. Maybe in time she would right herself.

Slipping in the servants' entrance, she trod the narrow hall past the butler's pantry and kitchen, peeking in a side room that usually held a gathering of white-aproned maids. This January morning the servants' backs were to her as they huddled around a small table, heads bent, unmindful of her presence. She stood in the doorway, hoping to see Mim but getting an earful instead.

"So it's true what they're sayin'!" The Irish lilt of the old-est maid, Fiona, struck like a chime in the still air. "He's got himself in deep water indeed!"

A rustle of papers followed. "He's bound to be sorry, as it was him who picked John Gunniston to run the river in his place. Looks like there's trouble from New Orleans to Pittsburgh now. If there's going to be a war, I wish they'd do it proper and nae pick off people here and there like a bunch of heathens!"

Mim?

Wren cleared her throat, not wanting to give the impression she was eavesdropping, and every maid spun round. Their somberness rebounded in a bright greeting. "Morning, Miss Wren!"

"Morning, Fiona, Betsy . . ." She greeted them all by name, envying their simple companionship. "I just wanted to ask if someone had time to sew the missing buttons on my cape for the concert." She tried to smile, a bit ashamed asking for help with so simple a task, but Andra insisted all work be done by the servants.

"Oh, aye, I was just coming upstairs to do that very thing," Mim said, breaking from their tight knot.

"No hurry, Mim." Turning, Wren retreated, leaving them to their talk.

The servants followed the season faithfully in the Pitts-burgh press, those who could read sharing with those who couldn't. From the sound of it, something else besides the usual society news had made the headlines this morn.

Deep water . . . run the river . . . war.

She stopped walking, the fragments of conversation coming clear.

James?

Spying the door to the morning room ajar, she slipped in, searching for the *Pittsburgh Gazette*. But the table was bare, only the aroma of coffee lingering. The little breakfast she'd eaten churned uneasily inside her.

Once upstairs, she began removing her riding habit, cold fingers fumbling with the mother-of-pearl buttons as her thoughts made fearful leaps. She'd last seen James a week prior when they'd parted without a word after the ball. He'd taken a separate coach to the Monongahela House. Was he in some sort of trouble?

"Miss Wren, I've brought needle and thread." Mim's forced cheerfulness made her more tense.

"The cape hardly matters, Mim," she said in Gaelic. "What's all this about James?"

Frowning, Mim disappeared from the room, returning minutes later with the *Gazette*. "Ye might as well know since yer by his side nearly night and day."

Wren took the paper in hand, steeling herself against the tide of ink.

Murder Downriver on Ballantyne Line.

Mim expelled a rare sigh. "The river pilot who took Mr. James's place was killed on the New Orleans levee just yesterday. A note was found on the body warning James he'd be next."

A chill spilled over her. "But why?"

"James has been running slaves on Ballantyne boats for years—bringing 'em up from New Orleans and other parts to freedom. He takes such risks and has always come away unharmed, but now he's the one being pursued. The coach accident that left him so wrecked was nae accident at all, ye ken."

"Someone means James harm?"

"There's a group called the Mystic Clan, the papers are

saying, who are murdering and wreaking havoc all along the lower Mississippi and are bent on James's destruction."

"What of Captain Dean?"

"He's on his way upriver now, though he'll have to come by land once in Cincinnati since the Ohio's froze. But ye can bet he'll be watching his back the whole way."

Moving to the hearth, Wren fed the paper to the fire, the flames hot against her outstretched hand. James . . . her Jamie. Who'd never said a word about the trouble. Who'd hidden his involvement beneath his everlasting reserve and impeccable manners. She watched the newsprint curl and turn to ash, wishing it would somehow end the matter.

"At least he won't be escorting ye tonight and drawing attention to himself." Mim lifted Wren's feathered hat from her head and returned it to the hatbox. "'Twill just be you, me, and Mr. Malachi at the concert . . ."

Wren listened as if from a distance. With Jenny Lind stealing headlines, Pittsburgh would be distracted from more ill-timed Ballantyne press, as Andra called it. Wren could just imagine the agonized turn of her aunt's thoughts, her hopes that Wren would dazzle society by appearing for the first time in public with Malachi, an occasion sure to supplant any sordid news.

She sank down in the nearest chair, hot and cold by turns. "I don't care about the concert, Mim. Not with James and the trouble he's in."

"Well, wet sheep dinna shrink, they just shake off the water." Mim stood looking at her, hands on hips. "Ye dinna give in to misfortune. Ye get up and go on as the good Lord wills. Knowing James Sackett, he'll do just that."

"But someone clearly means him harm. Every time he sets foot on the street . . . acts as my escort . . ." The past was rushing in, bringing home Papa's predicament of long ago, the old injury that dogged his every step. "James needs to go somewhere safe, far beyond Pittsburgh, like Papa did."

"Aye, that he does. But my guess is James will stay on and face what's to come, including acting as yer escort and making light o' the danger."

Making light of the danger was exactly what Wren feared.

"We have the Royal Box," Malachi told her as she entered the opera house on his arm.

"Seems fitting." Wren paused, the commotion at their entry leaving her slightly wide-eyed. "I feel almost like royalty, given the crowd outside."

The press of spectators around the theater was overwhelming, the reckless hack and omnibus drivers intimidating as they pushed their way past with whips and shouts. It was a blessed relief to step into the hushed, elegant foyer at last.

Malachi grimaced. "They're a rude bunch, I'm afraid, gawking and shoving to see us, and we're not even the main attraction."

She caught her breath. "You're one of them, Mr. Cameron. You and your Pennsylvania Railroad."

He winked at her, his slow smile disarming. "They weren't staring at me, Miss Ballantyne."

Heat prickled her neck, her temperature rising along with her alarm, her concern for James overriding the novelty and excitement of the occasion. She was barely conscious of her dress, her jewels, Malachi's lingering gaze. Andra had insisted she wear Grandmother's sapphires. Though beautiful, they felt cold and heavy about her neck. Wren preferred the purity and simplicity of pearls but had let Andra have her way.

Up a carpeted staircase they went, past dozens of other polished ladies and gentlemen, following the attendant who unlocked their private box. Wren entered first, eyes adjusting to the dim lighting. Someone had prepared well for their coming. Champagne. A silver bowl of red roses. Mother-of-pearl opera glasses beside a leather case.

Stepping to the front of the box, Wren felt a rush of awe. Countless eyes turned toward them as Malachi joined her at the balustrade. There was no denying Malachi Cameron was an attractive man. Sought after. Admired. Already a force to be reckoned with in the world of finance and industry.

He took her gloved hand and brought it to his lips and didn't let go. There was possession in it . . . purpose. Fingers captive, she looked out on the other concertgoers in the huge, horseshoe-shaped hall. Each box and alcove contained a little drama all its own. Couples chattered and laughed gaily, sipping champagne and raising lorgnettes to better view the preperformance activity.

No one had a more sumptuous box, a more regal view. For the moment it seemed she was queen of a gilt and glitter kingdom. This was privilege. Power. She breathed in its heady fragrance. Tried to feel at home. She wasn't a queen. But she could be one.

The box beside theirs was occupied by the Mellons and their friends. The nasal quality of Alice Mellon's voice rose above the hubbub of the hall as she turned toward them with a wave of her ostrich feather fan.

"Good evening, Mr. Cameron."

Without a word, Malachi looked to Wren, as if giving Alice time to acknowledge her too. Empty seconds ticked by, and then Malachi turned his back on the Mellon box.

Cut. By a Cameron.

Wren's elation was short-lived as cold reality rushed in. What were the petty snubs of society when one's life hung in the balance?

Jamie, Jamie.

She clung to his name, praying for his protection. Her every thought was consumed with his safety. Was Malachi aware of the situation? He showed nothing but pleasure at being alone with her. Mim was missing. The realization added to the turmoil roiling inside her.

With a smile Malachi looked skyward. "Old Drury may be an antique, but the acoustics are sound. Miss Lind, with her extraordinary vocal powers, may well raise the frescoed ceiling."

Wren lifted her eyes to the ornate design overhead. With a touch to her arm, Malachi seated her and then himself, facing out on the ornate hall. In his hand was the program, all mixed recital pieces, some she knew by heart. Taking a steadying breath, she managed, "Which arrangement most appeals to you, Mr. Cameron?"

He glanced at the paper, his voice thoughtful. "Mendelssohn's 'Wedding March.'"

She felt her color rise at his very telling choice. "A truly beautiful arrangement." Though she didn't look up, she could feel his eyes on her. "I'm partial to Miss Lind's celebrated 'Bird Song' for the violin."

"That would be a rare Guarneri, the papers say."

"Oh? I wish Papa was here." Wistfulness crept into her tone. "He's never stopped looking for the old Guarneri Grandfather sold long ago."

"If it's any comfort, your father should return any day." Leaning back in his chair, he took a sip of champagne. "He's made it as far as Lancaster by train, according to the telegram

I received yesterday. I'll be glad to see him again, given matters with your grandfather."

Malachi often mentioned Grandfather. Was he worried
that she—all her Ballantyne kin—might be pitched headlong
into mourning? If so, any engagement would be postponed
for a year or better.

The heavy stage curtains parted. The music started. At
the first notes, Malachi took her hand again, the program
fluttering to the floor, forgotten. She shut her eyes as Miss
Lind's high, trilling soprano broke through the grand hall's
expectant hush. Andra seemed to intrude as well, her vehemence as fresh as yesterday.

*The only acceptable way out of your debut is illness,
mourning, or the announcement of your engagement.*

Thankful for the shadows, Wren bit the inside of her cheek.
The Guarneri's tone was impossibly sweet. Stringed instruments so stirred her that she found it hard to keep herself in
check. That would be her excuse if Malachi noticed any show
of emotion. No one need know the struggle in her spirit over
James's severing words.

There's no future to be had with me.

In hindsight she understood. He was a hunted man. A
haunted man. Like Papa had been. The cold truth left her
heart in scattered bits. She could not save him. She could
simply try to allay some of the danger by doing away with
the season. Malachi was inching nearer to offering her a way
of escape. And in that escape, unbeknownst to him, lay helping James.

As Miss Lind's first song ended, Malachi poured her a
glass of champagne. Its heady effervescence seemed to race
through her veins, melting away the last shred of her resistance and his restraint. They left the front of the box to sit

on a loveseat half hidden by a curtain, away from too many lorgnettes and prying eyes.

His hazel gaze darkened with intensity. "I think you first bewitched me along the road that autumn day."

She couldn't help but smile. "In the gloaming, when you mistook me for a servant?"

In hindsight it was amusing and set them to laughing.

"I never expected to see a Ballantyne walking from town, clutching a fiddle of incalculable worth," he murmured. "Few would believe it. You're such a humble lass."

"Not a proper Pittsburgh one, truly."

He took the empty glass from her hand and set it on the table. "If I'd wanted a proper Pittsburgh belle, I would have wed one. If you haven't realized it by now, Rowena, it doesn't matter to me that you eat your ice cream with a lobster fork and hum hymns when you're especially nervous. I think it's rather charming. No one will care about that when you become Mrs. Cameron." His gaze swerved to the Mellon box. "And no one will ever dare cut you."

The forceful words were spoken like a vow, making the feel of his arms about her less startling. He was nothing like James, the scent and feel of him unfamiliar, almost feral. His bearded jaw found the soft curve of her neck, and she let her arms go around him in an uneasy embrace.

"I can give you the world, Rowena. Let me give you the world."

She started to speak but he silenced her, his kisses insistent if untried, and so unsatisfying she wanted to weep. Did he not notice, or care, that she did not kiss him back?

When the music resumed, Mim returned with their wraps, taking a chair by the door. The final piece was Mendelssohn's "Wedding March." Images of a life to come winnowed through Wren's mind like a scythe through grain. A grand house in Pittsburgh. Philadelphia. Edinburgh. Endless miles of rail to unseen places. She was farther from Kentucky than she'd ever been.

How had it all come to this? In love with a man she couldn't have . . . on the verge of giving herself to another? Her hope that James would love her was best set aside, secreted like a foolish, shameful thing. Malachi was the man who would help her forget, whom she might come to care for in time. Whose offer of marriage would free James from the season and any accompanying danger.

For James she would do this . . . her Jamie.

When the last note faded, Malachi turned to her. "Answer me, Rowena. Will you marry me? Be my bride?"

She looked up at him and set aside her final qualm. "Yes."

34

Courage is resistance to fear, mastery of fear—not absence of fear.

MARK TWAIN

In the half light of early morning, James sat in River Hill's book-lined study and listened to the big house come awake. Usually when he stayed the night he rode into town with the judge, but this morning Jack had insisted he remain behind. He was hearing an important case that would test the efficacy of the newly enacted Fugitive Slave Act, and Pittsburgh was on tenterhooks, the mood surly.

"Given the grim news in New Orleans and the fact reporters are camped about the courthouse awaiting word of you and your thoughts about the murder, I'd advise you remain here, James."

The judge was no stranger to trouble himself. Threats had been made over the years about his abolitionist leanings, but none had materialized, perhaps given the Turlocks' fearsome reputation and the simple fact that Jack knew how to turn the law in his favor.

Jack went out, his horse's retreating hoofbeats lingering long in the winter air, finally giving way to the rambunctious bustle of the boys as they rushed downstairs for breakfast. Ellie had come in earlier with a tray of coffee, trying to coax James into eating, but the hollowness in his belly had little to do with hunger.

The *Gazette* lay open on the judge's desk, the lead headline tearing at James a dozen different ways.

Ballantyne-Cameron Merger: Railroad Magnate to Wed Pittsburgh Belle.

The stunning loss of his friend and fellow pilot in New Orleans, his fury over the Madder affair, his concern Dean wouldn't make it safely upriver, gnawed at James night and day yet paled in comparison to this morning's news.

Even the normally stoic judge had been surprised, remarking how odd it was that an engagement would be announced in such businesslike terms. "No doubt a play on the railroad and a reminder of Malachi's recent acquisition in the East."

Ellie had taken a chair and read the column silently, looking up long enough to say quietly, "I suppose your acting as Wren's escort is done, James. And well done it is."

There was no pleasure in her praise, the small anguish he'd known with Georgiana swallowed up in a larger, more lasting misery. Ellie had left him alone soon after the judge had gone, as if sensing the subject was a sore one. But there was little time to smooth his tangled thoughts. In a few minutes Izannah pattered down the hall, her light step all too recognizable.

"James?" At the door she stood, her concerned gaze fastening on him in such a way he knew his outward calm wasn't convincing. "Is anything wrong?"

He couldn't speak. He couldn't even get to his feet as any gentleman would.

She shut the door, moving to the desk to set down a box of steel pen nibs and paper. It was then she took in the *Gazette*. Her mouth went slack, the tired lines in her face deepening. He'd never seen her so stricken. "Last night the Jenny Lind concert . . . this morning marriage?" Her disbelieving gaze found his. "Did you know about this?"

The accusation in her eyes was worse than any wound. "I wasn't there. I didn't know." But he'd sensed it like a storm brewing over the face of the river. He'd felt it coming, but he'd been powerless to stop it.

"Wren—and Malachi?" Her voice shook. "But she doesn't love him. She's simply going through with the season—with marriage—because she feels it is her duty."

"Isn't it?" he said a bit too sharply.

She turned the paper facedown as if she couldn't bear the sight of it. "Wren cannot marry a man who—" Biting her lip, she worked to keep herself in check, but she was failing miserably, as was he. "She cannot marry a man who courts her while inquiring about another."

"Meaning?"

"I was flattered at Christmas when Malachi asked me if I was being courted, if my heart was taken." She touched her brow, voice cracking with vulnerability. "I didn't realize he was pursuing Wren. The papers have linked her with many admirers, not only him. When he asked me what he did, I thought—hoped—"

His heart hitched at the sorrow in her expression—the blighted hope. Anguish tied another knot inside him. Malachi had been unsure of Wren. That was why he'd spoken to Izannah. Hedging his bets in case Wren refused him. Having entered the social season, he was determined to emerge with a bride. Which one was of little consequence, though in society's eyes, a Ballantyne trumped a Turlock every time. The thought was harsh, but he understood his friend all too well. Malachi wanted the matter settled so he could return to the railroad.

"James, you know Wren as well as I do. She's simply not suited to his sort of life. She finds no joy in wealth and all its trappings. Her tastes are simple. She loves people, music. She hates pretense. They're worlds apart." Izannah paused, her color high. "But that's not all. You care for Wren like I care for Malachi. Though you'll never admit it, I know you well enough to sense what you try to keep hidden, what you yourself deny. She belongs to you, James, not Malachi."

He set his jaw, the fervor of her words chipping away at his resolve. "Feelings aside, first and foremost she's a Ballantyne."

"So?" she flung back at him. "Do you think that matters to Wren? Though she hasn't told me she cares for you, I know she does. Her every feeling is written on her face as much as yours are buried, hidden."

"You know nothing of the sort, Izannah. Stop making wild assumptions—"

"James!" She tossed up a hand, her impassioned plea more of a shout. "She's a woman in love with you who's about to make a terrible mistake!"

"Ease off, Izannah. It's too late. The engagement has become public."

"Really? Because some two-bit headline is shouting the news?" She reached for the *Gazette*, flung it into the fire, and turned her back on him, shoulders slumped.

He watched the paper curl and blacken along with his last hopes. "All that matters is there's to be a wedding between two consenting adults, regardless of how any third parties feel about the matter. Malachi has proposed and Wren has accepted. The bond between them might grow, given time."

"Might?" She turned back to him, incredulous, tears streaming down her face. "And might your feelings for her wane over time, James? Or riddle you with regret the rest of your life?"

He looked away from her, caught in a tide of emotion he couldn't stay on top of. The pain inside him was too unforgiving, too raw to be submerged beneath form and custom and stiff restraint.

"The Lord knows I have my own regrets." Her voice faded to a thread of misery. "Namely my failed season . . . and now this."

He passed a hand over his eyes, the stinging saltiness grounding him. "Last fall at Lake Lanark, Malachi asked who I thought was worthy of pursuing. He said he'd returned to Pittsburgh for a bride. I told him you'd make a worthy wife, that he need not look any further." He confessed what he hadn't meant to share and watched a surprised awareness flood her eyes. "I hoped he would forego the season and call on you instead."

"Oh, James . . ."

"I never imagined he'd consider Wren for the very reasons you mentioned. But things went awry."

She leaned into the nearest chair, her hands splayed along its embroidered back. "Forget about my prospects. What about yours? This has to do with Georgiana, doesn't it? Are you going to let her death haunt you the rest of your life?"

"Georgiana's death has little to do with it. She never truly cared for me. She broke our engagement after Bennett told her about my past, remember. He went to Georgiana shortly before her death with the intent of turning her against me."

"That doesn't have any bearing on the present, surely."

"Have you forgotten, Izannah?" He swallowed, resurrecting details he'd tried to forget. "Your grandmother found me in the gutter behind Teague's Tavern when my mother died. She was said to be the most notorious prostitute in Pittsburgh. No one seems to remember how old I was. They simply recall that Wade Turlock was my father, if an unwilling one."

"I haven't forgotten. But it doesn't matter. Not to me. Not to Wren—"

"It mattered to Georgiana, enough that she decided to break our engagement. It matters to the Ballantynes."

"Listen to me, James." She was her father's daughter now, his mettle in her straightened shoulders, the solid timbre of her voice. "We're talking about Wren. She's not a woman rule-bound like Aunt Andra, letting society dictate her every action or etiquette her very existence. Nor is she like Bennett, bent on ruining anyone who gets in his way. If you'd given Wren any ground, any indication of your feelings—"

"I'm meant to be alone, Izannah. I'm reconciled to that. Even you can't deny I'm in over my head as an abolitionist." He looked to the closed door, needing distance. Pittsburgh seemed almost a refuge in light of the present moment. "I'm leaving for the city."

"What? Not Pittsburgh, surely. You need to go east, go abroad—"

"I'll not hide, Izannah. Let Madder and his ilk do what they want with me. I'll not bow to their threats or cower in a corner."

"Then you're as good as dead, James!" She caught his coat sleeve as he passed, but he kept walking. "Take heed for our sake if not your own!"

He went out, so weary in body and spirit it felt more midnight than morning. She didn't follow. But he heard the sound of her weeping as he pushed past the front door.

The relief Wren had expected to feel upon accepting Malachi's proposal turned to dust at the *Gazette*'s bold headline. BALLANTYNE-CAMERON MERGER.

Was that all their union was? Something to be acquired and trumpeted? Some trophy? She didn't bother to read the effusive column. Farther down the page was another grisly account of the New Orleans murder with a detailed sketch of the levee. Investigators were combing the city and every river town along the lower Mississippi for the criminals, offering a substantial bounty funded by the Ballantynes.

Pulse rising, she turned the *Gazette* over. She couldn't stop wondering where James was, if he'd heard of the engagement. The news had broken at New Hope that morning with the arrival of the papers. Someone had made free in the night with what Wren longed to keep quiet. She'd wanted to send a note to James first, let him know his duties as her escort were done. She needed time to get used to her and Malachi's new tie. Time to get her breath. But it was not to be.

The gushing Andra had done at breakfast violated every rule of etiquette invented as she inspected the Cameron ring. Crusted with diamonds and sapphires, it sat heavy on Wren's hand and bore the Cameron crest. Grandfather and Grandmother's enthusiasm was heartfelt but more subdued, and then came Bennett, who rode over at noon to congratulate her.

He was cordial if cold, his harsh treatment of her in the music room seemingly forgotten. "And when will the nuptials be?"

Numb, she tried to smile, to act the bride. So like Charlotte.

"Malachi wants to wed as soon as possible—once Papa returns."

He nodded, looking relieved. "Out of respect for the Ashburtons, I'd urge a quick, quiet affair. Nothing as grand as the one we'd planned."

"I beg to differ," Andra retorted. "Pittsburgh expects a lavish function. Indeed, the city deserves it with all the sordid news of late. I'll let the dressmakers know right away. And we simply must start on the guest list."

"No need." Wren stepped back from them both. "I'd like to be married in the chapel, wearing one of Granny's gowns, with only family present." She met her aunt's eyes with renewed determination, wanting to settle one matter beyond revisiting. "And I want it known far and wide that my season has ended."

Andra's smile was tight. "As a debutante, you're quite done. As the wife of Malachi Cameron, you're just beginning the social whirl, be it in Pittsburgh, Philadelphia, or Edinburgh."

In the hours to come, congratulations began pouring in, calling cards and telegrams accumulating thick as the snowflakes outside. By nightfall Wren thought it odd Izannah hadn't come by or sent a note, then dismissed it given the weather. Malachi was readying to leave on a trip to Washington County to meet with potential investors despite the snow, first making arrangements for their shipboard honeymoon, or so he'd told her.

Mim had been less than glib at the excitement, saying little about all that had transpired other than the concert. "That Miss Lind is true to her name. She's a nightingale every bit as much as yer fiddle."

Wren recalled it now, long after Mim had bidden her good night. The happenings at the concert wove through her mind like a melody, every word, touch, and note all melding into a discordant lament. She tried to sleep, but the thought of sharing a bed with a man who was little more than a stranger turned her restless.

As the Edinburgh clock chimed one, she said her prayers. Uppermost was James. Papa. What would be Papa's reaction? She prayed for his return just as she prayed for James's refuge. Any petitions for Malachi came last, shamefully so. Finally she drifted off, sleeping in snatches. Sometime in the wee small hours she found herself dreaming of Grandfather's worn, antique study.

"Papa?"

There at Grandfather's desk he sat, like he'd been there all along and she'd only imagined him gone. He looked up and set his pen aside. "I arrived but an hour ago with little fanfare. I didn't want to wake the household."

Coming out from behind the desk, he held her tight. He felt cold to her touch, the long coach ride in the snow a bitter one. She kissed his bristled cheek, but the gesture seemed as rote as the steps of a reel. The man who stood before her had been gone too long and was out of touch with the things that truly mattered.

"What's this?" He raised her left hand, the Cameron ring catching the light. Beautiful as it was, it looked out of place. More bit and bridle. She flushed at the thought, though the feeling of being harnessed stayed steadfast.

"I'm engaged to be married." The words came unwillingly, his warning to delay playing in her mind. "I'm to be Mrs. Malachi Cameron."

The surprise in his eyes held an angry tint. "He didn't ask me for your hand."

"How could he, Papa? You were gone."

"He might have waited till I returned. He could have written, found out where I was, sent a telegram."

"He's a busy man." She stumbled over the words, avoiding his eyes. "He wants to marry immediately."

"And you, Wren? What do you want?"

She looked down at her fingers, twisting the ring in a worried circle.

I want James to be safe.

I want the season to end.

I want to escape society's expectations.

I want a home of my own. Children. Music . . .

She awoke in a tangle of bedding, sweating yet cold, dawn pressing in on her with the demands of a new day.

35

I am no bird; and no net ensnares me; I am a free human being with an independent will.

CHARLOTTE BRONTË

Surely no one would be out on such a day. Even a killer. Yet from the moment James stepped out of the levee office, that same uneasiness took hold. A fitful wind had sent a torrent of rain sideways into Pittsburgh's coffee-dark streets, slowing hackneys and omnibuses and kindling tempers. Hours later, the bell jingling on his attorney's door was a nagging announcement that he'd left the relative security of the busy office. He'd spent the morning finalizing his will and leaving his fortune in stocks to the orphanage. That alone gave him some peace, though he'd be far more at ease if he was whole in body. In spirit.

The prayers he'd said, the stubborn refusal to entertain any thought of Wren, had been as difficult as trying not to breathe. She was his first thought on waking, his last thought before sleep claimed him. Even then she ransacked his dreams. The announcement of her engagement, miserable as it made him, was now the talk of Pittsburgh. Unable to stem the thought of her, he gave in to one comfortless notion. She had been his, if only for a tick in time Christmas night, though Malachi might possess all the rest of her.

He quickened his stride along Market Street, his hat brim no better than a water spout, and spied a familiar figure amid the mud and rain. Stepping under the awning of a tailor's shop, James squinted into the wind as the nattily attired man crossed the street, top hat in hand.

Captain Dean.

With nary a greeting, Dean motioned him toward the tobacconist shop two doors down where a painted wooden Indian stood guard. The place was nearly as familiar as the Monongahela House, the site of many an abolitionist meeting and a hiding place for runaways. A portly clerk greeted them and unlocked a back room, drawing the door shut again after lighting a lantern.

Cedar shelves lined one wall, full of glass jars and snuff boxes, countless earthenware crocks beneath. The cold air was redolent of the rappee blend of tobacco James shunned and the refined maccaboy he favored.

Dean plucked a Havana cigar from an open box and lit it at the corner stove. "I barely recognized you, bearded as you are." He turned round in a huff. "What the devil are you doing in the city?" The question burst from his lips in a plume of smoke, demanding answers.

Taking a rickety chair, James studied his muddy boots. "I'll not hide."

"By heaven, you'd better." Dean sat, chest heaving. "If you'd seen what they did to Gunniston, not just shooting him but brutalizing him—"

"I know the details. They don't need repeating."

"Listen to me, James. You have friends everywhere—you could go anywhere. Why are you still here?" His pointed look brought no reply. "You're not still squiring Rowena Ballantyne about town, are you?"

"The season just ended, at least where she's concerned." James flexed his cold hands and held them nearer the stove. "Her engagement was announced yesterday."

"Engagement?" Dean stared at him through the smoke. "To whom?"

"Malachi Cameron."

Dean swore, a rare occurrence, setting James further on edge. "And that's not enough to send you out of town? Packing?"

James held his temper. "Why would it?"

"Because you're gone—as gone as yesterday over her, that's why. From the moment I found her with you in the pilothouse last summer, I knew there was something between you."

"Not on her part." The lie came all too easily, as did the memory of her in his arms. "She's a Ballantyne, remember, nearly a Cameron. That's as great a distance as Pittsburgh from New Orleans, all of it unnavigable."

"Does she have anything to do with your death wish?"

This time James nearly swore. Dean had an uncanny ability to see things as they were and turn confrontational. "If she does, it's none of your concern. My death wish, as you call it, began before she came on the scene. I started slave running for the Ballantyne line years ago, knowing there was little to lose. I've long been a target. Does that sound like the sort of husband a woman would want? Would I put my bride in that sort of danger?" He took a breath, uttering the obvious in an attempt to end the matter. "Malachi Cameron wins. He's by far the better man."

"Cameron be hanged," Dean countered, his voice losing none of its heat. "You're the one in need of that Scottish honeymoon."

"Don't tempt me with impossibilities." Taking out his pipe, James packed it full of tobacco, ignoring the slight tremor in his hand. He was as overwrought as he'd ever been, far more from Wren than Madder's threats. Discussing it openly was like firing a packet's engine with pitch on an impossibly stormy night—certain to bring destruction.

"So when are they to wed?"

James could only guess. "As soon as her father returns, knowing Malachi. He has business in Philadelphia and Europe and can't delay."

"Is he in love with her?"

James glared at him. "Again, that's none of your affair—or mine."

"I beg to differ—"

Standing so abruptly he overturned his chair, James pocketed his pipe and made for the door. "I'll be at the levee if you need me. But you can leave all talk of Wren Ballantyne behind."

Malachi broke the wax seal and studied the creamy paper in the glow of gaslight, blinking at the finely scripted words like they were composed in Greek. He'd arrived home at nearly midnight from business in Washington County and discovered the letter atop his desk, his name penned beautifully across the top. He'd thought to grow used to Rowena's handwriting in time, to come to know her in far more intimate ways. And now this . . .

He read it through once . . . thrice, his head pounding along with his heart. What would he say? How would he explain it when the news went public? He'd not suspected anything amiss during the course of their brief courtship. Nor was he used to being thwarted. Folding the paper, he tucked it in his pocket and reached for his cape.

James would know what to do.

George Ealer stood by the window at daybreak, arms crossed as if standing guard. Behind him, pistol hidden beneath a stack of papers, James scratched at a ledger on his desk, determined to let his mind stray no further than the business at hand.

"You e-expecting Mr. C-Cameron, sir?"

"No." James looked up, surprised. Malachi rarely came to the levee unless he was taking a trip. With the rivers locked in ice, all traffic had long since ground to a halt.

"He l-looks g-grim as a r-reaper. Think I'll r-run that errand you want d-done a b-bit early." Grabbing for his hat, he slipped out the rear door as James capped his ink and set aside his pen.

Ever since the papers had announced news of the engagement, the city had been still abuzz, anticipating the wedding date. Malachi had likely come to ask him to serve as best man. The prospect tore at him, made him want to slip out the back like Ealer had done. Till now he'd tried to barricade himself from all wedding talk, keeping mostly to the Monongahela House or the levee, avoiding both River Hill and New Hope. He hadn't considered he might have to stand up at the ceremony.

Excuses swept through him as he formed a reply, only one credible.

I'm going abroad on Ballantyne business.

True enough. The waiting Guarneri violin, nearly forgotten in the tumult of circumstances, rose to the forefront of his mind and begged resolving. He owed Silas that. Sailing for Scotland might even throw Madder off his trail. Yet something perverse and illogical held him fast. What was death? Not a thing to be feared or dreaded. Simply a solution for the regret that was sure to riddle him for years to come. An honest way to end the pain.

Where was God in the midst of all this?

Though he'd lately gotten on his knees, he saw no shift in circumstances, felt no affirming presence. The Lord seemed to answer the prayers of men like Silas Ballantyne, not orphans, or worse.

Passing a hand over his face, he stood as the door swung open. Malachi came in, not bothering to wipe his boots. Leaving a muddy trail, he took the chair across the desk and removed a folded paper from his breast pocket.

James took it reluctantly, struck by Malachi's pained silence before he set eyes on what looked like a letter. He'd never seen Wren's writing hand, but a mere glance at it turned him inside out. Every lovely, arcing flourish was so like her, rendering the words within more poignant.

> *Dear Malachi,*
>   *After much thought and prayer, I am unable to be your wife. You are a fine man worthy of far more than I can give you. My heart is wholly taken. I am deeply sorry I didn't tell you sooner.*
>   *Your ring is enclosed.*
>   *Please forgive me.*
>
>   *Rowena*

Malachi's eyes were on him, gauging his reaction. Waiting for an explanation or some comforting word. Only James had none to give.

He swallowed, never lifting his gaze from the paper. "Have you seen her, talked to her?"

"I rode to New Hope before coming here, but she wasn't there. She's not at River Hill either. No one seems to know where she is, and everyone is frantic with alarm."

James's eyes lingered on one telling line.

My heart is wholly taken.

Malachi was staring at him as if he knew. As if he was to blame. Which he was.

"Do you love her, James?"

It was the last question he expected to hear, but it was one that needed settling. Malachi's eyes, tinged with sorrow and regret, bore into him. James could no longer deny the truth. "Yes."

A dozen excuses gathered inside him, begging release. *I didn't mean for it to happen. I never thought it would come to this. I tried to turn her away. I never wanted to love her.*

Malachi stood, resigned. "What are you going to do about it?"

James laid the letter down. "I'm going to find her."

"And when you find her?"

"I haven't thought that far."

Malachi took a step back and returned his hat to his head. "You're a lucky man, James Sackett."

Izannah met James in New Hope's parlor, making him feel even more disoriented, as if he'd ridden to River Hill instead.

"I wanted to be here when Grandfather and Grandmother learned the news. Andra has taken to bed with a headache and has said nothing to them yet. I came right over after she sent word Wren had left."

"Do you know how long she's been gone?"

"I have no idea." She touched her brow, rubbing a furrow as if she had a stabbing headache. "I took the liberty of searching her room. Mim said her valise, some clothes, and her violin are missing. And I discovered this."

Yet another letter. This one to Ansel.

> *Dear Papa,*
>
> *Word has come about the Guarneri Grandfather sold so long ago. A gentleman by the name of Du Breon has recently written from Cincinnati, saying he has information regarding its whereabouts. It seems a blessed time to leave Pittsburgh, given my season has ended and I'm not to wed. I thought to wait for you but am ready to go alone. I hope to find out more about the family heirloom you've long wanted. I will send word to you once I arrive safely.*
>
> *Your loving Wren*

A blessed time to leave Pittsburgh? Was she mad? Or merely heartbroken at all that had happened and in need of time away? One look out the windows' icy panes confirmed his worst fears and brought Izannah's distressed voice into play.

"I cannot believe she'd leave in winter. She's not traveled except to come upriver to us—and she's alone. Heaven only knows what she'll encounter in getting there, if she ever gets there."

364

"My guess is that she'll end up in Kentucky." He handed her back the paper. "I'll find her."

The look she gave him implied doubt. "Since the river is frozen this far north, she'll have to go overland. We don't have any idea when she left—or how."

"She'll likely take the stage west to Columbus and then on to Cincinnati." He started toward the door. "You'll have to explain everything to Ansel when he returns. I'll be leaving right away."

"Wait, James, please." She reached out a hand, dismay darkening her eyes. "Why not hire security guards, private detectives like Pinkertons—"

"Because I need to be the one who finds her."

Her hand fell away. "All this trouble for a violin?"

"I doubt the news from Cincinnati is credible." He felt to his bones it was a hoax. It could be nothing else, with the real Guarneri waiting in Edinburgh.

"You think it's just a ruse?" The horror in her eyes drove Gunniston's murder home. "A ploy to lure her there? To lure you there?"

"I don't know, but I'm going to find out." He wouldn't tell her he had as many enemies in Cincinnati as New Orleans, a tight ring of anti-abolitionists who were becoming increasingly vocal—and violent.

"James, it's too risky. You could be walking into a trap. Whoever means you harm has obviously linked you with Wren and has some scheme to—"

"And the longer we spend talking, the more danger she's in." He started for the door a second time. "You might as well know she's broken her engagement to Malachi."

She stared at him, pure astonishment in her gaze. "You didn't tell Wren my feelings for him . . ."

"I did not."

"Then she's ended their tie solely out of love for you, James. Is that it?"

He looked down at the hat in his hands, trying to take it all in. "I'll send word as I can. All I ask is that you pray for her safety. Pray that I find her."

"Find her?" At a third voice, James and Izannah stilled. Bennett filled the parlor doorway, barring any hasty exit. "I doubt you will. Even if the letter from Cincinnati is credible, she'll have little to do business with, as I took the liberty of relieving her of the Nightingale before she left."

There was a stunned silence before Izannah erupted in outrage. "You took the Nightingale? How dare you—"

"Rowena's naïveté comes in very handy at times. The note she sent to Malachi breaking their engagement was shown to me first by a trusted servant, giving me ample time to act. As far as I'm concerned, Rowena reneged on her responsibilities. The agreement was to make a match, to emerge from the season with an engagement, and a brilliant one at that." He walked toward the largest window, cold sunlight outlining his tall form. "You failed in that respect as well, James. A lasting Ballantyne-Cameron alliance was within our grasp and the two of you tossed it to the wind, and now we have nothing—"

"I don't care about any alliance, as you call it." James took a step toward him. "I only care that she's left and you've taken from her what she values most."

With a shrug Bennett faced him. "I doubt she even realizes it yet. I substituted one of Grandfather's less valuable violins, slipping it in the case to fool her. The Nightingale has already been sold, by the way—"

With a catlike swipe, James took Bennett by the throat, twisting his cravat into a tight knot. "Then I suggest you do everything in your power to buy it back."

"Too late, Sackett." Bennett tried to jerk away, but James held fast. "Though I made a hefty profit, it doesn't begin to make up for a broken engagement or the latest business deal that's sure to sour now that Cameron's been jilted—"

"Cameron be hanged!" With a ferocious shove, James sent Bennett reeling backward.

The jarring crash of an overturned table and Izannah's startled cry rang out like a tavern fight in the elegant room. Righting himself, Bennett lunged, knocking James back with renewed fury. The ribs that had yet to heal seemed to splinter anew. Blinding, breathless pain left him nearly doubled over. But it was nothing compared to the anguish he felt over Wren.

"Stop it, both of you!" Izannah rounded a near settee, her gaze flicking to the open doorway. "If Grandfather finds you fighting like this . . ."

As Bennett's boot knocked the breath from his middle, James steeled himself then charged. Chest heaving, every sense strained, he pushed Bennett across the grand room till they came up against the largest window.

Strength almost spent, fists full of Bennett's tailored coat, James thrust him backward with all that was in him. The sound of Izannah's ragged scream slashed through his conscience as a thousand glittering fragments broke over them, stinging and sharp.

"James, stop! You'll kill him!"

Chest heaving, he stood over Bennett. The old crown-glass window lay in ruins, a cold wind whooshing through the jagged space. Bennett lay slumped on the floor, eyes closed.

Wiping a sleeve across his perspiring face, James stepped back, his boots crunching glass. The Nightingale was gone. Wren was gone. His life meant nothing without her.

36

You pierce my soul. I am half agony, half hope ... I have loved none but you.

JANE AUSTEN

Ice and mud and misery left Wren raw and unsettled mile after mile. She dozed, waking occasionally to lift the coach shade and peer out on endless farms and towns and mileposts while her fellow travelers, snoring and indifferent, slept. She'd abandoned the Ballantyne name upon leaving Pittsburgh, afraid of attracting notice. Away from the city, no one seemed to care who she was or where she was going. She was but one of dozens of beleaguered travelers, the passing days a blur.

By now the news of her leaving would be well known. There'd likely been a rush to keep it out of the papers, sparing the Ballantynes and Camerons any damage. Once Papa returned to New Hope, what then? The note she'd left for him said so little. He'd be beside himself that she had no escort.

As she pondered it, her pulse raced in tandem with the coach wheels, the jarring stretch of road shaking her fully awake.

Despite the emotional wreckage she'd left behind, deep down she felt she'd done right by breaking her engagement. She wasn't meant to be Malachi's. And she risked grieving God by marrying for the wrong reasons. That alone reassured her the first hundred miles in cramped, smelly coaches and filthy inns, but then her health—and courage—began to wane.

Shifting on the overcrowded seat, she fastened her gaze on the posted rules for passenger behavior above the door. *Refrain from the use of rough language. Chewing tobacco is permitted, but spit with the wind, not against it. Men guilty of unchivalrous behavior will be put off the stage.* She supposed there was something to be said for gentility after all.

Thankfully, she had plenty of coin due to the funds she'd managed in Papa's absence from the sale of their Cane Run interests. But that was of little consequence. The Nightingale in her possession had once been appraised at a staggering sum. Parting with it would be anguish, but the joy the Guarneri would bring kept her from coming apart completely.

She needed to reach Cincinnati. She needed distance. A diversion. A mission. Perhaps once there she'd find some scrap of peace.

When she finally emerged from the coach and saw the forest of smokestacks and tasted the grit in the air, she was cast back to Pittsburgh. Cincinnati was an overgrown bully of a city sprawling to the river's edge, the landing lined with steamboats as far as her eye could see. She nearly flinched at its sameness. Head and heart pounding, she stood alone in the dusk as her traveling companions continued on their way. She was weary. Hungry. Longing for home. But home wasn't Pittsburgh.

And it certainly wasn't Cincinnati.

Izannah hadn't stopped praying, it seemed, since James had left New Hope three days earlier. A paisley shawl around her shoulders, she focused on a lone rider traveling over the rutted road from the west. From Pittsburgh? She leaned nearer the cupola glass, the beautiful bay horse coming clear.

Malachi.

The closer he came, the harder her heart thundered, so forceful she struggled for breath. He rode right up to River Hill's front steps and swung down from the saddle, tethering his mount to the hitch rail. Surprise sallied through her. She'd expected him to be long gone, parting with Pittsburgh and a very public broken engagement like a moth-eaten coat. Yet he was here, on her very doorstep, causing her stomach to somersault in bewildered expectation.

In seconds she'd made it to her bedchamber, catching up a brush and attending to her hair. A maid came to fetch her as she splashed rosewater on her wrists, making her glad she'd not changed out of her best gown. The persimmon silk rustled as she started down the steps to the blue sitting room to meet him.

He'd come to say goodbye, she supposed. To see if she'd heard anything from James. Perhaps ask a favor of her. Her cold hand clutched the doorknob. She was so weak in the knees she wanted to sit down. Too much had happened over the last few days. Her whole world felt on end . . . and Malachi's too, but in a different way.

Oh, Lord, for a smidgen of Mama's composure, please.

Mumbling "Amen," she pushed open the door. There he stood by the blazing hearth, hands outstretched toward the warmth, reminding her that his own mantelpieces were far from finished at Cameron House. But what did it matter without a bride or even a hope of one?

Slowly he turned toward her, and she framed his handsome, pensive profile in her head and heart to hold on to in the lonesome days to come. He looked careworn, his clothing rumpled.

"Izannah . . . I apologize for arriving unexpectedly."

"Never mind that, Malachi," she said softly. "You wouldn't be here without good reason."

"I just came from town. From seeing your father."

"Oh?" It was the last thing she expected to hear. "Business, then?"

"Yes, of sorts . . ." He began unbuttoning his heavy coat, revealing a bright scarf beneath. The red plaid matched his cold-reddened cheeks. "Rather, I have business with you." He swallowed hard and met her searching gaze. "I asked your father for your hand, Izannah."

She stared at him, his shocking words toppling the careful wall she'd built around her heart. "My father . . ." She could only imagine *that* scene. "What did he say?"

"He asked me what had taken so long." A small, rueful smile played around his mouth. "He asked why I hadn't listened to James Sackett in the first place." He stood in front of her, closer than he'd ever been, so close his spice cologne made her senses swim. "This is somewhat awkward, given what's happened with Wren and James."

Somewhat? "Oh, Malachi . . ."

Taking her hands, he looked down at their joined fingers. "I'm asking for your hand right now, Izannah, but I'm hoping in time for your heart. And I'll gladly get on bended knee

371

if you like." His slow smile held her captive. "But I'm not leaving here without your answer. I'm due in Philadelphia day after tomorrow and have little time left."

She'd never seen him so humble. So hopeful. Dare she say she'd waited for this day for *years*? She bit her lip, hoping he wouldn't want some distant engagement, some indistinct wedding date. "Take me with you."

"I should have taken you with me when I left Pittsburgh years ago." He studied her, his look half disbelieving, half elated, as if he was weighing all the possibilities. "We'll need to marry on the morrow. A Philadelphia honeymoon is what I have in mind. After that we sail for Scotland."

We. The word warmed her like a winter's fire. "My father can do the honors," she said calmly, as if one day's notice was all that was ever needed. "Mama can act as best maid."

"My grandfather will be best man, then. And Mina . . ." He expelled a breath. "Mina will scold us for being in such a rush, then forgive us when we bring home our firstborn."

She smiled, joy rising inside her at the pressure of his hands, the way his eyes held hers and didn't let go. Despite the suddenness of it, she felt strangely at peace. Having dreamed of this moment since the schoolroom, she realized perhaps it wasn't so sudden after all. "We shouldn't waste any more time, Malachi. A Philadelphia honeymoon sounds perfect, as does Scotland after."

"Then Mr. and Mrs. Malachi and Izannah Cameron it is," he said, and he took her in his arms and gave her the kiss she'd long dreamed of too.

James had finally made it to Cincinnati, where he notified port officials to be alert to Wren's arrival. Something told him she'd soon leave for Louisville on an available packet, given river conditions. This far south the Ohio was free of ice and far more obliging, river traffic undaunted. Gray-faced with fatigue, he'd shrugged aside any concerns for his own safety. Hopefully those who meant him harm were still in Pittsburgh. At least here he was on the move, perhaps as hard to find as Wren.

Leaving the port office, he returned to the street, where fog hung like a tattered veil, snaking between narrow alleys and crawling over the water. Clutching his valise, he started walking, the loaded pistol inside his waistcoat feeling odd and heavy.

He moved past gin shops and taverns fronting the river, considered by many to be the seediest place in the city, and wondered if Wren was even here. His belly cramped at the smell of roasting meat. He was in need of a meal and a bath. Sleep. Reluctantly he made his way to his usual lodgings, redolent of tobacco and brandy and the crush of masculine voices.

The clerk greeted him warmly and summoned a concierge to take his luggage to his room. "I've not heard of Du Breon, Mr. Sackett. He's likely farther toward Vine Street, where the music shops are located. Perhaps one of our staff could point you in the right direction come morning."

Come morning might be too late. Saying nothing, he went out again, ignoring the warning voice that told him to stay off the streets, that looking for her was nothing but a pipe dream. Standing by a dry fountain in the busy square, so torn in spirit it seemed he was no more than the slim shadow darkening the cobbled walk, he faced the truth. In a city teeming with over one hundred thousand people, it would take a miracle to find her.

He hadn't called in the police, though Ansel's latest telegram demanded he do so. James dismissed it as a frantic father's plea, well meant but ill timed. He didn't want her apprehended like a common criminal. He wanted to find her himself. He wanted to prove that faith and prayer mattered and would lead him back to her again.

As the fog tightened and gas lamps flared in the January twilight, the sick feeling inside him deepened.

Lord, please . . . Wren.

Here, as in Pittsburgh, Wren felt out of step with everything around her. Strange sights and sounds bumped up against her at every turn. She'd come so far. And for what? A hard, cold lonesomeness crept in instead of the satisfaction she'd expected, compounded by the shock of meeting Du Breon.

"Mademoiselle, you come to me all the way from Pittsburgh in winter? And you claim to be a Ballantyne, no?" In a small shop on Vine Street, he regarded her with bleary eyes and tapped his balding head. "Are you . . . *folle?*"

Insane? Her smile was sheepish. "Maybe a little."

"And is your grandfather *the* Silas Ballantyne?"

She nodded, gaze roaming the dusty room before returning to him. "My father, Ansel, is his son. He's in search of the lost Guarneri you wrote us about, only I've come in his stead. I'm staying at the Park Hotel."

His expression clouded. "I sent you no letter, mademoiselle."

"Are you not Du Breon?"

"I am, but I know nothing about the Guarneri you speak of." His gaze traveled from her confused face to her violin case. "But I see you carry an instrument. Might I see it?"

She set the case on the counter, desperate to make sense of the situation. This man hadn't sent a letter and had no knowledge of the Guarneri, yet his name was Du Breon and he was here where the post said he would be . . .

She took a deep breath, finding comfort in the familiar. "I have a rare violin known among collectors and musicians as the Nightingale."

"*Non!* You jest. *The* Nightingale?"

The silver clasps of the leather case gave way beneath her practiced hands. As she lifted the lid, her whole world shifted. She gasped, the pride and pleasure her instrument always brought a dim memory. Within the case's velvet lining was an imposter, a common Mirecourt, inferior in every sense. She stood mute, mind spinning.

Bennett.

Deep in her spirit she knew. Somehow he'd tricked her, robbed her of her sole joy and comfort. The Nightingale was no longer hers but someone else's. Though she didn't know whose or how, she knew why.

"Not the Nightingale, *non?* Yet an instrument still worth appraising." Taking the violin from her trembling hands, Du Breon began to inspect every detail, spectacles hiding his intent squint. "I have a buyer here in the city who may happily pay what this Mirecourt is worth. But I advise you to return to your hotel till I have time to contact him and arrange for a potential sale on the morrow."

Fighting tears, she returned the instrument to its case, unable to hide her distress. Worn down by weariness and the cold hard fact that the Nightingale was missing and the Guarneri was far beyond her reach, she turned away, thanking him but making no promises about tomorrow.

The violin shop was not easy to find, tucked in a tight corner at the end of a dingy alley, raising James's suspicions before he'd even stepped inside. Dust motes danced in the air at his entry, and his nerves were raked by the frantic jingling of a bell above the door. He stood quietly for a moment, adjusting to the shadows, willing the paralyzing wariness inside him to ease.

Violins of various shapes and sizes lined the walls, but the shop smelled old, neglected. Not the place one would find a rare violin or even inquire about one.

"*Bonjour, monsieur.*" An aged man emerged from a back room, a bow in hand. "Are you in need of a violin? Some sheet music, perhaps?"

"Neither." Still suspicious of some deception, James took a last look about the shabby room. "I'm looking for a young woman by the name of Rowena Ballantyne, who is in search of a rare Guarneri violin."

A slow awareness spread over the shopkeeper's face. "I am Pierre Du Breon, and I know the very one you speak of. She came here yesterday asking about the same."

"And?"

"I have no knowledge about the violin she hunts for." He raised his palms entreatingly. "I sent no letter to Pittsburgh."

He'd expected as much. A ruse and little more. The men who meant him harm had lured Wren here . . . him here. James shot a look at the front door, tension tightening inside him. Cane Run and its remoteness had never sounded as appealing as now.

In the stilted silence, Du Breon's cordial mood shifted. "Do you mean trouble, *monsieur?*"

"I simply mean to find her. And I'll reward you handsomely for your help." Taking out his wallet, James removed a few bills and set them on the worn counter.

"You mean her no harm? She is such a charming young woman . . ."

"No harm, I assure you."

Coming nearer, Du Breon set aside the bow and pocketed the money. "*Merci.*" Turning toward the back room, he spoke in rapid French. A shop boy appeared in a stained apron, smelling of varnish. "Take this man, Mr. . . . ?" His gaze returned to James.

"Sackett."

"Take Mr. Sackett to the hotel where Miss Ballantyne is staying. They have business."

"*Oui.*" The boy exchanged his apron for a cap and led James out into the misty Cincinnati morning.

Sunrise found Wren eating breakfast in a secluded alcove of the hotel's dining room, the only guest up so early. Despite the heaviness in her head from lack of sleep and the blistering ache in her heart, she was thankful for one matter. Away from Pittsburgh, the memory of James had lost some of its sharp edges. Bennett filled her thoughts instead, bringing a different kind of anguish.

Why hadn't she known he'd retaliate in some way for her broken engagement? Having denied him what he most wanted, he'd taken something from her. She should have hidden the Nightingale, should have sent a note to Malachi by Mim instead of someone from the stable. Though she couldn't be sure, she felt a servant had betrayed her.

Beyond the wide dining room window, a boy sped past, driving a tiny cart down the busy thoroughfare, a costumed monkey on his shoulder. Street vendors were already peddling their wares in a swirl of competing fog and sunlight.

Musicians commandeered corners, sending sleepy notes into the morning air. A multitude of people were passing. Women in fancy dress and plain cotton shifts, men in caps and top hats . . .

James.

Her fork dropped with a clatter. Here? Why? As her mind raced and fumbled to explain his appearing, she reached for her reticule, suppressing a wild desire to wave at him through the window. When she looked up again, he was gone. Had she only imagined him, then?

A sudden commotion in the foyer—the opening and closing of a door—confirmed she hadn't. He'd found her after several hundred miles and a blur of days. Why?

"Good morning, sir. Are you inquiring after a room?"

James's low, measured reply sent a tremor through her. "I'm looking for a young woman by the name of Rowena Ballantyne."

"We're not in the habit of giving out confidential information about guests—"

"In this case you need to make an exception or I'll have to involve the police."

A slight pause. "I understand, sir."

From her vantage point in back of the dining room door, Wren watched the clerk examine the hotel roster. "There is a Rowena, sir, but it doesn't appear to be the lady in question. Only a Miss Nancarrow . . ."

Wren didn't wait to hear more, already moving toward a back exit. She'd told no one where she was staying except the shopkeeper, Du Breon. An unwise confidence. Obviously he'd told James she was here.

Bent on escape, she nearly collided with two men at the door who brushed past rather rudely, obviously intent on some pressing business. One grunted what sounded like an apology, casting a brief glance at her violin case. Why *was* she still carrying it? For its familiar feel? Cold comfort. There was little of value within.

With that thought she stepped into the street. The hustle of the city, so like Pittsburgh, so unlike the calm of Cane Run, overwhelmed her. She wanted to shrink from the noise and the dirt, wincing at the abrupt sound of popping behind her. Loud and insistent, it ceased as quickly as it began.

Hurrying down a back alley, she tossed aside the desire to retrace her steps and throw herself in James's arms, erasing every mile and ugly memory, every speck of lonesomeness that lay between them.

Papa had sent him—or Bennett and Andra. Perhaps even Malachi. Well, he'd come in vain. She wasn't going to be found. She'd made up her mind, and James Sackett had no part in her plan.

"A Miss *Nancarrow*?" James repeated, staring at Wren's signature in the hotel register. Elation and frustration pulled at him. Perhaps she was less naïve than he'd thought.

The hotel clerk inclined his head toward the dining room. "Miss Whoever-she-is was eating breakfast a few minutes ago."

Wren—within reach? James swung toward the dining room, barely aware of a commotion in the hall.

"Ah, Mr. Sackett . . . at long last." The voice, a rough grumble, held unmistakable challenge.

Chilled, James turned toward the sound, instinctively feeling for his pistol. Two darkly dressed men stood at both exits, derringers drawn.

All the air left his lungs. *Lord, help.* Was his life to end here, now? Like this?

All thoughts of Wren dissolved in the ensuing noise and smoke. The ceiling and wall behind him took a pounding of bullets, plaster and paint shaking down around him.

He fired back once, twice, and heard someone shout. Then a swift crack to his skull and he blacked out.

Wren's walk to the levee was more of a run, and she clutched her valise and violin case till her grip grew stiff about the leather handles. Overcome by the landing's carnival-like atmosphere, she sidestepped horse droppings while trying to stay clear of cargo and wagons. The next outbound southern steamer was at ten o'clock, or so a passenger schedule told her.

The fog that had greeted her when she'd arrived two days before was rushing in again, wrapping her in its misty embrace. Disguising her. Or so she hoped. She prayed the police weren't out looking for her. Feet swollen in her too-tight boots, cape soiled from the grime of travel, she looked anything but a Ballantyne, even a Nancarrow. Her bonnet hid her well with its broad silk brim, but her fiddle case looked a bit out of place, like a huge finger pointing her way.

She waited in line for a ticket, eyeing the churlish Ohio, its surface marred with bobbing driftwood and the glint of ice. The sight of so many packets drove home the reality of James's predicament. He'd followed her here and he was in danger. Never had she imagined he'd come so far. Risk so much. She scanned the wooden pathways crisscrossing the muddy landing, expecting him to appear.

Once aboard the *Natchez Pearl*, she cast a last look at the landing, pushing down the stubborn notion that James should be beside her. She'd grown so used to him during the season—to his voice, his steady, reassuring presence, the uncanny way she had only to glance at him and he would cover her blunders.

"Careful, miss. Mind your step." An aging steward stood before her, passenger list in hand. "And you would be?"

"Rowena Nancarrow."

He glanced at her through crooked spectacles. "Bound for Louisville with intermediate ports between?"

She nodded, unsure what intermediate ports meant but afraid it spelled a delay. "How long will it be till we get there?"

"Late this afternoon, barring any mishaps or foul weather."

The prospect of a boiler explosion or sinking nearly froze her to the stage planks.

"Stay clear of all deck passengers," he told her. "There's talk of cholera going round. Best keep to the ladies' salon."

She wouldn't tell him she had a slight fever. The burning behind her eyes was unrelenting, making her woozy and thirsty by turns. As she stepped onto the slippery deck, she looked up at the pilothouse, pelted with bittersweet memories of that first voyage aboard the *Rowena*.

Making her way to the salon, she felt she was taking yet another irreversible step. She'd come so far, yet the memories she'd hoped to move away from remained. Despite the hurt of the past, the sweetness of James's arms stayed steadfast.

Would it always?

37

Where thou art, that is home.
EMILY DICKINSON

The signpost at the crooked gate read "Selkirk Macken, Luthier." Ice coated the rough-hewn letters, and a cardinal perched on the rowan branch above, the only spot of color in the barren Kentucky landscape. Half frozen to the saddle, James reached into his greatcoat and pulled out his watch, a gift from Silas at Christmas. The Edinburgh timepiece was slow, no doubt due to his falling into a frigid ditch along a slippery stretch of road the day before.

The bitterness of twilight seeped into his bones, the light at the end of the lane failing to lift his spirits. After a miserable, emotional journey, he'd pinned all his hopes on finding Wren here. Safe. Sound. Glad to see him. His pulse sped at the thought of her in his arms and Izannah's parting words.

When you find her, don't let her go.

That he would do, if she would have him. He wasn't sure she would. He'd hurt her deeply. Perhaps irreparably. She'd left his world without warning, though he was just entering hers.

Ahead the stone house—her old home—stood amid stalwart oaks. He tied his mount to the hitch rail and climbed slick stone steps toward the front door. His knock brought a barking dog bounding from the surrounding woods that simply wagged its tail on sight of him.

"I'm James Sackett," he said to the tall young man who answered. "A friend of Ansel's. A pilot of the Ballantyne line."

"Selkirk Macken," he replied, extending a hand. "This is my wife Rebecca."

Mrs. Macken's face creased in a smile. With a motion of her hand she waved him into a circle of warmth and light, the smell of bread and coffee inviting. Her soft, melodic speech was yet another reminder of Wren. "If you care to sit, I'll serve you supper."

He sat, too tired and cold to remove his coat, but he did place his sodden hat and gloves nearer the fire. Though his breathing had settled into a regular rhythm, his ribs seemed to scream from miles in the saddle and his tussle with the thugs at the Park Hotel.

Selkirk took a chair opposite, his own plate scraped clean. "Obviously you're not here on a social call."

"I'm looking for Wren."

Selkirk shook his head. "I haven't seen Wren since she and her father went upriver last August."

"I was certain she'd be here." Though he tried to remain stoic, dismay poked a hole in his surface calm. "My plan is to overtake her at some point."

Unfazed, Selkirk studied him. "Obviously she's decided Pittsburgh isn't to her liking."

"That's not the half of it," James replied, still stunned by all that had happened. "She left eleven days ago, bound for Cincinnati, posing as Rowena Nancarrow. She's alone, unused to travel. I was sure she'd come here." He'd never felt so flummoxed, so foolish. Somehow she'd managed to stay one step ahead of him the whole bewildering way.

Selkirk refilled his empty coffee cup. "She might have gone back to Pittsburgh."

James nearly groaned. He forced a few forkfuls of stew, not wanting to offend, and looked about the comely room. A far cry from the parlors he was used to, it had a simple beauty, an uncluttered appeal. A startling lack of pretense. Again, like Wren.

Selkirk reached for a stack of newspapers on a stool. James watched as he unfolded one, turning it around so James could read the headline.

Murder Solved for Ballantyne Line: Suspects Apprehended.

"I've been following the trouble in New Orleans that seems to be following you." The young man's eyes showed true concern. "The authorities say they've caught the men who ran you down on the streets of Pittsburgh then followed you to Cincinnati. Seems they lured Wren there with a note, something about a violin, but were hoping to waylay you instead."

"They caught up with me—two of the clan—in the lobby of Wren's hotel."

Selkirk's eyes widened. "You weren't hurt?"

James shook his bruised head, the memory a bit muddy. "Nothing worth mentioning." Could they sense his deep thankfulness? His awareness of prayer at work? "The desk clerk took a shot to the shoulder before police arrived and made arrests."

From her rocking chair Mrs. Macken mumbled a relieved "Amen."

Selkirk folded up the papers and put them away. "From what I know of the Mystic Clan and their dealings, it might be a good idea for you to stay here a few days. I doubt you'll be troubled further in these woods. We've plenty of feed for your horse and can put you upstairs in Wren's old room."

The offer, though hospitable, gnawed a deeper place inside him. He didn't want Wren's room. He wanted Wren. Setting his fork down, he looked toward a side door. "I'll stay tonight. But before I leave in the morning, I'd like to see your workshop, if you don't mind." He couldn't say what compelled him to ask. He simply felt the need to see where Wren and her father had spent so much time.

"Do you play?" Selkirk queried.

"On occasion. But I'm no match for Wren."

"Few can best a Ballantyne," he said with a knowing smile.

They moved to a narrow hall and breezeway connected to a large workshop. Lantern held high, Selkirk thrust open a thick door, and light spilled into the airy space. Stringed instruments of all kinds adorned walls and tables, the aroma of wood and varnish thick. Immediately James felt Wren's sweet presence. Felt her life and spirit. Felt, too, the pain of her having to leave it all behind, her shock at coming into Pittsburgh.

The ache inside him was widening every moment away from her. He'd had so little understanding of her or the life she'd led. She'd looked to him for guidance. Friendship. Affection. And he'd handed her judgments and rules and expectations. Not his heart.

Selkirk passed him an instrument, a gleaming maple fiddle with leaf trim. James took it and tested a string.

"Wren crafted this one herself. I've never had the pluck to part with it."

The wood was warm in his cold hands. The tone sweet. He struck a low G and Selkirk looked surprised. Was he expecting a spritely reel? A jig?

Tonight all James could manage was a lament.

The fever had finally left her. Beneath Molly's ministering hands, Wren felt almost renewed, whole in body if not in spirit. The Sabbath dawned, the sun chasing chilly shadows from field and forest. Cane Run was a sleepy echo of itself on a Sunday save for the singing coming from the newly built mercantile beside the inn. No one but Molly and her kin knew she was here. Lying abed in their tiny cabin, perched like a bird on the shoulder of a ridge, Wren had to content herself with the view from a narrow window.

She finally shed her traveling clothes, climbing into a wooden tub of warm water, the lye soap scouring her skin. A far cry from New Hope's copper bath. Thankfully Molly had kept her old dresses. She chose one, the worn, familiar fabric soft against her skin, the mossy green a reminder of James Sackett's eyes.

"I'm going home now, Molly."

With a nod of understanding, Molly stood on the sagging porch and watched as Wren slipped into woods as worn and familiar as the dress she wore. The air was sharp and sweet and clear. She drank in her surroundings with a thirst she'd never known. Sure-footed, she followed the low stone fence in crumbling shades of gray, the crevices filled with moss in winter and wild violets come spring. The creek ran full as it cut across the little valley, a boisterous rush of frothy water between slippery banks. Everything was bare. Unclothed. Awaiting spring. Like a fine lady in need of a fancy dress.

If only her heart could have broken in spring. The sight of blooming dogwood and redbud would have mended it back together again.

The lane to home bore fresh wagon tracks. Her breathing eased. Selkirk and his bride would have gone in to Cane Run for a gathering of praise. She was alone then. Alone with her tattered emotions and her tears.

Her heart twisted anew at first sight of the stone house, her gaze following the stalwart lines of the dogtrot leading to their shop. Everything was hushed. Somewhat forlorn.

What had she expected? A shout of welcome?

The house was no longer hers, nor the shop, so she stepped gingerly onto the porch between. A chill breeze swept by and she pulled her shawl tighter. Leaning into a post, she let her gaze swing wide. Everything looked so . . . small. When it had been larger than life before.

She still felt the Lord's presence here. She always had. But now, whisper-like, she felt something else. Slowly she turned.

James stood just behind her.

She stared at him, disbelieving, with the same intense yearning she'd felt for these woods. He seemed out of place on this humble porch. But he was here. Safe and sound. Standing tall in his dark wool coat. His handsome face was unsmiling, but his eyes were warm.

"Come home, Wren."

She swallowed past the catch in her throat. "New Hope is not my home, Jamie."

"Nor, I take it, is Cameron House?"

She shook her head, too torn to say more.

He took a step nearer, and a floorboard creaked. "I wasn't

thinking of either of those." Reaching out, he brushed her face with careful fingers, tracing the gentle curve of her damp cheek. "I was thinking of our own home."

Ours.

Before she could answer, he took her into his arms. For a few stunned seconds she did nothing but surrender to him in spirit. Her bone-deep weariness, time itself, melted away as he bent his head and pressed his mouth to hers. He tasted as sweet as she remembered, his beloved scent closing about her. Her hands crept to his collar, pulling him closer, her fingers kneading the smooth linen of his shirt before fanning through his dark hair. He kissed her with none of the hesitancy of before but wholly and possessively till she lost her breath.

Nothing else mattered right then. Not the Nightingale. Not the trouble she'd caused back in Pittsburgh. Not the uncertainties of the future or the hurts of the past.

This was coming home.

Epilogue

Give me but one hour of Scotland,
Let me see it ere I die.

WILLIAM AYTOUN

SCOTLAND
MAY 1851

There was an echo of Kentucky in these hills, the same wild beauty she'd been born to. Walking hand in hand with James down a ribbon of road that curled and dipped amid bracken and heather and wandering sheep, Wren pondered why it held no strangeness. No doubt it was the man beside her who had made all the difference to her homesick heart.

She looked back over her shoulder to their honeymoon retreat with a sigh. After a three-month idyll, the Ballantynes' country estate felt like home, inhabited by a skeleton staff of servants who called them a pair of turtledoves and left them mostly alone. Pearl-white and nested in all the greens

389

of spring, the Ballantyne mansion was far younger than Blair Castle with its stony grandeur farther down the road but retained a charm all its own.

"I wish Grandfather was here." She couldn't help but think of him. Scotland was full of reminders of the Ballantynes and their beginnings. "Granny too."

With a small smile James clasped her hands, helping her over a stone dike. "They're on their way."

"What?" She fastened surprised eyes on him as her boots sank into loamy ground.

"Silas wants to see Scotland again and hear you play the Guarneri. They should arrive in time for your concert at the castle."

She studied him, still disbelieving. "That's not till Lammas, the first of August." Would his health hold? Would Granny's? On a strange ship with few comforts? It had taken her and James forty days to reach Glasgow from New Orleans, much of it spent leaning over a basin or the ship's railing. Once on land she was little better, though she had a better excuse.

"The doctors are against his traveling but he's determined. Your father and Mina are coming with them."

She expelled a relieved breath. "I'm glad." She was just getting used to the fact that Papa and Mina were engaged, further tying the Ballantyne and Cameron and Turlock clans into an inseparable knot. "And Bennett?" She spoke the name with trepidation, having forgiven him the theft of the Nightingale if she'd not forgotten.

"Silas sent him to California in hopes to make a man of him." At her raised brows, he winked. "His words, not mine."

She smiled. "Grandfather is coming for more than the concert, surely."

"Great-grandchildren are a great motivator to cross an ocean."

Her heart lifted, thinking of the joys to come. Izannah's first child was expected in autumn, and she and Malachi had taken up residence in Edinburgh till then. The Caledonian Railway often took Wren and James to the Camerons' elegant townhouse. They'd agreed to be godparents when the time came.

Looking down, Wren touched her rounded waist with gentle hands. "It's a race to see who'll be born first—a Sackett or a Cameron."

"We'll be settled in our own house by then."

She looked up at him, rocked by the second surprise in as many minutes.

Bending down, he plucked a bluebell and tucked it into her flyaway braid. "I've just purchased the old abandoned property near the kirk we've been attending. You said it reminded you of Cane Run."

"The Duncan place?" Overcome, she threw her arms around him, the wool of his coat scratching her cheek. "Ours for keeps?"

He gathered her closer, his jaw resting atop her head. "It's not large as country houses go, but it has a music room and a connecting study where I can work on Ballantyne business abroad."

"And a nursery?"

"A nursery large enough for a dozen Sacketts."

With a joyful laugh she started away from him, the fringe of her shawl teased by the Highland wind.

"Where are you going, Wren?"

"Home, Jamie." She held out both hands to him. "Home at last."

Author's Note

I have long been an admirer of Samuel Clemens. Thanks to him, a treasure trove of information exists on "gentlemen of the navigation," as they were aptly named in nineteenth-century America. As he observed in *Life on the Mississippi*, the pilot surpassed a steamboat's captain in prestige and authority; it was a rewarding occupation with wages set at $250 per month. A steamboat pilot needed to know the ever-changing river to be able to stop at the hundreds of ports and woodlots. Clemens studied two thousand miles of the Mississippi for more than two years before he received his steamboat pilot license in 1859. This occupation gave him his pen name, Mark Twain, from the cry for a measured river depth of two fathoms.

There was indeed a Mystic Clan/Conspiracy and Island 37 operating in this time period, causing a great deal of trouble for a young man by the name of Virgil Stewart. Later, Stewart helped convict the river bandit John Murrell and published an account by this unforgettable title: *A History of the De-*

tection, Conviction, Life and Designs of John A. Murrell, the Great Western Land Pirate; Together with His System of Villainy and Plan of Exciting a Negro Rebellion, and a Catalogue of the Names of Four Hundred and Forty Five of His Mystic Clan Fellows and Followers and Their Efforts for the Destruction of Mr. Virgil A. Stewart, the Young Man Who Detected Him, to Which Is Added Biographical Sketch of Mr. Virgil A. Stewart. Ironically, Murrell was the son of a circuit-riding preacher and became a Christian and black-smith upon his release from prison.

Pittsburgh's high society was both decadent and rule-bound by midcentury. Many of America's leading citizens, both financiers and industrialists, came from this great city. My apologies to natives/residents for making Pittsburgh appear so dark and for calling Cincinnati "a big bully of a city." Both places are incredibly rich in history and culture and are beautiful riverfront destinations today. My time in both has been more rewarding than I can recount here.

Special thanks to the Pennsylvania judge who told me about Pittsburgh brides needing to be wrapped in sheets lest they be blackened by the soot of the city when the Industrial Revolution was at its height. These are the little details that make a historical novel leap to life.

I owe a deep debt of gratitude to the remarkable resource *Hill's Manual of Social and Business Forms* by Thomas E. Hill. Beautifully illustrated, this antique book is a treasure trove of information about nineteenth-century life, particularly genteel society. Exquisite history, indeed!

Acknowledgments

A book is an endeavor of many hands, heads, and hearts. Heartfelt thanks to my agent Janet Grant and the entire Revell team for bringing the Ballantyne Legacy series to life. Your commitment to publishing edifying books of all kinds inspires and blesses me.

Special thanks to Brandon Hill and crew for creating such memorable cover art. My time in the Seattle studio for *Love's Fortune* was amazing and unforgettable! I'm also very grateful for the fine video work done by Brandon Hill and Keith Bolling/Session 7 Media for this series.

HUGE thanks to Renee C. (and Coco!), both Pennsylvania natives, who have been incredibly encouraging as I wrote about the Ballantynes (and not only the Ballantynes). Reading friends like you make publishing amazing, and your savvy book reviews mean more than you know! I wish I could thank everyone by name who has been a part of this journey.

> Your name and renown
> are the desire of our hearts.
> Isa. 26:8 NIV

Laura Frantz is a Christy Award finalist and the author of *The Frontiersman's Daughter*, *Courting Morrow Little*, *The Colonel's Lady*, *Love's Reckoning*, and *Love's Awakening*. She is a Kentuckian currently living in the misty woods of Washington with her husband and two sons. Along with traveling, cooking, gardening, and long walks, she enjoys connecting with readers at www.LauraFrantz.net.

Meet
Laura Frantz

Visit LauraFrantz.net to read Laura's blog
and learn about her books!

- see what inspired the characters and stories
- enter to win contests and learn about what Laura is working on now
- tweet with Laura

"Laura Frantz surely dances when she writes: the words sweep across the page with a gentle rhythm and a sure step."

—LIZ CURTIS HIGGS, *New York Times* bestselling author

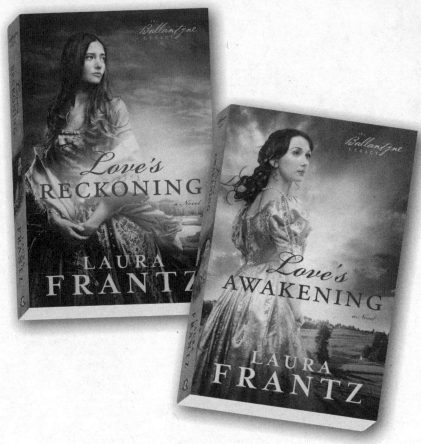

"You'll disappear into another place and time and be both encouraged and enriched for having taken the journey."

—JANE KIRKPATRICK, bestselling author of *All Together in One Place* and *A Flickering Light*

"Portrays the wild beauty of frontier life, along with its dangers and hardships, in vivid detail."
—ANN H. GABHART, author of *The Seeker*